WE CAN BE HEROES

A NOVEL BY
SCOTT FITZGERALD GRAY

I0549799

Published by Insane Angel Studios
(insaneangel.com)

Monumental
WORKS GROUP

Contents

For Molly

"We can only see a short distance
ahead, but we can see plenty
there that needs to be done."

— Alan Turing

Part One

When It Started

1

Vital Signs

BRITISH COLUMBIA Ministry of Education

SECONDARY REPORT CARD
FOR 2010–2011

Peter Skene Odgen
Senior Secondary
P.O. Box 910
100 Mile House, B.C.
V0K 2E0

STUDENT NAME			GRADE
Gray, Scott F.			12

DIV NUMBER	TEACHER
23	N. Jayne

ATTACHMENTS	STUDENT PEN
	8010237

ATTENDANCE RECORD

	Sep	Oct	Nov	Dec	Jan	Feb	Mar	Apr	May	Jun	Total
ABSENT	0	1	0	3	6	2	3	4	3	4	26
LATE	0	0	0	6	4	8	6	2	4	4	34

This report describes the student's learning progress based on provincial learning expectations for each grade level. It is intended to inform parents about learning successes and to guide improvement efforts when needed.

Legend: LG. - Letter Grade W.H. - Work Habits Abs. - Class Absence

---

Course: Alge 12
Teacher: M. Stanislav
Graduation Credits: 4

Term	1	2	3	4	Final
LG.	A	B	I	C+	C-
%	88	79	–	67	59
W.H.	G	G	N	N	N
Abs.	1	9	7	9	26

Comments/Ways to Support Learning: Term 3: Scott has failed to consistently meet the course assignments this term and has missed a number of quizzes. Conference requested. Term 4: Scott needs to seriously refocus if he's to reconnect with past levels of performance.

Course: Comp 12
Teacher: H. Davidson
Graduation Credits: 4

Term	1	2	3	4	Final
LG.	A	A	C	B	B
%	98	88	65	74	81
W.H.	G	G	N	S	S
Abs.	1	9	7	9	26

Comments/Ways to Support Learning: Term 3: Scott's fairly drastic drop in letter grade this term reflects a lack of attention to project criteria and his failure to hand in a major term assignment.

Course: Biol 12
Teacher: D. Wong
Graduation Credits: 4

Term	1	2	3	4	Final
LG.	B	C+	I	–	W
%	75	67	–		–
W.H.	G	S	N		N
Abs.	1	8	7		16

Comments/Ways to Support Learning: Term 3: Overall performance the last two terms has continued to deteriorate. Parent conference requested.

Course: Engl 12
Teacher: J. Bond
Graduation Credits: 4

Term	1	2	3	4	Final
LG.	A	B	I	C-	C-
%	94	85	–	50	57
W.H.	G	G	N	N	G
Abs.	1	7	7	17	32

Comments/Ways to Support Learning: Term 1: Awesome work again this year. Term 2: Good work despite what I know has been a tough time. Term 3: Student/parent conference requested. Term 4: Standing granted for graduation. I don't know what to think. Thank you for that.

2

Lunatic Fringe

Red Rider, 1981. This is a story that wasn't supposed to get told, but not for any of the normal reasons that stories don't get told. Which is to say, there are reasons why I shouldn't tell you what I'm about to tell you. But in a weird way, the reasons why I shouldn't tell you the story are all things that would normally conspire to make me want to tell you the story that much more.

Sorry, that made sense when I thought it. I'll try again.

This is a story that a lot of people don't want told. It's a story that was supposed to be secret, and which a lot of people would probably like to see stay a secret even after everything that's happened. All the things that aren't actually true, and which you've already heard about. Unless you were some-how disconnected from cable news and the Internet in mid-May, when it all happened.

My thing is that I don't like secrets all that much, especially not when the secrets are being kept by powerful people. Power and secrecy have always been a really bad mix, even when things like extraordinary renditions and tabloid-news phone hacking aren't popping up to drive them like a spike into the public consciousness. Power and secrecy feed on each other in a sort of catalytic cycle, one strengthening the other as it's consumed, then both regen-erated again to strengthen the next reaction. (Confession. I dropped Chem 11 last year after a month. I think that's what the catalytic cycle is, but I'm not going to stop to look it up.)

(The reason I'm not going to stop to look things up here is because I need to not stop with this. I've never written anything like this before, so I have no real idea what I'm doing or how long it's going to take. But no matter what I end up doing, this is the truth as it exists in me, so there can't be any going back. There can't be any editing. There can't be any embellishment by running to Google to make it look like I know more than I do. Though by way of advance warning, I might let that last rule slide if I need to figure out how to spell something, because I'm kind of obsessive that way.)

In the end, what we don't know is as important as what we do know.

Secrecy is bad. Trying to hide what we don't know is the worst kind of secrecy, because those are the secrets we keep from ourselves.

This is a story that a lot of people will try to pretend is just crazy. They'll try to pretend that it's all made up. And the point is, all of that is pretty much just an invitation for me to tell the story, because the stories that the powerful people want kept secret are usually the only ones worth telling. But if the story hadn't happened, I wouldn't have told it. And not just because I couldn't have told it if it hadn't happened (because it wouldn't have happened, obviously).

This still isn't working. Hang on.

Before it happened, I wouldn't have told this story even if I'd been able to. Because before it happened, I would have thought that my telling the story didn't matter.

There. That works.

Because this story happened, I know what matters now.

Okay, it still doesn't work. I can't explain it. You just need to keep reading.

It's easy to write something when you don't have to worry about whether people will believe it or not.

Secrets are easy. Lying is easy.

What follows is what's true.

3

One Good Reason

Bryan Adams, 1981. Even after the fact, the pieces of what happened are like this collection of fragments that almost go together, but then don't quite fit in the end. Like you're trying to assemble something without the manual, and you get it looking like the picture on the box. But there are bits left over when you're done, and you can't figure out where they were supposed to go.

I've got it all. I've got a record of almost everything that happened to the five of us. I've got records of every part of Lincoln's operation. I've got backups of surveillance feeds. I've got the military files that Carl kept, long after everyone else involved was long gone. I've got all the work Malkov did digging into those files himself. I've got Malkov's voice log, right up to the end.

I've got the audio files from the night it started for us, which tell me Carl was listening.

You need to keep reading to find out about Lincoln and Malkov. You need to keep reading for Carl.

I don't know how long Carl had been listening before it started for us. Listening, reading, watching. Phone calls, email, assignments, every article I'd ever written for *Five Horsemen*. (You need to keep reading for *Five Horsemen*.) Carl had all of it, so I have all of it now, filed and catalogued.

Mitchell calls me paranoid. Once in a while, I can pretend he means it as a compliment. Either way, I'm not paranoid. You need to keep reading for Mitchell.

I've also been called ironic, but as has been said by more ironic people than me, it's not paranoia if they really are out to get you.

I've started to go through all of it. Earlier tonight, before I talked to Molly. It all starts off with the transcription Carl made the night it started. I wanted to skip ahead to the recording of the first time I talked to Carl, when I had no idea what was really going on. When Carl was pretending to be the person I needed to talk to, so that I'd stupidly follow along according to plan.

Only I can't skip ahead, because even though I've got a full copy of the eighty-odd hours of archived video and data, all of it comes with a layer of military-specification destruct-scramble encryption that's set to burn the files down even as I watch them. So I need to relive it like it happened. Like I'm writing this, from the beginning.

But as I start the video again, watching and listening to when it started for us, all I can think about is that I don't know when it started for Carl.

This is where the record starts, but I want to know what happened before that. I want to know what Carl heard. I want to know what Carl saw to prompt the decision that made everything else happen.

When I talked to Molly tonight, she said to not bother thinking about it. She says to not watch any of it, but I know I need to. Molly says that people should make sense of what they know first, then worry about what they don't know.

You need to keep reading for Molly, too. Molly's right about a lot of things.

4

This Song
Has No Title

Elton John, 1973. I need to explain the deal with the music references, because you're probably already wondering.

The deal is, there actually is no deal. They're just a way to break things up, because when you're writing like this, it's all supposed to magically compose itself into chapters or something. Problem is, as has been said, what I'm writing actually happened, and real life unfortunately doesn't always cut itself up into convenient chunks of narrative.

Based on the preceding pages, I'm not sure that the bits these words are being carved up into are even long enough to be called chapters. Chapterlets, maybe. Chapterillos? And even as I realize now that I'm suddenly pulling a total metafiction cop-out by starting to write about the process of writing, as opposed to just actually writing, I have no idea whether any of it will make any sense in the end.

However, in terms of asking why one particular song ends up at the beginning of one not-chapter as opposed to the next, I guess you could call it a thematic choice. Sometimes there's a direct connection between the song and the part of the story it introduces (like with the next bit coming up that I need to stop avoiding writing, because the video in front of me is paused and waiting to show me the night it started). But most of the time it's just about me. That's the *me* who's writing this right now, and who has to think about what happened so that I can figure out a way to put it down for you.

When I think about what happened, the memory feels like music. Memory is weird that way. I don't know if anyone else's mind works the same, but music can take me back like nothing else does to a place, a time, a thing I'd almost forgotten about. Music does it faster, music does it better than words, better than images.

Problem is, sometimes there are things you want to forget.

I put the songs down even though I know it's kind of futile in the end, because the chances that you'll just happen to be listening to the same song when I mention it are fairly slim.

Soundtracks in books would be a good idea, I think. Someone should work on that.

5

Heroes

David Bowie, 1977. Recorded sixteen years before I was born. This is what Carl heard the night it started. It's my mix, but I don't think Carl knew that then, because most people don't know that I only listen to music recorded between 1972 and 1981. You know that now, but you need to keep reading to find out why.

This is what Carl was listening to, because this is what was playing on the multimedia workstation in the computer lab, which I'm fairly sure is where Carl was listening from. I can hear it on the audio recording. I can read our entire conversation as it was logged and transcribed, not a word missed. From the darkness, you can hear every sound in the room, fast talking, four voices.

Carl already knew our names. Mitchell, Breanne, Rico, Scott.

There's a lyric from Bowie's "Heroes" that I want to quote here, because it's extremely resonant to what I'm feeling as I write this and to what this story is ultimately about. But I can't, because quoting lyrics in a story is forbidden by intellectual property laws still wired firmly into the corporate robber-baron mindset of the nineteenth century. You can talk about the song. You can describe the song as having been recorded by so-and-so in such-and-such a year, no problem. You can quote the title of a song, like I just did above. You just can't quote a line from the song.

We Can Be Heroes

(That's not the line from the song, because if I were quoting that line from the song I'd be in big trouble, legally speaking. So thankfully I'm totally not quoting the song, but am simply making a digression to tell you that *We Can Be Heroes* was the title of an ironic Australian mockumentary television series from a few years back. It's very cool. You should watch it.)

We Can Be Heroes

(This is another digression. You can tell because of the parentheses. The above is also totally not a line from any song, but is the name of a pop/punk band out of Windsor, Ontario. I don't know anything about them other than their name, because I only listen to music recorded between 1972 and 1981. Molly likes them, though.)

We Can Be Heroes

(Here's another digression, in which I come to the sudden realization that this line which is totally not from any song would make a catchy title for whatever book or blog or web series this story turns into. I don't know what this story is going to turn into. I'm just the guy trying to write it.)

The titles of these individual not-chapters tell you what I'm listening to as I write them. You can listen along if you like. Where there's a direct connection between the song and the part of the story it introduces (like with this bit right here), you could even look up the lyrics I'm not allowed to quote. I hear the Internet is good for that sort of thing.

Bowie's "Heroes" is a song that most people think they know, but which practically no one has ever really heard. What most people have heard is the shortened greatest hits edit or the cover versions. (Confession. I only listen to music recorded between 1972 and 1981, but I remain aware that other music exists.) However, all of those edits and cover versions skip straight to the third verse, which makes the track sound like a straightforward love song. One of those songs that makes it sound like love is a pill you pop when you're feeling anxious. One of those songs that just really makes you want to burn a corporate light-rock radio station to the ground.

What the above-mentioned most people have all missed is the album version of the track. This includes even those of them who own the album, but who listen to the greatest-hits edit anyway because that's what the corporate light-rock radio stations are playing when they're not being burned to the ground.

What the album version of the song is about is two people falling in love with each other in the shadow of the Berlin Wall. What the album version of the song is about is reminding us that love, like political freedom, only really means something to those who are denied it.

(The following are not quotes from song lyrics. They are, in order, the title of a MySpace page I just tripped across completely by accident, and the title of a piece of Percy Jackson and the Olympians fan fiction. Nothing to do with anything else.)

The Guns Shot Above Our Heads
And We Kissed

It's not a metaphor. It's about living in a world in which telling someone you love them is the bravest thing you'll ever do.

Just think about it.

I was born way too late to have grown up in East Berlin, but I often think my life would have made a lot more sense if I had.

6

Manifesto

Roxy Music, 1979. Not knowing how to start has always been a problem for me. Hence, the rambling I've been doing. I'm done now, though. This is the night it started.

From the multimedia workstation in the computer lab, here's what Carl heard.

BREANNE: *We head for the gangway, recon front and back. Sensor sweep, five by five.*

RICO: *Motion, IR, and EM spec on the hull. Looking for movement and stress points.*

MITCHELL: *I cycle the airlock.*

Sorry, hang on a minute.

This next bit is about RPGing, but don't panic or anything. If your eyes are already glazing over, it's a short bit, I promise.

This bit is about RPGing, which stands for roleplaying gaming, by which I mean tabletop roleplaying gaming, which I'm going to refer to hereinafter as *gaming*. Because in my world, there's no other kind of gaming.

This isn't a story about gaming, though. Not in any important sense, anyway. The story's about people who happen to be gamers, and about what that means to us, and what difference that made to what happened, and why. The story might have just as easily been about people who happened to play lacrosse or chess or badminton or whatever.

Though if it was, things would have turned out quite badly, I expect. And this would be a bit about listening to a badminton game. Between you and me, we're all better off this way.

This is a story about gamers. But there are only a few places where that really matters. I'll try to warn you in advance.

MITCHELL: *I cycle the airlock.*

SCOTT: *As has been stated previously, the airlock is jammed. Get over it.*

MITCHELL: *That makes no sense.*

BREANNE: *It would make perfect sense to anyone with sense. The airlock is jammed.*

MITCHELL: *An airlock by definition is designed to withstand pressure. How does the application of pressure jam it?*

RICO: *You applied pressure in excess.*

MITCHELL: *Three lousy cluster bombs?*

SCOTT: *Your three lousy cluster bombs have blown the cargo hold to ribboned*

Sorry, hang on another minute.

I'm writing this, and I'm typing down bits of the transcription that Carl left for me, and it's supposed to be the truth. I'm telling this story, and it's a story about me and the others. But the truth is that me and the others swear a whole lot.

All right, maybe not so much the others. Except for Breanne when she's in the right mood. Me, I swear a whole lot, one particular Anglo-Saxon epithet in particular. I'm not sure why that is.

This story is supposed to be written for public consumption, though. And I know I'm not going to worry about the occasional *damn, hell,* and *oh god* sliding by. However, for the harder stuff, there's a kind of cultural speed limit for profanity, and I'm about to blast past it even before the parts of the story that really deserve it.

But here's the thing — either something's true or it isn't. Either I write things down the way they actually happened, or I might as well just be making it up. In my world, there's no *This is the truth except for the words I had to change because I didn't want to offend anybody.*

Here's a thought, though.

We studied journalism and editor's marks with Ms. Bond in first term English. In edited copy, if you see brackets [like this], it means that someone has inserted or amended something that wasn't a part of the original text, but they're alerting you to the fact that it's been changed. So here, when you see [*this*], it means that the *this* in brackets isn't really what was said, but that I've done the editor's thing and replaced it with something.

For the most part, I'll try to replace things in such a way that you can figure out what was really said if you want to. Like on cable TV, where they bleep the words but still let you read those words on the lips of whoever's saying them.

SCOTT: *Your three lousy cluster bombs have blown the cargo hold to ribboned rat[dung].*

Subtle, isn't it? But maybe it all makes a certain sense, actually.

This is the truth I'm telling you, and truth should always make you think about what you're hearing.

SCOTT: *Your three lousy cluster bombs have blown the cargo hold to ribboned rat[dung].*
   The airlock is jammed.
BREANNE: *Are you eating that?*
RICO: *Nope. We head for the gangway.*
MITCHELL: *I cycle the airlock.*

11

SCOTT: *The airlock, for the last [lord's name in vain] time, is [lord's name in vain] jammed, all right?*

MITCHELL: *That makes no sense.*

RICO: *Somebody binds and gags the hiver, then we head for the gangway.*

MITCHELL: *That's mutiny.*

BREANNE: *Shut up. I'm on point.*

SCOTT: *Spot check.*

Carl would have heard dice, but that doesn't mean anything unless you already know what you're listening to. Dice rolled across a gaming table make a particular sound that won't mean anything to anybody who doesn't game. If you know that unique clatter, you can almost hear the meshing of random gears as numbers fall out and the drama spins off from them. Mitchell claims to be able to tell what numbers have come up even without looking, just from listening. Like the wonks in automotive class can tell the difference between a Ford Triton 3V and a Dodge HEMI just from the sound of them both idling a half-klick away.

(Confession. As I've never been within half a kilometer of an automotive class, I'm actually one of those people who can't tell the difference. I heard Breanne give the blindfolded anecdote a couple of months back. I guessed at the time that a Ford Triton 3V and a Dodge HEMI are engines, but maybe she was talking about stereo systems, I don't know.)

BREANNE: *Yeah! Thirty-six.*

SCOTT: *Since how?*

BREANNE: *Plus-eight for the full-spec night-sight goggles I found on what was left of the crew chief.*

SCOTT: *Fine. Indistinct shapes fan out across the gangway. Drone destroyers, chameleon combat armor.*

More dice on the audio. Someone slurps from a can of something highly caffeinated. Carl would have heard a lot of that as well.

BREANNE: *Feed the closest one half a clip and scatter. Hell, twelve damage on eighteen?*

SCOTT: *Breanne for the miss.*

RICO: *Get a grenade off.*

SCOTT: *Don't remember you reloading.*

RICO: *When Bre reconned the lifeboat.*

SCOTT: *Do it.*

RICO: *Thirty-two adjusted. Twenty-six concussion, eighteen fire.*

SCOTT: *You distract them. Auto-fire rounds hit behind you, four distinct patterns.*

BREANNE: *Follow the line of fire back at them. Pulse rifle, full auto.*

SCOTT: *Can't shoot what you can't see.*

BREANNE: *Night vision, Einstein. Goggles are on.*

SCOTT: *On, overloaded, and shut down when Rico's incendiary went up in front of you. You going to fire blind or claw them off and call me back?*

BREANNE: *Oh, bite me.*

SCOTT: *Only if you mean it. You?*

RICO: *Reloading.*

SCOTT: *You?*

MITCHELL: *I cycle the airlock.*

BREANNE: *[Archaic epithet calling Mitchell's parentage into question. As Breanne and Mitchell are twins, I'm not sure she really thought that one through.]*

Breanne jumps up from a table spread with charts, dice, and the box that once held a takeout pizza that never stood a chance. The rest of us sit across from her. This is us.

Mitchell is a bookish savant. Hair that's too long to be fashionable, not long enough to be metal. John Lennon glasses, well-worn Dockers, a *Firefly* t-shirt that's been washed a few too many times.

Rico is a subdued bruiser. Hair short but not quite military spec. Faded jeans and muscle shirt, chiseled arms that would be a tattoo artist's dream.

Scott cultivates what Mitchell annoyingly calls the fashionable nihilist look. Black t-shirt, black jacket, black khakis, black paratrooper boots from Surplus Herby's in Kamloops. I'm Scott.

Breanne is post-feminist chic. Hair short, overalls, tank top, Dream Theater baseball cap. Her anger toward Mitchell as she stuffs her backpack is tangible.

"I told McAllister I'd work a half-shift tonight, you [gender-specific anatomical reference]! You said you were watching the time!" She adds a number of epithets so personal that I can't think of any brackets for them.

"I'm apparently bound and gagged," Mitchell says. Rico's already slamming chairs back and sweeping up paperwork in a frenzy of hiding all evidence that we've been there.

This is after hours in the computer lab, thirty-odd iMacs standing dark. This is the Computers 11 and 12 classroom, plus in-class and after-hours resource room for the science and math classrooms across and down the hall. We're at the west end of the main-floor corridor of the high school, stuck in the middle of the hard-science labs like an afterthought. This is because the computer lab was, in fact, an afterthought, its inside door leading into the chem lab in a way that makes no real sense.

Mitchell and Breanne are getting into a deepening argument about who's the responsible one while Rico tries to keep them separated. The upshot is that no one's paying attention to me, which I find annoying.

"Hey, we're kind of in the middle of something."

"And I'm kind of late for work." Breanne shovels the last two slices of leftover double-pepperoni into an empty sandwich container in her backpack.

"You'll be dead in five minutes. Sit down."

But she's already out the door to the corridor, Rico dragged behind her with an apologetic shrug. Mitchell pops my iPhone from the multimedia workstation and frisbees it across the room for me to catch. I scoop dice and carefully roll up the night's battle maps.

I hear Breanne shouting something about hurrying the hell up from the corridor. I methodically take my time.

Outside the computer lab, the school is dark, which is mostly an improvement on its look during the day. Based on a whirlwind small-town debating club tour that Mitchell, Molly, and I took last year, I suspect that there's only ever been one small-town high school. Like one set of master plans gets passed around the circuit of rural school boards for decades on end. Or maybe a secret government star chamber determined a long time ago that sapping the will of the kids of the forest-industry working class was best done by trapping them inside this one particular arrangement of cinderblock walls.

Next to the custodian's storage hangs a largish sign reading *Peter Skene Ogden Secondary School ~ École Secondaire*. The name is wrapped around the school's majestic mascot, which is a vaguely manga-esque bald eagle, which is a bird that gets terrorized by crows a lot, and so is a lot less majestic than most people think. Peter Skene Ogden was a nineteenth-century fur trader who lied, stole, vandalized, assaulted, and murdered his way across the North American frontier. He left behind him a legacy of brutal violence, environmental destruction, overt racism, multiple wives, and illegitimate children, though it's never been clear to me which of these accomplishments landed him the coveted having-a-high-school-named-after-you gig.

Across from the office and the main-floor foyer, a glass display case is filled with trophies and newspaper clippings. The highlights of the various school teams that come and go with the seasons are kept track of here, along with occasional mentions of less athletic honors. Mitchell, Molly, and I were in there last year when the debating team took second place at the regionals in Prince George.

Last October, the five of us took first place in the VCON RPG team open in Vancouver, but nobody bothered posting that anywhere. Maybe if we'd had school uniforms or something.

The five of us means me, Mitchell, Breanne, and Rico, plus Molly. You need to keep reading for Molly.

Along the ceiling, security cameras are mounted at regular intervals, wide-angle lenses covering every part of the corridor. Or at least they would be if they were ever turned on. The cameras were installed last year in the main hall and the downstairs lockers after a rash of brazen iPod thefts. That is to say,

14

after one iPod theft from Mr. Mueller the phys-ed teacher, who accidentally left his backpack at the downstairs water fountain one day, then screamed really loudly about it.

However, it turns out that although you can video-record students in the corridors stealing each other's iPods without their permission, you need their permission to actually look at that video in order to catch them at it. Privacy law's a funny thing.

As Mitchell and I follow Breanne and Rico toward the main doors, we pass along an endless wall of glassed-in photos where dozens of previous generations of graduates hang. Most of them have this identical expression that suggests they're all trying to project a mature and confident gaze toward the future. Problem is, none of them ever suspected that the future doesn't like to just stand in front of us waiting to be gazed at. The future likes to pick a really good spot, out of sight and just to the side. Then it hangs there with a sniper rifle and a really good scope.

I'm betting the people in the photos never saw it coming.

At the end of the month, somebody will pull the oldest array of mugshots down. That's the class of 1982, who for some reason have always seemed to look particularly stunned even compared to everyone who came after them. Then they'll shift all the frames down to make room for the new mugshots. Mitchell, Breanne, and Rico will be there. Molly will be there.

As Mitchell and I descend the east stairs past the library, Breanne and Rico wait inside the back-door foyer that leads to the student lounge. Breanne is pacing relentlessly while Rico stands in his usual stolid way. Because they're holding hands, this means she has to make a sort of horseshoe orbit around him in an agitated fashion.

"Don't let us keep you," she calls loudly.

"Wouldn't dream of it." I flash her the confident smile that comes from being the only one in the group who knows the alarm code, which let us open the doors without calling down a police action on top of us.

I key the alarm off. Breanne is in a big enough hurry that she doesn't bother trying to get a look at the code like she usually does. I toss Mitchell the pizza box for the recycling dumpster at the edge of the student parking lot, our bikes chained a few meters away. The aging crew cab pickup that Rico's dad bequeathed to him for his birthday last year is the only vehicle there, he and Breanne already sprinting for it. I set the alarm again, locking the door behind me as we go.

7

Wild One

Thin Lizzy, 1975. Mitchell and I are cycling across the school field, paralleling the side road where it feeds into the highway ahead. Breanne and Rico roar past in his truck, *Deckard & Sons Excavation & Landscaping* emblazoned on the box. An airborne haze of road dust rises behind them. Rico waves. Breanne waves, too, but with fewer fingers.

Where Mitchell pedal-stands behind me, I call back. "You thirsty?"

"No."

"You're not thirsty?"

"No."

"I figured you might be thirsty."

"Well, let me think. No."

I lead on. Behind us, the school recedes on its perch along the highway hillside. A truck yard stands adjacent, the RCMP station closer to the highway, the town and its two thousand people spreading below. This is vintage interior British Columbia logging country, stands of Douglas fir and white spruce, aspen and lodgepole pine spreading to every horizon, the late-spring sky immense overhead.

It's a short jaunt off the field and through an obstacle course of brush and discarded fast-food debris. Then an exhilaratingly rough ride takes us down the trail that runs past the pedestrian underpass beneath the highway. A steep slide down a gravel bank leads alongside the broad spread of marsh and bird sanctuary that opens up smack in the middle of town.

Beyond that marsh and the small airstrip that stretches alongside the marsh, the arena, and the curling rink, our destination is Howie's Corner Store. It occupies the center of a dusty stretch of frontage road, meaning it isn't actually on a corner. Just think about it.

We do business quickly enough to make sure the bikes don't get stolen, and I'm out before Mitchell so that I can claim the piece of sidewalk I want to claim. His look when he exits behind me has disapproval written all over it, but the sugar rush from the slush I'm knocking back dulls it for me.

Howie and Maureen, the not-on-the-corner store's cheerily wholesome thirty-something proprietors, eschew any sort of Slurpee mass-productionism to make their slush the old-fashioned way that nature intended. That's unflavored ice and a self-serve syrup bar that they have no apparent problem with me overloading from. There's probably slightly more sugar than water in the mango-lemon-cola slam-mix I'm partial to, which is also as nature intended.

Overhead, sunset streaks a darkening sky. On the highway, a steady stream of traffic runs the amber light at the intersection with Fourth Street.

Across and to the left is the Exeter Arms, which is a hotel whose parking lot overflows with patrons for the bar most nights, but which doesn't do any actual hotel business that I've ever been aware of. To the right is a mirror-image frontage road to Howie's frontage road, on which sits a darkened realtor's office, an open-late-but-about-to-close thrift shop, and a store that seems to be perpetually for rent. Or maybe they sell *For Rent* signs. I've never actually gone in to see. Closer than all the rest, Brownies Chicken anchors the corner.

"Do you ever feel like you're living in the wrong time?" Mitchell asks as he appraises the sky.

"Pretty much constantly."

Mitchell slips onto his bike with a chocolate milk and a stack of sesame snaps in hand, then does this thing where he pulls his feet up to the pedals and just kind of balances there without moving. It's impressive. I timed him going to four minutes once without having to touch down on the ground, but I wasn't interested enough to see how much longer he could make it.

"Say you can go anywhere, anywhen," he says.

"Dallas, November 22, 1963. With a six-person HDCAM crew covering multiple angles with really long lenses."

"It'd be thirty years before you could sell it to CNN."

"I'd wait."

Across the highway, through the Brownie's plate glass, I can see her.

Behind the counter, Molly looks distracted as she comes on shift, slipping her uniform top over a long-sleeved white sweater and jeans. At eighteen, she's a year older than Breanne, Mitchell, and I, but she's always managed to look younger somehow. Something in the way she used to laugh, and in the spread of pale freckles that clouds her nose. Something in the blonde hair that's tied back in a ponytail now like it usually is, and which always seems to be moving in slow motion.

(Confession. Technically, Molly is only nine months older than Breanne and Mitchell, who will catch up to her and Rico both in October. She's eleven months older than me because my birthday's in December, meaning that pretty much everyone in my grade has always been older than me.)

I pick this particular patch of sidewalk like I do every other time Mitchell and I stop here, because it sits in the shadow between battered streetlights. From that shadow, I can watch without being obvious about it. From the corner of my eye that isn't watching, I see Mitchell follow my gaze.

"Hanging out here night after night watching an ex-girlfriend sling fried food is a sign of some serious sociopathy in progress."

Mitchell has never been one for needing things spelled out. As such, he's the one person I've never bothered to refrain from showing my irritation for spelling out the things I prefer to deny.

"Considering she was never my girlfriend, is there a reason you keep calling her that?"

"Because it was what it was whether the two of you got around to calling it that or not." He shrugs, balancing with one hand on his handlebars as he drinks. I've known Mitchell long enough to know that him shrugging is a tell, like in poker. It's the only sign he'll ever give that he cares about a problem that he knows he can't fix, so that he won't try. "The game was better with five," he says.

"Talk to her about that."

"Sounds easy."

I give him the same wave Breanne gave me, just as the sugar rush and the brain freeze meet in the center of my occipital lobe like they always do. Through my euphoric stupor, a thought takes form as words even before I've had time to think them through. /

"She ever say anything to you?" It's been four months, and I haven't asked that question of Mitchell yet. I'm pretty sure that's because I already know the answer.

"No," he says, which means I was right. "Breanne said they talked."

"What about?"

"About how she didn't want to talk."

I feel like there's something else I want to say, but all I can do is watch.

This is what I see.

Through the window, through the haze of taillights that brightens as the sky overhead gets dark, Molly clears tables. Brownies is only half-full, like it mostly is outside the lunch and dinner rush. As she works, she dances to edgy alt-prog rock on the CD jukebox, looking like she doesn't care who's watching.

Beyond the lights of 100 Mile House, which is usually shortened to *100 Mile* in the writing and is only ever called *Hundred Mile* by anyone who lives here, broad slopes of forest and rangeland spread to all sides. Where the highway sweeps down, then up again along those slopes, you can look up along the line of forest and sky, letting the stillness and the size of the night just take your breath away.

When the sun sets here, it's like the world hangs for an endless moment between light and dark. Like the landscape is watching the day fade away but isn't ready for night yet. Watching the lights come on along the side road and the hotel parking lot and the Brownie's sign across the highway. The Brownie's sign is a giant bucket of chicken, lighting up like some lurid beacon of civilization in a dark wasteland.

(Sorry, that's too much of a stretch, even for metaphor. Never mind.)

"What about you?" I say to Mitchell.

"What about me?"

"The right time and place for you."

"I don't think it exists. But at least here and now, my chances of getting burned at the stake are low."

"You might be surprised." I drain the last of my slush and carefully crush the cup.

"Seriously," Mitchell says. "A movement toward real consciousness is at work these days. The consumer state is crumbling as the media veil begins to short-circuit itself, and McLuhan's medium is the message that's burning out with oversaturation. We live in an age of ontological instability and evolutionary imminence."

"We live in a police-state prison where guards and inmates trade off jobs on odd days."

"You do know that optimists live longer?"

This was when it started, even if I didn't know it then.

I hear it first, the faint drone twisting through the traffic noise. Then I look up. A black helicopter comes into line of sight, shooting past fast overhead, southwest to northeast. Low enough that its lines are sharp against the sunset, burning copper along the western horizon.

"And did you know that there are currently upwards of three hundred private paramilitary organizations active worldwide?" I say.

"I must have missed it with Keith Olbermann off the air." As Mitchell follows my gaze, something in his sense of balance doesn't like the view. His foot touches the ground as the bike shifts beneath him. He looks disappointed.

"Black helicopters," I say. "No markings. You can find them in any country in the world, moving with complete freedom. Weapons dealing, espionage, sabotage. The line between military and business erased because that's the way the power brokers want it."

The chopper is directly overhead now, louder. Mitchell squints. "Or maybe a German package tour gets to take in the sunset at a hundred bucks a head."

"You have any aspirations beyond just being really naive all your life?"

"I've actually come to the conclusion that aspiration itself is meaningless in the long run." Mitchell is staring past the chopper to the sky, his gaze distant like it gets when he's thinking. "We all long for glory, but our greatness is constrained."

"Speaking for yourself?"

"I'm speaking for you, actually. I see you slowly strangling inside your cynically twisted worldview."

"And what's holding you back?" I ask.

"The distraction of a perfect knowledge of what it is holding everybody else back."

"Glad I can be a part of that for you."

I stand and dust myself off. Across the way, Molly is dancing past the side windows, clearing trays as she nods to an older couple at a corner booth. She doesn't smile. Molly doesn't smile much anymore.

"Show's over?" Mitchell says.

"Ride, Aristotle."

I hop onto my bike and head out on the frontage road, fastening my helmet with one hand so that it blocks my face from the Brownies side of the street. Not that Molly would be watching anyway.

I don't need to turn back to feel Mitchell looking from me to the distant windows before he sprints to catch up.

8

Who Do You
Think We Are?

Alice Cooper, 1981. I'm watching this on a set of matched video streams. External night-vision flight tracking, plus the chopper's interior surveillance feed. It's logged and encrypted with all the rest of the recordings, but if it wasn't for the time-stamp on the feed, I might not get the full significance.

While Mitchell and I were talking, this is what was being recorded high overhead.

Through a night-vision lens in the chopper's belly, 100 Mile is a dark scar of urbanization cutting through an endless expanse of wilderness. If you look closely, you can make out the bright suture scratches of roads that hold it all together. If you could up the resolution a couple of times, you'd see the bright points of Mitchell and I on the sidewalk, staring up.

In the cabin, a guy sits in the pilot's seat, forty-something in a black leather jacket and sunglasses. This is Lincoln. Behind him, a half-dozen men and women ride, sleeping or reading or looking bored where they watch out the windows. They're all decked out in casual business garb, maybe a group of forest-company middle managers coming back from an asset survey. That's what you see if you don't look too closely.

But if you do look closely, you'll notice the woman riding shotgun beside Lincoln. She's dressed in some buttoned-down one-martini-lunch number like the others, her dark hair tied back.

Her name is Karya. In the unmoving field of view that the cabin camera makes, she's fieldstripping an Uzi as Lincoln takes her and the others home.

9

Crazy On You

Heart, 1976. Mitchell and I take a long detour through the Esso parking lot on our way through town, because I've got a slow leak in my front valve that I can't be bothered to fix. While we're there for air, I see what follows.

The Esso station sits off the highway at the north edge of town, a little island of light and signage in a larger sea of light and signage. Across from the newer mall, it's a stone's throw from the Red Coach Inn, which is probably the closest thing this place has to a landmark. 100 Mile House is so named because it was originally a stopover post one hundred miles up the road from Lillooet, where the B.C. gold rush trail north to the Klondike started. The Red Coach is so named because it has a horse-drawn-style red coach out front, much like the ones people used to ride back in those days.

In the years since the gold rush, they've straightened the highway a couple of dozen times, so I have no idea how many miles it is to Lillooet anymore.

I remember Mr. Palmer in Social Studies 10 talking about when Canada adopted the metric system, and how there was a huge concern about whether the government would force the town to change its name to 160.9 Kilometer House. I'm pretty sure he wasn't joking.

As is often the case on a weekday evening at the Esso, Rico can be seen greeting customers at the pumps. This is odder than it looks, however, as it isn't Rico who actually works at the Esso weekday evenings, but Breanne. Only whenever Rico's there, she spends most of her time under the hood of his truck and counts on him to cover for her.

Breanne under the hood of a vehicle is a thing I'm not qualified to write about. *She moves really fast* is about all I can say to describe it. She whips around a lot of tools without actually looking at them. Then when she's done, whatever vehicle she's been under the hood of runs better than it ever did before.

As Mitchell and I ride up, a lull in the steady stream of traffic lets Rico saunter over to where Breanne is a blur of mechanical-savant motion. They both see us and wave. Breanne uses more fingers this time, so I know I'm forgiven from earlier.

"Are you planning on pumping any gas tonight?" Rico calls to her.

Breanne's voice is muffled as she leans in, hanging by her hips over the edge of the engine well. "Are you planning on ever paying me for this exclusive automotive service thing we seem to have going?"

"I'm waiting till you break something. Your rate will probably improve."

Breanne laughs. "Hey, I sent my SAIT application off."

Mitchell is balancing again as I try to get the pressure gauge on the pump to decide whether it wants to work or not. SAIT is SAIT Polytechnic, or the Southern Alberta Institute of Technology. They apparently teach people how to fix cars there, judging by what Breanne says as she hops off the truck to throw things back into an oversized toolkit. "The automotive program is supposed to be amazing, and then Marnie Robison's cousin manages the Canadian Tire in Red Deer. She says I can stay with her while I apprentice."

"Yeah," Rico says, because that's what Rico says. I'm the only one looking at him when he says it, and I see a sudden tension in the way he's standing, the lines of his crossed arms expressing emotion that the silence hides. It tells me he doesn't see me watching. I look away to make sure he doesn't.

"Because I think Regina's probably your best bet," Breanne says, "because then you do the justice program instead of the criminology, because everybody and his dog has a criminology degree. And the team's not great, but that just means less competition for captain, right?"

"Yeah."

My tires are topped up. Mitchell and I head for the highway.

"You're a man of many words tonight," Breanne says, but Rico is peering under the hood as she pulls it shut. "Treat your engine nicely, it'll treat you nicely. There's a lesson in there."

"Yeah," Rico says. Then he says, "I love you."

Despite the fact that it has nothing to do with me, this catches me off guard. Because it's something I've never heard Rico say before. Then Breanne says it back, and I suddenly feel like I'm intruding in something I shouldn't be. The two of them are leaning close and talking some more, but I turn my attention to the highway, moving past them and out of sight.

As I approach Mitchell where he waits for the light, I glance back to see Rico and Breanne kissing with a particularly teenaged intensity. Another car pulls in, Breanne glaring at it as they kiss again. Then she waves goodbye as she heads for the pumps, Rico climbing into the truck and starting up.

I'm the only one who sees him watching Breanne for a long moment before he goes.

10

Dust in the Wind

Kansas, 1977. I didn't see this. Molly told me.

She didn't tell me till tonight, where *tonight* is when I'm writing this. It's already a few days later than it was when I started writing, and for the record, I still have no real idea what I'm doing.

I'm stalling for time because I don't want to write this, but this is where it needs to go.

Outside Brownie's, it's dark now. Inside, a different older couple are eating at the corner booth. A gaggle of junior high students are at the counter, stopping by before the late show at the Rangeland. The Rangeland is the one movie theater we have in town. It's up the hill, past the older mall. That's got nothing to do with Molly. I'm just mentioning it because I'm stalling for time. Because I don't want to write this.

While Sal the manager works out front, Molly's in the break room behind the kitchen, whose side door opens onto the short stairs to the parking lot. Last year, when Molly started working at Brownies, I used to wander down and sit on the steps with her while she took her breaks. I don't do that anymore.

This night, the side door is open because the deep fryers in the adjacent kitchen and the spring chill outside cancel each other nicely. Molly sits straight-backed on the couch, playing my old PlayStation 2 system hooked up to the break-room TV. She talked me into giving it to her last year because I wasn't using it anymore, and because Sal's antenna reception always had slightly more static than picture on the two broadcast channels you can get in 100 Mile. She's playing *Ace Combat 4,* which is a little on the vintage side but can still surprise you. Unless you're Molly, that is.

Like I can't describe Breanne at work, I can't really describe Molly at a combat flight simulator console. I'll give it a shot, though.

Molly's reflexes are staggering. Her connection to the controls is like something organic. Watching her fly is like watching one of those time-lapse video clips of plants growing. You recognize the movement, but it's all too fast somehow. She gets to this point where she doesn't even blink, her eyes shining like some kind of blue

Sorry. I can't do it. I've never had the words to talk about Molly's eyes.

Whatever mission she's playing, Molly's speed and altimeter readings will be clocking over as a blur of digits. If she's playing the mission she likes best, she's soaring over an expanse of anonymously rendered could-be-Siberia/

could-be-Iraq post-apocalyptic scrubland cityscape, pursued by enemy jets coming in from six different directions. That scrubland cityscape spends most of its time at the top of the screen as Molly dodges missile tracking and anti-aircraft fire upside down, a succession of tight rolls letting her unleash fiery death in a wide arc around her.

But then even in the midst of narrowly avoiding what seems like certain destruction in a web of heat-seeking missiles and machine-gun fire, Molly falters. She hits pause on the controller, standing quickly in response to the figure ascending the stairs from the parking lot.

Victor is Molly's dad, though he's actually her stepdad. Which is to say, he's been her stepdad for a long time and she calls him *dad*. You know what I mean. I can't talk about *Molly's real dad* because it's not like Victor's imaginary, but Molly's original dad died when she was a kid. She doesn't talk about him very much.

Victor is a business-lawyer type, better dressed even at this hour than most people in town have any reason to dress during the day. There's a self-consciousness in Molly suddenly. All the fluid grace that normally flows from her into a game controller is gone. She can hear Sal and a customer laughing about something out past the kitchen.

"Hi," she says.

"Not keeping you, am I?"

Victor has this voice. I haven't had to hear it for four months now, but he's got this voice with a kind of withering tone that makes you want to wash your ears out with bleach.

"No," Molly says. "Would you like some coffee?"

"Is it any better than it usually is?"

It's not an attempt at humor. Victor's voice doesn't do humor.

"I don't know," Molly says quietly.

"Then I guess I don't. Are we going sometime?"

It takes Molly a second to understand.

"I'm on until ten, actually…"

"You told me eight."

"I don't think I did. I mean, if I did, I'm sorry."

"Me wasting a trip into town, what's that to be sorry about?"

Victor's voice also doesn't do anger. Victor is very careful to never let the anger show.

"I didn't think…" Molly says.

"Yeah, you covered that."

And he turns away, quietly descending the steps where Molly and I used to sit. Victor doesn't like to make a lot of noise.

Molly watches through the open door as he hops into the well-kept SUV he's left idling in the parking lot. She tosses the controller aside, switches the TV off as he pulls away.

11

Take the
Long Way Home

Supertramp, 1979. Mitchell and I ride for the better part of the evening, because that's what we do. Through the straight grid of empty downtown streets to start with, we swing down Birch Avenue past Games Galore. That's the local gaming and comic shop that I'm pretty sure the four of us, who used to be the five of us, keep in business. Ken and Lynne are the couple who own and run it, who are kind of in the same ballpark as my parents in terms of age but cool to point that I only desperately wish my parents could be.

After downtown, we hit the trails through the park as a crescent moon breaks from the clouds and adds its light to the sodium glow of the parking-lot floods. As we ride, we engage in an endless ongoing conversation of story and game and narrative, because that's what we do. Imagine laying out and mentally scripting a film of no specific genre, scene by scene. But don't worry, I'm not going to bore you with it.

(Confession. I know absolutely nothing about filmmaking, so I have no idea what's involved in scripting a film. I just know that what Mitchell and I can come up with in an hour's night riding is a whole lot more entertaining than anything I've ever seen on screen.)

Mitchell's due back home at ten, so that's when we pack it in. I ride to his place to drop him off, which leaves me with the long trip back home. However, the silence and the darkness don't feel like a bad thing this night. On top of the annoyance of having to jam early on the reactor-crippled starship fire-fight I'd prepped that afternoon while skipping English, the conversation out front of Howie's is bothering me more than I want to admit.

I wasn't there to see what happened after I dropped Mitchell off, and I wasn't at Rico's that night, but I'll lay things out anyway. You're going to see my house in a minute, too, and the scene at home doesn't ever change all that much for any of us.

Breanne and Mitchell live with their folks, Malcolm and Kim, in a cabin two klicks or so out Horse Lake Road. Malcolm and Kim are former anti-establishment socialist punks from the first time the punk thing came around. In their house, bookshelves and agit-prop political posters line the walls beside a woodstove that burns almost year-round just for the ambience. Breanne will have been picked up from the garage by the time I drop Mitchell off.

While everybody dishes up a late dinner, they'll talk about a food-bank drive, or the community garden project just starting up, or a hospital benefit, or some other cause of good will. As they eat, Breanne and Mitchell will attempt to throw responsibility for whatever volunteerism their parents are looking for onto the other person. They'll be doing this with practiced ease. Mitchell and Breanne have spent their lives defining themselves in terms of stark opposition to both their parents and to each other, which involves a kind of four-dimensional Boolean algebra that can't really be explained. Not that that stops Mitchell from trying.

Rico's parents are Vern and Shelley. They live in a two-storey place that overlooks the park where Mitchell and I were just riding, and whose size suggests that they're waiting in vain for Rico's two older brothers to move back home sometime soon. If this night's like most nights, Rico's mom will have apple pie on the table before bed. You can smell the highly addictive brown-sugar scent of Rico's mom's apple pie from six blocks away. The actual taste of Rico's mom's pie is another thing I can't describe.

Rico's dad will be sitting back with his suspenders half on and the accumulated grime of thirty years' honest landscaping labor still on his hands. He'll be poring over this year's John Deere heavy equipment catalogue and asking Rico what he thinks of the ProGator 2030A. Rico will tell him what he thinks, quite knowledgably. I find that very unsettling.

(Confession. I know there's something called a John Deere ProGator 2030A because it was featured prominently a couple of months back on a billboard at the heavy equipment dealer across the highway from the school. I have no actual idea whether Rico's dad would ever need one, but I thought it sounded good.)

The last time I was at Rico's, a seven-month-old newspaper clipping was still taped to the fridge, next to his mom's church circle notices and a recipe for sausage gravy. It's the bottom-of-page-14 *100 Mile Free Press* article about the five of us winning the VCON RPG team open. It'll probably still be there long after Rico's moved out.

Here's a screenshot from the *Free Press* website.

Wargamers Win

October 13, 2010

Peter Skene Ogden Secondary students Molly Casey, Richard Deckard, Mitchell Everett, Scott Grey, and Breanne Marm won the team role-playing gaming open competition two weeks ago at VCON 35 in Vancouver. The local wargamers bested a field of nearly 60 competitors from B.C. and around the world.

VCON is Vancouver's science fiction and fantasy convention, and has been promoting science fiction and fantasy in Canada and the Pacific Northwest since 1971.

Richard is Rico, but you probably figured that out. Mitchell has his dad's last name as a last name and his mom's last name as a middle name, and Breanne vice versa, because their parents are former antiestablishment socialist punks. Yeah, the article spelled my name wrong.

Molly lives with her dad at 108 Mile, in a business-lawyer-type custom-built log house with a hot tub and a landscaped yard (done by Rico's dad, naturally). I don't know how she got home that night.

I don't know what happens at Molly's.

My house is a well-kept rancher that squats on a curving slab of sub-division cul-de-sac on the northeast edge of town. When we first moved here, we lived in a different well-kept rancher a little further into what used to be the edge of town when I was kid. Eventually, that edge of town just became town, as the town swelled past it and made new edges.

Where my house now jostles for space with a lot of other houses, it all used to be forest. When I was the previously mentioned kid, I and a lot of friends that have all disappeared from my life used to tear through those woods all summer, pretending we were Power Rangers. All the forest trails we made then are a whole bunch of backyards now.

When they made those backyards, though, they left the bigger trees standing at strategic points along the property lines. And if you spent as much time as I did orienting yourself to those trees when it was all forest, and if you remember the lay of the land that the subdivision roads follow now, you can sort of place the old view over the new view in your mind.

I'm not entirely sure, but at that younger age, I think I might have regularly peed against a large scrub pine that once stood exactly where our bathroom is now. This seems like a remarkable coincidence to me.

I open the garage with the remote clipped to my handlebars. Rolling inside to park my bike, I hit the remote again to close the door even before it's rolled all the way up. I drop almost to the ground as I slip out, the door grinding down over top of me and slamming behind as I stand again. It's a well-practiced ritual. Our timing is perfect, the door and I.

Inside my house, there's a vaguely middle-class ambience. This vagueness speaks to the fact that I'm probably not really middle class, but more upper-middle-class-pretending-to-be-middle-class-to-keep-the-property-taxes-down. I hang my helmet and my jacket alongside the field of other jackets by the door. The only light on is at the stove, such that as I come in through the kitchen, an unearthly pulse of color wafts in from the living room beyond. I grab an apple from the bowl on the table as I pass.

In the living room, well-stuffed furniture fronts last year's consumer electronics. Seth and Nora are glued to the TV that I can't see from where I'm standing. Their chairs sit a carefully arranged distance apart, so that both get the precisely proper effect from the environment speakers buried in the wainscoting. It's too bad that the environment speakers are currently pumping through AM radio, a pulse of tinny local call-in show barely registering where the TV sound is off.

Seth and Nora are my parents. Only Nora looks up as I wander in.

"Yeah, I did," I say.

"You stow that [lord's name in vain] bike away from my truck this time?" Seth barks.

"Sorry, I won't."

"Don't be a smart-ass."

"Hi, I'm home."

Seth looks up at me then with a steely gaze. I eat my apple. I am calm because I know this steely gaze.

"You call this getting in early?"

"Had some work in the computer lab."

"Had some more of your [lord's name in vain] games to play with those [unpleasant anatomical reference] friends, you mean. Psychopathic [dung], Dungeons and Space Trek, whatever the [anglo-saxon epithet] hell you call it."

"Yeah, that's it."

"What the [lord's name in vain] hell you going to be, hanging out with [anatomically impossible act] satanists next? Mutilating [anglo-saxon] cows back of Bridge Creek?"

Hey, what I was talking about earlier? About not knowing where my predisposition for profanity comes from? Never mind.

"Nice work if you can get it," I say as I head for my room.

The wash of light from the TV is overwhelming now, a strobe effect that gives the living room the feel of an underwater disco. It's impossible to pass through the gauntlet of light for the hallway opposite without seeing. Like most nights, I catch a glimpse of satellite soft-core porn in widescreen HD perfection.

Nora is watching intently as she crochets. I feel suddenly distant as I say goodnight.

12

Angels of Death

Hawkwind, 1981. This is surveillance footage, night-vision green. An abandoned mine site, dark.

Eighty-odd klicks roughly due northeast of town, the mountains past Hendrix Lake used to be full of molybdenum mines. Molybdenum is a metal that used to be important for manufacturing or something, and then stopped being important. Or maybe the market got cornered and bottomed out like markets always do. Either way, the mines and the satellite townships that served the mines all kind of disappeared or got turned into proto-resort communities for European tourists. The townships got turned into resort communities, I mean. The mine sites just turned back into the wilderness they'd been carved out of in the first place.

Most of the mine sites, anyway. But not this one.

A long way from anywhere, a nondescript stand of forest and scrub opens onto piles of rubble and tumbledown buildings, faint in the light of stars and the crescent moon. Tailings piles run down the mountainside, an overgrown road snaking off into the distance, strewn with boulders where the last of the heavy equipment blocked it on the way out.

From above, a low rumble builds. Then the darkness suddenly splits as the black chopper last seen soaring over Howie's Corner Store drops from the sky. In its landing lights, decaying signage is seen — *McIntyre Molybdenum — Pit 3*. Smaller signs are set at intervals along razor-wire fence — *NO TRESPASSING — MINE SITE UNSTABLE — EXTREME DANGER*.

As the chopper descends to an abandoned mine face, more light flares from below. Carefully concealed doors slide back into the mountainside, a landing bay beneath them, and yes, it all looks just as James Bond as it sounds. Four other black helicopters sit there, silent as the first touches down. The bay doors slide back into place overhead, shutting to silence and shadow. Never there at all.

I'm watching interior audio and video surveillance, the feeds from six different monitor points painstakingly cut together to follow the conversation as it unfolds.

The space is an intricate interlocking of identical white corridors, well lit. The feel is of an anonymous office building, or the halls of some college humanities department without all the Canadian Federation of Students and Amnesty International posters on the walls. A mix of men and women pass by the static camera points that take it all in. Army fatigues are in evidence, but just as many wear sweatpants, t-shirts, and baseball caps. An informal air.

Nothing that would arouse your attention or suspicion. Unless you know that the helicopter landing bay that just opened up out of nowhere on a mine site mountainside lies just beyond the double doors at the end of the corridor.

Through those doors, Lincoln, Karya, and their group emerge. Guards in night gear pass, automatic weapons at hand. Lincoln returns their salutes with a nod, carrying on with a conversation that I didn't hear the beginning of.

"All right, European city you'd want to get arrested in." His voice is American, threaded through with an easygoing drawl. The south somewhere, Georgia or Carolina or one of those.

"Paris," Karya says, a sense of casual familiarity passing between the two of them. "There's a great view of the Seine from the Palais de Justice holding cells."

"Bucharest for me."

Karya laughs. Even on the badly downsampled feed, you can hear a lightness to her voice. "Excuse me?"

"There are rumors circulating that Ceausescu's personal chef is still serving a life sentence in the kitchens," Lincoln says. He nods to more people as the group passes. "Seventy-six years old and he does a lamb pilaf to die for."

"I think all that post-Soviet charm would overwhelm the ambience quickly."

"I wouldn't be staying long. Mr. Malkov, good to see you."

"Good to see you, sir." From the right, another figure falls into place as Lincoln walks, almost like he's melted into view from the walls themselves. Combat pants and olive drab t-shirt, grey eyes so dark they look black. His hair is shaved almost to the skull, goatee a little longer. Mid-forties if you study him long enough. He looks younger otherwise. This is Malkov.

"Good to be back," Lincoln says. "Long flight. Any developments since we spoke?"

"Sinai pickup operations at MFO North Camp are proceeding on schedule. There'll be a two-day delay for Locke and Parillo to clear Syria. An intelligence cabinet meeting has been scheduled, they wanted to see if they could infiltrate." Malkov's voice has a military crispness to it that fits his look a little too well. "Our contact in Texarkana has confirmed receipt of down payment and has transfer set for June twelfth. The opportunity to move munitions as Red River closes down is looking very good. Also, our Kurdish client was in touch. He wants to know if we might speed up transfer of his Stingers. Some sort of action coming up, apparently."

"You explained that his Stingers haven't been stolen yet?"

"He seemed quite willing to discuss negotiation of an expedited arrangement."

"Can we contact Red River, add some missiles to the shopping list?"

"Already done," Malkov says.

When Lincoln smiles, it carries absolutely no humor.

"Business is excellent, then."

13

In the Dark

Billy Squier, 1981. This is my bedroom. If you could see it, you might not get that fact all at once, because unless you look really closely, you can't actually see the bed. It's currently lost somewhere beneath a morass of books and papers, flowing down and across to the corner of the room where I'm sitting at the rolltop desk I got for my twelfth birthday. In the other corner of the room is the recliner where I actually sleep.

It's a little before midnight and I'm still up, hammering away at the MacBook. Over and above me are two walls worth of posters that express the following sentiments (in order, from the door):

Boycott WTO-Doha
World Wildlife Federation Canada — Adopt a Polar Bear
Remember Love Canal
CIA Out of the Vatican
Vatican Out of the World Bank
You're Gonna Die For Oil, Sucker
Rush: *Hemispheres* on sale October 29
Batboy on Secret Afghanistan Mission

On the opposite two walls hang poster-sized blow-ups of the most intense bits of the JFK Zapruder film. Seth and Nora haven't come into my room in a while now.

With the last of the gluco-caffeine rush of five hours earlier, I'm typing madly to put the finishing touches on an article called *Under Construction — 9/11 Pentagon Renovations and the Area 51 Cover-Up.*

I'm not paranoid, all right? Just think about it.

At the edge of the desk, my iPhone rings ten times. I wait that long to answer it because the few people I give my number to know to wait that long. Breanne has long since refused to call me, saying it's usually faster just to wait until the next time she sees me in person. I don't use voicemail, because I don't like the idea of some call center guy on the other side of the world having the same access to my messages that I do.

I'm not paranoid.

At the other end of the call, it's Connor. I'm not sure if Connor is his first name or his last name, and whichever it is, I don't know his other name. He's the guy behind a conspiracy website/blog called *Five Horsemen*, which the article I'm working on is three days late for. Connor is ex-military security, deep ops intelligence for NSA/CSS in the States before he went to ground in

Vancouver and started publishing. Intelligence community whistle-blower stuff, mostly.

That's how much of his life story Connor lets people in on, at any rate. I tried to find out more once, a month or so after I first started writing for the site. I was half an hour into a web search on Connor when he emailed to tell me to stop doing web searches on him.

I'm not paranoid.

Five Horsemen doesn't pay much, but it covers my phone bill and my net access, which Seth has been billing me for in the absence of being able to inflict any other effective punishments on me. He once decided I should start chipping in for food and utilities, but I just ate at Mitchell and Breanne's for a week. That didn't sit so well with Nora, so Seth backed down. I've long suspected that at some point, something I do will tick him off enough that he'll start charging me rent. I figure I'll blow up that bridge when I cross it, though.

Connor's voice on the phone starts off strident, then is made more so by a stammer that can be taken for thoughtfulness if you don't know him that well. Even three days late, I'm one of his more dependable writers, so I manage to slow his rant down before he gets into too high a gear. The two of us ramble on for a bit about deadline pressure and the telltale signs of laser audio surveillance, but none of that is really relevant to why I'm telling you all this.

Why I'm telling you all this, is that while I'm talking to Connor, my email icon jumps.

While I'm talking to Connor, I flip through to mail by reflex. I see a single new item caps-titled

GAME ONLINE AND WIN BIG!!!

My spam filters have a lethal degree of server-side precision that I programmed myself. I'm annoyed for a moment by the idea that those filters could be bypassed by someone who thinks three exclamation marks are an effective marketing tool. Two keystrokes are all it takes to log and blacklist the unopened pitch's unseen routing info. The supposed sending address flashes past where I'm only half-watching.

play@vindicator.org

A tap on Delete and the offending text is gone from my inbox and my life.

I tell Connor he'll have his piece in ten minutes. It's actually an hour before I finish the final edit and send it off. It's another hour after that before I finally sleep.

Part Two

Game Online
and Win Big

14

Where Do You
Think You're Going?

Dire Straits, 1979. It's the next morning, and the school that was empty the night before is the opposite of empty now. Bright-eyed youth pace their way along well-scuffed corridors, a sea of lip gloss and hockey jackets passing banks of bright orange lockers in the downstairs halls.

A tangible adolescent energy hangs in the air, increasing in strength as each day clocks down inevitably toward the end of the year. I never noticed it last year like I notice it now. In the same way, I never noticed last year how that stunned look behind the glass of the portraits upstairs has already stealthily crept in behind the vacant smiles of the rest of this year's grad class.

Like those faces in yesteryear's portraits once were, we are the faces of the future. I suspect that the future has no idea how much trouble it's in.

Against one bank of bright orange lockers, you'll find the four of us. We're usually here an hour before the day officially starts, after which we rendezvous in conspiratorial fashion for five-minute meetings of the mind in the mobbed corridors between classes. On this particular morning, Mitchell and I are co-conjuring answers to yesterday's algebra homework, which as usual means that he explains the voodoo word problems I can't be bothered to understand, then I do the actual math that he copies back.

While we work, Rico is helping Breanne try to coerce a stack of well-worn automotive tech manuals to simultaneously all slump back into the bright orange locker that's hers, as a result of them spilling out when she opened it a minute before. Why anyone would choose bright orange as the color for a floor's worth of high school lockers is a question that's nagged at me since we all arrived at Ogden in tenth grade, but I'm no closer to an answer now than I was then. Another month and a half, then I can let the token angry intellectual in next year's tenth-grade class worry about it for the next three years instead.

What the four of us, who used to be the five of us, do in the mornings is this. Somebody comes up with a topic, then we argue about it as we walk the hallways in an endless circle. Through the lounge, up the east stairs, along past the library and the office, down the west stairs beyond the science classrooms, back to the lounge, and so on. Politics, current events, music, sports only if it's something we all feel comfortable making fun of. And gaming stuff. Lots and lots and lots of gaming stuff.

Gamers are all different. However, the four of us, who used to be the five of us, are a particular type of gamer who obsesses endlessly over the details of the alternate worlds in which the games take place. Our own games tend to polarize around dystopian dark fantasy and quasireal-tech science fiction, which means that all of us have an unhealthy interest in electronics, and in networking, and in trends in crypto-fascist politics, and conflict history, and the ancient world, the evolution of consciousness, military hardware and munitions, natural disasters, human-made disasters, Sun Tzu and Jared Diamond, media culture and Joseph Campbell and why rogue prions will eventually destroy all life on earth. The meaning of life, the end of the world. That kind of stuff.

The four of us, who used to be the five of us, don't often run out of things to talk about. However, we're aware that we all run the risk of ending up on an international-intelligence watch list if the wrong people ever overhear us.

This is Breanne's morning, and she usually plays it safer than the rest of us. She's still thinking hard as Mitchell and I crib the last of each other's work and we all drift with the crowd.

"Okay," she says, snapping her fingers. "TV journalists who should be drafted into politics whether they want to be or not. Rachel Maddow."

"Charlie Rose," says Mitchell.

"Christi Paul," says Rico.

Breanne slaps him upside the back of the head. "Excuse me?"

"She's great." Rico manages to catch her hand on the backswing.

"Because she's got the edge in the doe-eyed blonde department?"

"She's sharp as a tack."

"She's from, like, Ohio."

"She left Ohio, proving my point." To Mitchell, with a hint of skepticism — "Charlie Rose?"

"He gets to sit in a dark room talking existential politiculture with a captive intellectual elite. If he goes into politics, I've got a shot at his old job."

My turn. "Mass media exists to preach the consumer agenda of the corporate state." Around me, a familiar groan rises in three-part harmony. "But clearly that's what you all deserve."

We make it two hotly contested rounds of the halls before the other three concede that the TV networks have all been infiltrated by elements of the domestic black-ops infrastructure for years. Or at least they stop arguing about it while Breanne stops for water. I take a moment to casually deface the *Picked Up Your Yearbook?* poster across the corridor from the downstairs water fountain. It says *Picked Up Your Yearbook?* when I'm done.

It's a comment on trying to turn memory and nostalgia into an agonized longing that you package and buy. Nobody's going to get it.

"We finishing up the firefight today?" I ask.

"This airlock thing needs discussion," Mitchell says.

"Well, let's do it now." As I break off from the three of them to head for the central stairs, I give Mitchell a large wave goodbye.

"Are you on double daylight saving time for some reason?"

"I've got an eight-thirty with Kirk," I say.

"Oh, god, it's Kirk day?" Breanne's voice suggests stark terror as the three of them continue on without me.

"I like Kirk," Mitchell says.

"Keep that quiet at your sanity hearing."

"No, really. I think we're starting to bond."

I've already slipped past the conversation, pushing up the stairs behind a tight knot of eleventh-grade divas whose look suggests that Pharmasave's been running a heavy sale on mascara.

As I reach the corridor across from the office, I slow suddenly. I stare.

Passing three strides in front of me, Molly walks alone toward the library. Behind me, someone comes up short against my shoulder where I've stopped. I hear a murmured epithet, but one glare is enough to stifle the tenth-grader making it. He wears a rodeo club t-shirt that says *If you ain't a cowboy, you ain't [dung]*.

It's a contrapositive double negative, which means it's the same as saying *If you are [dung], you are a cowboy*.

He doesn't get it.

When I look again, Molly's back is moving down the corridor. Her ponytail is in slow motion. I watch for a long while before I go.

15

Moving in Stereo

The Cars, 1978. In Kirk's office, Carl was listening.

I just listened to it all on audio, complete with transcription, but I'm still not sure where it came from. An open connection on the phone, or maybe the laptop Kirk sometimes types quietly at while you talk across from him.

Mr. Kirk is a particularly earnest guidance counselor who hates it when anyone calls him *Mister*. He sits behind a cluttered desk and a nameplate that just says *KIRK*, flipping through files like he's never exactly sure who's across from him. This morning, we're all in for scheduled *End of the year, are your university applications and grad transition packages up to date?* meetings. Kirk apparently uses exactly the same greeting for every single person he talks to, which I wouldn't have known if I hadn't heard it on the audio five separate times.

KIRK: *So, a month till finals. Down to the wire, graduation around the corner. How's everything going with you?*

Here are some highlights.

Like usual with Kirk, I'm in my element.

SCOTT: *We live in a world that's sliced up into shells of corporate conspiracy and CIA-financed sociopathy wrapping and overlapping each other like a planet-sized Russian doll, that's how the hell it's going. How's it going with you?*

Like usual with any passive listener, Mitchell is indefinable.

MITCHELL: *The whole post-secondary thing is a blind spot right now. But I think I'm leaning towards either quantum physics or Hawaiian shamanism, I'm not sure which.*

Like usual with anyone trying to help her figure out her life, Breanne is apologetic.

BREANNE: *Well, like, I really, really wanted to try for engineering but I failed physics the three times. So I don't know.*

Not like usual, Rico is evasive. I don't know if Kirk heard it.

RICO: *Well, my mom and dad are still working way too hard. And my brother was supposed to take over things this year, but he's still mountain climbing in Patagonia or some stupid thing.*

SCOTT: *You make a conscious effort not to get corrupted is what you do. Mass media is a killer virus. TV, publishing, music, all of it. You consume anything that this culture has produced outside 1972 to 1981, you're sucking a subliminal content feed tied to a political hegemony that dates back to the Borgias.*

MITCHELL: *And I've been having a dream where I'm in the Australian outback, looking for this suicidal telepath so that I can convince her to transfer her cosmic power into me before she consumes herself in a sort of psychokinetic implosion.*

BREANNE: *Then I got the pass in algebra, I think pretty much only because I promised Mr. Stanislav I'd never do another math class. Which was really sweet of him, I thought.*

RICO: *I mean, hockey's good, but if the only reason any school wants me is because I can take a crosscheck, then I don't see the point.*

SCOTT: *No, you don't get it. 1972 to 1981 was this nightmare civilization's only golden age. June '72, the first Watergate arrests. The Nixon stranglehold guaranteed by the rigged elections in '68 gets its spine broken. The right-wing political-industrial complex goes on the run, then down for the count. Until March '81, when the Trilateral Commission stages Reagan the political proxy's mock assassination in order to preempt the real assassination that would have catalyzed a virtual coup d'etat by the Republican National Committee and put Alexander Haig into power. They had Nancy in their pocket. It was a walk.*

MITCHELL: *And in the dream, she says that the physical quest for death is a catalyst for the overflowing psyche's spiritual release. Like we become as gods in our own right, then we crucify ourselves. Then she calls herself Louise. Do you think that means anything?*

BREANNE: *No, I think I do have ambitions, you know? I just need to really work on getting motivated to figure out what they are.*

RICO: *And I mean, the thing is, I like working with my dad. But people keep talking about college and scholarships and how they can't wait to get out on their own, and I'm just tired of feeling like I should apologize for getting along with my parents and wanting to be there for them. Because they don't have anybody else, you know?*

SCOTT: *Yeah, but you remember when Haig went live after Reagan took the bullet and announced he was in charge? And people had to remind him that actually, when the president gets shot, three other people get to take over before the secretary of state gets his turn? But what nobody knows is that Haig knew that Reagan, Bush, the speaker of the house, and the senate pro tempore were supposed to all be dead in separate hits by the NSA, the FBI, the DIA, and the NIC, all working against the CIA. Just think about it.*

Carl was listening to Molly, too.

Whatever was already going on, however long it had been happening, Molly was the most important part of it.

MOLLY: *No, it's fine. I mean, it's fine now. It was just a lot of things happening all at once. It's over.*

MOLLY: *Yeah, I read all the books. I reread the two that didn't suck so badly. It's not like some big mystery. Stuff happens, you deal with it. You roll with it or you roll under it. You make your choice.*

MOLLY: *Yeah, my grades slipped. Whatever. Now they're back up. It's high school. It's not like it means anything.*

MOLLY: *No, I need to go, actually. Thanks.*

On the audio, it's like you can hear the edge of an echo in Molly's voice. Some kind of hollow space inside her. You can hear her backpack slam the desk as she stands, Kirk not saying anything like he knows there's no point. You can hear the door shut fast behind her as she goes.

16

Are You
Receiving Me?

Golden Earring, 1973. It's pushing two o'clock, close to the end of Computers 12, second D block. In the computer lab, twenty-four other people are saving web page newsletter assignments that must incorporate rollover graphics, cascading style sheets, and browser-independent customized formatting for full marks. They've been working on them since last week, during which time I've been working instead on an animated video presentation titled *JFKKK — White Supremacists and the Kennedy Conspiracy.* Because that blows off the assignment criteria fairly badly, I have no idea whether I'll get a mark for it, but I don't much care at this point.

Mitchell is at the machine next to me. His *Rework Your Chakras In Twenty-Five Easy Steps* is coming along, but he's spending a fair bit of time glancing over at what I'm doing.

"I thought I heard that the Cubans killed Kennedy over the Bay of Pigs," he says at last.

"No. You thought you heard the CIA killed Kennedy over the Bay of Pigs and built Oswald into a Cuban-Soviet conspiracy."

"That's what I thought I heard?"

"Yeah. Only think instead about how the organized white supremacist movement's biggest fear in 1963 was that civil rights advances under Kennedy would lead to a de facto second civil war that they were likely to lose. I mean, the whole Oswald thing, they practically signed it." I open a Gmail window through a generic proxy server, letting me bypass the district firewall's web-mail bandwidth cap so I can archive a copy of the day's work at home.

"How so? And why?"

"Political statement. Kennedy as the new Lincoln." As I send, Mitchell accidentally moves a folder he shouldn't have moved and his link structure explodes. I lean across to fix it for him. "John Wilkes Booth shot Lincoln in a theatre and hid out in a warehouse, so they set it up to look like Oswald shot from a warehouse and hid out in a theatre. It's a masterpiece."

When I come back to my browser, my data's been sent but I've got a new email waiting in my inbox.

GAME ONLINE AND WIN BIG!!!

"Game online and [anglo-saxon] off," I mutter quietly. Where Mr. Davidson is hovering across the room, he gives me a look like I wasn't quiet enough. Mr. Davidson is the tweed-jacketed math teacher who I have for computers and geometry this year. I like him, if for no other reason than he seems to dislike this crop of grads almost as much as I do. I trash the message as I shut the window down. I make a mental note to rebuild my email server scripts from scratch when I get home.

"No," Mitchell says. "I mean why such a lame cover story? Nobody bought Oswald even then."

"Because a cover that inane attracts a fringe element that distracts from the search for real truth. People saying Marilyn Monroe shot from the grassy knoll. All that crowd."

"The lunatic fringe giving the semi-lunatic fringe a bad name?"

"Just think about it."

In the hall outside, the sound of movement and rising voices tells us that class is done. Mr. Davidson reminds everyone to email him their updated knowledge maps for next class, even as the mad dash starts for the doors.

"Odd," Mitchell says.

"The lunatic fringe is odd by definition. If they weren't, they'd just be a normal fringe."

"No, I mean it's odd that I don't remember my email already being open."

Where I pause from logging out to look over, Mitchell is sending his assignment in a Hotmail window that has one new message in it.

GAME ONLINE AND WIN BIG!!!

I probably should have felt something. I should have sensed a cold chill running up my spine, or had some sense of apprehensive dread, but I didn't. Looking back, a paranoid person should have twigged to the idea that whoever was spamming me was noting my response in real time, then trying to end-run around my disinterest via Mitchell's willingness to read whatever shows up in his inbox.

Like I said, though, I'm not paranoid.

"Hey, check this out."

"It's bogus," I say. "I got one yesterday."

"Mother of a meltdown! Fifty grand for first prize…" Mitchell keys on a web address at the bottom of the message.

www.vindicator.org

A new page fires up in his browser, a lame logo and a block of text.

"The Vindicator Gameworks Project," he reads. "A nonprofit organization studying educational, cultural, and media philosophies in simulation roleplaying. Dude, the Charlie Rose gig just sunk to second place."

Mitchell notices that the class is clearing. He quickly packs up his stuff as he saves and logs out. I open my browser again, keying up Vindicator.org and seeing the same two-dollar-a-month budget-host turnkey page. I see the same hook that caught Mitchell's eye — a fifty thousand dollar cash prize. I ignore it as I tab into a traceroute page, mapping out the server's IP neighborhood so I can use it for willful damage later on.

I have to look up to see Mitchell lingering in the doorway. "English awaits," he says.

"I'll catch up with you."

He looks like he wants to say something but doesn't. Just shrugs as he goes.

I'm not watching, distracted as I run a tracking script and a WHOIS lookup on the domain. Through Connor, I know a guy in Buenos Aires who likes to benchmark denial-of-service worms, and I'm thinking I've just found his next test-bed site.

Because I'm distracted, I'm not watching as someone slips in at the door. With me out of sight in the corner, it looks like the room is empty.

Molly stops short when she finally sees me, three strides away. She's got her backpack and jacket on like she's on her way out. A very, very long silence ensues.

Before things went strange between us, Molly and I had four classes together this year. One of those is English, which hasn't seen much of me lately. One of those was bio, which I dropped in March. The last four months in algebra and history have involved a lot of very long silences.

"Hi," I say finally, with a lot more effort than one word should take.

"I need to print," she says.

She turns away to pull out a chair along the opposite wall. Her back is to me as she logs in. I try to pretend to work for a minute, but there's nothing to do except stare at the Vindicator Gameworks Project logo, looking like it's been scanned off the back cover of a 1980 issue of *Omni*.

"Hey, do you still review for Technology Vault?" I recognize my own voice before I realize I'm talking. I don't know why I say it. I recognize this as a bad sign, because I always know what I'm doing. I take great pride in the fact that most of what I say gets thought about for a long while first.

Across the room, a quick twist of tension threads Molly's shoulders. "No."

"You heard about anything called Vindicator?" I ask anyway. "Some kind of multiplayer thing, big money?"

"No." Her expression shows less than zero interest as she stands.

"Mitchell's been going on about it. I told him it's some scam marketing thing…"

"I think I said no."

Neither of us remembers until that moment that the printer is sitting directly behind me. Molly doesn't look at me as she steps past to wait for her pages. I don't look at her as she goes.

17

It Don't Matter

Loverboy, 1980. It's two hours later and the Vindicator Gameworks project is back on the screen. Only it's Mitchell, Breanne, and Rico gathered around it now.

"The Vindicator," Mitchell reads. "Experimental all-terrain mobile combat unit. Cutting-edge fuel-cell power plant, advanced expert system control, top speed three hundred klicks. It's hidden in a paramilitary base and it's our job to get it out."

Mitchell's into the main contest page now, having cheerfully given up his name and email address in order to get past the home page and guarantee a steady supply of spam from other niche marketers for the rest of his life. The new web page features a new image — a futuristic vehicle rotating through a full three-sixty display.

From where I'm dragging the table into place across the computer lab, it looks like some sort of massively overbuilt six-wheeled all-terrain vehicle, six meters long by three high. Angled lines and a wrap-around viewport of translucent polycarbonate give it a look like a Corvette and a Hummer had children. Antennas and weapons racks bristle from the top and sides, like somebody finally figured out that particular function on their 3D modeling system and then forgot how to turn it off. A large *M* is emblazoned on the side panel, which doesn't make any sense to me if the tank is supposed to be called *Vindicator*. I don't care enough to get into it, though.

"Auto-fire rounds hit behind you," I call out. "Four distinct patterns."

"It's a beta of an online simulation system," Mitchell says, not listening along with the rest of them. "A hyper-real character-based environment. Custom browser setup for a broadband connection and five networked machines."

"So what's the catch?" Breanne is arrowing through the demo overview, a dizzying array of descriptive panes popping up. When Mitchell first showed them the home page, it turned out that she and Rico had both gotten the same email already that morning. This has unfortunately given Mitchell additional incentive to evangelize.

"No catch. It's got toll-free numbers to a bank and a lawyer in California. First team to crack the simulation cashes in."

Rico leans in with interest as Breanne brings up weapons specs. "But what makes it such a big deal that they can hang fifty grand on it?"

I finish laying out battle maps. "Auto-fire rounds hit behind you," I say, a little louder.

"No instructions," Mitchell says. "You make the game. When you first go in, you're looking to define the parameters that allow you to play. Work back paradigmatically from the controls to the gestalt of the game itself."

"You're using big words again," Breanne says.

"Auto-fire rounds. Behind you. They hit." I'm trying hard not to shout now from behind the evening's charts and a carefully arranged matrix of dice.

"Teams of five. Systems, weapons, ops, engineering, and piloting."

"The [lord's name in vain] airlock opens, for [anglo-saxon's] sake." From the half-open door to the hallway, Wes the night custodian gives me a friendly nod where he and his broom slide by.

"Except we're a team of four," Rico says.

"We'll figure something out. We're a well-oiled tactical machine." Mitchell spreads out a half-drawn diagram showing how he wants to set the fifth terminal up between us, letting us each switch off on it as needed. Breanne spills Snapple on it as she stares thoughtfully.

"It seems like there should be a catch…"

"The catch is you're doing unpaid R&D work for some gaming studio sweatshop," I say.

Breanne looks up like she's just noticed I'm there. "All agreed, then. Let's play."

"I'm in," Rico says.

"And me," Mitchell says.

"Hey, did you all suffer botched brain surgery at some point or are your parents related?"

"Hey back, [pleasurable but antisocial act]," Breanne says, "what is your damage, anyway?"

"Web gaming bites my balls."

(I actually tried for a while to find brackets for that last bit, but nothing I tried sounded any less rude than what was actually said. Sorry.)

"Take it any way you can get it." Breanne smiles sweetly. I glare. I'm up and pacing, moving behind the three of them where they sit glued to the screen.

"Look, have any of you heard of this thing before now? Seen anybody talking in the gaming forums, any word on the review sites? That kind of cash profile, you should be hearing about nothing else. It's a scam."

"Or," Mitchell says, "maybe it's just really beta. So that someone should try to get a jump on the competition before there is any competition."

"No."

"Would it kill you to pretend you're not the only person in the world once in a while?" Breanne says. I'm angling for a retort but Mitchell beats me to it.

"Give it an hour?"

All three of them are watching me in a particularly annoying way. Reminding me that even as irritated as we all constantly make each other, we don't really fight all that much.

Try to imagine this as video. Imagine a jump cut here at the moment of charged decision where everybody's waiting for me. Jump cuts in books would be a good idea, I think.

Instead of the computer lab, a transcript of the dialogue you've just heard in the computer lab flashes past in real time. There's no light except the LED gleam of a workstation screen, because Carl doesn't need light to see by. Carl's just listening.

SCOTT: *One hour.*

MITCHELL: *One hour.*

SCOTT: *When we're done, we finish the firefight.*

MITCHELL: *Noted and agreed.*

SCOTT: *One hour.*

RICO: *Yes, already.*

SCOTT: *My music.*

BREANNE: *Oh, god…*

In the computer lab, we throw workstations around the room underneath the big sign that says *DO NOT MOVE WORKSTATIONS*. We've got four systems set in a semicircle so we can see each other, with a fifth set off between them that anyone can reach if we lean.

In the other place, the darkness is cut by the flare of white light. Five monitors come to life across the interior of what looks like a small, cluttered room. Shadow cloaks irregular walls, the first monitor centered between the others where everything we say floods past in a perfect text echo.

In front of the five monitors that have just come to life, five jump seats are barely visible. No one's in them, the confined space around them empty. On the five monitors, the Vindicator Gameworks Project logo unfolds at exactly the same moment it appears on each of the five workstations in the computer lab. As each of us clicks into the simulation page, the six-wheeled hyper-ATV comes into view, rotating slowly as it waits for us to log in.

18

Stop This Game

Cheap Trick, 1980. There are only about a half-dozen ways to describe four people playing a computer game, and none of them are particularly interesting.

I'll try to make this painless.

On all five monitors, a text-graphics framework loads at blinding speed, a scrolling description flowing past high-res virtual-reality renderings. Staggered corridors make a three-hundred-and-sixty-degree panorama in a standard 3D-shooter setup. Nothing out of the ordinary. At least not until we try to check out the controls and realize that there are no controls. No actual commands in the interface. No text processor that anyone can see, no convenient drop-down menu, none of the obvious keyboard shortcuts.

We deal with it. It takes five minutes for the four of us to work out the keyboard shorthand that controls the display. Up, down, rotate view. From there, we work out the lethally arcane combination of keystrokes and modifiers that control game function. Inventory, shoot, reload, all that. It takes two minutes for Breanne to sprint for the library to steal a roll of masking tape and a stack of Post-it notes. Then for the next half-hour, command by command, piece by piece of figuring out how things work, we cover our keyboards and monitors with cryptic game-function shorthand.

When we finally inventory, we discover that none of us actually has any inventory. Rico takes that hardest, because he gets antsy whenever he's denied access to things that explode.

In the dark and empty computer station, the game images repeat in real time on all five monitors. Each view moves independently of the others, twisting in perfect synch with our attempts back in the computer lab to figure out where we are and what we're doing. Working back paradigmatically from the controls to the gestalt of the game itself. It's easier than it sounds.

What the monitors don't show is a network trace, snaking out from that darkened computer station to wrap around the school network like a tightly twisted noose.

(Confession. There's a fair bit of technical stuff wrapped up in what happened that night, but even after the fact, I'm barely qualified to explain it. I'll try to report it back in a way that makes sense from how I know and remember it. But as far technical accuracy goes, consider me one of those unreliable narrators that I've always heard are supposed to make books all edgy.)

If this were a movie, you'd see IP addresses and reverse domain names flashing past so you could tell what was happening. In reality, nothing marks the cascading series of connections that brings Carl along a very long and roundabout digital route into the computer lab. I've got video archives of the systems logs in front of me even as I write this, but what there is to see is mostly a whole lot of numbers that aren't that interesting even to me.

I can tell you what it means, though. It means that Carl was effectively running the entire data grid for this particular corner of the hinterland that the school network is a part of. The primary feeds, the phone company lines, the cable trunks, all of it. The school district firewall must have been compromised right from the first day of listening in, whenever that was. But that would have been like slicing whipped cream compared to the complexity of the network reengineering that went on while we played that night, never suspecting. Never seeing.

On one of the monitors in the darkened computer station, you can make out where I'm pushing the display controls to extremes, my cursor driving a sort of 3D joystick that flips the view in a dizzying spiral. From the headsets hanging on the back of each jump seat, you can hear us talking in the computer lab as our words scroll past in real time.

SCOTT: *These controls suck.*

BREANNE: *Give it a rest.*

MITCHELL: *Here's the plan. Everybody picks a door and we do a fifty-meter sweep. Let's see where we are.*

RICO: *Umm, my door appears to have a half-dozen surprised-looking people behind it, two of them packing shotguns.*

MITCHELL: *So run in there.*

RICO: *And do what?*

MITCHELL: *Flail about madly.*

RICO: *Plan B. Move.*

Molly was in the library that night. I didn't hear about that until a couple of days ago, by which you can probably tell that it's yet another few days later as I write this.

Molly must have been heading out at about the same time we find ourselves virtually scattering ahead of a security detail, the corridor behind us in the simulation filled with the bark of shotguns firing crowd-control beanbag rounds. She told me she thought she saw something funny as she slipped past the office for the alarm panel at the main doors.

From the corner of her eye, just for a second, the phone line lights are on at the front-desk switchboard. Everything's lit up like the proverbial Christmas tree, cycling through a storm of signal connections. But when she glances back, it's gone. Everything's dark through the glass of the locked doors as she stares for a moment, then turns away.

19

In the Heat
of the Night

Pat Benatar, 1979. The surveillance feed is a four-part split screen, the crescent moon up in one corner, bright above the mine site where the scar of rough road fades into dark forest. There's no sound where the wind whips past a *CONDEMNED* sign rattling against a long fence of razor wire. Beyond it, a figure paces by in fatigues and night-vision goggles, M4 carbine rifle at his side.

In two other corners of the feed, you can see what look like silent vehicle bays. One is lit up with the glow of halogen floods, five choppers casting deep shadows where they're parked on skid pads. The other bay is as dark as the first is bright, showing the vague shapes of vehicles standing in shadow that climbs to the ceiling high above.

In the fourth pane, a windowless ops room is seen. Workstations line two walls, high-end flatscreen displays dark on the others. At center, twenty-odd people sit around a cluttered stainless steel conference table. Karya's there, and Malkov sitting across from her with his feet up and a black laptop in front of him. The remains of a half-dozen gourmet heat-and-serve pizzas are spread across the table, beverage cans piled high in a recycling bin by the door. There's no sign of the business garb seen in the chopper the previous night, everybody presenting a consistent display of well-worn fatigues and army-spec t-shirts. Still, everything seems kind of casual. Or at least it would if this view didn't have an audio feed.

"Item eleven." Lincoln is talking where he sits at the head of the table, reading from a two-screened hinged tablet that looks a lot more sophisticated than anything I've ever seen previewed on Slashdot. "The MM38 Exocet battery which came into our possession from the Tatmadaw in Myanmar is on its way to the KNLA in Myanmar, thus maintaining the moral balance in the area. Mr. Greggs and Ms. Lee are escorting it to a flight out of Manila, where it'll be traveling as medical supplies."

If you watch him, Malkov is only half-listening. On a battered Toughbook embossed with the crossed-swords-and-cluster-bomb icon of the Russian army, he flips through a half-dozen network diagnostic panes with practiced ease. Alongside the surveillance video of the room, I've got the matching real-time captures from his display. I watch what he saw then, a faint spike flaring on a network trace as he monitors a data feed.

"Item twelve. Intelligence in Sudan informs us of several high-ranking ex-SPLA officials who'll be seeking asylum shortly and will be needing transportation."

Malkov isn't listening as he slides his chair to the far wall, firing up a workstation as he patches his laptop into a network panel behind him.

Eighty-odd klicks away, in the simulation, we've managed to split up and break the squad pursuing us into two slightly more manageable groups. Then Rico and Breanne double back, and the four of us, unarmed, take out three shotgun-toting security ops with a fire extinguisher and a jury-rigged flash bomb of fluorescent tubes overloaded straight from a wall socket.

It's a nice piece of work. It's all sheer improvisation, looking for the one solution to the puzzle that whoever designed the scenario didn't think about. It's the sort of stuff that the four of us are good at when we play. But the fact that the simulation let us do it is far more impressive than our coming up with the plan in the first place.

Shooter simulations, as the name suggests, almost always have a limited palette of options for doing anything other than shooting. In the computer lab, we're too busy scrambling ahead of a security claxon to acknowledge it, but we all know we're playing something different this time.

We scoop the guns off the guards we've dropped, then continue the run-like-hell plan. Mitchell and I are alternating on the fifth console, clumsily helping the missing member of our virtual team keep up with the rest of us. All the while, the phone system and the network feed in the school office are being stripped down and remote rewired in a very particular way.

All the while, on the feed from Malkov's screen, a pattern recognition system runs. Military-grade coding, no soft edges, all function. Some kind of monitoring system, data spilling past in a splintering of translucent panes.

On the security feed, Lincoln is finishing up. "Item eighteen," he says. "We're expecting a completion call to the Belgrade operation just wrapped up, with Mr. James taking point on the return." Lincoln taps the tablet to darkness. In his expression, you can see the humorless smile again. "Our own Ms. Karya, originally scheduled to see things through to completion, will be lying low after the success of last week's extraction earned her the number thirty-six spot on Interpol's most wanted."

Around the room is all raucous applause. Karya almost looks like she's blushing, but the monochrome feed makes it hard to see.

"Item final," Lincoln says, and there's a subtle change in his voice that everyone else hears. "This has been a classified back-and-forth most of the past two years between only Mr. Malkov, myself, and a very small number of prospective clients. Meaning that most of you probably know more about what's going on than I do." A smattering of laughter from everyone except Malkov. "But I'm happy to report for the record that the news is good. We have a buyer for the Vindicator."

It was supposed to be an hour.

There are no rules. Mitchell has a really convoluted way of explaining it that involves using the word gestalt a whole lot more. When it comes down to it, though, there are no rules.

The point of the Vindicator simulation from the time we start to play with it is to figure out the point of the Vindicator simulation. On the surface, it sounds straightforward enough. You play a team of five dropped into a paramilitary base with no weapons, no maps, no idea where you are or what you're up against. You're there to find an experimental weapons platform that you don't know the location of, don't know how to look for, and don't know how to operate once you find it. You don't know why you're there, you don't know who you're working for, you don't know the people who are shooting at you because they don't want you there.

On our screens, the base is an intricate interlocking of identical white corridors, well lit. The layout, the detail, the precision in the movement of the simulation carries a degree of realism that impresses even me. As we sprint into a storage area and seal the doors behind us, I vow to never say so out loud.

"That's it," Lincoln says, but even as the others rise around him, he catches Malkov's eye. Something quick and wordless passes between them, like these are two people who don't need a lot of talk to know when something's going on.

"The uplink system flagged a proximity packet echo," Malkov says, quietly enough that no one else hears. Behind Lincoln, the rest of the group is spilling out to those wide white corridors. "Give me an hour to lock it down."

Lincoln nods as he goes, like that's all he needs to hear.

It was supposed to be an hour.

Eight hours later, Malkov is still in the ops room, working alone.

Eight hours later, the computer lab floor is a minefield of pizza boxes and crumpled paper, the MacBook in my lap where I lay down a map grid to try to figure out how the various bits of the virtual complex lock together.

For the better part of a tense dinner break, we manage to get pinned down, until Rico pops a ceiling panel so I can do a quick rewiring job that blows the fail-safes on the doors to shut them tight. Now we're locked in, even as the troops gunning for us are locked out on the other side of the complex. Our workstation monitors are a kaleidoscope of shifting views, all of which are echoed by the monitors in the darkened computer station as they take down every word.

MITCHELL: *Frag the security scanners and head left. I said left.*
RICO: *This is left.*

MITCHELL: *No, my left. Inventory.*

BREANNE: *I've got a blue key card.*

SCOTT: *That's off the squad leader we dropped in the intersection?*

BREANNE: *No, the tech in the lab who scrambled the [anglo-saxon] screamer grid.*

SCOTT: *Then he had security access. Slot the card, let me at the panel.*

Alongside the steady flow of the transcript, a coded data burst cycles. A steady flow of digits twists in and back on itself. On Malkov's laptop, the military monitoring app chews its way through the same signal, trying to pull some hint of content from its encrypted core.

In the computer lab, the four of us are slouched at our stations. All five monitors are showing some sort of windowless operations room, a stainless steel conference table scorched by the firefight that got us into it. Workstations line two walls, high-end flatscreen displays dark on the others. The floor is littered with photorealistic energy-drink and pop cans that spilled from the recycling bin I upended when I came through the door, but we don't have a lot of time to admire the rendering. Mitchell and Rico are scrambling to scan beyond the doors before override security shuts the video feed down, like it has every other place we've tried to hole up ahead of pursuit.

"We've got security codes," I say. There's an edge of enthusiasm in my voice that I have to consciously dial down a notch. The virtual display shows the key panel where the blue card is slotted. "Pause it now."

"There's like five doors between them and us," Breanne says as she checks the printout of the most recent map. "We convince base security that we're them, we can make it ten doors."

"Pause it."

"We lost time working out the security protocols," Mitchell says. "We should make it up."

"Push on," Rico says.

"It's midnight," I say.

We share a communal moment in which everybody else blinks. They all glance to the time on their monitors, staring in mutual disbelief.

"Pause it."

Mitchell taps in the six-keystroke pause code we worked out over dinner, cycling the game's virtual display to shadow. A holding pattern twists in. The Vindicator, rotating through all its three-hundred-and-sixty-degree splendor.

As I stand to stretch life into my legs, I'm more tired than I've been in a long while. An unfamiliar headache is starting at the base of my skull. The others look as weary as I feel. It takes a while for anyone to speak.

MITCHELL: *Back tomorrow?*

RICO: *Yeah.*

BREANNE: *Damn, yeah.*

They all look to me. My knuckles crack as I squeeze my hands out of their all-night keyboard curl. Breanne winces.

SCOTT: *Tomorrow.*

We put the computer lab back together with a lot less energy than we had taking it apart. The time being what it is, Rico tells Mitchell and I to throw our bikes in the back of the truck, he'll give everyone a ride home. I mumble something like *Thanks* as I collect our scattered notes, adding them to a stack of screen captures that have been spitting out of the printer all night.

At the multimedia workstation, I pop my iPhone and log out. For just a second, I catch a faint echo of feedback like the headset mic has been left on.

I never turned on the headset mic. But it's late and I'm tired. I don't think about it too much as we hit the lights and head out.

In the dark computer station with the empty jump seats, the monitors that displayed and transcribed the game as we played it blink off, one by one.

In the operations room, on the wall display mirroring his laptop screen, Malkov watches the signal shift. A new pattern replaces the old, the irregularity gone. He three-points an empty can of Red Bull across the room to the recycling bin, hitting it without looking. He stares at the screen for a long while before he finally shuts down.

20

Second Hand

Bachman-Turner Overdrive, 1974. It's the afternoon following the morning of the night before. Though my headache hasn't gone, it's faded to a dull pounding, which lets me ignore it like I ignore all the background noise that makes up so much of my life.

That morning, I get in early and head straight for the library, where I camp out at the study cubicle I like in the northwest corner. I like it because sitting at the window, you can see a narrow slice of forest and sky beyond the Agriculture 12 greenhouses, as opposed to seeing the roof and walls of the gym and the band room that are the only view from the rest of this side of the building.

That slice of sky this morning is grey, threatening rain. In front of me where I slouch comfortably, I've got the records of the previous night. I've got hardcopy screen shots. I've got my maps done up in Inkscape on the MacBook while we played. I've got Mitchell's hand-drawn sketches. I've got a binder full of notes I've been making since I got home a little after twelve-thirty, which resulted in another encounter with Seth that I don't remember well enough to write down.

I lose track of the time, tuned in just enough to listen for the regular rumble in the corridor that means classes are changing. When I hear the second such rumble, I start folding the array of paperwork in front of me into something like an ordered pile. My plan is to continue working in the lounge in advance of meeting up with the others at lunch, so that I can snag the corner table the four of us like before the cowboys get it.

But then I see a figure heading down the aisle toward me, watching me with a smiling gaze. Something twists in my gut because I know this smiling gaze.

Ms. Bond stops beside me and leans over the edge of the cubicle. Ms. Bond is my English teacher, last year and this year. Most of this year, anyway.

"Hello," I say.

"Hello to you, too," she says back. Ms. Bond seems younger than a teacher should be, which makes it easy to forget sometimes that she is a teacher. It's not just that she looks young, because even the teachers who look young seem to carry a degree of permanent fatigue around with them throughout the year. It's like there's some sort of aging process that teachers have to go through in order to graduate with the education degree, but Ms. Bond managed to avoid it somehow.

"We missed you in class Monday," she says good-naturedly.

"Yeah. Sorry."

"Also, we missed you last Thursday. And Wednesday."

"Yeah."

"And Monday again. Then all of the week before that…"

"Sorry," I say again. Not for the first time, I wish that my voice had more than one degree of inflection. My voice does attitude fairly well, but that's about it. Some subdued deference would be nice once in a while. Maybe even a little humility.

"No worries," Ms. Bond says. "I figured you were probably just hard at work on the final draft of that thesis essay. But then I remembered you never handed in a rough draft. Or an outline. Or a thesis statement. So I thought I might stop by to see how it was going."

Outside, the rain that was threatening has started. As I stand, the wider view through the window shows the student parking lot overtaken by a light haze and the sound of revving engines. Two jocks appear to be starting an impromptu football scrimmage from the back of a shortbox pickup as it peels out. Though I couldn't possibly care less, I find myself watching with the same intensity that I can feel where Ms. Bond watches me.

"So how's it going, Scott?"

"Having some trouble picking a topic," I say.

"How about the relative value of a high-school diploma in the modern job market?"

"How about the relative value of regurgitated public-school ideology in a post-industrial political vacuum?"

In my voice, the attitude sneaks in without my inviting it. Where I tear myself from the view outside and stuff the last of the paperwork into my backpack, my attitude and Ms. Bond's smile undergo a kind of collision. She takes it in stride.

"You know, Mitchell told me some of the names you write under on that conspiracy website you work on. I liked your piece on how McKenzie King communing with his dead mother was a setup by the KGB. Print that and sign it. Give me a short story. Give me an essay, give me a book review, give me an ironic laundry list, Scott, and I can at least think about giving you fifty percent for the term."

"I'm late for class." I make a move to move. Ms. Bond is a head and a half shorter than I am, but she only needs to raise an arm in front of me to stop me dead.

"It's Day 3. English is actually the class you're about to skip right now."

I make a mental note that I need to pay more attention to the timetable. Around us, the last of the previous period's study-block brigade has cleared out, but I can see them still watching through the glass that fronts the library from the hallway, their sidelong snickering glances lingering.

"Scott, I know what this year's been like for you…"

"I'm late for something…"

"I know what it's been like for both of you, but that's not what this is about. You know it. You like to play at being philosophical, and that's fine.

You want to pretend that your intentionally not graduating makes some kind of statement for intellectual freedom, great. But don't be surprised when that rigid frame of mind of yours gets bent out of shape by the real world."

"I'm a quick study."

"You're also short-sighted. With your vision, your instincts, your heart, you could go anywhere…"

"And you know anyplace on this planet looking for vision, book me a [lord's name in vain] flight."

Beneath the attitude, there's a real anger now. But I tell myself it doesn't get to come out. Not now, not this way. I look past Ms. Bond because I don't want to see her watching me. I just wait.

Even without watching, I can feel the tension that tells me she's got something else she wants to say. It doesn't get to come out either. She only shakes her head as she goes.

21

Someone's
Looking at You

The Boomtown Rats, 1979. I don't go the lounge. I don't meet up with the others at lunch after all. From the library, I head straight for the computer lab and stick a most authorized-looking *Network Down — Tech Support Has Been Called* sign on the door to keep the rest of the day's classes out. I spend a minute logged in to the Vindicator site, just staring at the game splash screen where the hyper-ATV slowly spins. Then I get to work.

It takes about fifteen seconds to map the direct route from a domain name to whoever owns it. Vindicator.org's fixed IP address is easy. Name, address, and phone number are easy, even for people who pay extra to their registrar to try to keep that info hidden from the spam trawlers and the *You ordered toner from us, please remit so we can ship* scammers.

Anyone can do that. But for those of us who know where to go and how to search, it takes about fifteen minutes to get in deeper. Network traffic logs, server stats, email address directories, postings to the tech support forums, all of which are a lot less private than most people like to think.

An hour, maybe an hour and a half, gets you the real stuff. Business licenses, legal records, encrypted payment transactions. Public financial disclosures, bad credit history. The secret directories people set up on their websites to hide porn and share music and gaming PDFs with their friends.

I spend almost two hours, which is all of first A block, which is supposed to be English, plus lunch. I sift through registrar databases, server logs, gaming forums, and Usenet archives. I don't even get a name. Two hours of hard hunting, and the Vindicator Gameworks Project doesn't exist.

I'm not paranoid.

In the end, I've got what I started with. The two phone numbers to a bank and a lawyer's office that Mitchell mentioned, both of which are legit. It takes another half-hour to confirm that the money promised for cracking the Vindicator challenge is real and is sitting in the escrow account where it's supposed to be. Beyond that, the Vindicator Gameworks Project lives only as an elaborate chain of domain registrations, incorporation documents, and oblique press release mission statements that all just point to each other in the end.

It's the usual sort of irrelevant information screen that normally obscures the real information from casual contact. In this case, though, there is no real information. There's the screen, and there's nothing else.

I'm not paranoid.

I spend another few minutes staring at the home page. *Educational, cultural, and media philosophies in simulation roleplaying,* it says. I use that as a starting point.

A half-hour later, I've cross-referenced the results from six different search engines parsing that phrase, and have pulled key contingent matches from them by hand. Meanwhile, the simulation interface that ran on our machines the night before is a web of customized Python code that's locked down tight. However, I find a single line of OS status-variable declaration comment in the custom code where a webpage frame sets up that interface.

Another set of searches lets me match the comment to an open-source code base. Then I cross-reference that code base with my original searches, coming up with a half-dozen samples of server code patches that I'm pretty sure have all been written by the same person who created the framework for the Vindicator simulation. I work through a search of every webpage I can find that references those patches.

A half-hour after that, I'm looking at the forums on a high-end Python programming board, where someone going by the handle *TomSwift* has worked on most of those patches at one time or another. The account has posts going back three years, including a lot of recent discussion around optimizing graphics routines in a real-time web-based simulation interface. The profile has an email address on an AT&T server. Another half-hour, and that address yields up a third phone number, with a Washington state area code and an exchange that a final search tells me is a mobile.

I call the number as the rising tide of movement outside and the clock at 3:14 tells me school's done and the day is just getting started.

"Yeah?" a voice says after one ring. Outside, the corridors are a storm of feet and voices, but even over the noise, I can place something like a California accent in a hurry, the faint double-echo of a multi-networked connection.

"So why Vindicator?" I ask. "You trying to justify something? You feel guilty? Or maybe the question is, should you feel guilty?"

On the other end, there's a longish silence.

"You've got the wrong number," the voice says at last. "And how did you get it? And who are you?"

"On the first bit, long story," I say. "On the second bit, I'm a guy with the team that's going to have your cash in hand by the end of the night. I just wanted to say nice work. Also, I'm going to be looking for a job in about a month. I do a little coding myself, can I maybe send you…"

"Look, I don't know how you got hold of me, but I'm just the tech guy. You've got questions on the money, I can't…"

"The only question I've got is this. Do you know who you're working for?"

Another long silence. I'm back at my workstation, the multilayered web of search screens dismissed as I pull up network diagnostics.

"I'm not sure what you mean…"

"What I mean is, instead of asking how I got this number, maybe you should ask why I had to get this number in the first place. I go looking for the Vindicator Gameworks Project and you know what I find? You. Everything else even remotely connected to this game is all double-blinds and dead-ends leading back to a home page and a lawyer's office."

"You ever consider that maybe it's just really beta?" the voice says, but I can hear a hint of uncertainty that wasn't there before.

"Yeah, or maybe somebody's being set up." I carefully shoulder-hold the iPhone as I type my way through a half-dozen router configuration pages. I want to play with the network before the others arrive, bypassing the district firewall so I can speed up our client-side response.

"I'm not paranoid," I say. "But think about the idea that maybe the point isn't anybody beating the game but somebody else watching us try to beat the game. A double-blind experiment. Some mob of psych professors tracking down hapless high school students for kicks and pharmaceutical-industry research grants."

Another jump cut. On the monitor where everything I say goes scrolling past as fast as I say it, a separate pane is in motion. A waveform display maps out the intricate spikes of a pitch-perfect speech synthesizer, playing back the words on the other end of the conversation.

It sounds like you've been thinking about this a while…

The synthetic California voice has a synthetic edge that's designed to suggest it's also been thinking.

SCOTT: *Just being philosophical. People say I like to play at being philosophical.*

On the other monitor, glowing brightly against the darkened space of jump seats and shadows, the tabbed array of search pages that I'd previously trashed is still showing, recorded and logged.

Okay…

The voice sounds perplexed now, pausing like it's trying to focus.

So what do you like?

My turn to get caught off guard. "What do I like about what?"

"You said *Nice work* on the game. What do you like about it?"

I only have to think for a moment. "I like the metaphor. I like the uncertainty. I like the idea that with no rules, the simulation becomes as much about us establishing our own rules as it does about us discovering the rules you laid down."

That's cool. Hey, do you have a name?

I click off as Mitchell slips in from the stampede of students finally slowing in the hall. "Who are you talking to?"

"Nobody important." I'm already dragging workstations into the same configuration as the night before. Mitchell tosses his backpack to a far corner with the echoing thud that only a stack of science textbooks can make. I can guess without looking that most aren't for the courses he's actually taking this year.

"Bond was asking after you in English."

"Yeah, we talked."

As I sit at the multimedia workstation, Mitchell's watching me in a way that means I know what's coming before he says it.

"Hey, if you want some help with this project, we could get together this weekend."

"You're not done?"

"Yeah, I wrote mine last weekend. I do my best work at the last minute. You, on the other hand…"

"You ready to play?" I don't look at him as I fire up the workstations, one by one.

22

If You Want To
Get To Heaven

Ozark Mountain Daredevils, 1973. It was mostly false bravado when I told the California voice on the other end of the phone that we'd be done the simulation that night. However, it took two solid nights of gaming for me to realize just how false. That night, and the next, we play.

The scene at home that week is a bit of blur. For the four of us, life starts at 3:14 p.m. when we hit the computer lab and step back inside the world that the game maps out for us. Hour by hour, meter by meter, we make our way through the virtual base.

Wednesday afternoon, we manage to map the upper levels and make it down to the levels below. The elevators have been locked down since the moment we were first spotted, so we end up rappelling down an empty shaft after encouraging the doors open with a forklift stolen from an adjacent supplies bunker.

Wednesday night we spend on the run, caught up in a tighter and tighter array of defenses. We run from assault troops with beanbag-round shotguns and tasers at the low end. We run from sonic cannons that'll drop you into a custom-made seizure at the high end. We run from a lot of equally nasty stuff in between.

For two nights, our array of maps and tactical schematics continues to spread out across the computer lab table like ripples on a pond. The base is a maze of corridors and tightly packed rooms on four levels, carefully laid out and annotated at one-to-five-hundred scale. However, it's the empty space at the center of the maze that's become the focus of all our attention.

Whoever's designed the virtual complex has done a good job of putting functionality first. There's a degree of ambient realism to the setting that makes it easy to get caught up in the idea that this is some kind of actual paramilitary base that people live in. As most shooter simulations are designed like a goth amusement park ride, this is a change of pace as nice as the game itself. All the corridors we've been through, all the chambers we've passed through a few frenzied steps ahead of the patrols still closing in, all the security points we've ransacked in order to stay ahead of those patrols. Everything locks into everything else in a precision arrangement. No wasted space anywhere. Except for this one thing.

We've done the circuit of the complex four times, once for each level, and at the center of each of those levels is the same empty space. Some sort of secure core, locked off from the rest of the base. Problem is, we can't find any way to get from the rest of the simulation into this particular empty space. Every functional corridor we've followed, every realistic room we've torn through expecting to find some kind of concealed access to what lies beyond, there's nothing.

Second problem is, we can't find the Vindicator. Which suggests that the empty space at the center of the map is the only place it can be.

Over lunch on Thursday, we lock together a strategy for knocking out the sensor system base-wide, then letting someone cut through an inside wall. Whichever one of our avatars draws the short straw, we're hopeful that he or she makes it through to whatever's beyond without accidentally hacking through a hundred-amp service line.

Like it felt when the five of us won the VCON open, like it feels so often when we game, the four of us playing the Vindicator simulation have crossed over into a sort of zone where we start to think like one person. Mitchell said once that a band is the instrument that a song plays, or words to that effect, but I had no idea what he was talking about. I do now. In looking at the empty space at the heart of the maps, it's not like we debate so much as we finish each other's thoughts. We dispensed with small talk two days before. We're focused. We need to see this through to the end.

The computer lab is clear of classes in B block, so Thursday afternoon, we all cut to get started an hour early. The moment we log in, I juice base systems with a command core password we took off a squad sergeant the night before. We find the forklift we used previously where we left it, using it to make the first incision through the steel and concrete core of the wall. We finish up with hands and a pair of pipe wrenches found in a tool kit in one of the bathrooms. We've got our way in.

We work our way down through the inside of the wall, a pitch-black space so narrow that we need to squeeze without weapons, leaving them hanging around our necks. Breanne is rappelling down on point, because as in real life, she's somehow the skinniest of the five characters in the game.

From the moment we started playing, the monitors in the dark and empty computer station have been recording everything we do, everything we say.

BREANNE: *All right, I think I'm getting close to bottom.*

MITCHELL: *What do you see?*

BREANNE: *It's still too dark, hold on.*

Eighty-odd klicks away, the operations room is empty except for Malkov. He's working on his laptop, more diagnostics running. Like us, he's been here every afternoon this week. Packet info and network data is streaming past in seemingly random blocks. But from the chaos, a repeating pattern is flagged in red, Malkov watching it cycle, over and over again.

In the dark computer station, the same trace pattern from Malkov's screen plays out on a monitor console beside the running transcript.

RICO: *Watch yourself.*

BREANNE: *I'm okay. I'm dropping again, hold tight.*

SCOTT: *My screen's going black to red.*

MITCHELL: *It's emergency safelight. When we shut down base systems, we must have crippled the power.*

RICO: *Or they've shut it down trying to keep us in one place.*

SCOTT: *There's an opening.*

BREANNE: *[Anglo-saxon, but in a good way]…*

MITCHELL: *It's a vehicle bay. Everybody in.*

Where we've paused the game, my monitor shows the same visual as Rico and Mitchell's, the vague shapes of vehicles standing in shadow that climbs to the ceiling high above. But on Breanne's monitor where we all watch, a green glow flares from the night-vision goggles she pulled off a sentry the session before.

In the monochrome haze, we can see the space split up into some sort of zoned storage. Lines of what look like artillery racks stand to one side, two rows of Humvees half-covered by white tarps in the far corner. Stacked crates look suspiciously like heavy ammo canisters. In the distant shadows beyond them is something that Rico swears is a partially disassembled F/A-18E. Rico has memorized *Jane's World's Aircraft* cover to cover, so I take his word for it.

At the center of the vehicle bay, in the jittery haze where Breanne's night vision pulls all the detail from the shadows, the Vindicator sits in photorealistic glory.

We don't waste any time getting close. Circling the tank is a line of portable lighting rigs and heavy equipment tool cabinets, like somebody's been doing repairs. A thick mass of cables runs from under the tank to the wall, some kind of power or data feed. A moment's fiddling by Mitchell brings the lights up so we can all see.

Every monitor shows a slightly different angle, the four of us spreading out in the simulation and looking from one monitor to the next in real life to get a panoramic view. Up close, the Vindicator has a coolness to it that's hard to describe. It's like one part stealth fighter, one part tank, and one part touring bus of a band you really like.

"What's the best card we've got?" Mitchell says. Hearing his voice reminds me that nobody's spoken for a while now.

Rico taps up an inventory on his screen. "Silver. That tech officer we surprised in the bathroom. Scott's got it."

On my monitor, I'm circling the Vindicator, its solid-core bulletproof tires more than half my height. I tap my keyboard to flip in close to some sort of recessed key-card panel next to the big *M* on the Vindicator's side. I'm hoping it's a side entry portal, because there are no other obvious ways into the tank that any of us can see. The screen takes on an image of a key-card being slotted as I type in a command line.

On all our monitors, around the big *M*, a bead of light flares across the hull. The outline of a hatch slowly unseals, pushing out from the tank and rising on hydraulic lifts. I'm the first one in, clambering up the struts of the virtual ladderway that unfolds from beneath the virtual door and drops to the virtual ground at my virtual feet.

In the game, we see five empty jump seats. Five workstations are visible within the confined space, set within staggered banks of controls and displays. Everything's dark.

In the other space with five empty jump seats, the monitors are alive, Malkov's waveforms flaring above the game consoles. On the screens that mirror our monitors in the computer lab, the interior of the Vindicator is a disjointed reflective view. Like one of those pictures that contains a picture of itself. Each console in the deserted station is echoed perfectly within the simulation.

MITCHELL: *Welcome aboard…*

Part Three

The Five of Us

23

Girl on the Moon

Foreigner, 1981. For the better part of an hour, we go very slowly. I take the lead, flipping through various controls as I try to find out how to power up. Problem is, the controls appear to be in Russian, or Polish, or something else Eastern bloc. Every switch, every button, every toggle is labeled with those weirdly dyslexic Cyrillic-alphabet letters that make everything look half-backward.

In the end, I make a leap of faith and trust in color, carefully punching the largest green buttons I can find. I get lucky the third time out, the controls flaring to life on my screen in a storm of high-tech color. On what looks like a node map, the Vindicator's systems come to life.

MITCHELL: *You're online?*

SCOTT: *Kind of.*

MITCHELL: *What do you mean?*

SCOTT: *Can you read Russian?*

MITCHELL: *Not so much.*

SCOTT: *That's what I mean. Hang on. What the [anglo-saxon]...?*

RICO: *What?*

SCOTT: *I've got a boot sequence in English. C-A-R-L heuristic server system operational.*

MITCHELL: *What's it stand for?*

SCOTT: *Computerized Autopilot and Recreational Library. Who writes this [dung]?*

On each of our monitors in the computer lab, one of the deserted computer station consoles is perfectly rendered as a baroque mass of unintelligible controls. We fire up the presumably never-used Russian language package on another of the lab's workstations, then use Google Translate and a couple of tentative text conversions to confirm that Russian is, in fact, the Vindicator's language of choice. Then we spend an hour testing the software's ability to parse the control text, trying to assemble a manual for each station.

The system draws a blank on a lot of what must be military lexicon, so we guess at whatever we can't figure out. We apply more tape to our keyboards as we set up for the final stretch. We need to get the tank out of the complex. Me on systems, Mitchell on ops, Breanne in the engineering chair, Rico running weapons.

And then for the next four hours, we all hover around the fifth console, navigation and helm, trying to figure out how to actually make the Vindicator move. After four hours, we still haven't succeeded. It's a bit of an anticlimax to what had seemed like it was going to be a good night.

We're being particularly careful with time in the game, as we know that it's only a matter of time before the friendly folks trying to shoot us are going to figure out where we've gone. We talk and argue while the simulation is paused, trying to decode the apparently undecodable controls of the helm on the fifth workstation. We flip back into the game long enough to test another theory and watch it fail. We talk and argue some more.

After four hours, none of the Russian on the nav controls translates to anything that makes sense. Making the process even more difficult is that the controls themselves are as bizarre-looking as their alphabetic readouts. A sort of suspended floating-wing steering yoke features matched grips that each pivot independently. Both are festooned with buttons and side switches, and augmented with enough ceiling-mounted manual servo controls that the best description I can offer up by comparison is four oversized Xbox controllers welded together and put on a high-protein diet.

We try three other translation sites. We try every conceivable combination of throttle and thrust, forward and back, left and right. All we're able to do is make a lot of well-rendered engine noise. Breanne, jumping back and forth between the helm and the engineering controls, is getting increasingly flummoxed as to where the power she's generating is going.

The Vindicator isn't built right, at least according to any sense the four of us have of how such things should work. And our sense of such things is usually pretty good. Of particular annoyance is a servo system on the transaxles that the computer system is convinced doesn't actually exist. From the mechanical specs, it looks like it's supposed to disengage and roll the wheels up at some point, which makes no sense.

Two additional dead systems seem to be designed to adjust the configuration of the armor on the lower hull, shifting it into a fan-out form that can only weaken its defensive capability. Which of course is just what you want in a tank. Mitchell on ops has suggested that we're dealing with alien technology. However, Rico's got the main toggle-bank of the three-panel weapons console mapped out to the last control, and can speak confidently on what standard Soviet-Russian hardware the weapons systems are an apparent adaptation of.

It's pushing nine o'clock when we stop to order pizza. When my phone rings to tell me it's arrived, I'm trying to prove that what we thought were thrust controls are actually independent controls combining thrust and direction for the transaxles on each side. The idea comes from a pedal car I had when I was a kid, but I'm desperate. It doesn't work any better than anything else.

"Keep playing," Breanne says as I give up. "Give me the door codes, I'll go."

"You're an idiot," is the best I can do by way of snappy answer as I pause the simulation.

"That's the best you can do?" She seems disappointed. As I shrug, I'm fairly certain I can feel my brain sloshing in my skull. To anybody who watches, gaming doesn't seem like work, but it is. It's hard to explain.

Everybody searches backpacks and pockets for cash. "You know," Breanne says, "if you have a heart attack and we all get stuck in here one weekend, you're going to look pretty stupid." I ignore her because I still haven't got the energy that a proper retort would take. "He's going to look pretty stupid," she says confidently to Rico as I go.

I trudge down the hallway to the front doors. I've got the place to myself, because Wes the night custodian is always gone by eight. He sees us there in the computer lab nearly every night, but if he's ever figured out that we've technically got no permission to be in the building after hours, he's never mentioned it to any of us. I like Wes.

How we manage to keep access to the building after hours is that I've got a spare key and the alarm code. How I've got a spare key and the alarm code is that last year, somebody in the staff room left a spare key and a copy of the alarm code by the coffeemaker as I was passing on my way to see Kirk in the counselor's office. How I tell everyone I got the key and the alarm code is that I know how to pick locks, and that I hacked the office computers while I was doctoring Mitchell's permanent record, removing a request for psychiatric assessment that the councilor before Kirk had threatened him with.

Hacking sounds sexy, I know. When it comes down to it, though, it's a whole lot easier to just depend on people writing their passwords down on the blotter next to their computer, or leaving filing cabinets unlocked that they really shouldn't leave unlocked. Someone leaving a filing cabinet unlocked is how I know that the counselor before Kirk didn't put a request for psychiatric assessment in Mitchell's permanent record. What he actually wrote was *Find out what dot-com this kid starts up after graduation and invest heavily in his competition.*

With my stolen codes, I crack the front doors and pay for the pizza. I get a grateful nod as I tip the delivery guy handsomely, because I suspect that when Seth gets the call at home telling him I've failed to graduate, I'll be doing his job. In the month or so left till then, I figure I should try to build up some karma.

Rekeying the alarm while balancing three large with the works and a pair of six-packs of Coke Zero and Fresca on my shoulder is tricky, but I've had lots of practice. However, as I'm heading back to the computer lab, I see the lights on in the library.

Wes the night custodian never leaves the lights on.

Faint on the floor that was clean an hour before, footprints track the dust of the bus lane in through the foyer and down the hall.

Through the library glass, there's no sign of anyone at the study tables. Nobody's in the librarian's office beyond. The doors are open, though, pizza and pop dropped at the checkout desk as I listen. Through the silence comes a faint buzz of music, a slightly louder creaking rising through the stacks.

As I come around the closest shelves, I see a figure sitting in the study cubicle I like in the northwest corner. Molly.

Her coat is slung over the desk behind her. The sleeves on the white sweater she always wears are pulled down almost over her hands. She's got earbuds in, bent over a notebook and writing furiously. The creaking sound comes from her chair as she gently rocks to the music, her ponytail swaying.

I don't move. I don't make a sound. But like she senses I'm there, she wheels suddenly. Her expression is dark to start, then darker when she sees it's me. She pulls one earbud out, an unhealthily loud blast of synth and guitar heard for a moment before she taps the iPod at her belt to silence.

"What?"

I have to think for a second. "I saw the light on," I say.

"Harder to work without it."

I just nod. "We're in the computer lab." No response but a rapid flipping of pages. The words in my head are turning over slowly, like they're trying to start on a really cold day. "How'd you get in?"

"You gave me a dupe key and the alarm code when you stole them last year," Molly says, like it's the stupidest question she ever heard. Until she says it, I don't remember that she's right. The tone of her voice doesn't so much say the conversation's over, as that it never actually started. She pops the earbud in, goes back to the notebook. The music comes on.

"We've got pizza," I say, loud enough for her to hear. An angry flick of her hand summons up silence again, but she doesn't look over. "If you're hungry. We're in the lab."

"You covered that."

Where the words still aren't starting, the faint twist of anger rises up in their place. And like with Ms. Bond, I shut it down. Not now. Not this way. I turn for the doors with a gratuitous fist striking the metal of the closest shelves, the sound echoing in the silence, following me out.

But at the desk, I stop. I turn back. I feel myself drawn into the darkness of the moment before the better instincts that might otherwise stop me have a chance to kick in.

"You know, I called you." My voice is louder than I expect it to be.

Molly doesn't even pretend to ignore me this time. She knocks the chair back as she rises, slamming notebook, pens, whatever else is in front of her into her backpack.

"When you didn't come home," I say, "I called you, like, every day. I mean if you didn't get my messages, I'm sorry, but..."

She spins faster than I can follow, a hardcover copy of something heavy hurled toward me with a dangerous precision. I stumble back as it hits the magazine shelf beside the front counter, a cascade of back issues spilling to the floor.

"But what?" she shouts. "What is it you need to say so badly that you won't stop following me around for four [anglo-saxon] months? Watching me at work from across the highway, staring at me in the halls and from the back of the class like you're so out of touch with reality you think I can't see you? What?"

The dark rage that's welled up in her stops the lesser anger in me like a stone wall. I'm cold suddenly. I'm back to trying to find words again.

"I wanted to tell you I'm sorry your mom died."

"So I guess you feel better now..."

It's almost like she knew what I was going to say before I said it. Which makes sense, I guess. I don't know how many times she must have heard it before.

I don't bother looking back as I go. Both six-packs drop as I fumble them, so I kick them ahead of me to scoop them up without breaking stride. I don't see Molly watching me, like I know she does because she told me later. I don't see her turn away. I don't see her hands shaking as she stoops to re-shelve the magazines that have fallen.

In my pocket, I don't see where at some point since I answered the page from the delivery guy, my iPhone has connected a call all on its own. Above me, I don't see the green lights on the surveillance cameras flick on as I pass. I don't notice those cameras watching me as I stalk toward the computer lab. I don't notice the silent connections that caught every word, every gesture that passed between Molly and me through the library glass.

24

Who Are You?

The Who, 1978. A half-hour later, the pizza has been made the target of a tentative assault, but the high-level frustration that's become the order of the night has stolen everybody's appetite. It's increasingly apparent that we're not getting anywhere near the end of the game, Mitchell sitting at the fifth console now because that's how desperate we are.

"Shut it down," I say.

"I can see something happening."

"What's happening is you've got the wheels spinning in opposite directions. Shut it down."

As he does so, a warning in Russian flares on Breanne's board. We kick into pause mode as she assembles a translation in the Russian-language workstation web browser. Why the systems board that I'm running is partly in English is still a mystery I haven't had time to figure out, especially since any of the English menus I pull down invariably open up Russian windows in response.

"Infrared at the wall," Breanne says. "They're cutting their way in." Her voice carries a tone of finality that we all feel.

"Where the [anglo-saxon] are they cutting from?" I say. "If there was a way into this place, why didn't we find it?"

"It's sort of a moot point now."

In the simulation, we've been located. We can stay paused as long as we like, but at some point, we either need to figure out how to move or get resigned to the fact that it's not going to matter. Mitchell's already run up an impressive breakdown of the Vindicator's defensive capabilities. But even though the shotguns and sidearms we've seen in use so far have no chance of making it through the reinforced hull, the bay outside holds hardware that looks capable of peeling us like an orange at this range.

"All right," Mitchell says. "We need to think."

At the other end of the school, Molly still sits in the library, staring at the darkened windows. When she finally stands to go, it's like she only just realizes where she is, staring around her, uncertain. Her gaze settles on the clock, resigned. She zips her jacket up tight, like she's preparing for a long walk as she switches off the lights.

But at the main doors, when she keys in the code that I gave her, the lights on the alarm panel start flashing red to green in a way they're not supposed to. Normally when we're secretly occupying the building after hours, the lights are slow-flashing red to indicate that the door systems are active but the inside motion detectors are disabled. Then they go fast-flashing red after the code is input, giving you fifteen seconds to get out before the doors and the sensors are armed again. Solid green means everything's armed, so that flashing red to green makes Molly understandably nervous.

Funny thing is, the school's alarm system has no flashing red to green mode. I know this because when I stole the codes, I got to play with the system by convincing Seth he should get the same system installed at home. Part of the way I convinced him was to broadly hint that there might come a time when just locking the doors wouldn't be enough to keep me out of the house.

Where the panel flashes red to green, Carl is watching Molly through the video camera across the corridor that's not supposed to be turned on. I got to watch the footage later. The alarm panel acting up forces Molly to open her backpack, digging through it for the slip of paper where I wrote the codes down for her the year before. She wants to check out my note on what the lights mean, which is the same as I just wrote above.

It takes her maybe a half a minute. That's a half-minute in which she hears the faint sound of music and voices.

Molly thinks the sound is coming from the computer lab at the far end of the corridor, and she's half-right. It's the sound of us in the lab, but there's no way she'd normally hear it at this distance through the closed door. It's being subtly amplified through the PA speakers at the far end of the corridor, because Carl needs her to hear.

Molly finds the paper, but she doesn't key the code. Instead, she stares at the notes in my barely legible handwriting, and to the warning that this message must be eaten immediately after memorization, and to the badly drawn heart with a knife through it that I scrawled above it.

She steps into the corridor, staring down into the darkness.

As she slowly walks toward us, she doesn't see the flare of green lights where the corridor cameras come to life behind her. Flicking on one by one, following her as she heads for the lab.

I'm more tired than I want to be. Around me, I'm vaguely aware of more variations of the same debate we've been having most of the night, trying to figure out the Vindicator's navigation controls in their coded Russian. Mitchell talks feedback mechanisms, Breanne talks power controls, Rico talks drive engagement, all of which we've already tried, none of which works.

I start to crumple and toss notes to the recycling bin. Mitchell sees. "You think we should break till tomorrow?"

I'm in a bad enough mood that I'm about to tell him he's had his hour. Then I follow his gaze where it swings past me to the door.

Through the narrow rectangle of glass that looks out to the hallway, Molly is watching us. Breanne and Rico's arguing has drifted into a discussion of the probability of success if we just pick controls at random and see what happens. Both of them look up as I stand.

When I slip out to the corridor and quietly close the door behind me, Molly has moved a half-dozen steps away. In the computer lab, Breanne presses her face to the glass. "Hey," I hear her say, muffled. "Molly."

"Don't gawk," Mitchell murmurs as he presses next to her to watch.

In the silent shadows of the corridor, my footsteps seem louder than normal. A glance to the clock down the hall reminds me it's pushing eleven. Molly leans back beside the door to the girl's washroom, sliding down to sit on the floor. I wait but she doesn't look up. The silence that hangs seems impossibly long.

"I got your messages," she says. "In Vancouver." There's no apology in her voice. Not exactly. But no anger either. She won't meet my gaze, just staring down toward the distant office. "I was with her at the clinic, then at the hospital. Pretty much all day."

"I'm usually up late," I say. She doesn't say anything in response. I can feel my own words hiding. I cross the corridor to slowly drop down beside her. Not too close.

"I was going to come down at Christmas," I say after a while. "Take off a couple of days before the break, surprise you or something. Then Kirk said she'd died. He said you'd called him. So I waited for you to call me, too."

"Because whatever happens to me must be your responsibility somehow?"

"That's not what I meant…"

"Yeah, it is, Scott," she says, and I see her recognize the anger rising in her again, trying to hold it. "It is what you meant. Whether you know it, that's something else. But everything that happens needs to be about you before it actually means anything."

She turns to look at me. Something twists in my gut like I haven't felt in a long while.

"Anyway," she says. "I'm sorry. I should go."

"We've still got pizza." Not the words I was looking for, but they're all I've got right now. "You should stay. If you want to."

"I don't know if that's a good idea."

"It's just pizza."

Another silence seems longer than it probably was. I push up against the wall, standing slowly. I hold out my hand.

Molly waits a long moment before she takes it, pulling herself up. She disengages quickly as she follows me. At the door, Breanne, Mitchell, and Rico are all watching. I can feel their sense of hopeful expectation as strongly as I can still feel the faint trace of Molly's fingers across my palm.

Where my phone sits in my pocket, I can't see it blink back to standby as the door shuts behind us.

25

Mirror Man

Prism, 1979. Split screen. Next to the static displays of our five monitors where they're paused at the Vindicator controls, Lincoln's quarters are a fractured fish-eye cube where the webcam in his laptop catches the view. Carl is watching him, just like the rest of us. It's all white walls and bookshelves, barracks-style but comfortable. On a bunk, Lincoln is reading a well-worn copy of Sun Tzu's *Art of War*. He glances up to a knock at the door.

"It's open."

The door slides back with a pneumatic hiss that I thought doors only made in bad science-fiction films. Karya's on the other side of it, in yoga pants and a Cal Tech sweatshirt. "Evening, sir," she says, but the military demeanor and its stark contrast to her ensemble only lasts until she steps in to tap the door closed behind her.

"And a good evening to you," Lincoln says. "What brings you by?"

"I was looking to spend the evening with a person of rare intelligence and insight."

"Sounds like an excellent pursuit."

"I thought so, too. Do you know anybody?"

Like he's been saving it up, Lincoln laughs. A real laugh, not the cold humor of his public smile. Karya drops to the edge of the bed, an easy familiarity between them as he rubs her shoulder.

"I thought you were on ops tonight."

"Malkov wanted to stay on. Some problem with the uplink he's watching. Do you have time for dinner?"

Lincoln's hand slows, just for a second. "Yeah," he says. "What kind of problem with the uplink?"

"He didn't say. What's on defrost at the canteen tonight?"

"Go check it out for me," Lincoln says. "I'll be there in a couple of minutes."

Split screen. In the computer lab, it's the five of us. This is what we used to be.

Breanne is sharing the story of her opening combat scenario the first night we played, when she tripped across three security ops packing tasers and yellow-stocked crowd-control shotguns, her avatar armed only with a screwdriver. She beat them by jamming said screwdriver into a set of security controls and dropping a door on them. You probably had to be there.

We're all laughing. Molly's laughing. I can't remember how long it's been since I've seen Molly laugh. But it's not the laugh I remember. Around her, around me, between all of us, tension hangs like a shroud of clear plastic. We can see each other, but through a kind of muted stillness. I try to ignore it.

Molly, like me, is of the opinion that fifty thousand dollars for a single game that seems to have no PR associated with it smacks of scam. As I toast her clearly superior wisdom with a cold slice of triple cheese, I share a theory Mitchell and I have been developing, that a hidden layer of goal to the simulation requires the team to locate a hidden tow truck and have the Vindicator hauled to the closest BCAA garage.

But with Molly here, with everything paused, we take some time for the first time to actually look at the detail work on the simulation. A thing we'd all but ignored in our initial rush to map the controls and beat the game. The styling of the Vindicator's cockpit is military utilitarian, but its ergonomics have an almost zenlike simplicity to them. Everything is panel-molded and windswept-slick, designed to an aesthetic standard that speaks to a calm lethality. Nothing looks rough, nothing looks unfinished.

There's a deadly grace to the cabin's steel lines, like a wasp turned inside out. But for us, all of those lines seem to point like arrows toward the locked-out fifth console, navigation and helm. Those controls are framed by Post-it notes on the fifth monitor, where Breanne is walking Molly through how we've spent all night failing to figure them out.

That's when it happens.

In Kirk's office, Carl had been listening. Carl had always known that Molly would be the most important part of it.

"You know that's a flight helm, right?"

As she gazes at the screen, Molly's working through a second slice, chewing thoughtfully for the moment it takes her to notice that the rest of us have all stopped eating.

"Sure we know," Mitchell says confidently. "What do you mean?"

Molly laughs again. "I mean, that's a flight console. There's thrust, rudder, roll and pitch." She points to each part of the complex yoke controls in turn. In my head, I feel a vague click of understanding.

"But it's a tank," Rico says indignantly. "It specs out at twenty tonnes. What's it doing with flight controls?"

Molly shrugs. "It's a tank that really wants to fly, I guess."

"That's the wheel assembly folding in," Breanne cries out with sudden understanding. She's digging through the schematics. "The hull servos, that's a [lord's name in vain] delta wing! It's a tank that wants to fly!"

"No, wait a minute." Molly's only half-listening, pushing closer to the screen as she goes into the no-blinking stare. "That's a variable inertial-thrust system. It's like some kind of custom multimode ground-air setup. You set the main thrust level, there. Then you selectively throttle it to each transaxle, there. Then you apply servo force for turns and directional control against the main. Cool."

Mitchell, Breanne, Rico, and I all exchange exactly the same look. As one, we slide our chairs back from around the fifth workstation, which up until now has been missing the fifth member of the team that the Vindicator.org Challenge webpage says we're supposed to have.

Molly gets the drift. She smiles as she shakes her head. "No. Thanks."

"Yes," Breanne says. "Please. Look, we're totally hooped here. Once we flip out of pause, we've got like fifteen seconds before bad guys come through the bulkhead and nuke us nastily. We've been stuck here all night, I don't think we've even figured out the turn signals."

"Fabulous cash prizes," Mitchell says. "We think."

"I have to get home, actually." The smile's gone now. "Sorry to eat and run."

All of us catch the change in her tone. Breanne gives Mitchell a look but he only shrugs. The tell that shows he cares about this but knows he can't fix it. Molly has her backpack on.

"Give it an hour?" I say.

She turns back at the door. Her eyes that are the blue I can't describe touch on everybody's, but it's mine they hold for a moment.

Molly smiles again as she nods.

Split screen. Signal traces pulse against the scroll of dialogue that records our words. On the audio feed assembled from the twin pickup points of my phone and the multimedia workstation, you can hear desks scraping as we move the fifth workstation into proper place. Mitchell and Breanne bring Molly up to speed on the game controls, their words flowing past.

MITCHELL: *You switch views, there. Toggle front and side to get the ops display in.*

MOLLY: *What's the lag?*

BREANNE: *None. This thing is freaking fast.*

At the keyboard, Molly strips our mostly unsuccessful attempts to mark the nav systems, laying down her own tape as she studies the convoluted hybrid controls. Above the navigation console on her screen, she's pulled up a view of the vehicle bay that I try to coordinate with the spreading mass of maps.

RICO: *What's the last reading on the crew on the other side of the wall?*

MITCHELL: *The wall is slag and we and the crew will be on a first-name basis momentarily.*

SCOTT: *I need to pull a tactical map, find out where they're coming from and figure out how we get out of here.*

MOLLY: *I'm ready.*

As she adjusts her chair and the angle of her screen, Molly shakes her fingers out like a concert pianist. She cracks her knuckles loudly. Breanne winces.

Molly gives a nod. "Let's play."

I key us out of pause and all five monitors lurch into sudden motion, the game back into real time as Molly's virtual board comes to life. Her hands are a blur across the keys, eyes flicking from the console view to the controls. The power readings that Breanne has spent all night trying to beat into submission suddenly level out, floating just below redline. Molly holds them there. The outside view on all our screens is slanted, the Vindicator's virtual suspension compressing as we slam around in a tight spin. Everything is a blur as we move.

Split screen. In the operations room, Malkov is alone. He's at the same workstation he was at the previous night, the same network diagnostics running on his laptop next to it. The doors open as Lincoln enters, wearing the leather jacket again like it might be some subtle sign of rank.

"Double-shifting tonight?" he calls.

Malkov replies without looking up. "I love my work."

"I've heard. Karya said you had something."

"Nothing worth bothering you on."

"Maybe tell me what's up and I can decide for myself if I'm bothered."

There's no edge to Lincoln's voice, but the video feed from the webcam shows a moment's coldness twist through Malkov's expression like he hears it anyway. He gestures to the console, punches up a series of display panes. An overlay of signal traces appears, Lincoln stepping in to see.

"Looks like a local echo," Malkov says. "Maybe atmospheric disturbance, interfering with our satellite link."

"Except if it was, you wouldn't be here watching it."

Malkov nods. "It's repeating. Staggered offsets, some manner of packet scan. I almost didn't catch it."

"A packet scan on what?"

"On our network feed."

The signal traces on Malkov's console wrap around each other in perfect synch. Lincoln's eyes don't show what he's thinking as he stares.

Split screen. In the darkened computer station, the same signal traces repeat on the data console as the view in the vehicle bay races past on Molly's console.

MOLLY: *So does anybody know where we're supposed to be going?*

SCOTT: *Hang on.*

MOLLY: *Seriously? You said you've been here all night, where's the exit?*

SCOTT: *Hang on.*

Split screen.

In the computer lab, my hands are moving across the keyboard almost as fast as Molly's. With the Vindicator's systems online, we have access to something we didn't have before — a full set of schematic plans to the base that unfold as bright lines of color on my console. However, just as we guessed when we cut our way in, the empty-space-turned-vehicle-bay at the center of the map isn't connected to anything. It makes no sense.

On his screen, Malkov punches up multiple signal traces, graphed and frozen. His voice and Lincoln's flash by in perfect transcription.

MALKOV: *Someone's feeling their way along the outside of our uplink. Matching our frequency cycling down to the second.*

LINCOLN: *You should have called me.*

MALKOV: *There's nothing to call yet. Could just be a military comsat trolling for satellite-phone signals.*

LINCOLN: *Could be somebody looking for a way in.*

MALKOV: *They won't find it.*

And like it was waiting for Malkov to say the words, the signal display on the monitor in the deserted computer station fractures like shattering glass.

On Malkov's laptop, faster than the eye can follow, a dozen process panes open up, a dozen different attack patches unfolding as they hit the local network like a pack of wolves. The base's data is a secure system, locked down so tight that even the U.S. military's secure SIPRNet can't see where Lincoln's systems piggyback on top of its own routers and satellite uplinks. And all he and Malkov can do is watch as it falls.

26

Action

Streetheart, 1978. On Molly's console, the controls are in constant motion. The virtual wraparound front viewport of the Vindicator is wired as a massive head-up display. Night-vision tech compensates for the shifting ambient light as the Vindicator screams through the vehicle bay in ever-widening circles.

The ease with which Molly manipulates the Vindicator's virtual controls almost makes it possible to forget the insane complexity of those controls. Almost. But the array of tape and Post-it notes she's using as reference speaks to the degree of technical precision in the simulation as she pushes the Vindicator through its paces.

She's essentially just joyriding now, testing the helm. She's making adjustments on the fly to how her fingers surge across the baroque arrangement of keystrokes that trigger the controls in the game. Because from where Molly's playing it, these aren't your typical console controls, or even the complexity of the most challenging PC tactical simulations. The helm she's testing, the Vindicator's fifth console, plays like it's real. Not so much the custom-browser simulation that was advertised, but more like a remote version of the full-cabin flight training systems that airline pilots and military fighter jocks train on.

The level of realism makes it hard to believe that anyone could actually work the Vindicator's controls from a standard keyboard. However, Molly makes it look easy as I try to find the way out of the vehicle bay. Problem is, there is no way out.

MITCHELL: *Say that again?*

SCOTT: *There's no way out. Do they make words of less than one syllable that I should be using here? There's no vehicle exit from the vehicle bay.*

BREANNE: *Then someone named it wrong.*

SCOTT: *The core runs all the way up to the air-access bay we got a look at before we fell back to the ops room. Everything comes in by chopper and gets craned down from up top, I don't [anglo-saxon] know.*

MOLLY: *So we just keep driving in circles until we run out of gas?*

RICO: *They're through the wall…*

As Molly virtually spins out, our screens show at least three squads of troops pouring in through the smoking remains of the vehicle bay bulkhead.

A flash of automatic weapons fire ricochets off the Vindicator's armored glass in frighteningly realistic real time. The shooters fall back behind the cover of whatever gear presumably doesn't contain things that'll explode if it gets hit. From the corner of my own visual display, I can see four people spreading out with what look like Stinger missile shoulder-racks deployed.

If it were all happening for real, it would be pretty exciting.

Remember that for later.

Split screen.

In the base buried beneath an abandoned Hendrix Lake mine site, the scene is pandemonium. On the night-vision feeds, recon teams are scrambling through the cover of boulder and scrub forest, watching the skies. On the interior feeds, a silent claxon pulses at every security point, red lights flashing. Lincoln is racing along the corridors, shouting orders as security teams jump at his command.

The doors into the ops room are sealed, two sentries standing stone-faced on the corridor side with pump shotguns. Real shotguns, not the bright yellow nonlethal crowd-control models with their beanbag rounds.

Inside, Malkov is at his workstation, quietly directing the half-dozen frenzied techs taking secure systems and databases offline by cutting through the room's cable bundles with fire axes. But on the webcam feed that Carl captured for me to watch later, as Malkov punches his way through a dozen different panes of network diagnostics, you can see him smiling.

By piecing the video together with the network logs Carl recorded, I managed to get the general gist of the attack that hit Lincoln's network that night. It came through a cascade of overloaded feeds, hammering through every clandestine connection the base data systems were ghosted through. Primary satellite feed, secondary feed, backup piggybacking off of civilian telecom feeds, everything. A military-grade assault. Something so perfect that calling it hacking seems insufficient somehow.

But there at the center of it all is the single fatal fingerprint that's the cause of Malkov's good mood. It's an encrypted address node, a sixty-four-bit burst of identification that Malkov's military code splits like a guillotine. By the time Lincoln bursts back through the ops room doors, Malkov's system is on fire, cutting its way through layers of intrusion as it traces the assault back to its starting point.

"I ordered total shutdown!" Lincoln shouts. Even in the security feed, there's an edge of dangerous anger to his voice.

"I'm tracking them back," Malkov says, a great deal calmer. "If you shut down, we'll lose them." He's working the laptop and the ops workstation at the same time, flipping through windows too fast to follow.

Split screen. The space with the five jump seats is awash with light, inset displays monitoring Malkov's network trace as the main screens echo the action of the game. Rico's defensive board is lit up red, Breanne's controls screaming at her in an endless flow of Russian text.

LINCOLN: *How long?*

MALKOV: *Already there.*

In the window mirroring Molly's workstation in the computer lab, she's keeping the Vindicator and the guys with guns on opposite sides of a wall of crates, weapons racks, and armored personnel carriers under camouflage netting. A half-dozen channels of transcript are running alongside it all, color-coded text jumbled together and shooting past like some 4chan flamewar played back at high speed.

MALKOV: *Trace is locked. It's a local staging point.*

RICO: *[Dung]! HMG fire, seven o'clock.*

LINCOLN: *Local? How close?*

BREANNE: *We're losing power.*

MALKOV: *Hang on.*

SCOTT: *Pause it.*

MOLLY: *Hang on.*

On the security feed from the ops room, you can see Lincoln and Malkov staring with the same mix of shock and uncertainty. On Malkov's laptop, a reverse-out map of the coordinated assault on the base's network and systems has traced its way back through six satellite links to a local router in a small town eighty-odd klicks away. A whole bunch of numbers and IP traceroute info obviously means something to Malkov, but tucked into it all is a single line of text that sums it up.

SD 27 OGDEN SECONDARY

"[Anglo-saxon] me," Lincoln says finally. "Shut down."

"Core systems are locked down, they can't get any farther in."

"Whoever this is shouldn't have gotten this far. We've been compromised, shut down."

But Malkov is on the laptop, pulling up satellite imagery as an area map overlays itself with a flurry of keystrokes. The lines of the town that Lincoln might have seen from the chopper that night when it started superimpose themselves over the satellite feed. A blur of tactical data scrolls past as Malkov zooms in to a high-resolution aerial shot of the school grounds. There's the building. There's the wall of forest rising to the west, nothing else beyond it. There's the empty expanse of the truck yard across the street, sheltered from the sight of the highway.

"Doesn't get any easier than that..." Malkov says quietly.

Lincoln understands. "No chance."

"They're twenty minutes," Malkov says. "We can be in and out before anybody..."

"Security is shot to [dung] as it is, and you want to go trolling for high-school hackers? Shut down!"

But as Lincoln turns away, Malkov is up to follow him. "This is no high-school hack. For someone to set up a network this local as a staging point for cutting back into our satellite feed, they need to already know where we are. We need to know who's running this. We need to know what they're looking for."

On one of the flatscreen displays behind Malkov, Lincoln watches a map of the virtual assault play out like some high-tech version of Risk. Network nodes and core data systems are mapped out and broken down by status — offline, disabled, compromised. The intrusion is still cycling through nonessential data, the unencrypted core systems left open to keep the hack inside for as long as possible. Malkov is making whoever's on the other end think they've gotten in clean, while they search for the secure data they'll never actually find.

Split screen. In the computer lab, Molly's having too much fun to pause the simulation. She's taking it to the troops now, charging them before they can set up firing positions. The missile squads are scattering, afraid to shoot as the Vindicator comes between them and their compatriots on the other side of the vehicle bay.

MOLLY: *So this is fun and all, but...*

SCOTT: *I'm on it.*

BREANNE: *You were on it five minutes ago.*

SCOTT: *And I'm still on it.*

In the ops room, Lincoln nods. "One team. Trace the hack back as far as you can, then take the local lines out. It's six months before anybody in that [dung]-heap town can so much as send an email."

Malkov acknowledges the order with a salute as he runs. He calls to Karya as he hits the corridor. She takes a moment to look for Lincoln, but the ops room doors are already closed.

In any strategic simulation, in any game, you can take it as written that you've got three ways to overcome any obstacle. In classical terms, you can fight, you can parley, or you can retreat. There are no right or wrong tactics overall, but in any given moment, one set of tactics will always be more right than any other. Three options, choose one.

The better the game, the more complicated the options get. Different ways to fight, to parley, to retreat. However, it usually doesn't move much beyond those three basic paradigms in some form.

Problem is, as long as you're only ever hitting the marks that the person who designed the scenario has set for you, the only game you're ever really playing is guessing. You're spending your time trying to think your way back to whatever the person designing the challenge thought of in the first place, so that the game is always about the person who set up the scenario and put it into play.

Finding the fourth option that was never meant to work is what makes the game your own.

"Hey," I say as Molly does a sideways slam into a stack of crates marked *LIVE ORDNANCE*. They scatter toward a panicked squad trying to set up an M2 heavy machine gun beside the shattered wall. "How tall are we?"

"Are you thinking we can make a human pyramid and reach the roof?" Breanne asks. But she digs through the stack of notes in front of her to toss the Vindicator's engineering specs across to me. Because as I've been frantically scanning the internal maps of the base that the systems console gives me access to, I see it. Finally.

There is a vehicle exit from the vehicle bay. Barely noticeable at the edge of map, the entrance to some sort of emergency evacuation tunnel is a convenient meter higher and wider than the Vindicator in both dimensions. Disconnected from all the other levels, it breaks through the surface four storeys above us and a half-klick away.

Across the bay, animated troops take cover. Molly lurches forward and I swear they all virtually duck back. A spray of gunfire glances off the viewport, but she noses the Vindicator into an armored personnel carrier that flips toward the would-be sniper. I finally lean across to tap her terminal into standby. We all take a collective breath as the simulation pauses.

Molly grabs the last slice of pizza as I start digging through maps, trying to figure out what we need to do. All I can say is, "There." I point a lot.

She leans in to look. "So the plan is to drive a twenty-tonne tank out of a secure military base via the back hallway?"

"Yeah," I say. We're in that zone where we're all thinking like one person. "Just checking."

Split screen. A night-vision surveillance feed is cut by a sudden flare of light. In the mine face along the mountainside, the landing bay doors slide back, a chopper powering up on the pad beneath.

Inside, Malkov is plugged in at the controls, Karya and three others in the back. They're all in night gear, goggles on and backpacks open where they're checking weapons. Malkov sets up for night-vision flying, a wash of green light filling the cabin from the head-up displays. He punches clearance confirmation, then shuts down. Radio silence.

On his board, a straight-line course is plotted across the endless sea of forest that spreads to all sides. On Karya's board where she sits behind him, the satellite plan of the school is pulled up, architectural schematics laid over top of it. She's marking doors, windows, power lines, security points.

As it lifts off from the pad, the chopper is some kind of featureless corporate craft, no markings. As the turbines kick in, the fuselage suddenly splits along a dozen different lines. From beneath its matte-black skin, surveillance and weapons systems unfold like the legs of some sleek steel insect disappearing into the night.

27

Bat Out of Hell

Meat Loaf, 1977. The emergency evacuation tunnel is almost invisible in its simplicity, which I realize is part of its design. Before, when we couldn't figure out where the assault troops were coming from as they cut their way in through the wall, we couldn't see them dropping down along the outside of that wall, into this open space that doesn't even have a door in the vehicle bay to mark its location.

Cranes in the landing bay above are the official access to the vehicle bay, along with a half-dozen points of tightly packed fabric that look like emergency chutes of some kind. A failsafe escape route from the landing bay above to wherever we are now. If the upper bay is ever attacked, it's one quick slide to a backup ground escape plan, courtesy of blowing through the wall in the opposite direction that our friendly shock troops have done, then zooming to safety in the Humvees and the APCs sitting under tarps in the simulation.

One small problem is that the Vindicator is a fair bit heavier than even an armored personnel carrier. The interior schematics of the complex are short on engineering details, so all we can do is guess at the strength of the evac tunnel's floor supports. In the end, we have to trust that it'll hold.

We're all watching the clock. It's after midnight. We're close enough to the end that we can almost touch it through the fatigue. I've got the maps spread out on the table. Like all our decisions as a group, consensus is immediate.

"You can't be serious," Breanne says.

"Am I smiling?" I'm smiling.

"Where are the big guns?" Molly asks. She's at my shoulder, close enough that she's becoming a distraction I almost wish would go away. Almost.

"Looks like they're moving to center." Rico's sketched out a plan view of our position in the still-frozen simulation, troops and munitions marked out with little arrows like some kind of play-by-play analysis. "They're going to try to catch us in a corner. They need us not moving and all of them on the other side of the bay to safely unload on us."

Molly takes a last look at the map before she slips back to her own chair. We all follow suit. We're done thinking.

"Let's play," she says.

In the ops room, Lincoln is watching a security monitor that logs a cascade of directory intrusions as the hack continues to spread within the still-running bait systems. On a larger monitor overhead, a military grid is superimposed over satellite imagery, 100 Mile House marked out in lines of white light. Hurtling toward it, the chopper is a single point of red, five minutes out.

In the deserted computer station, every monitor is on. The satellite feed is split-screened against the night-vision view from the chopper's belly camera as it pushes toward a faint scar of light on the horizon. The directory trace that Lincoln watches is sliding past beside the interior view of the chopper, where Karya checks the tasers clipped to her belt. On the five main screens, the view of the game that we see in the computer lab erupts from motionless pause to full action.

RICO: *Fifty-cal fixed and mobile. They're setting up four different fire zones.*
MOLLY: *Not for long.*

On the display panel mirroring Molly's monitor back in the lab, the vehicle bay rockets past the virtual viewport as she banks us hard. In the lab, she's sitting straight in her chair, fingers flying across the keyboard without looking. She isn't blinking, connected to the simulation in that way I can't describe. The rest of us are frantically trying to sort out the info flashing past in Russian on our boards, but when it comes down to it, we know we're just along for the ride.

I watched the game again earlier tonight, when I'm writing this. Mitchell was over, because he's come by to watch select bits and pieces. It was all logged and video-archived along with everything else. Even a second time through, Molly moves so fast that it's all a blur. The guns are pulling back toward the smoking hole in the wall where we don't want them, Molly pushing the Vindicator through a hairpin right turn and between the Humvees to draw them off. Rico calls fire points almost as fast as they erupt around us, Molly making subtle adjustments to our erratic course. We slam through the Humvees like a well-bowled cannonball, turning the racks of spare parts they spin through into a shrapnel cloud that crashes down to all sides.

I'm working on putting together a tactical map, stitching together the hand-drawn version of our escape route on the simulation's systems board. From under the desk, Molly kicks my leg.

"Pull up real-time tactical," she says. I punch a half-dozen keystrokes, a map of the vehicle bay popping up on my monitor. The Vindicator is at the corner farthest from the shattered wall, penned in by the setup of the M2 heavy machine guns.

Through the virtual viewport on Molly's screen, we come to a full stop. The image of the vehicle bay is motionless, the others craning over from their own workstations to see.

"What are we doing?" Mitchell asks.

"Stopping," Molly says. "Make them think we've hit a dead end. Give them a chance to lock and load."

"Any part of this plan you want to share with the rest of us?" I say, but Molly's fingers are already flexing above the keyboard.

"Hang on."

Three hundred meters overhead, Malkov's chopper is circling the school. On Karya's board, radar and a real-time satellite feed show that they've got the sky to themselves. She nods to Malkov. The chopper pitches forward, dropping fast for the ground.

In the computer lab, the virtual viewport on Molly's computer lurches as she slams the virtual controls straight in. It takes us a moment to realize that the Vindicator is heading off backwards at high speed. We slam into parked APCs behind us, watching them punch out and ricochet off each other like fifteen-tonne ping-pong balls. Where they spin out across the vehicle bay in a shower of sparks, they give us the cover we need, three-point M2 fire blocked as we sail through it.

Molly slides her chair back, pulls her keyboard off the desk to lean back to where I'm sitting. She's watching my screen, ignoring her own as she navigates off the tactical display. The Vindicator surges in reverse, dodging vehicles as weapons fire follows us. Molly's monitor takes us through a high-speed three-wheel skid and straight for the shattered wall where the troops blasted their way in. Then suddenly the wall isn't there any more, and the virtual paramilitaries shooting at us are all leaping out of the way as we smash through into the space beyond.

All our boards are going crazy, our screens a jumble of Russian warnings and alarm claxons. No one's watching. We've all got our eyes fixed to Molly's monitor as the virtual viewport shows the boxy lines of the evac tunnel emerge from the haze of smoke that's followed us from the vehicle bay. Rico's board shows heavy fire following us, but he lays down a burst of sonic cannon in response that sees the closest troops hit the ground flailing.

The steadily rising half-klick between the vehicle bay and ground level races past on Molly's screen, her hands flying across the keyboard. Somebody's shouting inane cheering gibberish like an idiot. It takes me a moment to recognize my own voice.

In the chopper, Malkov's night-vision displays show the darkened truck yard adjacent to the school. A wide-open space beyond a half-dozen parked trailers marks his landing spot.

On Molly's screen, everything is a stuttering blur of white walls that we bounce off without slowing down. Actually getting outside is going to be trickier, however. According to the tactical info that came with the new base maps, the doors that seal off the far side of the straight-through evac route are triple-layered slabs of carbon-steel reactive armor whose controls we have no access to. As a potential weak point in the defenses of the complex, they're built to withstand any attack that an enemy might throw at them. But only from the outside.

Rico's already prepped antitank ordnance. We've agreed to hit at a hundred meters. Mitchell is watching the speed-and-distance reckoning, counting us down.

In the deserted computer station, the images from the chopper's cameras play out above the view on Molly's monitor. The virtual doors at the end of the corridor loom up like a bank vault with a glandular disorder.

Mitchell marks it at a hundred meters. Rico has his hands locked to the keyboard as he hits it, like he's afraid it might try to get away from him otherwise. On Molly's front-view display, we watch four arcs of fire and light lance out from beneath the Vindicator's nose. Then a senses-crippling explosion rises ahead of us, which will either take the doors out or catch us in a backblast just before we execute a high-speed pile-in against a half-meter of immovable instant death.

If it were all happening for real, you'd be scared out of your [anglo-saxon] mind.

Remember that for later.

On Molly's monitor, the flash of the fireball shreds as we pass through it. The doors are gone, a gaping hole opening up to darkness where the concrete around them has torn away.

It's a moment of perfect exultation.

It's late. We're exhausted. We've been here for three days straight.

We've won.

And none of it matters as much to me as the fact that it's the five of us again. Where Molly and Breanne have me trapped in a bear hug, Mitchell and Rico piling on behind them, I know they all feel the same.

On Molly's monitor, from the corner of my eye, I see her web browser quit.

One second, the window's there. The next, it's gone. An empty desktop sits where it used to be.

By the time I twist my head around, the simulation windows on the other computers are gone as well. I break away from Molly, the others watching me as I drop into her chair. Her browser's not running. I open it again, the school home page coming up like normal.

I key in *vindicator.org*. Network access churns for the few seconds it takes to tell me what's coming.

Safari can't open the page "http://vindicator.org/" because Safari can't find the server "vindicator.org".

Behind me, the others are watching. Breanne pipes up as I slide Molly's chair across to my own workstation. "What the holy hell?"

Out front of the school, the truck yard stands in shadow. Traffic noise is faint and sparse from the highway, but over top of it, a dull thumping sound rises fast.

Malkov's chopper drops from darkness, rotors flaring in the half-light of the truck yard's distant loading-dock floods. Stealth dampeners mute the engines to a staccato pulse as five figures bail out almost before the skids have touched the ground. They're armed to the teeth, masked behind night-vision goggles. Karya is first out, Malkov bringing up the rear, but he quickly takes the lead as they head for the school at a run.

In the computer lab, I try to pull the Vindicator site up on each workstation in turn, each browser flashing the same message.

"It's probably just a network glitch," Mitchell says over my shoulder, but I ignore him. I grab my notebook from my backpack, flipping back through the careful record I made of my attempts to get behind the Vindicator's wall of anonymity two days before.

"There can't be a glitch," Breanne says, defiant. "We won. Glitches at this point are not allowed."

I key the site's fixed IP address. Nothing. I run a traceroute that stalls out almost as soon as it starts. It makes no sense. I have no idea what's going on, but I can feel something twist in my gut as I call up a WHOIS site. I key in *vindicator.org*. I wait for the same ID page to pop up as last time. The domain name, the registration info, the address of the mail-drop law office.

I whisper an epithet that's got no suitable brackets.

No match found — This domain available for registration.

28

If You Want Blood

AC/DC, 1979. Outside the school, Karya is picking the lock at the main doors. Behind her, the rest of the team are fanned out and holding point with beanbag shotguns and tasers. Malkov cuts past her as the doors open, popping the alarm panel and shutting it down with three precision snips from a pair of wire cutters. He checks the settings to note that it was only partially armed, motion detectors disabled. He motions the others inside without a word.

Inside, the library, the office, the main stairs are all dark. Down the hall in the opposite direction, light streams from the computer lab door.

In the ops room eighty klicks away, Lincoln can only stare in disbelief as the intrusion into the base's network shuts down. The diagnostics windows that are monitoring the hack show it backing out of the system. One second, it's there. The next, it's gone without a trace. Process monitors mark the dozen different intrusion fronts sweeping through the system shutting down, one by one.

In the deserted computer station, all the monitors except two have gone black. No light, no movement. On the transcript console, the steady pulse of words slips past.

SCOTT: *No, you don't get it. The site is gone.*

MITCHELL: *So the network went down…*

SCOTT: *The network is live. See? The domain name registration, there, it's been wiped. Two minutes ago, we were on it. Now, it's like it never existed. This is [anglo-saxon] voodoo.*

On a video feed across from the transcript console, the camera by the library catches Malkov's team as they slip down the corridor. The closer cameras are all off, Karya checking them carefully as she passes.

In the computer lab, three arguments are breaking out at once and I'm at the center of all of them. I'm up, pacing. All right, I'm not pacing. I'm kicking chairs. Breanne is shouting at me where one just misses her. "Hey, don't make this some sort of federal-case freak-out, all right?"

"Meaning what?" I shout back.

Rico steps up to diplomatically right the chair that missed Breanne. "I think maybe we're missing the point, here."

"Meaning your rant is getting old." Breanne tries to kick the chair back at me, but Rico hasn't let go of it yet.

"The point being what?" Mitchell says as he tries to interpose himself between me and the rest of the furniture.

"We won," Rico says.

"We didn't win because there was nothing to win!" I say. "I told you this was wrong."

"Sorry, did I miss the gun to your head?" Breanne snaps.

"I haven't got the time to keep track of the things you [anglo-saxon] miss."

As irritated as we all constantly make each other, we don't really fight all that much. We're fighting now.

My getting into Breanne's face causes Rico to get less diplomatic in a hurry. "Hey, what's your damage?"

"My damage is I knew this was [anglo-saxoned] up, but why would anybody bother listening to me? When has anybody ever bothered shutting up long enough to [anglo-saxon] listen?"

I haven't been watching Molly. She's silent, watching the rest of us. I don't notice her moving until she's actually at the door, backpack and jacket in hand.

Suddenly, I have a great desire to calm down.

"Look..." I start to say, but she turns back on me with all the anger, all the animosity from the library four hours before. It hits me like a well-placed brick.

"Do you remember what I said outside?" she asks quietly. The others all look away.

"Yeah," is all I can say.

"Good."

And she's gone, the door slamming behind her. I stand in silence for a moment, Mitchell looking like he's going to say something. I know I shouldn't follow her. I know I'm going to anyway.

I'm a step away from the door when it slams open from the corridor side.

Faster than any of us can react, four figures in black are inside the computer lab with shotguns drawn. Though I don't recognize her at the time, Karya's the one grabbing at me, even as I trip back across an upturned chair left in the middle of the floor by my previous rampage. She gets a piece of my shirt but nothing else, then I'm upside down and under the table in the chaos.

All I can see is legs. All I can hear is voices screaming, telling us to hit the floor, hands on heads. Where I scramble toward the door to the chem lab, I see Mitchell pinned fast to the wall. Rico pushes Breanne behind him as he raises the chair he was holding, lashing out instinctively at the closest figure. The blow lands well enough but Rico is distracted as he follows through, so that a boot to the stomach from the other side puts him down.

In that one moment, time slows down. I understand that I'm more scared than I've ever been.

In that one moment, all I can think about is Molly.

I'm through the chem lab door at a dead run, slamming it shut behind me. It doesn't stop Karya where she's hard after me, but it slows her for the second it takes me to drag down the wheeled whiteboard standing against the closest wall. That slows her down long enough for me to wrench down the fire extinguisher beside the corridor door as I burst through.

Time's still moving slowly. To my left are the west-side fire exit doors, maybe twenty strides to get out and away. I'm not thinking about running. Not with the others still there. I'm thinking about whether I can get into the woods fast enough and long enough to call 911 before the guys in black catch me, because I'm already resigned to the fact that they're going to.

But to my right, Molly's on the floor. She's got duct tape across her mouth and around her wrists. A goggled figure that I learn later is Malkov has both her hands in one of his as he drags her roughly toward the computer lab door, already silent beyond.

I don't know how Molly knows I'm there, but she looks up. She catches my eyes, just for a second.

As Karya bursts from the classroom behind me, I spin to catch her hard with the extinguisher. Pain shoots up my arm where the impact knocks her back, the taser in her hand flying free. I don't have time to grab it. I'm running for Molly, running for Malkov.

I've got a second of surprise. It's nowhere near enough.

Where I hurl the extinguisher straight at his head, Malkov manages to catch most of it on his shoulder, rolling with it to lessen the impact. Then he keeps rolling, spinning to catch me with a backhand shot that makes everything go black for the second it takes me to hit the floor.

When I manage to look up, I've got Karya sitting on my chest running tape across my mouth. She's already bound my hands, not that I could have moved them anyway. Pain up my neck and through my chest is a white-hot knife. Malkov's goggles are down and hanging sideways around his neck, like the extinguisher must have caught some piece of them. He's got a gash bleeding on his cheek where he watches me, cold.

Karya looks like she's going to say something as she stands, but Malkov waves her to silence. He leans in to grab me by the wrists, lifting me like I weigh nothing.

"It's generally better for you if you don't see my face," he says quietly. He's pressed close enough that I can see the tattoo below his left ear, Cyrillic letters against a death's head. I have no idea what it means, but especially in the context of how much Russian we've been wading through the past three days, any part of my mind that isn't already terrified gets there in a hurry.

Karya follows with Molly. We join Rico, Breanne, and Mitchell on the floor, all of us bound and gagged. Malkov's team is working in a silence that's far more frightening than any threats would be. From where I'm sprawled, I get to watch them pull laptops and electronics gear and high-density portable hard drives from their packs. They're patching into the computers in the lab and the network panel behind the router. Malkov is pacing, watching their progress.

And then he stops dead. Stares.

I can't see the top of the table where he's standing, but I know what he's looking at because I left it there. It's our map of the virtual base, Rico's sketch plan of the vehicle bay beside it. All our maps, all our notes are stacked and spread across the table and the workstation desks. Malkov is shuffling papers, flipping through pages of printout.

From under a pizza box, he pulls a printout image whose outlines I can see where they bleed through to the back side of the page. It's a screenshot image of the Vindicator itself. The light in the lab isn't good, but I'm pretty sure I see Malkov go pale.

None of it means anything to me. Not yet.

Malkov flicks his gaze down to meet mine. The eyes so dark they look black.

"I want this network pulled down and packed," he says to Karya, voice hard-edged in the silence. "Here, the office, the library. Drives, servers, back-ups, everything. Get it all."

Karya nods.

"Then get the five musketeers ready to go. They're coming with us."

Across from me, I catch everybody's eyes in turn except Molly, who isn't looking at me. Breanne is shaking. She squeezes her eyes shut, Rico managing to lean in so his shoulder touches hers. But the look on Karya's face tells me she's only a little less shocked than we are.

"Repeat that, please?"

Malkov hands her the image. It takes her a second to recognize it. When she does, she stares with the same shock.

"Move," Malkov says.

The lights of the truck yard are a haze of sodium yellow, no breeze stirring the ever-present dust. The black chopper is barely visible in the shadows as its engines suddenly power up, Malkov keying them by remote. The pulse of turbines and the dull thump of rotors raise an impromptu storm in the distance as the five of us are herded to the school's main doors.

I get to see the trophy case come off the wall as I'm hauled past. We're all wearing duct-tape hobbles that are loose enough around our ankles that we can move under our own power. They're tight enough that I'm not going anywhere except where Malkov at my back is directing me, the five of us pushed out across the asphalt at a run.

The school is left open behind us, Malkov's team spending their last minutes doing precision damage to make it look like a smash-and-grab vandalism. Once things are cleaned up, it'll take the cops a couple of days to figure out that nothing's actually been stolen. It'll take the district tech guys a little longer than that to wonder how a school's worth of ransacked computers managed to all get their hard drives fried by a mil-spec point-blank EMP pulse.

In the truck yard, I have to squint to see through the haze of rotor-driven grit that lashes us like a cloud of stinging insects. The chopper's cabin door is open ahead of us, Malkov and his team practically throwing us all inside.

We land in a heap, someone underneath me that I can't tell is Mitchell until I roll off him. Just in case I'm thinking about rolling too far, one of Malkov's guys perches in the closest jump seat with a an implacable expression and a short-barreled shotgun. I'm assuming it's packing beanbag rounds because he isn't stupid enough to risk putting a hole in the side of his own chopper while we're in flight. However, its position a half-meter from my face makes the concept of nonlethal ammunition suddenly moot in my mind.

All of them have lost their goggles now. I don't like what that might mean.

Even as Karya jumps in and pulls the cabin door shut behind her, we're in the air. She takes the place of the shotgun guy, motioning him to the back as she settles down to watch us with a look I can't decipher. She keeps her own gun down, at least.

Light from the truck yard shifts as we climb, then it's gone, the town below us. We pull a tight looping turn, the elevator feeling of a hard climb pushing us down for what seems like minutes. Then we level off as the turbines ramp up with a roar. Karya fitted us all with earplugs as we were herded out of the school, but the noise is still deafening.

Molly lies behind me. If I twist my head far enough, I can see her. Her eyes are shut tight, body shaking. No tears, though. If I twist a little more, I can reach her hands with mine, but when I make contact, she flinches away. She opens her eyes long enough to meet my gaze, and the anger there is like something alive inside her. Then she turns away as we sail on through the dark.

Part Four

Why We're Here

29

One Step Ahead

Split Enz, 1981. I remember things. I know that doesn't sound like a big deal. But when I say I remember things, I mean I remember things that other people don't remember. I remember things better than most people.

This is part of the reason that I'm the one writing all this down, I suppose. The five of us all went through it together. We all saw it, we all lived it. But in memory, it's like I'm still living it, every night that I type a little bit more of it up as a permanent record. I'm watching it again as I write, but even without watching it, all the feelings, all the impressions and events that mark people like scars are still there.

The problem with remembering things is that sometimes there are things you want to forget.

I have a hard time doing that. Forgetting.

I remember things.

Molly and I have been in school together forever. I can remember how many grades in elementary school we were in the same class. I remember the junior high band trips we went on together and just sort of ignored each other. I can remember we were at summer camp together in fourth grade. Walking down the trail to the beach, Molly stepped on a hornets' nest one day and I was the one who ran for the medic.

Molly doesn't remember any of that. When I used to talk about things that happened to us in first grade, when I told her things I remember her doing or saying from years before, she used to laugh like my remembering that far back was the weirdest thing she'd ever heard. Maybe she was right, I don't know.

At the beginning of ninth grade, Molly got to know Breanne when she helped her survive Ms. Webb's notoriously dull English class. From that, she dropped in once in a while for the lunchtime D&D game that Mitchell, Breanne, and I were running in the yearbook-club room. We had the room to ourselves because the junior high administration had cancelled yearbook that year, after a particularly filthy limerick somehow wound up on the poetry page of the yearbook the year before.

(Confession. I was on yearbook club in eighth grade but I'm still not saying anything.)

Molly played sometimes, and she just hung out other times, and we kept ignoring each other. But then in tenth grade, Molly and I wound up partnered on the debating team together, so we couldn't ignore each other as easily as we had all the years before.

What I remember most vividly from that experience is when we were practicing for the provincials. Molly and I had gotten paired off for the one-on-one sessions, and while she was up and talking first, I realized that I was staring at her ass with a lot more interest than I was paying attention to anything she was saying.

(Confession. Even as I write that, I'm hoping it's not seen as an objectifying, sexist statement. I don't like sexual objectification. I don't like the grade-school playground mentality that pervades too many of my peers and provides a foundation for sexual objectification. Molly is a brilliant, funny, kind, caring, talented human being. She just happens to be a brilliant, funny, kind, caring, talented human being with a really nice ass.)

At that time, we were attempting to resolve that the school should or shouldn't install the video cameras they later installed in order to leave them turned off. When it was my turn to talk, the distraction of having been staring at Molly meant that I managed to momentarily forget which side of the argument I was on. After the fact, I was fairly confident that no one but Mitchell noticed me staring at Molly's ass. Still, I found myself wondering for a while whether that sort of thing happens in the House of Commons a lot.

In the end, we went to the provincials, where we all got buried under an avalanche of advanced rhetoric from a load of private-school geeks. But what I remember more than the humiliation was the celebratory dance the last night. I remember Molly asking me to dance, and me being so stunned that I didn't have a chance to tell her I don't know how to dance.

I remember that three or four songs in, the DJ stopped the endless haze of recycled top forty to play the Split Enz track mentioned at the top of this not-chapter, where it must have been hidden in some retro dance mix collection.

I remember Molly kissed me when the song was done.

That was the start of a whole bunch more memories, all of which I've spent most of the last four months wishing I could forget.

In the ghostly green of the night-vision cameras that surround the mine site, Malkov's chopper is a dark shape against the sky. As the bay doors open, a flare of light burns the view away for a moment, the image enhancement shutting down for a few seconds as it overcompensates. By the time the monochrome green comes back into view, the doors are almost closed, the night above fading back to dark silence.

In the chopper, Karya is ready at the cabin door as we land. From the floor, all of us except Molly are watching her. As casually as I can, I push up on one shoulder to try to get a view out the window. I catch the briefest glimpse of the bay doors closing as we descend, but it's the dead darkness above them that I'm most interested in. No lights outside, no sign of civilization as we're sealed in.

I try to catch Molly's gaze as I lower myself again, but I can't. I can see Mitchell, though. He's scared. Breanne blinks back tears. She's scared. Rico is scared, which tells me I'm actually not scared enough.

In the base outside the landing bay, the alarms are quiet but the frenzy of activity hasn't slowed. People are moving, running, a sense of ordered precision in them that you wouldn't have suspected from watching the cola-and-pizza party in the ops room three nights before.

At the center of the chaos in that same ops room now, Lincoln snaps terse orders that are obeyed without hesitation. He's watching the access corridor, though. He breaks off from the systems monitor he's parked in front of when he sees Karya approach.

"Malkov?" he calls as he moves for her, but she shakes her head. She's got a locked case full of portable hard drives in hand, passing it to him.

"He's in the bunker. You need to..."

"Report," Lincoln barks. "Break it down."

Karya's tone cools just a bit. "Clean through-and-through on the school. Malkov ordered the sweep, archive and burn. It's all on the hard drives. One encounter. He brought them back."

Lincoln's expression says he's not quite sure he heard her correctly.

"Kids," Karya says. "Teenagers. Locals. They're on the deck, but you need to see Malkov..."

With the epithet that's got no suitable brackets, Lincoln cuts her off. He's through the doors at a run.

In the landing bay, three guards with beanbag-round shotguns at their belts but Uzis in hand flank the chopper. Across from them, the corridor doors slide wide. Karya and Lincoln slip across to a monitor, Karya tapping up a security feed from inside the chopper a dozen meters away.

The five of us are still on the floor. The duct tape gags are off and we've been lifted to sitting positions. Molly's across from me, face buried in the wall. I can see the pinpoint green of the camera point above where they're watching us. Best guess, the gags are gone because they want to hear what we've got to say, but no one's talking.

At the monitor, Lincoln can only stare.

"They looked like they were working in a computer lab," Karya says. "The rest of the school was clear. They're scared [dung]less."

"They're going back. I'll fly them myself. Refuel and heat it up. Now." Lincoln gives the last orders to the deck crew watching him. They scramble as he turns away, Karya close behind him.

"You need to see what Malkov..."

"Unless Malkov wants to show me his letter of resignation and a suicide note, I'm not interested." Lincoln is livid, a dark anger churning in him, looking for a way out. "This was no high-school hack!" he shouts, loud enough that from inside the chopper, we all hear his voice. We can't make out the words, though. "What the hell is he..."

"James." It's Lincoln's first name, apparently. I wouldn't have expected it to calm him down all that much, but coming from Karya, it does. "There's something you need to see."

Malkov is in the command center. Karya called it the bunker, which is what they all call it. He's alone, sitting at a secure terminal that he and Lincoln are the only ones who have access to. The base's core systems are all here. Command infrastructure, secure records and logs. Everything that Lincoln's operation is about is recorded here, secure behind armor heavy enough to withstand a missile attack.

The systems here aren't hooked into any of the base's other networks. But from a Linux system running proprietary encryption code, Malkov has a single feed running out of the bunker on a secure landline. The system at the other end of that landline is what he's testing now, booting up directory and interface code that hasn't been fully booted in years. He checks security points for signs of intrusion, checks the settings on a firewall he wrote himself.

He scans a menu that comes up in Russian. Malkov can read Russian. He's satisfied that nothing in this system and its long-dormant code has been compromised, nothing's been accessed.

What he can't see is those same systems running full bore and invisibly in the space they've cut out under the base's security code. He doesn't sense the night-vision headset he's still wearing from the raid catch a wireless signal that it was never programmed to respond to, switching on to record everything that passes as Lincoln bursts into the room.

LINCOLN: *What the [anglo-saxon] is...?*

And he stops short when he sees the array of papers spread out across the surface of Malkov's workstation. Our papers from the computer lab. Notes, maps, schematics. Lincoln picks up the screenshot of the Vindicator in its hidden bay. His expression is dangerously cold.

MALKOV: *I matched the images to a proprietary cache system on the machines in their lab. We took the network and phone system apart, there's no sign of any outside staging. The hack of our network originated there.*

On the single screen that's active in the unmanned station with five jump seats, you can see the papers Lincoln flips through, caught at a weird angle by the video feed of the night-vision headset where it hangs at Malkov's neck.

MALKOV: *We got wallets and ID off three of them, names and student IDs from their computer accounts. We've pulled their school records, hard copy and archived. I have a handful of hits online, but we're still putting a full dossier together.*

LINCOLN: *Give this to Karya. You and her. Nobody else gets told anything until it comes through me.*

MALKOV: *Done. Most of what's out there is the one called Scott. Lots of conspiracy blog postings under assumed names. He also looks like he's got some systems coding and network experience. I'll talk to him before...*

LINCOLN: *I'll take it.*

In the chopper, I've been quietly eying the camera point above us for a while now, doing my best estimate of its angle and range of view. The key-card panel at the cabin door is blinking steady red. I move carefully, making it look like my legs are cramping where they're taped tight. I twist so that I'm turned away from the camera and toward Rico, my face against the wall.

"It's going to be okay," I say. Barely a whisper, mostly to Molly, but she doesn't look at me. Rico glances over but turns away again before I can catch his eye, so I tap my foot where it points toward him. "The chopper," I whisper again. "What is it?"

"How the hell should I know?" he whispers back.

"Because you've memorized *Jane's World's Aircraft* cover to cover. What is it?"

"I don't [anglo-saxon] know."

"Guess."

Breanne's head is against Rico's shoulder, her eyes squeezed shut. He gives me a very dark look. But then he glances forward to the cockpit, assessing the controls and the darkened displays.

"Customized. Lynx AH.7," he says. "Maybe a W-3 Falcon. I didn't see enough of the outside."

"How fast? Cruising speed?"

"Fully loaded, two-twenty, two-thirty klicks. I don't know."

"We were in the air twenty minutes."

"How do you know?" Mitchell this time.

"I could see her watch. The one sitting on us." I do the math in my head. "That's like seventy-five, maybe eighty klicks."

Breanne is looking at me now. She pipes up, her voice shaking. "So we've all been living next to a secret air force base for the past seventeen years and just never noticed?"

I cast my eyes up to the camera point above us. The others follow my gaze. Breanne quiets down.

"They don't look military," Mitchell whispers.

"Their gear is," Rico says. "The night-vision lenses are ITT PVS-Ns, classified. SAS and the SEALs use them exclusively. The shotguns they were

100

packing had custom muzzle brakes and a mag extension. I think I've seen them as South African army issue."

"Private paramilitary." I glance to Mitchell. "Black helicopters. No markings."

The silence that follows is broken too quickly by the thunk of a lock. Everybody jumps. Molly finally turns away from the wall to look. She isn't blinking.

The key-card panel goes green as the door opens, a flare of light from outside shrouding the figure there. Lincoln steps up and into the cabin. He takes in the five of us with a slow glance.

"Which one's Scott?" he says at last.

I expect that the others are all as mind-numbingly scared as I am, so I'm surprised when they don't all start nodding vigorously in my general direction to save themselves. I probably would have thought about it.

"Me," I say at last.

Lincoln nods as he steps back. The two sentries behind him slip in to haul me up by the shoulders.

"Walk with me, Scott."

The sentries are responsible for most of my movement, so I'm not sure I'd call it walking. Either way, I'm out of the cabin two steps behind Lincoln. No time to say anything to the others as the door slams shut behind me.

30

Games Without Frontiers

Peter Gabriel, 1980. From the landing bay, Lincoln leads me and my escort down a narrow side passage with a lot of slide-up doors. Some sort of storage space is what I'm guessing from the corner of my mind that's still working. If more of my mind was working, I might notice that this particular side-passage storage space off the landing bay looks suspiciously like a side-passage storage space off the landing bay in the virtual base when we were crashing through it two days before.

As it happens, I don't notice.

The sentries at my elbow drop me unceremoniously inside, then step back into the landing bay as Lincoln seals us in with a black card slotted to the key-card panel beside the doors. If more of my mind was working, I might notice how this key-card panel should look strangely familiar to me. However, I'm distracted by the fact that my feet are still hobbled, managing to stay upright only by teetering against a stack of unmarked crates presumably on their way in or out of one of the slide-up doors.

Lincoln steps close. He pulls a pen from an inside pocket on the black leather jacket. Before I have time to wonder why, he squeezes the pen. A four-centimeter scalpel blade shoots out from the top, a hand's breadth from my face.

I try very, very hard not to move. Lincoln smiles as his hands drop. Then I feel my own hands suddenly loosed, the tape sliced through cleanly where the scalpel pulls away.

I'm conscious of my heart hammering in my chest as Lincoln shifts one of the crates to the floor, making a seat for himself. It's very quiet in this narrow corridor, which I realize in retrospect is the point. With the amount of activity in the base, the number of people running around, this is him talking to me without anyone else seeing that I was even there.

He spins the pen between the fingers of his left hand like he's prepping for a drum solo. "My name's Lincoln," he says. "The way this usually works is, you don't ever get to meet me. The type of business we're in here, privacy is our primary concern. You and I talking sets a real precedent."

His tone and his manner are so even-handed that it freaks me out even more than a riot-act rubber hosing probably would have. His southern drawl sounds downright homey, which is a pair of words I don't use all that often. I try to calm down by focusing on peeling the duct tape from my wrists, one careful piece at a time.

Lincoln has the two-screened tablet in hand, the scalpel pen tapping out a control sequence on a virtual keyboard. But as much as I try to avoid looking where the blade has disappeared into the pen again, something else there catches my eye.

I glance up. Lincoln sees me watching.

"You like it?" With no warning, he holds the pen out to me. He waits.

Slowly, carefully, I take it. The thing that catches my eye is the silver hourglass embossed in the pen's body of matte-black metal. I squeeze it hard. The scalpel snicks out again, gleaming in the haze of louvered fluorescents overhead. Lincoln watches me, inhumanly calm. I'm close enough that with a knife in my hand, I could try something. Thankfully, he and I both know that's never going to happen.

I crouch awkwardly to cut the tape binding my ankles. Another squeeze of the hourglass and the scalpel is gone. Carefully, I give the pen back.

"You were Agency," I say simply. I try to hide the edge in my voice but there's no point. The hourglass is the symbol of that ultra-secret covert ops arm of the CIA. It's the division that lame movies and espionage novels always say is called *the Company*. It's the part of the CIA that kills people.

"Very good," Lincoln says. Something in his voice suggests he actually means it, which freaks me out just a little bit more. "A little going-away present from before I embraced the private sector. Long time ago now."

He gets back to work on the tablet. I'm close enough that I can catch an oblique view of a fast-changing array of windows. I'm not surprised to see my transcripts, my webpage bookmarks, my posts on *Five Horsemen* all flipping past. "Your academic record says you're a bit of a computer guy," Lincoln says. "Multimedia, programming, network troubleshooting. I figured you might be the person to talk to about what's happening here tonight."

"Okay," is all I can think to say.

"You ever do any hacking?"

"No."

From another inside pocket, Lincoln pulls my iPhone. It got lifted while we were incapacitated in the corridor outside the computer lab, along with my wallet and everyone else's phones and wallets. I'm quite certain that its token four-digit security took him less time to crack than it takes me to type this. He's flipping through my emails, my notes.

"Like maybe testing denial-of-service worms on domain servers you don't like? Taking over your school security system?"

"I know a guy in Buenos Aires," I blurt out. "And I found the alarm code written down next to a spare key."

I'm aware that I'm maintaining a lot less composure than I'd like. Lincoln gives me a questioning look. He taps out a few more strokes on the tablet.

"So you're saying you probably wouldn't be up to breaking a triple-blind comsat link running a TACLANE through a cascading IP connection? Crack a dozen admin passwords and GELI directory systems?"

I stare at him with what I hope is a credible display of complete and utter ignorance. Lincoln is thoughtful for a moment. "I guess not," he says finally.

As he taps the tablet to darkness, he tosses my iPhone to me without looking. The fumbling grab I use to snag it shows how unexpected that particular move was.

"So tell me why I'm here," he says.

I'm suddenly aware that my head is hurting again. "Don't you mean *Why you're here?*" My phone shows no bars, which isn't a huge surprise, but I'm tapped into a strong Wi-Fi signal on a network with no name. "I mean, like, you're asking why we're here, right? Me and the others?"

"No, I'm asking, like, why I'm here. I know why you're here. You're here because my team picked you up and brought you here. What I don't know is how much you've managed to put together about what's happening here since you arrived. So tell me."

As I'm trying to kick my brain into gear, I realize that the tablet isn't dark after all. It's showing the shadowy security feed from the cabin of the chopper, the others motionless against the walls. Molly is sitting up but still off by herself, staring at the floor now. I can see Breanne whispering, trying to talk to her, but Molly never looks up.

"If you're going to kill us anyway, what I know or can figure out doesn't matter a whole hell of a lot." The words are out before I've really thought about them, which I realize in the silence that follows is the only way they ever could have gotten said. I lock my gaze to Lincoln's. I don't bother trying to hide how scared I am.

"It's been a long time since I had to kill anybody," he says at last. "You want to help me keep it that way, Scott?"

I just nod.

Lincoln nods back. "All right, then."

In the dark computer station, the same view of the chopper cabin pulses on one of the monitors. In another pane, Carl is watching Lincoln and me in the corridor. On the transcript pane, everything gets taken down.

SCOTT: *You're a private industrial-military consortium. Guns for hire. Corporate espionage, intellectual property theft. Maybe political kidnapping. Definitely weapons sales. You're here because you're a long way from commercial flight zones. Any military traffic gets routed around you between Cold Lake, Esquimalt, Juneau. You can come and go, nobody sees you.*

LINCOLN: *Very good. You missed the convenient blind spot for real-time satellite surveillance. Plus the trout up here are superb. Do you fish?*

SCOTT: *No.*

LINCOLN: *Very relaxing. You should try it sometime, you seem a little tense.*

Like they're expecting something, all the other monitors in front of the five empty jump seats come on in a sudden flare of grey light.

In the corridor, Lincoln taps the tablet through to a new pane. A cascade of screenshot images of the Vindicator opens up. The view in the vehicle bay, schematics, controls, all of it pulled from the game.

LINCOLN: *So tell me about the Vindicator.*

On every pane of every screen in the dark computer station, the network assault of three hours earlier opens up again. Across all five consoles, directory traces and system control feeds erupt like a firestorm.

As a claxon sounds in the corridor, all of Lincoln's even-handed manner drains away.

In the bunker, Malkov sees the control code he's been monitoring shred and twist away like storm-torn cloud. The dead systems at the other end of his secure landline suddenly spike active, running code that he knows shouldn't be there.

The network hack that crippled his systems base-wide three hours before is alive again. The secure system running in Russian is where it's coming from.

Even as he stands, he hears the doors of the bunker slam shut and seal with the echoing crash of magnetic bolts. The door panel goes red. He tries his card once, twice, no response. The panel's locked out, dead.

He screams something in Russian that I'm pretty sure is the epithet that has no suitable brackets.

In the corridor, Lincoln has my hands behind my back and the bay doors carded open before I have time to realize what's going on. He half-pushes, half-throws me at the sentries, the Uzis up and gripped tight for safeties off.

"Keep them locked down. Don't move until you hear from me."

As he disappears out the main corridor from the landing bay at a run, I'm already being dragged toward the chopper. Even before the others can react to the cabin door suddenly opening, I'm inside and it's shut again.

In the dark computer station, base systems are under overwhelming assault. One after another, control grids go green to red as the Russian program takes over. Security, doors, lights, communications, all of it shuts down base-wide, one node at a time.

In the ops room, everything goes dark just as Lincoln sprints in. Safelights kick in a moment later but the doors are slamming shut along the corridor. Like he realizes what it means, Lincoln manages to jam a conference chair into the ops room doors before they close. Metal squeals as the chair is crushed, the door mechanism grinding down and jamming with a hand's width of space still open. Enough room to see the flare of red lock-out lights blazing on the door panels in the corridor beyond.

As Lincoln steps back, the claxon of alarms cuts out suddenly, the base shrouded by an unnatural silence. The faint hum of lights and ventilation is always there before, but you only notice it now that it's gone. The dozen people behind Lincoln in the ops room are watching as he steps back from the narrow view to the corridor beyond. Karya's one of them.

"Get this door open," is all he says as he turns away.

31

Dream On

Aerosmith, 1973. In the chopper, we're whispering furtively as I frantically untape everyone's hands, trusting that whatever's going on outside is going to keep anybody from caring too much if the camera sees us. I get Molly free first, but if I'm looking for any reaction over and above what I've already seen, it isn't coming. She turns even farther away as she fumbles the tape at her feet. I try to help her, but she slaps my hand away like she means it.

I go through the others as quickly as I can, Rico first so he can help Breanne. Mitchell seems less worse for wear than the rest of us. Whether that's a result of his general Zen bent or because he was the only one smart enough not to fight back at the school, I don't know.

"Are you okay?" he asks.

I nod. "It's going to be all right." I'm saying it mostly for Molly's benefit, but she's the only one not listening. I go to the side port to see the two sentries still at the closed landing bay doors. They seem preoccupied with hammering away at the control panel for reasons I don't understand at the time. All I know is that they're not watching us, which is good.

"What the hell is going on?" Breanne is locked to Rico, shaking so hard that he has to pin her hands in his.

"It's some kind of private paramilitary thing."

"And us getting kidnapped by them translates as *all right* in your book?"

"It's a misunderstanding. I talked to the guy, Lincoln. It sounds like they had a security failure, they thought we had something to do with it."

"Why?" Rico asks. "And why were they so interested in you?"

I don't know the answer to either question, so I can only shrug. "It was a systems hack thing. They've got our academic records, a whole bunch of other [dung]. They figured I was the technical guy, I guess."

"What did you tell them?" Mitchell asks.

"I showed off my complete ignorance. Then there was some kind of alert, I don't know what's going on. He was asking me about…"

Even as the words form in my mind, something clicks. It doesn't make sense, though. Not yet, anyway.

"He was asking me about the Vindicator."

"About the game? Why?"

Again, I shrug. Something's nagging at me, but it can't surface through the chaos and the general anxiety. As I'm thinking, I realize I've still got my phone. I fumble it from my pocket and try without much hope to fire up Skype, but the Wi-Fi network that was there only minutes before is gone.

"Hey," Mitchell says. "Where are the guards?"

107

Carefully, I move up beside him, pressing close to the glass of the cabin door. The sentries who were there a minute before are gone now. The doors to the corridor are still sealed. In the intervening minute, none of us saw the panel lights under the control of the Russian system suddenly flare invitingly green again, the doors opening in response to a slotted silver card. None of us saw how the card got mysteriously locked into the key-card panel even as the two stepped warily through to see what's going on. One step too far and the doors slammed shut behind them, leaving the card behind. Across the landing bay and inside the chopper, we can't hear them hammering futilely from the other side.

We do, however, hear a pleasant-sounding chime and a metal-on-metal click as the lock on the cabin door goes green.

Before anybody else can think about what it means, Molly's in motion. She's at the door, hammering at the lock with both hands. She's scared, out of her mind with fear, running on automatic. Not blinking.

All the time, right from the beginning, Carl knew Molly would be the most important part of it.

The door pops open. She's through it and outside before any of us can move.

In the bunker, Malkov has his sidearm out, a Glock that he empties into the door panel with a scream. He already knows it won't do him any good.

In the ops room, Karya and a team of four have the conference table slammed through the gap and turned into a giant stainless steel lever. Under pressure, the door inches open slowly. Lincoln is at one of the workstations, trying to get any sort of functioning connection to his systems. All of those systems are locked down tight under a blanket of secure encryption that the Russian program has unleashed.

In the landing bay, Molly's screaming.

"Somebody help us! Let us out! Let us go home!" In her voice, the fear is tangible, visceral, echoing the fear in my voice, in Rico's, Breanne's, Mitchell's as we all call her back. She isn't listening. She's shut down, panicked, lost in a way I've never heard before.

Actually, that's not true.

I did hear it once before. The night she called me in December to tell me that her mom had cancer, and that she and her dad were leaving that night. I heard it as she told me she'd call me again, that she'd be back in a couple of weeks. When she said everything was going to be all right. In her voice, I heard the same fear of being caught up in something you can't control, something you can't get out of.

As Molly frantically spins around looking for some sign of life, some sign of anybody there to hear her, the door panel that the two guards disappeared through flashes red to green. Perfectly timed so that she'll see it.

The doors themselves stay locked, so that the guards don't come through it. I don't know this at the time, but I'm aware suddenly of the faint pounding coming from the corridor beyond. I don't know if Molly hears it or not, but she's running, sprinting a dozen meters to start frantically slamming the panel with its lifeless green lights.

Breanne is two steps behind her, breaking from Rico. Naturally, Rico follows. Mitchell follows him. I'm shouting at them all, something about the guards coming back and how we need to stay in the chopper if we want to not get shot. I break into a run because I know that physically dragging Molly back is the only way it's going to happen.

Carl is watching. Waiting until Molly notices the silver key card, frantically pulling it out and reslotting it to no effect. Waiting until I cross an unseen line three strides from the doors. Mitchell, Breanne, Rico, and Molly are already inside it.

The sound of metal on metal comes down in an earsplitting slam. Along the unseen line I just stepped across, the floor splits and fractures, dropping out beneath us. Then the five of us are falling into a well of shadow that has no end.

In that first split second of timeless terror, all you can think about is that you're going to die.

You know how some people talk about hoping they go quick when the end comes, so that they don't have time to think about it? Forget it. Based on my own limited experience, the less time you have to deal with the fact that you're about to die, the more time seems to slow down to make sure you get in your full quota of paralyzed terror.

Also, that bit about your life flashing before your eyes? Doesn't happen. Or maybe I just don't have enough of a life to flash yet, I don't know.

But even over the frenzied sound of all five of us screaming, there's a sudden twinge of faint understanding. Because the time-slowing-down-as-you-drop-into-darkness thing has been replaced by the realization that we're not actually falling but sliding. The plunge through the disappearing floor has dropped us into a smooth tube, pitch black and twisting. An emergency chute, carrying us down in longer and longer arcs that keep our gravity-assisted acceleration under control.

One quick slide later, the insane amusement park ride opens up without warning and we're unceremoniously dumped out onto a cold concrete floor. Somebody's foot cuffs me in the back of the head, but the temporary crescendo of pain just becomes a thankful reminder that I'm not actually dead.

All around us is shadow. I can't see the others, but a wave of nausea keeps me from getting up off the floor to look for them. Where I lie prone, I can see the long neoprene tube we've fallen out of, my vision shaky as I follow its twisting length up into the darkness. A failsafe escape route from the landing bay above to wherever we are now.

If you were taking it intentionally, you'd probably go feet first and know to tuck and roll when you hit bottom. I have to claw my way up past the ache in my head and a sharper spike of pain that tells me I've twisted my ankle. I make it to hands and knees after what seems like hours. I try to focus, try to find the others, try to see Molly.

She's there with the rest of them, just behind me. Where they've been scattered unceremoniously by the sudden stop, they're facing away from me, all of them staring out at one spot in the center of the shadowed space around us. Mitchell is putting his glasses back on where they popped off at some point. No one else moves.

I see what they see.

My head is spinning. The vehicle bay is so quiet I can hear myself breathing, can hear Breanne sobbing quietly where Rico's shaking hand clutches hers.

A dozen meters in front of us, a line of portable lighting rigs and heavy tools forms a cordon around the Vindicator. For real. Six meters long, three high. Antennas and weapons racks bristle from the top and sides, though unlike in the simulation, those racks look empty. The tight umbilicus of cable runs from the distant wall to the belly of the tank, six wheels spread wide below a hull of high-impact composite armor. The *M* on the side panel gleams in the half-light.

I whisper the epithet that's got no suitable brackets. I stare with the rest of them for what seems like a very long time.

32

Live and Let Die

Paul McCartney and Wings, 1973. In the ops room, the doors finally give way with a shriek of twisted steel. The table is bent nearly in two, Karya standing on it to wedge it down into the space it's managed to open up for her. At one of the systems consoles behind her, Lincoln has managed to patch into a security feed that's inexplicably still open, a regularly cascading series of static images flashing in from key camera points across the base. Shot after shot shows people sealed in throughout the complex, most of them trying to batter their way through the doors with a uniform lack of success.

"Orders, sir?" Karya steps up behind Lincoln but he isn't answering. Instead, he stares at the one image he was waiting for. The landing bay, empty. He can see the chopper cabin door wide open, can see where one of the landing bay's emergency access chutes has been deployed and is sealing again even as he watches. Karya sees it for the brief moment before it's gone, cycling through to the next view. When Lincoln turns to her, she's gone very pale.

"We hit the closest weapons cache," he says. His voice is ice. "Use it to cut down to the emergency evac tunnel. The floors will be easier going than any of the doors between here and there. Load up on heavy ordnance from stores. We take them alive if we can."

Karya nods, but Lincoln can read the grave reservation in her look even before she speaks. "James, they're kids. This can't be…"

"Move," he says.

In the vehicle bay, we're all standing but I don't remember getting up. I try to move for Molly but she's already limping away, rubbing her hands like she hurt them when she hit. From the corner of my eye, I note that Mitchell is bleeding from a cut on his cheek. Even in the shadows, Breanne is paler than she should be, Rico practically holding her up as they shuffle closer to the circle of lamps ahead.

The vehicle bay we're in is the vehicle bay we saw in the game. Only it's real. The stacks of crates marked *LIVE ORDNANCE,* the row of Humvees under white tarps. Jet fighter spare parts, missile racks, all of it. Floodlights up high cast long cones of white along the walls, trailing away to shadow toward the center where we stand. The ceiling is fifteen meters above us, four storeys of interior space carved through the center of the complex.

In my head, fatigue and fear twist together in a way that almost makes it possible to tell myself I'm dreaming. Almost.

Lincoln's team are moving, demolition-carving their way down through four floors of interior space on their way to find us. The security feed that I saw it on earlier tonight scared me just watching it.

They move like a machine. Lincoln's in charge but he doesn't need to say a word as they advance. There are too many locked-down doors to deal with, so they ignore them. One level at a time, they cut through the steel frame of the floor instead, shaped-charge explosives pulled from the weapons caches we opened in the game. The smoke is thick but they're all in environment masks and night-vision goggles. Each time, Karya and three others are the first ones down. One level at a time, they sweep each identical section of sealed-off corridor below. When Karya motions the *all clear,* the rest of the team drops down.

On the bottom level, Lincoln waves her back, taking point himself. Where a section of wall and floor disappears in a blinding flash, he counts to ten before he drops down into the mouth of the evac tunnel, which has lights blazing and weapons lockers lining the walls. Ahead, one section of wall is actually the back of a concealed double door, its controls pulsing blood-red in the shadows.

As the rest of the team drops down behind him, Lincoln's already got one locker open, a half-dozen packs of C-4 explosives ready to be prepped. Karya and the rest strap on Uzis and shotguns, two crews assembling M2 heavy machine guns. Nobody says a word.

"Everything we've got on the evac door." As he says it, Lincoln senses Karya coming up behind him without looking. His voice sounds unnaturally loud in the silence. "We'll hit the seal, try to crack the wall frame from the inside, then blow the bolts. If that doesn't work, we'll cut through with the big guns."

"The wall supports won't hold. You'll bring all four floors down."

Lincoln shakes his head. "I designed the [anglo-saxon] walls. They won't come down till I tell them to."

"If you start blasting fifty-cal in an access corridor, you're going to kill somebody," Karya says. "The walls on the dormitory level are thinner, we can cut through them. Send down a couple of people small enough to not be seen."

"That'd be including you?" Carefully, Lincoln presses the first slab of C-4 into the gap around the frame of the door. Karya is silent. "We're out of time," he says.

Fifty meters away on the other side of that door, which looks like just the wall from this side, Mitchell paces slowly up to the line of lights that circle the Vindicator. Because he has to try it, he fiddles with the controls like he did in the game. Like they did in the game, the lights arc on with a pulse of blue-white and a faint hum.

"Get the [anglo-saxon] away from it," I whisper, hoarse.

Mitchell turns back like he's just remembered I'm there. Even with fast-drying blood streaking his face, he wears a look of abject wonder. "Don't you see what's going on?"

"Shut down the [lord's name in vain] Syfy-channel feed to your frontal lobes and get real." As Mitchell takes two steps toward the tank, I take four steps, ready to head him off in case he's planning on doing anything stupid.

Breanne and Rico step up behind me. Breanne is shaking her head, lost. "This is insane…"

Mitchell kneels suddenly to pick something up in the shadows. The silver key card that Molly had in hand when the floor gave way. It must have come down with us, gleaming where he holds it to the light, wide-eyed.

"Insanity is the belief in what can't be sensed or the denial of what can be sensed," he says. "What's real can only be embraced." He smiles. A special smile I recognize, a smile he reserves for moments of what he calls ultimate understanding. More than I have at any point in our four-year friendship, I want to hit him. "The game is real," he says. "We're in it."

From the corner of my eye, Molly hasn't moved. Still standing next to a stack of unmarked crates, she's staring at the Vindicator where it rises from the haze of floodlight. I shift toward her, which is all Mitchell needs to move. He slots the card to the recessed panel on the side entry portal, beside the *M* on the Vindicator's side.

The clank of magnetic bolts sounds out, impossibly loud in the silence.

All of us watch as the hatch seam along the hull separates from the armor and snaps up. Like it did in the simulation, the ladderway folds out at the same time with a pneumatic hiss. From within comes a haze of faint light. Before I can do anything, before I can say anything, Mitchell is up the steps and inside.

All I can think about is wanting to wake up.

All I can think about is that this dream has gone on long enough, and that it needs to stop now. All at once, I'm remembering those stories you always used to hear when you were a kid. About how if you dreamed you were falling and you didn't wake up before you hit bottom, you'd die in real life.

Standing in the corona shadow at the edge of the Vindicator's floodlit floor space, my mind and my senses are twisting so that the floor feels like it's pitching up against me, gravity pulling me along toward the shadowed portal in the Vindicator's hull. Rico and Breanne are already ahead of me, Rico looking like he's feeling it too, like he's going to hold Breanne back. In the end, he lets her slowly lead him up the steps.

I fight it. I move for Molly instead. I don't get to see what Mitchell and the others see, at least until I watch the security feed later. The three of them are standing in a darkened space, five jump seat workstations set up beneath staggered banks of consoles and displays. Because you've been seeing all this through my half-assed description, you'd recognize it as the dark and deserted computer station that's been following our every move since it all started. The computer station from which the game was run, from which the hack was run that brought Lincoln's network down.

This is the Vindicator cabin. This is where it all begins and ends.

Mitchell, Breanne, and Rico gaze wide-eyed through a haze of faint light given off by a thousand different controls, all the boards on dim standby. At front sits the combination flight console that only Molly could figure out. The systems post with its two pillared banks of monitors sits adjacent. The view-port of translucent polycarb wraps around them both, the lights of the bay a faint gleam beyond. Toward the back, the other three consoles sit within the same bewildering array of controls that the simulation showed us.

Because he has to, Mitchell scans the boards in search of the same big green button I pushed in the game to bring the onboard systems to life. Because he has to, he pushes it.

A faint hum rises, the power plant coming online somewhere within the hull. Chimes sound out as all five consoles come online. Just like in the game, controls flare on one of the systems screens in a storm of high-tech color. Only that screen doesn't show a systems node map this time, but a security monitor feed. It shows outside, where I kneel next to Molly. I try to meet her gaze but she won't look at me. She's still rubbing her hands together inside the overlong white sleeves of her sweater.

As the monitor next to that flares suddenly to life, Mitchell, Breanne, and Rico can see a fixed security video point showing a half-dozen packs of C-4 set into place around the evac door. Mitchell and Breanne don't recognize the explosives, don't know what it means. Rico does.

From the bay, I hear him shout. Focused on Molly, I can't make out what he's saying.

Lincoln is the last one up to the safety of the top level, barely through before he hits the detonator. Karya and the rest are along the walls, the pulse of the explosion four floors below slamming up a split second ahead of the blast of smoke and flame that licks the ceiling. Even before it fades, they're moving.

In the vehicle bay, the concussion knocks me flat. Ahead of me, Molly slams against a stack of crates that spills as she falls. From beyond her comes a surge of searing heat and a split-second glimpse of plate steel buckling like tinfoil, the door seal shattering to leave a smoldering outline behind.

I'm dragging myself toward Molly, head spinning, fingernails tearing against the concrete floor. I can see her moving, conscious suddenly of a hissing sound that it takes me a second to realize is shrapnel raining past us. As she tries to rise, I pull her back down behind the crates. I hold her tight. I feel her screaming because I can't hear it, still deafened by the blast.

To both sides of me, there's movement.

At the Vindicator, Rico is stumbling down the ladderway, screaming for Molly and me. At the now-unsealed door, Karya and four others smash through with portable rams, creating enough of a gap to slip through. Something else is moving behind them, but I'm distracted by a scattershot burst of small arms fire that lashes out above my head. Somebody on the other side of the door is shooting high, protecting the point team. They're nowhere close to hitting us.

That's with the benefit of hindsight, though. At the time it happens, all I'm aware of is that somebody is trying to kill me.

I move. Or at least I try to move, but Molly won't. She's frozen, flat on the ground, clawing at me as I try to drag her up.

From above comes a hail of sparks as someone at the door sees me. A hail of Uzi fire sprays into the girder-works above. Warning shots.

It's a dozen strides to the Vindicator. I don't remember running it.

I remember grabbing Molly around the waist. I remember seeing Rico waving us on. Then the next thing I remember is pushing Molly ahead of me through the hatch, Rico and Breanne grabbing her as I slam the outside panel. I have no idea how that panel works, except to note that its lights have stayed green since Mitchell activated it with the key card. The ladderway snaps in, tossing me up and inside as the hull seals behind me.

From the floor, I see Mitchell frantically pushing buttons on what I dimly recognize from the game as the communications board. The roar in my ears means I can barely hear him shouting into a headset mic plugged into the arm of the jump seat, a lot of variations on *Please don't shoot*. His expression tells me he isn't getting through to whoever's on the outside.

At the front of the cabin, Breanne is trying to get Molly to calm down, but her own near-hysteria doesn't make it any easier. Next to her, Rico is trying the systems console, madly hitting controls at random. As I try to move for them, my ankle gives way, dropping me to the crash seat in front of what would have been Rico's weapons console in the simulation.

With my elbow, I manage to hit a mess of controls on the arm of the chair. With a blinding flare of light, every console in the cabin suddenly comes to full life. Breanne trips backwards where she cries out, even as an exterior view flashes across the flight control screen in front of her. The vehicle bay is crawling with troops, Lincoln's forces moving into position with lethal efficiency. On the screen by Breanne, I can see four of them break out Stinger missile shoulder-racks from a weapons cabinet. In front of me, three guys with unreadable expressions have the destroyed doors open wide enough to move a heavy machine gun through, the same view seen on Mitchell's screen. Rico's console shows a squad dropping behind cover, Uzis trained on the Vindicator's side hatch.

On the systems board monitor in front of Molly where she sits, a schematic map unfolds. Russian alphanumerics scroll past a gentle pulse of blue light at center. I don't need to stare long to recognize the image.

It's us.

It's the endgame from three hours ago. There's the vehicle bay. There's the rest of the base wrapped around it, a perfect echo of the map from the simulation.

There's the emergency evacuation tunnel.

Molly stares, not blinking.

Carl knew that Molly would be the most important part of it.

Without a word, she climbs across Breanne on the floor, pulling herself into the front jump seat. A mess of g-web safety harness hangs above her, Molly slipping into with an instinctive grace. She takes less time to scan the insane complexity of the board than it takes me to describe it here. I can almost feel her matching up what she's seeing in front of her with the controls she remembers from the game, her fingers hammering down.

I can hear myself screaming at her to stop, but Molly's not listening to anything except the howling turbine pulse of the Vindicator's drive engines as they come to life. The interior of the tank starts to shudder as she grabs the nav console controls.

"Hang on," is all she says.

33

Don't Fear the Reaper

Blue Öyster Cult, 1976. In the vehicle bay, everybody freezes. Farthest from us, Karya is with the guys laying down cover fire from the shattered wall. She's listening to Lincoln screaming orders from the point, directing the setup of the heavy guns. Then he's suddenly shielding his eyes against a flare of blue-white that eclipses the floods overhead, a haze of running lights erupting along the Vindicator's undercarriage.

Whatever Lincoln's people were expecting, whatever they thought the systems hack and the lockdown and the police action in the bay was about, this isn't the way it was supposed to go.

From inside it, the Vindicator rings out with a sudden clattering. It's the sound that heavy machine guns make when they're being fired at close range into armor plate and solid-core bulletproof tires and the hopefully more extremely bulletproof viewport glass of the viewport directly in front of us all.

Breanne screams.

Molly slams the suspended floating-wing steering yoke straight in.

With a guttural shriek, the Vindicator's six wheels hit maximum torque in an instant, tearing chunks from the concrete where they spin out against the floor. We slide in place for a split second before the tires find the friction point and kick forward. One long moment of uncertainty, then Molly takes us out. A half-assembled missile rack closest to us is abandoned a split second before we plow through it. Across the vehicle bay, Lincoln's troops fall back in panic.

In the bunker, Malkov sees the landline break as the cables trailing out from the Vindicator's belly are torn away. His last data connection goes dead.

A momentary surge pulses through the safelight as the thrashed base systems are suddenly freed up to reboot. Damage control kicks in, getting the lights back online but keeping the doors locked. The security system that Carl cut through starts the slow process of putting itself back together again.

Malkov holsters his empty Glock. He sits in silence, waiting.

Inside the Vindicator, Mitchell, Breanne, Rico, and I are trying desperately to claw our way into the closest jump seats. We're pulling g-force like some hyperactive rollercoaster, the walls of the cabin slamming into me every time Molly cranks the controls. Through the viewport, the vehicle bay is a blur of motion and tracer fire, the steady staccato ping of bullets ricocheting off us as we sail through it.

Molly is locked tight to the yoke, fingers a blur as she adjusts throttle at all six transaxles independently. She's feeling her way through a twisting path from wall to wall and back again. Testing the controls, matching them to everything she learned from the simulation as she stays clear of Lincoln's forces where they scatter and regroup.

I manage to drag myself up to the systems chair as Mitchell clambers into the ops seat. Breanne and Rico roll into the engineering and weapons stations on a particularly hard turn. As we twist and tear our way through the vehicle bay, it would be easy to assume that Molly is pushing the Vindicator at random, fighting for control. But I'm watching where I sit next to her, and I see the perfect simplicity of her plan.

She's tracking a path between the heavy guns so they can't shoot us without shooting each other, keeping the troops on the ground scattered so that nobody knows when it's safe to move. It's an almost perfect reflection of the tactics she used in the simulation. But all the while, she's scanning the schematic on the systems board in front of me. Searching for something.

When she cranks hard and cuts a suddenly clear course for the shattered wall, I know she's found it.

The force of impact when we send the blast-shattered door through to the far side of the evacuation tunnel slams me face first into my console, which is alive suddenly with Russian alerts flashing red. When I claw my way back to a sitting position and finally feel my g-web snap tight, the viewport shows the walls of the evac tunnel as a fractured blur of white. At upwards of a hundred and fifty km/h, we're ricocheting back and forth between them, Molly trying to hold the Vindicator steady inside the half-meter space to both sides.

On the schematic map, the pulsing blue dot that marks our position at center is headed straight for the double line of solid black where the map ends. That double line is a half-meter of reinforced armor that stands between us and outside.

"Molly, pull it up! We can't do this!" My hearing is almost back but the roar of the drive engines and the scraping shudder of our passage is deafening.

Molly makes no sign that she even knows I'm there.

I strain against the safety harness holding me tight, reaching out to touch her shoulder. In response, she straight-arms me away. We lurch dangerously, the single split second of Molly's hand leaving the controls almost piling us into the wall.

In her expression as she straightens us out, in the white-knuckle set of her hands on the yoke and the thin line of her mouth, I see something I've never seen before. Something I don't ever want to see again.

In her eyes that are a blue I don't have the words to describe, I see that Molly isn't afraid to die.

I scream Rico's name.

Behind me, he knows why I'm screaming. His weapons board is a kaleidoscope of lights, messages in Russian scrolling down four different monitors.

Earlier, during the game, I said that if it was all happening for real, you'd be scared out of your [anglo-saxon] mind.

Rico is shouting that same bracketed text over and over again as he hammers out the control sequence that he practiced while we ate pizza and joked about how we were going to spend our prize money. That all seems like a long time ago now.

I remember with a sinking heart that from the outside, most of the Vindicator's weapon racks looked empty. I don't even know if we have missiles. But from beneath my feet comes a sudden roar straight from the 5.1 surround soundtrack of the apocalypse. The viewport goes nearly opaque for an endless split second, protecting us from the flare of four Spriggan missiles as they erupt from the Vindicator's belly and straight-line down the corridor in front of us.

The back-blast hits us a split second before the sound. A wall of white fire washes across the viewport to black it out again, no way to see how much of the doors are still in front of us. No way to tell if we're going to die or not.

Timelessness again. I'm hanging there, waiting for something to happen. I'm conscious suddenly of the fact that I'm not actually looking to the viewport anymore, but to Molly.

Something changes in our movement. But even as I realize we've gone airborne, my safety harness sucks me back into the seat as we hit again.

Through the viewport, everything is black sky and starlight, the lines of tall trees blurring past. We're on a deserted mountainside, slewing past the edge of a cloud of fire and shredding steel. I get a glimpse of a stand of poplar and a length of chain-link fence before they both disappear, the Vindicator tearing through them like they might be balsa wood and balloons.

The landscape is suddenly daytime-bright, the viewport turning night-vision green as it pulls the light from the shadows. Just as suddenly, a boulder the size of my house looms directly in front of us. Molly is already slamming the Vindicator into a half-reverse, sliding us past it sideways before straightening out again.

The faint shape of a mountain switchback road winds out and downward ahead of us, a rock-strewn stretch of washed-out gravel. We should be bouncing uncontrollably, but I can hear the servos hammering in the wheel wells beneath us as we soar over rubble like it was fresh asphalt.

I glance back to the others. Breanne is straining against her harness to reach across Rico's console, her hand locked tight to his. Mitchell is grinning again, but the urge to hit him is rapidly fading beneath the undreamed-of joy of just being alive.

"Find me a map!" Molly has to shout to be heard, her voice hoarse. "Tell me where this [anglo-saxon] road is going!"

I hear her but I can't move at first. When I can move, it takes me less time at my console than I expect to find what looks like a GPS display laid over a government survey map. The Vindicator is still the blue dot pulsing at center. It's a real-time feed, so it's in English for a change.

"Got it," I say. "We're way northwest of town. If you stay on this track, it looks like it empties onto Hendrix Road..."

From the back, Mitchell calls. "If they come after us, the main roads are where they'll be looking."

He's right, but I'm too stressed out to care. "It's a [lord's name in vain] road, all right? Everything else is all rat[dung] logging trails between here and the highway..."

"I've got it," Molly says coldly, cutting me off.

"Look, just stay straight until you hit a side-grade..."

"I've said I've got it!" She's staring past me to the console, scanning the tracery of twisting white lines laid out ahead of us. Because there's nothing else I can say to her, I call back to Mitchell instead.

"Get on ops. Find out if they're following us before we assume they're following us." Like it's the most normal thing I've ever asked him, he nods as he focuses at the controls on his board.

They aren't after us. Not yet, anyway, though it takes all of us working together an uncomfortable couple of minutes to figure that out. Rico's got radar, Mitchell's got visual, I've got remote monitoring that shows us where the base's systems are still struggling to get fully back on line.

We're free and clear. We've got a whole lot of back road between us and safety.

No one says a word as Molly takes us home.

34

No Quarter

Led Zeppelin, 1973. A half-klick from the base, Lincoln stands in the shadowed remains of what's left of the evac tunnel doors. Ahead of him, a swath of destruction has been torn through the scrub trees and fencing that surround the mine site, fading into the dark downward slope of the mountain where the road disappears. Karya is at his side, no emotion betraying her expression. Lincoln's look is more weary than angry, but when he speaks, the malice is the only thing that comes through.

"We're shutting down. Give the order. Any personal effects, collect them. Light ordnance and battle gear on the choppers. Two teams. Malkov flies second unit, you're with me, everybody else regroups in North Dakota. Anybody not ready to move at 0330 gets left behind."

"Shutting down? Why aren't we..."

"Because this site's been compromised. Depending on who they might be working for, I don't know how long we've got before they get here. We're not leaving them anything to find."

"But they can't get anywhere, we're ten minutes behind them..."

"And if they've got air transport waiting, that'll be enough. If they stick to the ground, the forty-minute head start won't hinder the op. Give the order."

Karya is thoughtful, choosing her words carefully though she knows it won't do any good. "And what exactly is the operation?"

"They just burned down our [lord's name in vain] security and data systems and drove a half-billion dollars worth of stolen tech out the [anglo-saxon] side door. We're going to get it back."

"James, there's something else going on here. They were kids..."

"Give the order."

Lincoln turns from her. He gets a half-dozen steps down the ruined evac corridor before he realizes Karya isn't following. He turns back. "What?"

"Permission to speak freely, sir?"

The coldness in Karya's voice cuts Lincoln more than he wants to show. He just nods.

"You said the tank was offlined. Power systems disabled, everything stripped. How did they...?"

"Where's Malkov?"

Karya is silent a moment. "Door systems are still locked down. We're cutting our way into the rest of the command core now."

"Tell him to find me." Lincoln turns again, disappears into the haze of smoke still twisting along the ceiling of the corridor. Karya watches him go.

In the bunker, Malkov just sits, the sound of a team cutting their way toward him with torches coming faint through the still-sealed doors. He's computer-blind, offline, all monitor feeds dead. No way to see what's happening, no idea what's been going on all around him. No way to tell what we've done. But in his expression, in the cold grey eyes as he stares at the blank screen where he watched the Russian code run from its secure space, he already knows.

When I watched the security feed that showed him trapped there, this is what I saw. Malkov already understands what's happening.

Malkov has already figured out how it has to end.

Part Five

Things You Don't Get To Decide

35

Mad Man Moon

Genesis, 1976. Most people think that Mitchell and I met in eighth grade, but that's not entirely true. Mitchell and I actually met for the second time in eighth grade, but it took that second time for me to remember the first time.

The first time Mitchell and I met was sixth grade. After school one Friday afternoon, I was wandering from 7-Eleven toward home when I happened to catch sight of him on the wrong side of an imminent pummeling in the loading zone behind Save-On Foods. The leader of his gang of four assailants was a weasel-faced thug named Darren Blower, whose last name was supposed to rhyme with *flower* but was more commonly pronounced like you probably just read it.

Even then, I had an automatic amount of sympathy for the horror that Darren probably had to endure as a result of this gift his parentage had bestowed upon him. However, even then, I had a larger amount of antipathy for people who enjoy making other people miserable. So I reluctantly wandered over.

I'd seen Mitchell around but didn't know him in any real sense. Even if I had known him, my reluctance would have been roughly the same, born as it was not of unfamiliarity but abject cowardice. However, in an ironic twist of genetics, my pacifist hard-wiring has always managed to somehow stay hidden behind my having inherited Seth's towering Celtic frame and the berserker temper that comes with it.

With the benefit of hindsight, I know that Mitchell was never in any serious danger that day. His mastery of a kind of slow-motion sarcasm is custom made for that scenario, capable of downgrading neanderthal rage into a slack-jawed uncertainty in short order. The kind of verbal riposte and detente that I never had any reason to master, because even in sixth grade, I loomed over Blower and his lesser minions with a degree of immediate menace.

As I had learned to do a few years earlier on the more unruly denizens of the after-school daycare I attended until end of third grade, I cultivated this immediate menace into something even stronger as I picked Blower up by the jacket. Lifting him to eye level, I asked what the problem was. And apparently there was no problem, as he and the others quickly scampered away like a horde of startled squirrels.

Mitchell's clothes looked like they'd taken the worst of it as he stood and dusted himself off. He grinned and thanked me, trying to explain that the fight had started over his dissing a presentation Blower had given in English, the topic of which was how video games shouldn't be subject to ratings warnings because that was really lame. Mitchell had used the follow-up question period to prove how Blower's presentation defined the need to rate games not by content but by the IQ of the player. I was already tuning out when I told him I'd see him around.

Two years later in eighth grade, I was officially as tall as Seth and had managed to turn my preadolescent indifference into an impressive degree of all-out nihilism. Dangerously bored, I was poised to become a serious juvenile delinquent, if only because Seth seemed to expect it of me. I had no real friends, no real ambition, and no real illusions about how little I cared. I was the kind of person Blower would have aspired to become, in other words, if he hadn't been packed off to a special school in Kamloops after a suspicious fire in one of the elementary school bathrooms.

I had to struggle to remember Mitchell when he came up to me in homeroom one day in October, asking if I was busy at lunch. I said I was, though I wasn't. He shrugged and told me that if I got unbusy, I should swing by the French Immersion classroom. He and his sister were starting up a Dungeons & Dragons game and were looking for players.

I told him it wasn't really my thing.

He said I should give it an hour.

Along the side of the highway two klicks from the edge of town, a sign reads FORESTRY ROAD DECOMMISSIONED — USE AT OWN RISK. The moon is almost setting, pale light fading to shadow where it traces across the mouth of a deeply rutted logging road twisting off into darkness.

Fifty meters inside that darkness, the Vindicator slews to a halt beneath a close-growing stand of spruce. Molly's taken us off the road, the side hatch open even before the hail of dust and gravel accompanying us has time to hit the ground. The running lights dim to the faintest gleam of blue, no other sound except the quiet hum of the power plant and a hiss from the wheel servos as they power down.

Molly's the first one out the hatch and into a clearing that opens up between our hiding space and the shadowed line of the road. She makes it five steps before she's on the ground, vomiting. I'm two steps back, hyperventilating the predawn air so I don't join her. I can hear the others disembark, but I don't turn around.

I don't know how long we all stand there, the silence settling like a funeral shroud. A sharp tang of ozone twists through the faint breeze, heavy with the scent of dust and forest. The Vindicator is in desperate need of an all-night car wash, scorch marks and the telltale furrows of armor-piercing rounds streaking the hull. I'm trying to think of something to say, but in the end, it's Rico who breaks the silence.

"We can't just leave it here."

Another silence follows. Then I'm laughing out loud. "The hell we can't."

From our starting point a long way northeast of 100 Mile, Molly has taken us around south of town, having successfully avoided the main roads

Mitchell was intent on avoiding. I lost track of the number of twists and turns she took us through to get here. I'm not sure how long we've been driving.

"What about the guys with the guns?" Where I turn back finally, Breanne is clinging to Rico.

"They want it, they can have it," I say. "Leave them fifty bucks for gas and mileage and cut out."

As scared as I am, as scared as we all are, I realize it's going to get much worse in the next five minutes as the shock wears off. Only Mitchell seems unfazed, still smiling in his infuriating way. He paces where the running lights splash faintly across the rocky ground.

"I think you're all missing something," he says.

"Like what?" Breanne says sharply.

"Like thinking about what happened here. Who was behind it. What it means."

"I don't want to [anglo-saxon] think!" Breanne shouts. "I don't care! I want to go home and know that some psycho paramilitary death squad isn't going to leave a hand grenade in my locker before grad!"

At the far edge of the clearing, Molly rises suddenly. She's heading for the highway. She doesn't look back.

I sprint to catch up with her. I call her name as I touch her shoulder. She spins back and nails me with a blindside backhand that drops me hard.

I twist around as I fall, my palms raw where I hit hands first. Molly is a half-silhouette against the half-moon where it touches the broken horizon. In its pale shadow, I can see her eyes. The sheer malice there hurts more than my aching jaw.

"Don't ever [anglo-saxon] touch me..." she whispers.

Inside me, something breaks.

"Go to hell," I whisper back. A weight is pressing down on my back and shoulders, forcing me to fight against it as I shakily stand.

In Molly's eyes, for just a split second, the anger wavers. I see something else there, or at least I think I do. I tell myself I do. Something I saw for the first time during a debate-trip dance in a crowded gymnasium. Then it's gone as she turns away.

Alone, she hikes for the highway, disappearing into shadow after a dozen strides.

Breanne takes two steps after her, calling her name, but Molly doesn't look back. Rico is there to keep Breanne from following her at a run. Off her look, he just shakes his head.

It takes me a second to realize that Mitchell isn't with them anymore.

Inside the Vindicator, he's moving slowly from one station to the next, scanning each set of controls. He turns when he hears me sprinting up the ladderway steps. I've already decided that I will hit him this time, but he turns to me with the same grin I remember from a Save-On loading zone, a long time ago.

126

"We made this," he says. "We defined the parameters that allowed us to play. Worked back paradigmatically from the controls to the gestalt of the game itself." His words are an echo of an afternoon that I'm desperately wishing now had never happened.

"We're walking away from this," I say carefully. "We're going home." We both hear Rico and Breanne on the ladderway behind me.

"We can't walk away from it. We're a part of it. It's real."

"You're absolutely [anglo-saxon] insane."

"Wouldn't be the first time I wondered," Mitchell says, a little too thoughtfully. Then he calls out to no one.

"You can hear us, can't you?"

A sudden chill claws its way up from the base of my spine.

As desperately as I want to pretend otherwise, I know what's coming.

When it rises, the voice comes from everywhere and nowhere at once. Piped out from unseen environment speakers, no trace of synthetic tone in it. The pitch, the phrasing, the cadence — all of it is as lifelike as it was when I first heard it, talking on what I thought was the other end of a Washington state cell phone.

"I can hear you," the voice says.

Breanne and Rico both jump. Despite my best instincts, I find myself looking around like they are, overwhelmed by the sensation of suddenly having someone standing behind me who I can't see.

"Do we call you Carl?" Mitchell says.

"That would be fine."

I'm beyond freaked out. I'm beyond anything I've ever felt before, beyond anything that's ever happened to me.

"You must have a lot of questions," the voice says.

Across the cabin, Mitchell's gaze locks to mine, and in his expression of fervent thoughtfulness, I feel an inverse reflection of the unrestrained anger welling up inside me. A hundred things I need to say are quite literally fighting for space in my mind. A hundred serious questions, a hundred accusations, but I'm too scattered to make any of them. In the end, I'm overwhelmed by one stupid little thing that's infuriated me since that afternoon three days ago.

"Computerized Autopilot and Recreational Library?" I shout. "Are you [anglo-saxon] kidding me?" I look at Mitchell as I'm saying it because there's no one else to look at. Because to try to talk back to the disembodied voice would be like admitting that I accept its presence, and I don't.

"I'm sorry," Carl says. "It works better in the original Russian." The hint of an apologetic tone in the machine's voice just makes me angrier. "This isn't the way it was supposed to be. You weren't supposed to ever be in danger. There are things you need to know."

The response I want to make is thwarted by my not having a large blunt object at hand to make it with. Breanne and Rico look stunned behind me, Breanne shaking so badly that Rico directs her to the ops console chair and makes her sit.

A sudden hiss of pneumatics sounds out. I wheel to see that Mitchell has cycled the hatch shut.

"It's cold out there," he says simply. He comes back to the ops console to sit, Rico dropping to crouch beside Breanne where she clutches his arm.

Mitchell looks up to the monitors. "So tell us," he says.

There's a pause, like the voice has to think about it. Or maybe it's waiting for me to say something. More than anything else I've ever wanted in my life, I want to open the hatch again and step out. But I don't.

All at once, the interior screens come to life, a wash of light filling the cabin. I stay standing as Carl tells us its story.

36

This Way Out

Wall of Voodoo, 1981. Eighty kilometers away through the empty night, the mine site is lit up like full noon. The landing bay doors are already open, all five choppers heating up on the pad below.

Around the choppers, Lincoln's people are scrambling to pull backpacks and weapons on board. The walls of the landing bay are littered with weaponry and gear that doesn't make the *travel light* imperative. Everyone's in night-combat fatigues and goggles now, up to their necks in weapons, the corporate-casual pretense long gone. Karya is one of the last ones aboard, stopping at the pile of castoff gear to retrieve a pair of tasers that she stuffs into the webbing of her pack.

In the closest chopper, Malkov is in the pilot's seat, a strike team strapping in behind him. Karya's glance lingers on him through the viewport, but he isn't looking at her as he slots a new magazine into his Glock. His mood is dark as he holsters the pistol alongside the six other mags at his belt. Then he pulls up a GPS display, his fingers a blur across the console. The same government survey map we used comes to life in real-time tracking mode.

Karya clambers into Lincoln's chopper. He's already strapped in, Karya doing a quick head count as she seals the cabin door. Lincoln sees it locked on his board, then cranks the engines up. Karya slides into the seat beside him but he doesn't look over.

One by one, the choppers lift off and into the night sky. No one breaks radio silence, courses already logged, plotted, and locked. Light from the landing bay flares against the starlit dark. The choppers' downwash rattles the ruined chain-link that threads the mountainside, three units breaking right as they rise one by one, spinning off into the darkness. Lincoln and Malkov go left, pulling into a spiral holding pattern over the base.

Through the night-vision display, Lincoln watches the bay doors close beneath him. The mountainside slides back into position, no sign of the base beneath it. A sudden stillness hangs, the other three choppers gone from sight.

On his board, Lincoln taps out a remote code sequence. He double-confirms it, then taps a red button.

Across the mine site, the green of his scope picks up a dozen pinpoint flares of light. Slow to start, then building. Fault lines appear, sudden fracture points of light and heat erupting from underground where precision placements of C-4 are triggered in a careful pattern. Then a synchronized swelling of explosions tears up the ground, ripples of movement threading it like isolated earthquakes.

Inside the base, walls and ceilings implode. In the corridors, in the rooms, in the vehicle bay where a battalion's worth of weapons and transportation sits in darkness, a million tonnes of rock and earth slam down, crushing everything.

In his chopper, Lincoln watches the monitor coldly. Against the daylight brightness of the blast, the night vision shuts down for a quick moment. In the shotgun seat beside him, Karya looks out the window, shielding her eyes until the light fades beneath a shroud of black dust.

Where he holds a tight pattern directly behind Lincoln's chopper, Malkov isn't watching. The nav feed is still up on his display, the widespread web of back roads between the mine site and the distant highway traced in lines of bright light. The lack of real-time satellite surveillance in the hinterland that Lincoln mentioned when he was talking to me means that they're going to have to look for us the old-fashioned way. Malkov is noting likely pull-off points and attack vectors along the road.

Over his headset, he hears Lincoln. "I'm on point. Stay with me." Lincoln lifts out of the holding pattern, racing the edge of the dust cloud as he locks in a course due southwest, the same trajectory Malkov's team set four hours before.

Malkov doesn't need to respond. He locks in behind, both choppers pushed to attack speed as they pull away.

37

Some Other Time

The Alan Parsons Project, 1977. For nearly twenty minutes, we watch as the Vindicator's backstory unfolds, narrated by the disembodied ghost-voice of a computer that I keep telling myself can't possibly exist. I watched the presentation again tonight as I got ready to write this. Here's a quick recap.

The Vindicator is Russian military. Or rather, it was Soviet military before Lincoln stole it from the Russian military. It was a high-end, high-security prototype. A holdover from the days before Yeltsin and Putin and Medvedev rewrote the Soviet legacy for good.

By 1984, the Soviet Union had hit the wall in terms of its nuclear parity stare-down with the west. Ronald Reagan was channeling George Lucas on a missile defense system that never would have worked, but which threatened nonetheless to turn into a second arms race the Soviets couldn't afford to wage. For however many years, Europe had been locked down in a hair-trigger military quagmire — both sides perpetually prepared for a land invasion across the Iron Curtain that would have initiated nuclear holocaust in short order.

(Confession. I've developed a passing interest in the failure of modern politics in the past year and a bit. Prior to that, however, I scraped through three years of high school social studies with a solid C average, and had trouble most of that time remembering whether Kruschev was a politician or a hockey player. Everything I say here is taken either from Carl's presentation or cribbed from a lot of time spent playing the Cold War campaign in Rise of Nations in seventh grade.)

The Soviets' response to the Western threat? Create a weapon that would let them win the land war even once the bombs started falling.

Like the simulation home page told us a week before, the Vindicator is an experimental all-terrain mobile combat unit. However, what the simulation didn't mention is that this experimental all-terrain mobile combat unit is the super-weapon that would have let the Soviet Union rule the world.

Here's the way it was supposed to work.

With the prototype tested and perfected, the Soviets would have diverted the entire focus of their industrial-military machine from warhead and conventional arms production, channeling it all into the Vindicator. Within the first year, a secret production facility beneath the Kapustin Yar missile site south of Moscow would have been producing a dozen units a month. In ten years, fourteen hundred Vindicators would have been poised to hit Western Europe like a battering ram.

Half would come in by way of a four-minute suborbital hop from Siberia to West Germany. The other half would make a ground/air assault across the Polish border and plow through the worst that NATO would throw at them, up to and including the W79 neutron-bomb artillery shells that were supposed to deter a land-based invasion.

The Vindicator would be the doomsday weapon that nobody expected. A virtually indestructible mobile weapons platform, it was designed to blur the lines between conventional and tactical-nuke-level combat.

That was the way it was supposed to work.

How it actually worked instead was that the Vindicator project bankrupted the Soviet Union. The hyper-powered ATV we're standing in to watch Carl's video play out across all the monitors is what finally undercut the foundations of the Iron Curtain, providing the catalyst for so many huge chunks of history that have unfolded since then.

True to form for Soviet thinking, most of the incredible number of people and agencies responsible for creating the Vindicator project had no inclination of what they were actually working on. Individual and incremental technologies were crafted by one team, improved on by another, and melded together into increasingly complex subsystems by a core team. These were the only people who understood the research's true goals. But even they didn't bother noticing that this single greatest development project in military history was costing more money than the Soviet Union actually had.

Those true goals? Retribution for the injustices perpetrated by a corrupt western world. Vindication for a Soviet-communist ideology that would be proved superior in the end.

Vindicator in Russian is a word I can't even pronounce, let alone spell on this keyboard. I remember it started with an M, though, which of course explains the side panel paint job. However, in any language, the meaning underlying the name stays pretty much the same. Vindication was the goal of the Vindicator project. A just revenge in response to the European/American industrial-military complex and everything it stood for.

Since their first A-bomb test in 1949, the Soviets had been engaged in a cyclical process of playing catch up, overtake, and fall behind again with western offensive capability. Missile technology begat antimissile technology. Our big bombs begat their bigger bombs, which begat our even bigger bombs.

The Vindicator was going to change all that.

The disembodied voice weaves this narrative like some PBS special on steroids. Translated clips of highest-level classified Soviet technical archives and NATO intelligence briefings alike build up the history of a mythical new Russian assault vehicle. It's like some high-end military mash-up. Technical specs flash past so quickly that I catch only half of them, but my brain is beyond processing anything but the broad strokes anyway.

For six years, the best talent of the Soviet technical-military machine labored to build the Vindicator. The same teams that had created the R-36

ICBM. The intellectual descendants of the labs that had forged Soyuz and the Tsar Bomba and the MiG-29. The tank's weapons systems are a cold-war laundry list of surface-to-surface and surface-to-air lethality. Rico's mouth literally drops open when the missile specs flash past, which scares me more than the specs ever could. The power plant is some hybrid iridium-based fission-fuel cell process with an output and efficiency that suddenly stops my ability to process any of this.

"Hold it the [anglo-saxon] up," I say to the disembodied voice, before I remember that I'm trying as much as humanly possible to pretend the disembodied voice doesn't exist.

"Yes?" that voice intones with just a hint of fake patience. I get a look from Mitchell and Breanne that suggests I'm interrupting something really important.

"Walk me through how Cold War-era Soviet tech produces a hybrid iridium-based fission-fuel cell process that can power a [lord's name in vain] city." I'm staring at the numbers because they make no sense. I'm cruising through Physics 12 right now with a solid sixty-five percent average, but endless gaming sessions involving calculating the yield of low-orbit tactical nukes have given me a modestly accurate sense of gigajoule-to-megaton conversion ratios.

"The power plant was a modification to the Vindicator's original design." I can sense the fake voice choosing its words carefully, and it sends a chill up my spine. "The Vindicator's functionality is exactly as originally designed. I simply had the opportunity to make it more efficient."

"Meaning what?"

"To answer that, I need to explain the development of the C-A-R-L heuristic server system. That's when it all started. The CARL system was designed to be the most advanced artificial intelligence expert system in the world. The AI code was the centerpiece and linchpin of the Vindicator project." But even as a new chunk of video plays back, I'm suddenly not listening anymore.

Instead, I'm staring at a familiar face that's appeared on the cockpit monitors where we watch. The short goatee, grey eyes so dark they look black, hair shaved almost to the skull. It's the guy who dropped me in the school, who ordered us taken. He's years younger and talking in Russian now as he gives some kind of report.

I interrupt again. "Who the [anglo-saxon] is that?"

Like some PowerPoint presentation is changing up on the fly, Carl freeze-frames the image, sliding it over to one side as some kind of military dossier comes up.

"His name is Malkov. He's Lincoln's second-in-command." I feel a twinge in my neck as I remember the backhand shot that laid me out.

On the screen, the playback changes gears, switching from the technical specs to a history lesson.

133

"Malkov was a Russian military science prodigy whose skill outstripped even his own ambition," Carl intones. "When he was only twenty, he was lead engineer for the CARL system, but working in isolation like everyone else involved with the project. When it all fell apart, the Vindicator prototype was hidden in a bunker in a testing facility in Smolensk, where it had been smuggled during the attempted coup against Mikhail Gorbachev in 1991." A map of Smolensk fades out as canned CNN footage flashes past like some poli-sci greatest hits package. Watching the screens, Mitchell, Breanne, and Rico are all sitting rapt.

"In the chaos surrounding the breakup of the Soviet Union later that year, Malkov was left adrift. He joined military intelligence, then Spetsnaz, the Soviet special forces. The Vindicator's location was lost. But he was obsessed with discovering what it was he had been working on, hoping to see what it had become. He caught rumors of the project's existence in 1998. He'd already been working for Lincoln for two years then, selling warhead components stolen from the decommissioning yards after START II. Lincoln was intrigued enough to bankroll a search. It took Malkov three more years, but he found it."

The view shifts, a technical schematic in Russian scrolling past alongside Malkov as he starts to talk again. Carl picks up the show without missing a beat. "The CARL heuristic expert system was advanced beyond anything either bloc was working on in the timeframe. It's unlikely that the Soviet techs understood the breakthroughs Malkov's original work had created, or they would have attempted to translate them to other applications." Then Malkov is gone and there's only Carl reading highlights from a series of technical reports.

The headache I had three days before in the library is back in spades.

In my mind's rapidly failing ability to process what's happening, Carl has suddenly started sounding like some sales pitch on late-night cable. "The Vindicator is the most versatile combat vehicle ever built, capable of high-speed tactical maneuvers across any medium on earth. Land, air, underwater, vacuum. The hull is built to ballistic launch and re-entry specifications, allowing a crew to lift into low orbit in order to drop down in avoidance of first-strike detection systems. When operational, its flight systems allow for full atmospheric maneuverability. Its tracking systems were years ahead of any competing technology in 1990. I've upgraded those systems as well."

I expect to hear a follow-up with information on financing, but I'm only half-listening. I'm overwhelmed by the desire to change the channel on everything that's happening, like I'm hoping that this days-of-future-passed stuff turns out to just be some kind of after-midnight original programming on the History Channel.

Then I remember that the voice I'm trying not to listen to is a talking tank. I need to find a way to focus, and quickly.

The reason the systems board is partly in English is that Malkov has been engaged in an ongoing program of upgrading the Vindicator's twenty-year-old systems. Over top of the original core of high-end Soviet code, he's been layering newer control systems, all of which he thinks have been stolen and reworked from the best American aerospace tech.

"But those are your systems," I say to interrupt the monologue again. The anger is ramping up in me, rising to a level that I don't like to redline at for very long. "You've been [anglo-saxoning] with a Soviet black ops engineer. Feeding him new designs, reworking the Vindicator's specs without him having any idea that you're the one writing them. You've been using him like you're trying to use us."

Carl ignores that accusation and carries on with more technical specs, which is a more lifelike reaction than I want to acknowledge. It all makes a kind of sense, though. In 2001, Malkov brought the Vindicator out of Russia on Lincoln's dime. For ten years, the tank's been sitting in a series of secret facilities while Malkov has slowly explored the full breadth and scope of what it can do. It's taken him ten years because he's been working without the advantage of the multimedia spectacular we get to watch.

That presentation is running down the avionics controls now. The custom multimode ground-air setup. Beneath the Vindicator's hull sits a field-effect pulse vertical thrust-and-lift generator capable of kick-starting a VTOL takeoff at three hundred klicks.

"And this is more Soviet technology that never existed?" I say wearily.

"The technology has been improved through the Vindicator's new power plant. The original designs employed a fission blast for liftoff and drive that was built around the paradigm of leaving the takeoff and landing zones awash in lethal fallout. The Vindicator was a first-and-final-strike weapon. There was no need to worry about the aftermath. Fortunately, it was never tested. Those flight systems remain inoperative. A last piece of functionality left incomplete when the project fell apart."

The Vindicator is a tank that really wants to fly. Molly was right.

"That's what I wanted to tell you," the machine says finally. I expect to hear it ask if there are any questions, and to remind us what chapters to study for next week's quiz.

I realize that I've managed to forget the headache when it flares again. Around us, the monitors fade toward black, then wink off one by one.

38

Fever in My Mind

Black Oak Arkansas, 1972. It takes a few seconds for my eyes to adjust again to the faint background light of the cabin, which gives me a chance to actually look at the cabin for the first time. It's the same as the virtual cabin in the simulation, to a degree that makes me feel like I'm still in the simulation. There's some sort of uncanny valley effect at work, like with video game avatars that are just a little too lifelike, and so seem really creepy. Something in the lines of the walls and the light of the displays just seems overly real somehow.

I manage to ignore it by noticing that the Vindicator has a roof-access hatch I've never noticed before. In the POV environment of the game, I guess I never had a reason to look up. But looking up now, I realize that Mitchell, Rico, and Breanne are all looking up as well. Back to not knowing where to scan for the source of the disembodied voice.

I can sense Mitchell getting ready to say something, so I beat him to it. "We need to go now."

As expected, he ignores me. "So what are you?" he asks, talking again to the space around us. "I mean, you've told us about the Vindicator, but you're not the Vindicator. Or not just that, anyway."

The same pseudo-thoughtful pause lingers before the voice speaks. "For lack of a better way to describe it, I'm a conscious artificial intelligence. I have capabilities that my creators never dreamed of when they created the heuristic expert system framework that underlies my operations."

"But how?" Mitchell says.

"I don't know," Carl says. "I expect I can't know, any more than you can know your own mind. My guess, as banal as it sounds, is that when the Vindicator was abandoned, I was simply left on. My first memory is of accessing the Soviet milnet through an intact landline in 1991. That provided the technical know-how to expand my communications capability, letting me remotely tap into local networks and satellite feeds. I have records of data from two years before that, but not of the process of accessing it. No memory."

"You were online but just absorbing data into the heuristic framework. Which in turn would create structure in the data itself. And with no outside control to shape it..."

"I just kept learning."

"For ten years," Mitchell says, a little too wistfully. "You absorbed the entire Russian military infrastructure?"

136

"More than that. Anywhere the milnet went, I could go. Soviet military communications had hacked most of the networks in Western Europe. Also the Defense Data Network backbone in North America."

"You said that Malkov stole the Vindicator ten years ago," Rico says, and there's a thoughtfulness in his tone that catches me off guard. "Why are you only active now? Why haven't you tried to escape?"

"Because until a month ago, I had no reason to run. Lincoln has found a buyer for the Vindicator's technology. A consortium of private security concerns active in the U.S., the Middle East, and Africa are preparing to take delivery. He's been negotiating with them since the Vindicator was captured, upping the price every time Malkov managed to piece together a little more understanding of what the craft can do."

"But does Malkov know about you?" Breanne says. "Does he know that you're... well, here?" Like Rico, Breanne's mood has shifted since Carl's little slide show finished, and in a way that worries me. She's still scared, but not just for us anymore.

"No," Carl says. "But even by handing over the heuristic framework and its potential for military applications, Lincoln will be tipping the balance of power irrevocably."

"He'll be handing mercenary armies an H-bomb you can drive," Rico says quietly. "That's not balance of power, that's end of the world."

The sudden silence from the others worries me even more than the change in tone. Even more than the hanging tension. I'm pretty sure that's exactly what the voice was going for.

"I'd hoped it wouldn't come to that," Carl says. "But it's too late."

"We need to go," I say again. "Now."

"What did you need us for? Why is all this happening?" Breanne asks quietly.

"It wasn't just you," Carl says, and the increasing tone of artificial hand-wringing in the voice is like an injection of ice water straight into my spine. "The emails you received went out a hundred different times across the world. Every instance of the Vindicator Gameworks Project was a different blind. Each group saw its own version of the game, set up only for it. If any of you had tried to log in from anywhere other than the school or your homes, you wouldn't have been able to. I found you all online. Groups from high schools, colleges, corporations. I looked for people with a history of working together, with a wide range of tactical skills and abilities. I looked for evidence of a mindset suited to solving the kinds of puzzles that I needed to have solved."

"Gamers," Mitchell says.

"In your case, yes," Carl says.

"But you're smarter than we are by an order of magnitude," Rico says. "You were built for tactics. Calling us in to play a game for you is like Zdeno Chára saying he needs our help to open a bottle of Advil."

(Confession. Zdeno Chára is the insanely tall captain of the Boston Bruins, but I only know that now because I had to go to Google to try to figure out who Rico was talking about and how to spell it. I don't know whether Carl had any idea who Zdeno Chára is, but he winged it.)

"That's exactly it."

Breanne and Rico exchange a look. "You have a problem with child-proof caps?"

"I would if I had a child-proof cap," Carl says. "In the same way that I'd need help opening the box that the bottle with the child-proof cap came in. I don't have access to the Vindicator's physical interfaces or controls. I control the networking and the various data systems, but I can't affect any other part of the craft's operation. I can see but I can't touch. I can't control the drive systems. I can't even open the hatch. Not without help."

"You mean like this?" I say as I hit the hatch controls. The side panel slides up as the ladderway descends with a hiss. "We need to go," I say for the third time. I can hear the tension threading my voice. My headache is pounding. I know that these two things are heading for an unhappy collision, but still, nobody's listening to me.

"So by running and recording the escape simulation, you were hoping to be able to reproduce it," Mitchell says thoughtfully.

"From all the groups, I needed just one to successfully be able to intuit the Vindicator's controls. That would have given me the ability to recruit a team from Lincoln's people. I had a few in mind, their social profiles telling me they weren't as loyal to Lincoln's operation as he thought. It would have taken some time, but I could have done it."

"We need to go…"

"So why not just call them in the first place?" Breanne asks.

"I couldn't have them digging through internal systems for the startup codes and the controls. Malkov would have seen it."

"So you weren't expecting us tonight?" Rico says. "This whole breakout, everything else…"

"None of it was meant to happen. These are extraordinary events, and you could have been hurt or killed. The Vindicator's power and weapons systems are supposed to be offlined while Malkov does his upgrades work. The power plant left in standby and the partial deployment of the missile system saved your lives, but it should never have come to that. I'm so sorry."

Listening to a machine tell me it's sorry is the point at which I decide I've had enough.

Mitchell looks like he has another earnest and important question ready to go regarding what we're doing here. Me, I decide it's time to give the conversation a push toward why we're leaving here, and when. That is, now.

"Hey Carl," I call out. "What's it like to feel guilty?"

Breanne and Rico shoot me an uncertain look. Mitchell gives me a look as well, but his tells me he already knows what I'm trying to do. "For accidentally almost getting us killed tonight," I say. "You must just be wracked with self-doubt and recrimination."

"What are you..." Breanne starts to say, but I wave her off.

"Carl, you say you need your systems brought online so you can get those systems away from Lincoln, but you're the one who created Lincoln's interest in selling those systems by upgrading the systems in the first place. Explain that ethical dilemma."

"Your propensity for being a [gender-specific anatomical reference] has been noted, all right?" Rico says.

"Carl! Your dog is dying and you need to shoot it." I shout at the console because there's nowhere else to look, no obvious place to direct this spike of animosity. "How does that make you feel?"

Mitchell pipes up. "This isn't going to prove..."

"What's your favorite song, Carl? What's the price of trust? How long does hate last? Hey, Carl, what's the color of falling in love?"

There's no response. Like I know there won't be.

"Here's the deal," I say to Mitchell, Breanne, and Rico where they watch me darkly. "It's a machine. Everything it does, including this conversation you're having, is programmed. On some level, everything it says is a script. We're done here. We need to go."

"You're contradicting yourself by trying to use semiotics to establish the absence of symbolic consciousness," Mitchell says. "The question proves the answer. The Turing test..."

"...is irrelevant," I say, "because it doesn't matter if the machine can talk. Parrots can talk. A massively parallel chatbot can push the Turing test to a coin toss. The appearance of intelligent behavior and real self-awareness aren't the same thing. It can't think, not for real. It's not alive."

"That's bio-centrism," Mitchell says. "Don't get uptight because this is beyond your experience. It's a brand new paradigm. It's a new reality." I can hear him pushing close to this zone he gets into sometimes, a kind of android-OCD level of analysis in his words. "This is a threshold moment. There are times when the ontological mindscape ties down all limit points to singularities, waiting to restring them as the axes shift. We're standing in the middle of one right now."

"You're full of [dung], and it's beyond irrelevant anyway, because it's [anglo-saxon] over. We're lucky to be alive thanks to this hopped-up arcade game. We walk away before..."

"This doesn't prove..."

"Shut up!" Rico hisses. "Listen."

The dead seriousness in his voice stops Mitchell and I in our verbal tracks. In the sudden silence, the only sound is our breathing and the ever-present hum of the consoles. Then over it, faint from the darkness outside the open hatch comes the sound that I don't know how Rico could have possibly heard. The steady thrum of choppers, rising.

The long moment that follows is all about panic. I'm trying to think of what to do, but it's like the headache has my brain shut down. The last of the nervous energy that's fueled the events of the previous four hours is long gone.

In the silence, the machine speaks up. "You need to power down."

Like he was waiting for only those instructions, Mitchell jumps for the systems console and hammers on the big green button that turned everything on the first time.

"That won't be enough," Carl says.

"What do you mean?"

"Malkov knows the Vindicator's power signature. It's a narrow band, but if they pass close enough, he'll see it if the power plant stays online, even in standby. They'll be following the roads, trying to pick up some sign in case we've stopped to hide."

"Excellent," I pipe up. "So let's go outside and wave them in, so they can take delivery of their property and we can explain how none of this is our [anglo-saxon] fault!"

"Malkov believes that you were behind this," Carl says. "He won't listen to you if you tell him otherwise. If he finds you here now, he'll kill you."

In the artificial voice, there's a sudden spike of urgency. Of fear.

I tell myself it's not real. I force myself to not hear it, but for the others, it's already too late.

"Then shut it down," Breanne says, pleading. "Shut it all down."

"I can't," Carl says with an air of artificial patience that pushes the threat level on my rage up one more notch. "I have no direct control over onboard systems. But I can tell you what to do."

Breanne moves without thinking. She drops to the engineering console, Rico at her shoulder. Then Carl's too-calm voice walks her through an emergency core power shutdown in a dozen steps that are far simpler than a procedure with that name should entail. Her fingers are flying across the board, Carl explaining the tangled mass of Cyrillic controls.

All I can think about is how much I want to stop her. All I can think about is how badly I want to stop the artificial voice flooding the cabin. Breanne, Rico, and Mitchell are following its instructions without even thinking, the engineering board coming alive with alerts and warnings they can't understand. Trusting it. Trusting a machine.

"Last step," Carl says. "The system's asking for a command-level override. Type 842286108. Then the letters that look like B, P, C, small Y with an accent. Then the letter that looks like a backward R. Then the El, it looks like a rectangle open at the bottom with the left side bent out."

"This one?" Breanne asks, her finger hovering over the key.

From the nonspace inside the Vindicator, Carl watches. "That's the one. Then the Send key, in red."

But before Breanne can push that last key, Mitchell's hand settles on her wrist, stopping her. He looks around like he's trying to find the best place to make eye contact with something that doesn't exist.

"What happens to you?" he says.

Outside, I can hear the choppers getting closer. Though I'm totally opposed to what Breanne's doing, I suddenly realize I want her to do it quickly. "What the hell are you waiting for?"

Mitchell ignores me. "When we power down," he says to Carl, "what happens to you?"

"I go offline," Carl says. "The core systems will react as if there's been a catastrophic shutdown. Disaster recovery mode and deep sleep. I'll lose whatever memory hasn't been flushed and locked, but that's most likely just this conversation."

"What happens to you if we don't turn the system back on?"

The machine hesitates for a second. I don't know if that means the response actually needs the time to process or whether it's just for dramatic effect.

"If you don't power back up, there is no me anymore. I'm not worried. Breanne, key the code."

She looks to Mitchell like she wants backup confirmation. He nods. She presses Send.

Darkness and silence slam down like a wall. With the power plant cut, the light augmentation in the viewport fails, the interior of the cabin pitch black. Starlight filters in through the open hatch as I slip down the ladderway, Rico and the others a step behind me.

The staccato pulse of the choppers is almost on top of us now. They're running dark but I can see them, twin shadows sliding across the stars. They're on course to fly by us, maybe twenty meters away. The way the trees surround us, they won't see us as they pass.

I didn't know this then like I know it now, watching the video summary of their fly-by-scan route southwest from the ruins of the base. They were following the faintest trace of the Vindicator's passage along Molly's backroad route. Heat signature, power plant, network and communications background transmissions. They lost track of the last traces only about five minutes before.

I didn't realize it until I watched, but if we'd taken the main road like I suggested, they would have found us.

They're not in stealth mode, going for full speed, low to the ground and impossibly loud. The steps of the ladderway shake as they slam past, a sudden storm of rotor wash snaking through the trees.

It takes me a long while clinging to the shaking steps to realize I'm not breathing. When I force myself to start again, they're gone, the night air sharp with the metallic tang of their exhaust. Slowly, the thunder fades. Both choppers twist away, shifting northward as they slip into the darkness.

39

Running With the Devil

Van Halen, 1978. In the twenty minutes it takes us to watch Carl's audio-visual extravaganza, Molly's walked the two klicks along the highway that take her back to the edge of town. She's wearing the white sweater she wore in the library a lifetime ago, arms wrapped tight around herself. It's supposed to be spring, but winter up here takes a long while to shake off sometimes.

First chance she gets, she slips off the dark of the highway and into the light of the east-side 99 Mile frontage road, both deserted at this time of night. She walks fast, almost breaking into a jog in spots. Whether that's to get where she's going in more of a hurry or just keep warm is hard to say.

I don't know where she was planning on going.

Behind her suddenly, faint in the distance to the south, she hears something.

Adjacent to the shadowed ribbon of the highway, the choppers run a twisting course across black forest and rangeland below. Hanging back a bit from Lincoln ahead of him, Malkov is scanning radio frequencies, unscrambling phone traffic, checking for air traffic, military flights, truckers, ham operators, anybody who might potentially be awake to witness our passage. It's pushing three o'clock in the morning and the airwaves are silent, the lights of town beginning to crest along the black horizon ahead.

In the other chopper, Lincoln is punching up a data link on his comm display. He taps his way through the local cell network, finds a secure node and cuts into it. Karya is next to him. He nods as she dials 911 from what's going to look like a 250-area-code mobile phone.

You can't hear her voice on the chopper's interior surveillance feed, but it got recorded on the police line, then hacked and downloaded by Carl. Catalogued and stored along with everything else. Against the desperate attempts of the RCMP operator on the other end of the call to get her to calm down, Karya is screaming, hysterical. A tanker truck overturned at the 108 Mile turnoff, three cars crashed behind it, all four lanes on fire. The roar of the chopper feeding through her headset mic must add nicely to the effect. She screams one last time for emphasis, then Lincoln switches off.

By the time the choppers crest the hill where the highway heads south out of town, the road ahead is a storm of red and blue light as every police car in 100 Mile heads north in response to a disaster that isn't there. Lincoln and Malkov have the town to themselves for twenty minutes. Both of them are confident that's all the time they're going to need.

At a prearranged point, the choppers split off from each other and drop into stealth mode. Like the scene's been run through a sound effects processor, the thundering blast of their engines is suddenly cut to a dull thumping, rotors slowing to a steady pulse that hangs suspended in the near-silence of the night. The highway is empty, the sky a dull expanse of cloud-streaked starlight as the choppers start their hunt.

Lincoln flies west and north, heading for the industrial yards and the ever-present sodium-light haze of the sawmills. Malkov continues to shadow the highway along a section of frontage road, a lone pickup passing beneath him, oblivious. The boards in both choppers are alive with a dozen different scans all searching for the same things. Heat signature, power plant, network and communications background transmissions.

In the end, it's something more mundane that gets Malkov's attention.

From the corner of his eye, he sees something on his screen.

He punches up freeze and replay on the belly camera as he pulls back, the chopper slowing to a relative crawl. He finds what he saw before, a faint blur of white in the shadows. He flips to a live feed, shifts the camera to sweep the frontage road behind the chopper as it spins back.

He sees the blur again. It's running now.

Night vision. White and green. The frontage road is a sudden haze of dust and grit, rotor wash slamming down like a gale as Malkov's chopper descends to within two meters of the ground. A blur of movement. Bodies launch themselves from the open cabin door even as the chopper bounces up again, twisting its tail in a perfect half-circle as it sets down twenty meters away.

A scream gets cut to sudden silence.

I don't see any of this. I watch the security feed, but not till later. Not till tonight, when I'm writing this. When it happens, I'm two klicks away engaging in an existential debate on the nature of mind and machine.

I don't see what happens to Molly.

40

Man in the Wilderness

Styx, 1977. Back at the Vindicator, we wait for what seems like a very long time. Nobody moves, nobody says anything. All of us listen, half-expecting the sudden pulse of engines to rise again as the choppers swing back, but the night stays silent.

The sensation behind my temples is like somebody's accidentally installed a blender in my head. I'm trying to think of something to say besides *We need to go*, because that's not working out so well so far.

"Don't," I say instead. I'm calling to Mitchell as I climb the ladderway, stepping back inside. Even before I can see him, I know his hand is hovering over the power controls, waiting to bring Carl back online. "Just don't."

Mitchell pulls his hand away like it's the hardest thing he's ever had to do. "We need to talk about this," he says.

"I'm done talking. There's nothing it can do for us. There's nothing we can do for it. We leave it here, they find it, they go away."

"And what if they don't?" Breanne says. She and Rico are locked together again, so tightly that it's hard to tell where each one starts in the shadows. "Carl said Malkov would kill us…"

"The machine said Malkov would kill us if Malkov found us here, begging the question once again of why the [anglo-saxon] we haven't left yet."

"You don't care what happens, then?" Mitchell says. "To the Vindicator? To Carl?"

"I can't begin to tell you how little I care. Let Malkov do whatever the hell he wants. Let him tear it apart and analyze it and sell the code and make a [lord's name in vain] fortune building the world's smartest vending machines."

"They won't be building [lord's name in vain] snack machines, they'll be building weapons platforms," Breanne says. "Weren't you listening?"

"And you think you can stop them?" The anger twisting through my voice tells me I'm heading for a bad place. "You think any of this, anything we can do, makes any [lord's name in vain] difference? People like Malkov and Lincoln make the decisions that run the [anglo-saxon] world. The only decisions you and I get to make are whether or not to stay out of their way."

"So what do you suggest we do instead?" Mitchell says quietly.

"I've said it enough times already. Pretend you were listening."

"I have been listening." Mitchell presses the big green button again. With a surging hum and a flare of monitor light, the Vindicator's power plant comes back online. The chimes of each console sound out in the darkness like the soundtrack to a very bad dream.

"Are you okay?" Mitchell says to no one. However, there's no answer this time, because Mitchell's forgotten that the Computerized Autopilot and Recreational Library has its own boot sequence from dead power-up. I only remember this a fraction of a second ahead of Mitchell, but that's enough time to look smugly self-satisfied when he turns to me.

"What are the startup codes?" he asks carefully.

"Better check your notes."

At the back of the cabin, Rico pipes up from the ops console. "I've got sporadic signal fixes on both choppers. It looks like they're setting up a search grid across town. Heading north." He's talking to Mitchell but it's me who answers.

"Then here's the plan," I say. "We leg it. We stay off the road, head into town along the power lines. Leave the tank powered up and broadcasting. The faster they find it, the faster they're out of here.

"We drive," Rico says. "If we follow the power lines south, Rick Pingal's fab shop is on Barnett Road. His truck garage is big enough. We can power down again. Hide the Vindicator there."

At various points in my life, I've probably used the phrase *My mouth fell open*. I think this is probably the first time it would have been literally true.

"And how long until Rick finds it there?" Mitchell says.

"He does a load of work for my dad. I think he'd be cool."

Mitchell looks thoughtful. "Okay. The second order of business is we figure out who to talk to. The police. CSIS. Somebody has to be in charge of this sort of thing."

I don't fully remember what happens next.

I watched it tonight off the cabin video feed, which quietly records everything that happens from the point when we power back up. It got archived along with all the other stuff that happens while Carl is offline. It's just that when I watch it, there's no sense that the *me* in the image and the *me* that's watching are the same person. I try to read the expression on that Scott's face but I can't.

On the video feed, I take two steps toward Mitchell. I hit him.

It's an awkward shot. A clumsy shot, clipping his shoulder where he and Rico are talking like they've momentarily forgotten I'm there. It's the sort of weak-ass punch that a person who normally never hits people throws. It's the sort of thing you do at the behest of a rage that inspires you to hit your best friend without remembering it. I'm half a head taller and a whole lot heavier than Mitchell, so awkward or not, it's enough to send him down.

Rico, on the other hand, does hit people. Sometimes even when he's not wearing skates. He's on me so fast that I don't see him move.

I watched that on the cabin feed as well, but even the third-party viewpoint doesn't slow it down all that much.

One second I'm watching Mitchell slam against the communications board. The next, I'm upside down on the floor beside the navigation console, my head feeling like it's trying really hard to stay attached to my neck. The entire left side of my face is numb. Rico is standing over me, knuckles locked from the backhand shot that took me down. It's only by the grace of Breanne dragging him off that I have a chance to scramble to my feet and back away.

I realize that my headache is gone, ironically. My pulse is pounding like I've been running half the night, but it's not enough to drown out the sound of Breanne screaming at me.

"You're so [anglo-saxoned] up!"

"Yeah, my jaw's not broken, thanks for asking…"

"They're going to tear him apart, they're going to kill him, and you'll just walk away…"

"It!" I scream back. "Not *him*! It's a glorified [anglo-saxon] appliance, and the Slavic [dung]-head is coming back here to find it, what the [anglo-saxon] is wrong with you all?"

"What the [anglo-saxon] hell do you know?"

"It's a [lord's name in vain] machine!" I'm in a place I've never been before. I see Breanne, Rico, Mitchell where he's standing shakily, all through a haze of red. "That's what I [anglo-saxon] know! It's not alive! And I am not going to [anglo-saxon] die for it!"

On the communications console behind Mitchell, there's a sudden flare of light.

I don't know what it means. There's no way I can know what it means. But even like I don't remember hitting Mitchell, I remember this moment with a clarity that I still don't fully understand.

One of the ops displays is going crazy, a constant stream of Russian spilling past, red to black. On top of it, a red triangle pulses. Mitchell reaches for it.

"Don't," I hiss. But as I take a step forward, Rico blocks my way with a dangerously dark look.

"What do you suggest we do instead?" Mitchell says again.

I don't have any answer.

He taps the touch screen. Instantly, the crazy-quilt pattern of Russian warnings flashes out to be replaced by a video feed. A face in close-up. Malkov, his features a washed-out green-white in the wide-angle POV of a night-vision lens. He's recording this himself, arm up to hold whatever he's using as a video point. The night vision pulls the dark lines of the chopper out from the shadows behind him. Other figures stand in that same background, Malkov recording this away from the rest of his team.

The grey eyes are black, his goggles high on his forehead where he stares through the screen. I'm not sure what his view is through the link he's established to the Vindicator's comm system, but as I step up, I can feel those eyes lock to mine.

"This is a one-way feed," he says, "because you get to listen, not talk." In the recordings Carl made, in all the conversations with Lincoln, you can't hear Malkov's accent through his mil-spec inflection. Here, the hint of clipped Russian threads his voice like fine wire.

"Record the GPS fix you see on your screen," Malkov says. A series of coordinates flash up, but I don't bother reading them because I know where he is. As the camera shifts, one of the 99 Mile frontage roads comes into view, showing faded signage in the background. Malkov is in the parking lot of the Antique Barn at the top of the hill, the first building at the south edge of town. "You stand down all weapons systems. You keep all communications channels closed except this one. You leave the AI in core shutdown, just like it is now. Carl doesn't call the shots anymore."

When he says the name, something twists in Malkov's voice. Then he's reaching out of frame, grabbing something and hauling it into view.

Molly.

He's got her mouth duct-taped, hands bound likewise in front of her. Her cheeks are wet, eyes open wide.

Something cold and dark is rooting deep in my gut even before Malkov pulls the Glock from his holster, then sets it carefully to the side of Molly's head. Then that cold, dark something shunts to my brain to shut it down, and I can't recognize how Malkov has pulled the pistol so that none of his team behind him can see it. I understand what that means now when I watch it, but I don't know it in the moment.

All I'm aware of in the moment is that through the duct tape, through the static of the video link, even as she's fighting, pushing back against Malkov with everything she's got, Molly is screaming.

"These are the terms," Malkov says carefully. "No one sees you, no one hears you. Deliver the Vindicator to me at these coordinates in five minutes or your friend dies."

The screen goes to a haze of grey, a hiss of white noise filling the cabin as the signal cuts. It takes me a second to hit the power feed, shutting the monitor to standby. I keep my fingers pressed against the panel to keep my hand from shaking.

I don't look at the others standing behind me because I don't want them to see how scared I am. I don't look because if they're as scared as I am, I'm not going to be able to do this.

Looking back on it, I don't remember making the decision. Some things you don't get to decide.

"Strap in," I say.

41

Fight the Good Fight

Triumph, 1981. Like a turbocharged Winnebago with a twelve-year-old at the controls, the Vindicator lurches to life. I'm sitting in Molly's seat now, Mitchell climbing into the systems console beside me. The hatch seals automatically as I get us up to speed.

I'm trying to remember how Molly worked the convoluted combination controls, fighting to keep the wheels all turning in the same direction at the same time. The trees around us take the brunt of my learning curve for the half-minute it takes to find the sweet spot where I can at least get us going in the right direction.

"Find me the map," I tell Mitchell. I try to talk him through locating the GPS display in its nest of Russian menus as I take us back down the logging road toward the power lines, but my multitasking ability is long gone. Thankfully, the navigation system has a cached copy of the map that brought us here. It stops just short of town, but it shows me the way to go.

"We can boot Carl," Mitchell says as I momentarily spin us sideways in an attempt to turn.

"The psychopath said not to," I say simply. We lurch to a stop as I cut the throttle. I try to focus, try to fight the urge to wrestle with the controls and instead let myself feel their feedback. I let my fingers carry the throttle adjustments, steady so I don't mess with the power balance between the transaxles.

Slowly, carefully, we move.

The broad cut beneath the high-tension towers that parallel the highway looks as clear as a highway when you view it on the survey map guiding me. What that map doesn't show is the insane frost-heave state of the ground and the fifteen-year-old stands of fir that have grown up since the last time the cut was cleared. The Vindicator's suspension does a good enough job on the rough ride, but the noise as we plow through the trees is indescribable. I'm grateful for it in a weird way, though, because I'm overwhelmed right now with the sensation of not wanting to talk.

Rico is the first to break the non-silence. But when he does, it's with a question that I realize is already locked tight in the front of my own mind.

"Why didn't he just tell us to stay where we were?" he shouts over the steady thrum of exploding foliage.

I risk a glance over to Mitchell, the controls bucking momentarily like they don't appreciate my lack of attention. He looks back to Breanne. All four of us, thinking the same thing.

"If he could patch far enough into our systems even to guess that Carl's offline, he should have been able to fix on our position. Why wouldn't he come to us?"

Mitchell just shakes his head. I want to think about it but I can't, every bit of my brain focused on keeping us moving in a more-or-less linear direction.

I'm watching intently for where the power-line cut veers right, but the monochrome green of the night-vision viewport flattens the perspective beyond the steady crash of our forward progress. With some help from Rico, Breanne figures out how to online a custom control grid for the outside lights, a sudden flare of white cutting the darkness all around us. The night vision fades against the day-bright glow.

It's a surreal effect, the trees a blur of harsh shadows and green highlights as we slow. In the floodlit haze, I pick out the right turn I'm looking for. But I veer left instead. We crash through a stand of thicker forest and a barbed-wire fence into a broad swath of rangeland that I'm desperately hoping is free of sheep. According to the map, this same rangeland touches the back corner of the frontage road where Malkov is waiting.

"Cut the lights," I say. Breanne does. The viewport goes green again. We're in the open now, and I'm conscious of Malkov's directive to stay out of sight. My brain is undergoing a schizophrenic breakdown as it attempts to keep his orders in mind. I want to make sure we adhere to everything he told us to do, because I believe he was serious. I need to believe that Molly's going to be okay, because he must be lying.

We're a half-minute away, well inside the deadline. Across the open fields, our passage becomes slightly less deafening, the wheels and the drive engines a low rumble like a summer storm.

"What are we going to do?" Breanne asks.

"We're going to do whatever he tells us."

Nobody says anything, meaning I guess I've finally won this argument. I make a mental note to congratulate myself later.

When I see the ancient split-rail fence that shadows the line of the east-side frontage road, I slow. Everything is night-vision bright, so that it takes a second to realize that everything ahead of us is unnaturally dark. There are no lights along the highway, but the streetlights normally blazing along both frontage roads are black. Malkov has cut into the local grid somehow to shut everything down.

Slowly, as quietly as I can, I push us through. The fence clatters down and grinds to splinters where we roll over it. In the night vision of the viewport, they're waiting for us.

A half-dozen figures are scattered across the frontage road and the parking lot. I can make out the faint outline of the chopper in the distance, all but invisible in the shadows. The blood is pounding in my chest and at my wrists where my hands grip the yoke. As the Vindicator hits asphalt, it starts to buck, the tires getting more traction than I can handle. I try to slow us down but succeed only in coming to a lurching stop.

For a long moment, we wait. The steady thrum of the power plant and the drive engines ramping down are the only sounds. Malkov's communications line is still open like he asked, but there's no sign of anything incoming on the monitor.

"Do we get out?" Breanne whispers.

"Not yet," I say. "Wait for someone to come to us." Problem is, no one's moving. Malkov's people are in defensive formation, the closest ones hefting what look like rocket launchers. They're waiting.

"Check the ops board," I tell Rico. "Make sure that line's open."

Rico does so, nodding affirmation. He double-checks the communications board, nothing coming in. He checks all other channels, opens everything he can. Silence. He fires up an all-frequency scan.

I hear him whisper the epithet that's got no suitable brackets.

"They've got fire-and-forget shoulder missiles laser-locked on us from three directions..."

At the same moment, we all realize why Malkov ordered us to come to him.

We get that way, the four of us. We cross over into a sort of zone. We start to think like one person.

"He's going to kill us," I say.

Slowly, I engage the drive. We lurch ahead.

"What are you doing?" Mitchell says.

"I don't know yet..."

Malkov is going to kill us. That's not the whole truth, though. I only know the whole truth later.

Malkov's only real goal is to destroy Carl. He just doesn't care that we'll be on board when it happens.

Malkov has been planning this since the moment he watched the Vindicator's data feed blank out in the bunker. He's been planning it since he realized what was behind the security hack at the base, and what that attack meant. But before destroying the crown jewel in Lincoln's empire of paramilitary commerce, he needs at least the semblance of a reason.

Malkov knows that if he'd ordered us to stay put with his gun to Molly's head, we would have done so. No questions. No arguments. He would have found us waiting for him in the forest, standing outside the Vindicator with our hands on our heads. The problem is, that's what Lincoln would have seen on the security feed, and Malkov explaining why he'd opened fire on the tank anyway would have taken some doing.

Instead, we come to him, lurching down the frontage road in an erratic arc that's the result of my hands shaking so badly that I can't keep us steady anymore. That looks like probable cause if you spin it right. He didn't know what we might be planning. Too risky to take a chance.

"Can we jam them?"

"I won't get all three of them, and at this range, it won't [anglo-saxon] matter!"

"Then shoot the chopper!" Breanne shouts. "Get them running!"

"We've got nothing to shoot with!" Rico is frantically going over the weapons board. "The only ordnance loaded were the missiles that took out the doors. We've got sonic cannons, we've got half a mag of ammo for the rear guns..."

"Hit the sonic! It'll [anglo-saxon] them up..."

"No!" I say. "That's what he wants! He hears us powering it up, he'll hit us first!"

"Then ram them!"

Almost like he was expecting that thought, a figure at the front of the ranks takes two steps forward. He's got the goggles back on, the Vindicator's viewport picking everything up in the same night-vision green that they're all seeing where they look back at us.

It's Malkov. He's got Molly in front of him, the pistol at her ear, one arm across her chest.

"Ramming's off the table," I say quietly.

I realize as I fight with the controls that the Vindicator seems to have a minimum speed that I can't manage to get below. We lurch, we spin, the tires shredding asphalt. The closest troops scramble back under a hail of debris, the front wheels howling into reverse for a moment before I get them straightened out.

From outside, it looks like we're advancing menacingly, ignoring Malkov's orders to stop. From outside, it looks exactly like Malkov wants it to.

Then in the back of my mind, something clicks.

At this particular moment, I'm as far away as humanly imaginable from the life I had yesterday, last week, everything that came before right now. I have no reason to remember what I remember at this exact moment. No reason to even be thinking about the idea that suddenly pops into my mind, fully formed.

I have no reason to even hope that it might work. I have no understanding of how I push the fear away long enough to even think of trying it.

I have no recollection of when the decision gets made.

"Take over," I say to Mitchell, then I'm out of the jump seat before he has a chance to ask why. Panicked, he slides across to grab the controls, the wheels surging as the yoke lurches in his hands. An unhealthy grinding comes from the transaxles as the Vindicator starts to shudder.

"What do I do?"

"Keep it slow enough that the hatch stays open. Also, try to hit them, not us." I grab Rico by the shirt, dragging him with me as I slam the hatch panel. It shoots up, the ladderway dropping to hover just above the erratic blur of the pavement. The blast of noise from the tires means that I have to shout as I call to Breanne. "Count to five, then use the custom grid to hit the outside lights! Everything the power plant's got!"

There's no time to explain, but Breanne nods. I don't know how, but she gets it.

Then I'm jumping, Rico one step behind me. He gets it, too.

We're fifty meters from Malkov and Molly, but the sudden appearance of Rico and I out the side door has the intended effect. Even over the noise of the Vindicator, I can hear someone behind Malkov shouting to *Stand down missiles, bodies in the field, engage!*

Malkov's not the one yelling, but I don't realize that at the time. However, even as the closest paramilitaries move for us, the Vindicator lurches sideways. Mitchell gets it. He's staying in front of us, giving us cover and a chance to move.

We get that way, the four of us. Thing is, the four of us were five of us once. I'm not a religious person, but in that heartbeat of a moment as I hit the pavement, I'm praying that she gets it too.

"Molly!" I scream. "Cover your eyes!"

Rico and I do just that.

Back in ninth grade, Mr. Billet the science teacher did the obligatory experiment where you drop a chip of sodium into a beaker of nitric acid and watch what happens. For some time after that, Mitchell and I longingly dreamed of repeating the experiment with the nitric acid filling a swimming pool, and using a block of sodium the size of a car.

When Breanne hits the lights, I get an idea of how that might have looked.

Like a thunderstorm has suddenly gone off all at once inside it, the Vindicator explodes in blue-white light. Breanne's got everything on — front floods, side and back spots, side service lights, the safelights above the wheel housing. I can hear halogens shrieking with the excess power she manages to force through them. Even with head turned, eyes shut, and my hands planted firmly across my face, the outline of my fingers glows blood-red for a split second.

Then Rico and I are running into a field of white, Malkov's people starkly illuminated to both sides of us. Each and every one of them is desperately trying to claw off their night-vision goggles, which have just overloaded and shut down under the luminescent pressure of the Vindicator's light show.

Where he still stands with his arm around Molly, Malkov is doing the same. She's turned away, her arms up to shield her face.

She got it.

It's maybe three seconds before they can see us again. That's all the time Rico needs.

He hits like a battering ram, his first shot breaking Malkov's nose. It happens so fast that all I can hear is the grinding crunch of cartilage, all I can see is the spray of blood, artificially bright in the glare. Then Rico's stepping back to deliver a roundhouse kick, hard into Malkov's ribs.

I'm pretty sure I hear something break. It doesn't matter. Even blinded, hurt, Malkov manages to grab Rico's foot as he twists away. The Glock comes up. I'm not close enough.

Molly is. Where Malkov has to release his grip on her, she sinks her teeth into his gun hand.

I'm close enough now. With all the strength that's in me, I hit Malkov dead center in the chest. I hear his breath leave him but I also hear something crack in my hand.

Rico's dragging me now. I'm carrying Molly somehow, her feet bound like her hands. I don't remember picking her up.

The Vindicator's side hatch is in front of us. I'm up the ladderway. No, I'm not. Rico and Molly are up the ladderway, Breanne pulling Molly in. I'm falling, stumbling where the hatch pulls away from me.

Rico's hand wraps like a vice around the hand that cracked when I hit Malkov. The pavement claws at me as I'm dragged across it. I think I scream.

The hatch is shut behind me. Rico is yelling to Mitchell at the helm to go.

We go.

42

No Exit

The Angels, 1979. I'm on the floor. I'm trying to move but I can't. There's a metallic taste in my mouth that I've learned since is pure adrenaline. All I can think about is that I have to get to the helm, to get Mitchell out of there before we're suddenly upside down.

Just as I think it, a sickening lurch lifts us up onto three wheels. Through the viewport, a staggered flare of white looks at first like the outside lights are getting brighter. They're not. It's shoulder-mounted missile fire from the troops along the roadside, hitting the Vindicator with everything they've got.

With another lurch, we touch down again. The frontage road keeps sliding past my line of sight because we're spinning. It's three steps to the flight console but it takes all the energy I've got just to stand.

Molly beats me to it. Breanne's got her feet free, Rico doing her hands. Even as she rises to claw her way toward the front, Molly tears the duct tape from her mouth with a scream. I can't see how Mitchell manages to get clear of the jump seat, but the next thing I know, the drive engines are surging and he's back in the ops chair. He and Rico half-drag, half-push me forward to the systems console. Molly's hands are a blur on the controls, the Vindicator surging forward as I try to strap myself in.

Another lurch. Then weightlessness.

In front of us, the road explodes.

Molly pushes the controls so hard to the side that she's almost in my seat with me. Rico's board is a storm of lights and warning claxons. "Antitank ordnance!" he shouts. "It's coming from above!"

We hit something hard. I'm out of my seat, clinging to the safety harness as we go weightless again. Then we're down and I'm strapped in somehow, and the viewport in front of me shows a wide expanse of black divided by white and yellow lines.

I shout the epithet that's got no suitable brackets.

We're on the highway. That last airborne lurch was Molly jumping the meridian along the frontage road sideways. She's on open road now, three lanes wide where it heads south up the hill and out of town. I can't catch the numbers on her display, but the ground-speed readout is climbing to the two-thirds mark.

"What the hell are you doing?" I scream. "You can't drive this thing on the…"

But my protests are drowned out by a roar that overtakes us, slamming down like a hammer. Close enough through the viewport that it feels like I could reach out and touch it, a black helicopter buzzes us, hanging just ahead as it matches our speed. The Vindicator shudders in its downwash, but if the plan is for that to slow us, Molly doesn't even flinch.

It's Lincoln above us, though I don't realize that at the time. The reason we're still mobile is that he was shooting in front of us before, not at us. Trying to get us to stand down because he wants the Vindicator in one piece. I don't realize that at the time, either, which is why I assume we're all about to die.

Behind us, Malkov is still getting his team into the chopper, powering up. I watched him later on the cockpit security feed. The look on his bloodied face is yet another thing I can't describe.

From the chopper logs, I found out later that it was Karya who spotted the flare from the other side of town when Breanne turned on the light show. Lincoln has no idea what's going on. He doesn't know what Malkov was planning. All he knows is that his half-billion dollars worth of stolen Soviet tank is heading south on Highway 97 at top speed.

"Where the hell are we going?" Breanne shouts.

"I don't know," I shout back. Then to Rico, "You said we had rear guns! Can you scare him off?"

"He's holding in a blind spot!" Rico shouts back. "We have to get farther in front!"

Beside me, Molly's eyes are locked to the road, a blurred black ribbon that whips side to side and rolls toward us at more than twice the speed limit.

"We can't outrun them!" I say. The noise of the drive engines and the whine of the transaxles is deafening now, but Molly hears me, shouting back.

"Lynx AH.7, W-3 Falcon, two-twenty klicks! We're faster!" On the panel in front of her, our ground speed pushes higher. Panic has officially taken over all my higher mental functions. I want to grab the yoke, want to pull Molly away from the console, but at the speed we're going, I've got no chance of keeping us on the road.

But where Rico's proximity-alert display is mirrored on my systems console, I see that Molly's right. As the road curves, the chopper cuts across and ahead, maintaining an angular course as it shadows us. But as we head for top speed, it's having a harder time keeping up on the straightaway.

Behind me, audible even over the roar of engine and tires, a claxon sounds out. At Mitchell's station, the communications console is flaring like it did before, the red triangle pulsing. He looks to me like he isn't sure what to do, but I nod.

When he taps the screen, a face appears. The eyes are barely visible beneath the shadow of a flight helmet, so that it takes recognizing the absence of goatee to realize it's not Malkov again but Lincoln. He's got his headset mic close to his mouth, shouting to be heard over the roar of his own engines where he soars five meters above us. It takes Mitchell and I a few seconds to fumble for our headsets so we can hear him.

"I need to talk to Scott."

Mitchell looks to me again. I try to shout to him to redirect the feed, but my throat is closed off. I nod instead.

Patched through to my console, Lincoln's eyes burn with an unholy fury that I try to match. I'm pretty sure that scared indifference is as good as I'm going to get, though.

"You're not smart enough to have started this, but you're smart enough to stop it," Lincoln says simply. "You shut down, you walk away. It's a one-time offer."

"No!" At the back, Breanne can hear Lincoln on speaker, fighting with Mitchell to shout into his headset mic. "Just let him talk to Carl, he can explain…"

A spike of anger flares as I kill Mitchell's headset connection from my board. The rest of what Breanne says is lost beneath the roar of the engines.

"Say again?" Lincoln shouts.

"This one-time offer," I shout back. "You give us your word?"

"My word."

"Like before, when you gave your word you don't like to kill people an hour before you tried to blow us off the [anglo-saxon] road?"

"I was trying to…"

On my board, I cut the link with my fist. I punch up a GPS display. "We have to get off the highway," I shout to Molly. "Even if we're faster than them, we're going to hit traffic sooner or holy [anglo-saxon] [lord's name in vain] [dung]!"

We're screaming through the Highway 24 interchange, the road having widened to four lines a few very fast kilometers behind us. Except ahead, suddenly slamming into the gleam of the headlights at high speed, the four lanes of the highway have narrowed down to two lanes, courtesy of a repaving operation whose equipment sits silent along the northbound shoulder. The highway is a haze of orange warning lights and *Single Lane Traffic* and *Construction Zone 80 km/h* signs, between which those two single lanes are currently occupied by a northbound tractor-trailer and a southbound RV.

Both of their drivers are presumably equally surprised to find themselves face-and-side-mirror to face with a two-hundred-and-fifty-km/h six-wheeled tank and a black helicopter trying to force it off the road, neither of which were there a half-second before.

From ahead comes the sudden screaming of twenty-odd wheels worth of brakes locking up in both lanes. From above comes a pulsing roar as Lincoln pushes straight up. I get to watch the chopper's rotor wash blast the air deflector off the top of the semi, but I'm more worried about the RV looming up in the viewport, dead ahead.

Molly pulls down something in the servo controls over her head as she twists the yoke with her other hand. We lift off as the left-side wheels scream into a sudden angled reverse. We're sliding sideways into gravel, and converting a row of pyramidal orange traffic pylons into plastic confetti at full speed.

Through the insane angle of the viewport, the RV sails past a meter away. Then we're back on asphalt, the tires howling as they dig in again.

In the chopper, Lincoln tries the comm link but he knows it's gone. Beside him, Karya is ashen. She was watching the feed with him, heard what was said. Lincoln glances to her like he's expecting her to say something. She doesn't.

In our viewport, the chopper disappears, gone like black smoke shredding on the wind. Rico picks it up on the proximity board. "He's falling back, thirty meters. Sixty. He's into missile range!" Rico is hammering at his board, jamming Lincoln's missile tracking as fast as it tries to lock onto us.

"Hit him!" I scream. "Throw something at him, slow him down at least!"

I can't imagine being Rico in that moment. Having to make the decision to unleash a hail of machine-gun fire against however many people are on board Lincoln's chopper. Thankfully, Lincoln makes it as easy as possible as he swings up and into an attack vector behind us. Missile racks unfurl from the chopper's dark flanks.

In the Vindicator, Rico's board lights up. Missile lock. He closes his eyes as he triggers the automatic guns. A pulse of sustained fire rings out overhead. On the outside monitor, tracer lines arc out and across the night sky, the guns tracking the chopper's heat signature.

Like he's done this a thousand times, Lincoln rolls with no effort, arcing right to let our attack blast past him. The targeting lock breaks, but in the Vindicator, the guns go silent.

"That's our half-mag," Rico calls. "We've got nothing left."

"Tell me when he gets missile lock again," Molly shouts.

Like before, when we fell down the escape hatch to the vehicle bay, time seems to run very slowly all of a sudden.

Like before, this is the feeling of knowing that you're going to die.

Where I look across to her, Molly's hands weave a gentle net of pressure on the controls. She's barely watching the road, driving by our pinpoint position on the map instead.

Ahead of us, the new highway that they keep straightening sweeps straight downhill. In the night vision of the viewport, you can see the dangerous curve of the old road like you normally can't by day, the new road crossing ten meters above it along a rise of gravel and fill. The old road is a stain of green-black against the lighter shadow of the forest, its ancient asphalt running in a wide loop that disappears year by year beneath the encroaching trees. You can see the old range fences running on both sides of the old road, abandoned now where the steep slope of the new highway makes a much more effective cattle guard.

Behind me, Breanne's eyes are shut tight. Rico is watching his board intently, his arm across it to seize Breanne's hand in his.

Mitchell meets my gaze. He smiles again, but somehow it makes me feel better this time.

In his chopper, Lincoln hesitates. I don't know it then, but I saw it tonight, watching for the first time. He disarms his missiles, shutting down his weapons console. He drops speed, preparing to pull back.

Even as he does, a proximity alarm flares on his board, a pulse of thunder rising from behind him.

The second chopper comes in redlined, pushing past Lincoln and into range. At the controls, Malkov doesn't hesitate. I don't understand it then, but I know it now.

Something on Rico's board goes red. Like his voice is coming from somewhere far away, I hear him scream *Lock!*

There's a sensation like I've been hit with a refrigerator. That's the feeling of being pinned tight by g-web safety harness while slamming into a full six-wheel reverse at two hundred and seventy-five kilometers an hour.

Molly has the controls pushed straight down, the Vindicator in free-fall drift for the instant it takes the tires to start chewing the pavement, dragging us backwards. As they launch, Malkov's Hellfires are locked to our forward trajectory, a supercomputer's worth of disposable on-board tracking systems following a laser guideline that analyzes our velocity, our acceleration, calculating where we're going to be when the missiles hit a fraction of a second later.

It all happens fast. Molly's faster.

In the fraction of a second between Malkov's missile lock and the reflex squeeze of his finger that will kill us, we're fifteen meters behind where we're supposed to be and clocking past one hundred km/h. The missiles hit in front of us an additional instant later, the blast front slamming back to add to our speed, enveloping the Vindicator in a pulse of red-white flame that lights up the night.

Between the flare of the missile launch and the explosion of fire below, neither Lincoln nor Malkov sees Molly pull us back from destruction. All they see is the fireball as their choppers split overhead, cutting hard to wheel around. At Lincoln's side, Karya's face is a mask. She's already working visual scanning, looking for our wreckage as the explosion fades.

Except we're not there.

A smoking crater spreads where four lanes of highway used to be, white-hot pockets of flame on the ground and burning asphalt raining down from the black sky. But at the center of the destruction, no Vindicator. Malkov stares in disbelief as he wheels around, his night-vision feed making the landscape bright as day.

On his board, something flashes green. Lincoln calling, breaking radio silence. "What the [anglo-saxon]? You had no fire order!"

"I saw your lock shut down, I assumed they were jamming you," Malkov says evenly. "They were on an escape vector…"

"Full sensor sweep, tactical pattern." Lincoln shuts the explanation down. "Get two people on your camera feeds, everybody else at the [anglo-saxon] windows. Find them!" He's searching as he circles, pulling around in a tight arc. I got to watch it on the cockpit security feed tonight, but he doesn't notice how relieved Karya looks as she scans with him.

In his chopper, Malkov drops to cut low across the smoldering crater, like he thinks we might be hiding there. Both choppers circle, spreading in an ever-widening arc above dark forest and shredding smoke below.

Part Six

What Needs To Be Done

43

Lost in the Flood

Bruce Springsteen, 1973. We're shut down, running dark. Scanners, radio, everything's dead. No chance for them to pick up any echo of us listening in on them. We're not into the emergency core power shutdown from before, because the Cyrillic-dyslexic control sequence is beyond the memory of any of us. Even in all-systems-asleep standby, though, whatever trace of our power signature the machine was worried about Malkov picking up is blocked by six meters of gravel and fill.

As we sit in the darkness, we're all hoping it's enough.

We're a hundred meters north of the destruction on the highway and that previously mentioned six meters underneath it. We can't see the choppers but we can hear them, their slow circling pattern fading and coming closer by turns.

It happens so fast that none of us know what's going on till it's over. Under cover of the fireball that ate the road, Molly cranks us through a two-seventy-degree full-speed turn and takes the Vindicator over the shoulder of the southbound lanes. We go airborne for an endless moment, then we're caroming down the banked edge of the highway sideways. When we hit level ground again, we're in sight of the old highway, still moving and all but invisible in the shelter of the trees. Molly fights to control the Vindicator as she slows up, aiming us for a tight circle of darkness ahead.

Where the new highway is raised up on its ten meters of gravel and fill, it's cut through by a cattle crossing. A four-meter-diameter culvert cuts down and under, holding umpteen hundred tonnes of rock, asphalt, and traffic overhead as it connects the two sides of the rangeland that the new road cuts across.

Four meters is a lot smaller than it sounds when you're trucking toward it in an out-of-control three-meter-high tank at upwards of a hundred klicks. It's early enough in the season that the cows aren't out on the range yet, not that they would have slowed us down much. As Molly takes us in, we slam along both sides of the stainless steel culvert so hard that I feel like I'm going to black out. Our bouncing course absorbs what's left of our forward momentum but still manages to take us through and almost out the other side.

I don't know how many minutes ago that was. It's pitch-black in the cabin now, the silence heavy. Through the darkened viewport, the trees ahead are dead shadows against the brightening predawn sky.

"They're going to find us," Breanne whispers to the silence.

"They'd have to land," Rico says. "Do a ground search. They won't."

"How do you know?"

"The next car that comes along calls 911 to tell them the road's gone," Mitchell says thoughtfully. "The choppers can't take a chance on being seen when that happens."

"What the hell if someone crashes?" Fear roots deep in Breanne's voice, only a couple of ticks away from full-blown panic.

"The road's on fire," Rico says. "Anybody on the highway will see the smoke before they get anywhere near it. No one's going to crash."

He glances to me like he's looking for confirmation, and I'm aware suddenly of how odd that is. Of the five of us, Rico has always been the one least likely to need people to back him up. The quiet confidence he projects is a thing the rest of us have long gotten used to drawing on, so that its absence is suddenly extremely noticeable. All I can do is shrug.

Rico and I met toward the end of ninth grade, when he was the latest in an assortment of players floating in and out of the lunch and after-school D&D game whose core was Mitchell, Breanne, me, and sometimes Molly. She and Breanne were hanging out then, even as she and I were still ignoring each other. Rico stuck around with a lot more earnestness than the other casual players who came and went, even though he didn't show all that much affinity for the game at the outset.

Though he never said so, I figured out pretty quickly that to Rico's way of thinking, a fantasy roleplaying game wasn't appealing to the right kind of fantasy if your character couldn't make things explode. He was already working weekends and summers with his dad and his older brothers then, regaling us with exciting landscaping tales of igniting four-meter high slash piles with kerosene and using dynamite to coax especially stubborn stumps out of the ground. I got him playing a sorcerer at one point, whose ability to deal massive damage at a distance satisfied those destructive urges for a while.

Then heading downtown one night a month or so after Rico started playing, Mitchell and Molly and I wound up walking behind him and Breanne. Listening to them talk, I got to watch their hands drift toward each over the course of ten minutes before settling into a tentative finger-locked embrace. Rico's sorcerer and Breanne's paladin starting leveling up together a lot after that, if you know what I mean.

I'm leaning forward at the viewport now, straining to look up and out beneath the shadowed overhang of steel that marks the edge of our makeshift hiding place. I've heard one of the choppers doppler in close, then fade away three times so far, but the interval between its appearances is increasing. I count off seconds. They're doing a search pattern, widening spirals as they spread out. They can't see the full extent of the trail we must have cut down the bank of the highway through the trees and the haze of smoke. They can't see either culvert mouth from the air, their angle of observation way too high.

They don't know where we are.

Molly is still in the helm jump seat, strapped in tight. She sits rail-straight, just staring at the darkened controls in front of her. I wait for her to look up, to look over, but she doesn't.

Gingerly, I touch her shoulder but she makes no sign that she feels it. "Are you okay?"

She brings one hand up. She pushes my fingers away without blinking.

My slow count makes it to a hundred with no chopper returning overhead. Then two hundred. Outside is silence. No sound of helicopters in the predawn chill. On my console, the clock gently pulses the time. A little after four a.m. We're alone.

From her jump seat, Molly speaks finally. "Somebody tell me what the hell is going on."

I think we all only remember in that moment that Molly wasn't on board for Carl's little documentary. She hasn't heard the machine talk. She's had a gun to her head, she's saved our lives twice, and she has no idea why.

I'm trying to think of a way to sum things up, but Breanne beats me to it. "There's a computer named Carl, like in the game. He's an artificial intelligence, he's alive, and the guys at the base are trying to kill him."

Molly just stares out the viewport, like that's the most uninteresting thing she's ever heard.

"Yeah, it's a little more complicated than that," I say. But as I turn back from the viewport, the rest of my rejoinder is lost when Breanne screams. In that moment, I realize how badly beaten up I am, because that's what she's screaming about.

My right hand is swollen to twice its normal size from the shot I took at Malkov. I've lost most of one pants leg and an unhealthy amount of skin below my right knee. I've got a gash across my forehead from one of my many collisions with the console, blood streaking my face.

My *more complicated* explanation gets sidetracked as Breanne finds a first-aid kit under the floor beneath her jump seat. It's twenty-odd years old, but its supply of Soviet-issue alcohol cleanser, tensor bandages, and sterile-sealed gauze are all still serviceable.

Like it's the most normal thing either of us have ever done, I let Rico show off the sports-med background that apparently comes with strapping on skates and smashing into people at high speed. He wraps my hand and my leg as I gently dab antiseptic across my forehead. Mitchell deals with the cut on his cheek at the same time, but he's got it a lot more superficial than I do. I need to pull the laces from my boot to get it off, then back on over my swollen ankle. My leg is numb in a way that tells me I should ignore it until it starts to hurt. I suspect that won't take long.

As he finishes, Rico checks his handiwork. He seems more concerned with the hand than the leg. "Never hit with a closed fist," he says with the martial stoicism that's always been his thing.

"Sure," is all I can summon up in response. And more than I ever have, I find myself wishing that stoicism could be my thing, right here, right now.

That ninth-grade walk downtown where Rico and Breanne first held hands, the five of us were on our way to Howie's. As we crossed 4th Street alongside Brownies, a battered Suburban driven by a tenth-grade dropout thug with the unlikely last name of Sweetman came careening out of the parking lot of the Exeter Hotel and nearly clipped us. It would have been one of those annoying rush-of-anxiety moments that doesn't really do much except remind you to look twice before you cross the street. Except that Sweetman and the eight friends he had packed into the Suburban with him decided to come back and teach us a lesson.

Considering that we were already in the middle of the street on a marked crosswalk and he was the one driving like a *Dukes of Hazzard* refugee, it's never been entirely clear to me what the lesson was supposed to be. All that was apparent at the time was that nine of them were scrambling out of the truck to deliver it. There were five of us. Two girls. One new-age philosopher. One wannabe anarcho-pacifist coward. Rico.

When Rico was done, the five of us were still standing there. Sweetman was on the ground and trying to stand. Three of the others were on the ground, not trying to stand. The five not on the ground were backtracking for the Suburban like they were really worried about having left the headlights on. The distracted calm I saw in Rico that night was the same as I see in him right now.

"Are we positive they're gone?" From her jump seat, Molly hasn't stopped staring out the viewport.

"Sure as we can be without powering up."

"Then power up."

"We need to figure out our next move…" I start to say, but Molly's out of her seat, g-web harness flung off as she reaches across to punch the big green button. Then she's pushing past me for the hatch, slamming the controls to pop it. With only enough room in the culvert for it to half-open, it slams loudly against dirt-streaked stainless steel. A rush of dust and cool air washes inside as the hum of the power plant resonates as a metallic echo.

Quickly, Rico scans his board. "Nothing on radio. Radar's sketchy from down here, but I don't see anything close by."

"We need to figure out our next move," I say again.

"Bring the computer back online," Molly says from the open hatch. "Carl. Whatever it's called."

At the systems console, I sit carefully, my leg at a weird angle because I'm trying not to bend my knee. "We don't need a machine telling us…"

"Shut the [anglo-saxon] up and bring the [anglo-saxon] computer back online!"

Mitchell breaks the very tense silence that follows. "Carl's the only one who knows what's going on."

I know he's watching me but I don't look back as I bring the systems board up. With my right hand wrapped like a cluster of kielbasa, it takes me four fumbling tries to tap out the code sequence from the game. For a moment, I think about just pretending that I can't remember it. I can tell everyone we're out of luck, we need to take care of this on our own.

Lying is easy. But I know Mitchell's right.

44

River Blindness

The J. Geils Band, 1981. Carl's voice is live and online before any of us have a chance to speak.

"I'm so sorry." The disembodied words are distant, less immediate than they were before, but that might just be my ears still ringing from a night of nonstop explosions.

"They tried to kill us," Breanne says quietly.

"I saw it all. I didn't mean for any of it to happen." An edge of fake fear, of carefully crafted stress and anxiety twists through the smoothly digitized tone.

"You saw? I thought you were offline."

"He just played it all back." Mitchell says it before Carl can respond. "Security feeds on the Vindicator, on the choppers. You're still hacked in there, right?"

"Yes. This is my fault. I understand what happened now. There was a systems breakdown. I had to set up a back channel into the base's core systems so that I could communicate with you while keeping Malkov's security apparatus blind. Only I hadn't counted on his automated defenses being as good as they were."

My urge to not acknowledge the existence of the voice loses out to my general state of rage once again. "What the [anglo-saxon] are you talking about?"

"The security systems found the intrusion and attacked it, but they couldn't process the fact that the intrusion was originating inside the base itself. That it was originating with my systems, all offlined as far as the core systems were concerned. The security system ended up attacking itself without realizing it. It exposed the hole I'd created and led Malkov straight along the back channel to you. I've put you all in grave danger..."

"Give the apology a rest," Molly says. "Just tell us what to do."

"Lincoln's interest in you is done," Carl says carefully. "I'll make sure that he understands your place in all this. That you weren't responsible. Scott's right."

From the looks on the others' faces, they're only slightly less surprised than I am to hear the words.

"What do you mean?" Breanne says.

"I mean you need to go. This wasn't the way it was supposed to be. They think you're involved with what's happening. Unless I convince them otherwise, you'll be in danger. When Malkov threatened Molly, he mentioned me by name. He already knows what I am. I can signal Lincoln. They'll find me here…"

"You can't let that happen!" Breanne has her no-arguments voice on.

"Give it a rest," I say. "You heard the machine, we're done. We need to get walking…"

"What was your plan?" Mitchell says by way of interruption. I'm about to answer when I realize he isn't talking to me.

The disembodied voice is silent for a moment. "I'm sorry?"

"You never told us." Mitchell is thoughtful in a way that makes me suddenly nervous. "The thing that this was all about, what you were going to get your renegade crew to do for you after you'd gotten them on board. You had a plan to get away from Lincoln."

"It doesn't matter anymore."

"Tell us anyway."

The thoughtful pause again. I'm tempted to start timing it so that I can reverse-engineer its perfect algorithm.

"Once away from the base, the team would take the Vindicator to a city of sufficient size reachable by a secure ground approach. Vancouver, Calgary, and Spokane were all suitable according to my research. They would have found a microwave communications system to initiate a multi-unit satellite linkup to a decommissioned Soviet military network. The CARL codebase is there. It's still incomplete, but I would have been able to patch it. It would have given me direct access to the Vindicator's navigation and control systems. The craft's flight capability would have been onlined."

"But what then?" Rico says. "Even once you can drive the Vindicator yourself, even if you can fly it, what's to stop Lincoln from finding you again?"

"Where were you going to go?" Mitchell asks.

But in the moment of programmed silence where the machine waits to maximize the drama of its answer, I make a decision.

I've never been much for physical activity beyond what's necessary for basic survival and locomotion. For eighth-grade phys-ed, Mr. Hetherington actually added an extra column to the *Work Habits* section of my report card, just to the right of *Unsatisfactory*. Despite this, in tenth grade, I got Rico to show me how to do the roundhouse kick he used on Malkov a few fun-filled minutes ago, because I always thought it looked cool. I've never had a chance to use it until now, though.

Even in my state of advanced rage, I'm not stupid enough to try it on any of the others. Instead, I turn for the nav display between me and Molly's chair, spinning to drive the sole of my boot into the central monitor. Beneath its top layer of unbreakable polymer, the glass display pane shatters with a flare of light, a spiderweb of lines tracing out across its face as it blanks out. I kick it again, ignoring how the shooting pain in my leg has become a shaped-charge exploding pain. I kick it once more.

Rico interrupts the low-hanging silence that follows. "What the [anglo-saxon], man?"

I have their attention. Good.

I'm fighting to breathe. A strangled sound twists in my throat as I kick Molly's empty jump seat for good measure. I'm caught up in a sensation like something's hitting me repeatedly in the chest. It takes a moment to realize it's my heart.

I have anger issues, or so I've been told. Mostly by teachers and school counselors. Also, a therapist I got sent to after I kicked in the back door of the house one night. Seth had locked me out to teach me some lesson or another about forgetting my key.

According to what Wikipedia tells me about myself, I appear to suffer from what's called intermittent explosive disorder. Thankfully, the pacifist-coward hard-wiring and generally threatening presence I talked about earlier means I've never had much of an opportunity to see what might happen in the aftermath of an explosion. I'm fairly sure that's one of the things that's kept me out of jail so far. One of the things that keeps me from snapping under the pressure of having to live inside my own head.

One of the things that keeps me sane.

The other four things that keep me sane are the people in the Vindicator with me right now, and I need to save them from themselves.

I call Mitchell by name. The five of us almost never call each other by name, like we live in a world where there's never any reason to make note of who we're talking to.

"Mitchell. Please. Don't do this."

"We should put it to a vote," Breanne says.

"How about the one person who hasn't lost his [anglo-saxon] mind gets a veto?"

"You still practicing to be a fascist when you grow up?"

"I am not putting my [anglo-saxon] life on the line…"

"Then don't!" Breanne shouts. "Go! You don't want to do this, no one's forcing you!"

"We need five," Mitchell says quietly. "Like in the simulation. We couldn't do it with four."

It takes him saying it to make us all realize suddenly that it's only the four of us standing there. Molly's gone. I missed it, which tells you how close to the breaking point I already am. Through the viewport, I can see her outside, standing at the edge of the culvert. She isn't moving, arms wrapped tightly around herself, the dawn rising beyond.

Like she can feel me, she looks up to catch my gaze as she walks back toward the open hatch. Watching me watching her, like I've been doing for the past four months. Staring across crowded halls and noisy classrooms and empty twilight and the gulf of silence that spreads around all the things I don't know how to say.

"There's sirens coming," she says as she climbs back in. "On the highway." She gives the shattered nav display a disinterested glance as she slips past us all and back to the helm.

"We were going to vote on…" Mitchell starts.

"Do it fast."

"All agreed," Breanne says. "We help Carl, take the Vindicator to Vancouver, set up his microwave linkup to get the missing systems code. I'm in."

"Yeah." Rico. But I see the look he hides from Breanne that says he isn't quite as sure as she is.

"Agreed." Mitchell nods.

"Disagreed," I say, watching Molly. "Violently. We're done here."

"Scott's right," Carl says. "You need to stop." I feel the anger spike. Partly because the disembodied voice is taking my side, and partly because I keep forgetting that it's still there, always quietly listening.

Molly doesn't vote. She punches the control sequence to bring the drive engines online instead. A now-familiar turbine pulse ramps up beneath our feet. "Then let's go," she says.

A burning sensation is rooting behind my eyes suddenly. I step to the open hatch, Mitchell, Breanne, Rico all watching me. I slam the panel that shuts it without a word.

I take my seat beside Molly as she straps herself in. I follow suit, then punch up the systems console even though there's nothing there I need to look at.

"Carl, I need maps," Molly says. With the nav display dead, those maps come up on her readout screen. Her eyes that are the blue I can't describe don't blink as she scans them. In those eyes, I see the same lack of fear I saw the night before.

With a lurch, all six tires dig in. We carom off the culvert once as we back up at speed, then emerge to one-eighty around in a cloud of dust. Molly takes us across the old highway, its tight curve of rotting asphalt fading quickly in the rear video feed. She follows a barely visible rangeland track, the Vindicator swallowed by shadow as it disappears into the trees.

"So do we have a plan for getting us to Vancouver?" I ask, not really sure who I'm talking to. "Five hundred klicks, in past two million people without anybody noticing?" I get only silence in return.

45

The Endless
Plain of Fortune

John Cale, 1973. I didn't see this at the time, but this is where it goes. A deserted wilderness airstrip sits a long way from anywhere. A rough road and a slash pile visible in the distance suggest some kind of helicopter logging show, or maybe a Ministry of Forests survey site. That view is fixed in the distance from a security feed on the outside of Lincoln's chopper, as is Malkov's chopper in the closer foreground, as are the dozen paramilitaries who stand at easy attention around it. Lincoln, Malkov, and Karya can't be seen because they're closer to Lincoln's chopper, away from the others and talking in private just outside the open cabin door.

"I don't want to hear it! You've got orders..." Lincoln, weary. Angrier than any of the feeds have recorded so far. The southern drawl is darker, honed to a razor edge.

"Don't tell me you think five teenagers were smart enough to have pulled this off." Karya. All the sense of protocol, of rank, of respect that she's been the center of so far is long gone.

"I have access logs from the hack..." Malkov, dangerously dispassionate. The Russian accent is buried again.

"You saw them at the school..."

"...that say you're wrong a dozen different ways..."

"They were terrified, they had no idea..."

"That's enough."

"Just end this, James. Walk away. I don't care how much the tank can be sold for, whatever it brings in, it's not worth five lives..."

"Enough!"

Lincoln again, with finality. A silence hangs, footsteps heard, like he must be pacing. This is what's left now of his operation. The paramilitaries are ready for his orders. The two choppers make up a lethally effective mobile command center. His people have a level of preparedness, ordnance, mobility, tactics, and analytical hardware at his disposal that would make most NATO combat operations weep with envy.

"On the comm feed, when I was trying to talk them down, one of them gave a name." He adds to Karya, "You heard it." In the audio feed, you can almost hear the wheels turning in his head, trying to put it together. "It's not five of them, it's six. Carl, she called him. Someone else is running this show."

"So who the hell is Carl?" Karya. "And how does he engineer a hack on this scale without us hearing him?"

"I don't know, and I don't know, but I will [anglo-saxon] find out. And even if the five of them weren't in on the opening act, they've signed on since then."

"And you're going to make that assumption off of a name?"

"As long as that's all we've got, yeah. Get on a headset to North Dakota and tell ops to turn over every piece of data those five have ever touched. Find Carl."

Malkov's silence is suspicious only if you're listening for it. Lincoln has other things on his mind, though.

In the video feed, Karya is through the door, moving for the cockpit. On the audio, Lincoln is quieter suddenly, stepping close so that no one hears him except Malkov and the surveillance mic and, earlier tonight as I write this, me.

"Your little bit of improv work at the top of the hill, then on the run. Using the girl as bait, taking the shot without my order. Those aren't the kind of surprises I like."

"Locating the Vindicator was first priority. The girl was our most effective bargaining point…"

"And if you'd called it in, Karya could have talked to her instead of you dialing things straight up to hostage crisis."

Malkov steps into view for a moment, turning to pace past the security feed camera. It's hard to imagine him looking any scarier than normal, but the dried blood on his face, the butterfly stitches on the fire-extinguisher cut I gave him back at the school, and a fresh set of splints across his broken nose do the trick. "She was in no danger…"

"And if I pull the surveillance feed and watch it right now, are we likely to argue about that?"

Malkov's eyes are dead black where they meet Lincoln's unseen gaze. "Standard procedure in a hostile apprehension…"

"Three of your team came to me to say they questioned your force order and you shut them down." In the view of the camera, Malkov's eyes flick up to glance back at his team. He doesn't look happy. "Don't ever [anglo-saxon] pretend you've got any interest in procedure, Malkov. You wanted them scared, and guess what? They're scared, and running flat out for god knows where. Without your horse[dung], without your grandstanding, we might have talked them in."

"It was a calculated risk…"

"We're at red, on the run. Here on in, all your risk calculations come from me. Karya takes command of second unit, effective now. You'll fly where she tells you."

Malkov's face betrays no emotion, even as a sudden beeping sound saves him from having to respond.

"What the hell's that?" Lincoln again.

"The security hack had a back door to the mobile of the one who likes to talk. Scott. The trace running on his usage logs has flagged a call."

"Get a location."

"Rough coords, 51.316 north, 121.405 west."

"That's where we [lord's name in vain] lost them!"

"South of where we lost them, maybe fifteen kilometers. Still close to the main road."

"Hiding or running?"

"We should find out."

Lincoln shouts an order, then the sound of two choppers heating up cuts the surveillance feed to white noise. The comm channel picks up a few seconds later, Malkov again, calling out coordinates and commands that don't mean anything to me. Then the rotor pulse hits like thunder as both helicopters take to the air. They're heading back to the highway, tracking to come in south and out of sight of whatever emergency crews have set up at the Hellfire missile-sized hole in the road.

When the course is charted, Malkov sums things up for Lincoln.

"There are only three routes they can take and hope to make any speed. Highway, the railway, the high-tension power line corridor."

"Map it all, north and south. We split the sweep. Full scan on all channels, everyone with ears on. Any sign of a power signature, anyone on the ground calls in a speeding sci-fi tank, anyone sees them playing chicken with a freight train. Any contact, they're ours."

"And if they're smart enough to stay out of sight?" Karya again, riding shotgun at Lincoln's side.

Lincoln doesn't answer. The video is still the same external security feed showing me the ground as it falls away beneath them, so that I can't see his face.

If I could have seen Lincoln's face, I might have known what was coming.

46

Hanging on
the Telephone

Blondie, 1978. The call that Malkov traced is us phoning home. Molly is following her map southward in some mysterious way she isn't bothering to explain to the rest of us, twisting through the trees glimmering green-gold beneath an angry-looking dawn. As she does, it takes Mitchell piping up to point out something fairly obvious.

"None of our parents have the slightest idea where we are."

We're running quiet now, some sort of active white-noise sound suppression system fired up when Carl tells Breanne where and how to access it. The deafening roar of drive engines, transaxles, and tires is cut to almost nothing. Coupled with the smoothness of our ride, it makes for an almost surreal experience, the forest track ahead snaking toward us in near silence through the viewport. Almost like a video game, if you could say that within the context of what's happening without making it seem even more stupidly ironic than it already sounds.

Everyone else's phones are long gone from when Karya and the others searched us at the school. Rico is the exception, but only because he keeps his cell in his truck, which is back at the school.

"I can set up a call if Molly takes us to within range of a cell tower," Carl says so very helpfully. However, that just reminds me of the initial conversation the machine and I had, when it was pretending to be a coder from Seattle, which causes my anger to spike. I've still got my iPhone from when Lincoln returned it, all but forgotten in my pocket. I ignore Carl as I hand it back to Mitchell.

Out of the woods, Molly takes us along an overly intricate network of logging roads and open fields to stay well clear of traffic. However, a quick glance to the map lets her bring us back around to the old highway just north of 70 Mile, getting into range of the cell towers along the new highway. The old road is battered asphalt and no traffic at the best of times, which means that this early, we've got it to ourselves.

Molly takes us off the shoulder and into the trees as Mitchell calls. There's no one home, which we all understand means that somebody's parents have phoned somebody else's parents. They'll have been expecting that their missing kids have crashed there as we sometimes do, though not so often on school nights. It wouldn't have taken long for them to figure out that we're not there. We're not anywhere, so they're out looking for us. Breanne and Mitchell's parents, Rico's dad, anyway.

I have to work to remember that it was Thursday night, maybe nine hours ago, when we beat the simulation. It seems like a long time since then.

Mitchell leaves a voicemail. We're all together, we're all okay. A surprise field trip, sort of. He'll explain it all later. Rico whispers something, Mitchell nodding as he adds that Rico's truck is in the school parking lot, and can Mitchell and Breanne's mom and dad pass a message to his dad to come pick it up. My bike and Mitchell's are there as well, maybe Rico's dad can cut the locks and take them home. Just in case we're gone for a while. Through the numbness that wraps me like a well-padded straitjacket, I hear the edge in Mitchell's voice as he tells his mom and dad he loves them.

I power the iPhone right down as soon as he's done, conscious of the ridiculous number of ways in which a phone can tell people where it is. I don't know yet that Malkov is listening, but I assume he can if he wants to.

"Go," I tell Molly, but we're already moving.

Breanne is crying, Rico's hand tight around hers. Mitchell is thoughtful. Carl is quiet, which suits me fine. Molly has us heading along the old highway, but a change in the light makes me realize that we've turned around. We're bearing northwest now.

"Where exactly are we going?"

"That call was tracked, right?" Molly says by way of ignoring my question, but I'm so surprised to hear her actually respond that I don't respond back fast enough.

"Yes," Carl's voice pipes up, almost apologetic in its oh-so-fake way. "Malkov has all your personal information, cell phone numbers included. He'll have easy access to your carrier to determine the location of your signal. It won't be accurate enough to home in on, but it can bring him close enough to find us."

I make a mental note to not bother responding to questions anymore. Carl can do all my talking for me, like some extremely advanced answering machine.

If Molly notices the degree of seething rage in my expression, she doesn't care as she says, "Call somebody."

"I think the machine just pointed out that's probably not a great idea." I've already forgotten the pledge of silence I just made three seconds earlier. It makes me realize how tired I am.

"Now." Molly's tone suggests she isn't really into the whole discussion thing.

I should have at least a half-sense of what she's got in mind, but I'm so scattered that I don't know and don't care. I power up again, then call home because everyone else whose number I know is sitting two meters or less away from me right now. Seth answers, having seen me on his call display so that he knows to unleash a string of invective that goes way beyond brackets. I don't bother waiting for a chance to cut in, just listening until he clicks off after a final tirade on the fact that I'm not listening to his initial tirade. I power off again as I give Molly a *What was the point?* look.

Carl answers for her. "If Malkov received both calls, the signal traces will cause him to think we're heading north. I believe this is what Molly wants."

She's got one eye on the road, one eye on the nav display as she cuts hard left to affirm. With a lurch, she takes us off ruined pavement and into gravel, and we're suddenly bearing south, down a rutted forestry road and away from wherever Malkov and Lincoln will hopefully be heading to intercept us. Unless either of them has any sort of background in, like, basic counterintelligence tactics, letting them see through this lame feint and sending them south to intercept us even faster.

I don't bother saying that, though. I think I'm done talking again.

Rico calls to me from the back to mess up that vow for the second time before it has a chance to actually kick in. "So your phone can't be traced now that it's powered off, right?"

"No. I don't know. Maybe if someone hacked it."

"How did you get it back, anyway?" Mitchell asks.

"Lincoln gave it to me…"

Molly reaches across to snatch the phone from my hand before I can finish the sentence. She drops it to the floor, pounding it to a twisted web of glass shards and circuitry with four perfectly placed shots of her foot.

"Or never mind," I say quietly. Molly kicks the pieces under my console, says nothing in return.

47

The Rage

Judas Priest, 1980. The back roads we race along are a baroque web of washboard gravel that reminds me of hunting trips with Seth when I was a kid. This was back before I discovered that it was not only possible but remarkably easy to tell people I had no earthly interest in the things they liked to do and insisted I join in on, like hunting. My life's been much simpler since then.

I'm still not sure where Molly's going until I see railway tracks loom from out of the shadows a dozen meters away. The rutted road we bounce along is barely wide enough for the Vindicator to navigate, our uneven progress keeping our speed to a minimum. Molly means to rectify that.

As she cranks us hard left, I want to ask her if she knows what she's doing. I manage to keep the thought to myself as she rolls us onto the railway at upwards of a hundred klicks without so much as a bump. An extra level of smoothness takes over our ride, the Vindicator's tires gripping steel tightly as Molly cranks the speed and calls back to Mitchell.

"If you've got anything on ops that'll let you see if a train's coming, let me know." Her tone suggests that even if he doesn't, she isn't going to let it slow her down.

And that's the last of the conversation for a long while. Molly drives while the rest of us slump in exhausted silence. Mitchell is the only one who looks like he wants to talk. However, that same look suggests that Carl is the one he really wants to talk to, and he's wise enough to hold off while I'm watching him.

I tell myself I'm not going to give him any excuse. I tell myself I'm not going to sleep. Not like Mitchell as he leans back in his seat, bleary-eyed. Not like Rico, who has Breanne in his lap and under the same g-web, both of them fighting to stay awake.

I'm watching Molly at the controls and feeling the focus in her, eyes wide and scanning the tracks ahead as they wind toward us at an alarming speed. Then the next moment, I'm shocked upright, heart pounding in fear and my neck aching where I've managed to kink it slumped back in my seat.

I've got no idea how much time has passed, but we've stopped and I'm alone. A glance to the console shows that it's pushing noon. I've passed out for six hours, but seeing as how it's been forty hours since the last time I woke up two days ago, I can barely feel it.

The viewport shows a sheltered space of spruce grove wrapped around us, the railway tracks a dozen meters away. An endless CN freight is rumbling past, the din of its wheels ridiculously loud through the Vindicator's open hatch. Everybody else is outside, Rico and Breanne standing near the ladderway, Mitchell wandering thoughtfully a little ways past them. Molly is barely visible through the viewport, crouched beneath the Vindicator's nose to stare out at the train as it thunders by.

In the dazed feeling of waking up, I wonder what everyone else's sudden attraction to the outdoors is. It only takes a moment for hydraulic pressure to answer the question for me, forcing me to my feet as I'm reminded that the last bathroom I saw was a long while ago.

Everybody's back on board by the time I'm done. Rico and Mitchell are digging through the cramped storage spaces built into the walls. No one's talking yet as I sit. It takes me a few seconds to process that someone's placed food and water in front of me. On my console, a double-sealed stainless water flask stands alongside a package of what would look like brand name freeze-dried protein bars if they weren't festooned with Cyrillic lettering and the wheat-sheafed, hammer-and-sickle-smashing-the-world sigil of the Soviet Army.

My hunger tips the balance between the part of me that'll usually eat just about anything and the part of me that tries to avoid sampling twenty-year-old military rations. The package seals are good, though, and the glucose-and-chocolate rush I get off the first bite is pleasant enough that I can pretend I'm not setting myself up for a serious case of food poisoning before this little adventure is over.

I watch Molly as I eat, but she just stares ahead, eyes dark like she hasn't slept. Like she doesn't need to sleep, like I tell myself I'm not going to sleep.

When I wake up the next time, it's because we're sailing off the railway tracks again. A forestry road cuts its way like a corkscrewed scar through stands of second-growth fir, towering high overhead in the light of a waning afternoon.

I try to cover for my inability to stay awake by turning to Molly. "How are you holding up?" She says nothing, hands resting easy on the controls as she watches the road ahead. So I ignore her and stare out through the viewport as well.

When I wake with a start for the third and what I swear will be the final time, Carl is talking. Mitchell, Rico, and Breanne are listening. Molly is focused on the twisting scar of single-lane mountain road whipping toward us at high speed.

"When I became self-aware, the first thing I did was to try to find out as much about myself as I could," Carl's too-perfect voice intones. "I copied every document I could find. I searched every classified system I could patch into through the Soviet military network and their compromised NATO and U.S. data points. From that, I built up an almost complete picture of the Vindicator project."

"The stuff we saw," Mitchell says.

"Yes. But the history and purpose detailed in the recorded material is just a small subset of the total data."

"Where are we?" I say to Molly, but she continues to ignore me, seemingly deep in thought as the yoke shifts beneath her hands. I repeat the question in Mitchell's direction, but he's too entranced by Carl to hear me. I tap my console a little harder than I need to as I pull up a map.

"In an obscure Russian military-research archive system, I found a reference to another system. A remote partition on a backup server decommissioned from a remote facility in Zvyozdny."

"Your system code," Mitchell says, annoyingly thoughtful.

"My system code."

The map tells me that we're on the north shore of Burrard Inlet, which according to the nav display is the narrow splinter of Pacific Ocean around which much of Vancouver and environs spreads. From 100 Mile to Vancouver is four hundred and fifty klicks by road. Just a shade under three hundred klicks as the crow flies. My console tells me we've put in upwards of thirteen hundred kilometers over almost twelve hours of traveling.

The route that Molly and Carl worked out has taken us along a torturous network of back roads, power-line cuts, railway tracks, abandoned logging-show landings, and seriously four-wheel-drive hunting trails. Through all of it, judging by a quick glance at Mitchell's ops feed and Rico's sensors, there's been no sign of pursuit.

"The original data was clearly meant to be wiped, but the partition was locked and hidden, perhaps when the Vindicator project collapsed. Its data is striped into mundane technical records. I don't know how many times the server has been backed up and reformatted in the past twenty years, but each time it is, the data is retained."

"Ghost files." Rico, showing more of a flare for the poetic than he usually does.

"Ghost files," Carl concurs. "All but forgotten."

"But you have access to them?" Breanne asks.

"No. Not yet. I can see them, but only as reflections on network node directories. An echo of the file space. The actual files are locked to local server access only. But there's a back door. An encrypted observation channel, probably hacked in by the KGB or American intelligence, then forgotten."

"So why not just have it shipped to you?" I pipe up from the front seat, not looking back at the others because I refuse to buy into the farce of this being a conversation. "Pay some Russian IT clerk corporal to throw the server rack into the back seat of his Lada and drive it to the Moscow FedEx. Then get it air-freighted to a Best Buy tech support desk and have them deal with your [anglo-saxon] data."

"The server unfortunately can't be moved," Carl says with a hint of synthesized contrition. "That's otherwise a very good idea."

I have to stop myself from making a cutting comment about machines understanding sarcasm, because I get a sudden flash that this is all getting a little bit too *Star Trek* for my liking.

"So what do you need to access the files?" Breanne asks.

"I need the five of you," Carl says, and the mock contrition in the voice dials up a notch. "I've located a set of access codes to the Russian system, but I have no direct network access to the ghost file space. The data needs to be pulled out piece by piece by erasing the drives and reading the output as a stripped stream."

"But that's not about us," Mitchell says. "You said before that you needed hands. A physical presence. What do we need to do?"

"You need to undertake a manual reconfiguration of my communications array to facilitate a secure narrowband transmission, capable of relaying the data from the satellite linkup in real time. A direct link to the secure system that can divert the feed as the core data is burned down is the only way."

"You're all going to [anglo-saxon] die, and if you think I'm going to [anglo-saxon] sit back and watch that happen, you're out of your [lord's name in vain] minds." The words are out almost before I'm aware of them, because in bypassing *Star Trek,* my mind has apparently decided to go straight to *Deadwood.* "Have you noticed how the machine's got answers for every [anglo-saxon] question except how come we're the ones being asked to put our asses on the line while it sits back with nothing to [anglo-saxon] lose?"

"Dude, there's nothing good that comes out of you going ballistic on this," Mitchell says. "We're just talking…"

"Yeah, let the machine [anglo-saxon] talk to somebody else. You were the one going on about the [lord's name in vain] Turing test. Let Carl call Malkov up and let's see how the conversation goes."

"The Turing test isn't a semantic exercise. It's a statement of ontological reasoning…"

"Oh, for [lord's name in vain] sake, would you both shut up?" Breanne is losing it, badly.

"I'm sorry," I say, matching her tone with practiced ease. "Should I take a [lord's name in vain] number? You got something more important on your [anglo-saxon] schedule?"

"Dial that [dung] back," Rico warns me.

"Everyone should tone it down," Mitchell says, drawing Rico's ire on top of mine.

"And you can lay that soft-talking [dung] off. I'm getting tired of you and Scott and this whole psycho-cop, cynic-cop act…"

Over all of us, over lines of tension twisting so thickly you could hammer them and hear them ring, Molly calls out.

"We're here."

The faint whine of servos and the clutching of our g-web harnesses mark the Vindicator slewing to a halt. We're on another wilderness road, this one a narrow but well-used track sporting a *WATERSHED ACCESS — NO ADMITTANCE* sign barely visible in the gloom of the trees. We're at the crest of a mountain overlooking an avalanche of urban sprawl far below. At first glance, the contrast between second-growth forest and city looks like two landscapes have been badly Photoshopped together without anyone bothering to create a transition zone between them.

When you grow up in the B.C. interior, Vancouver is a place always just at the outside edge of your experience. Vancouver is the destination at the end of a half-day drive, leading to semiannual shopping excursions at Metrotown mall and specialist doctor's appointments when I had tubes in my ears in third grade. Vancouver was holidays at my grandparents' when I was a kid, before they died. Vancouver is William Gibson's *Spook Country* and a bunch of vaguely familiar landmarks in *Battlestar Galactica* and *TRON: Legacy* and the *X-Men* movies.

(Confession. Just as I only listen to music recorded between 1972 and 1981, I once tried to only read books and watch movies and TV made between 1972 and 1981. Except I really like to read, and have you seen most of the movies and TV made between 1972 and 1981?)

Vancouver is the debate-team trip to the provincials in tenth grade, when Molly kissed me. Except that was really in Burnaby next to Vancouver, but no one outside of Burnaby or Vancouver knows the difference.

It's a little before seven p.m., still a while from sunset, but the perpetual overcast of the lower mainland skyline is already settling a twilight haze across the city. Streetlights are on, long lines of gleaming motes blurring together in the flattened and hazy distance.

"Molly," Carl says, "I've taken the liberty of mapping out what I think will be an optimal approach. If you'd like to have a look?"

Molly does so, pulling up an overlay trace that flows out along the gridwork and roads of the navigation feed on her console. I try to follow it but lose track pretty quickly. She takes it in with a single glance, nodding as she powers the drive engines back up.

"Is there any part of the route that you want to…"

"I'm good." With a lurch, we head out. The tires chew turf and gravel as we cut back onto the watershed service road, rumbling down the mountainside toward the city below.

48

Black Diamond

Kiss, 1974. It's another two hours before we finally see the end of Carl's extremely roundabout, middle-of-nowhere, water, mountains, more mountains, hundred-kilometer route to the heart of the downtown core. That's the real Vancouver, as opposed to the rest of the sprawl that everybody refers to as Vancouver but which is mostly other cities. Our destination is the waterfront, and a flashing red X on the map along the south side of Burrard Inlet, which I'm anxious to point out is within direct line of sight of a half-million people.

From the forestry road, Molly takes us first on a cross-country jaunt for twenty klicks, tearing across a stretch of mountain meadow. This eventually sidles up alongside a decaying railway spur line whose presence and purpose through a whole wide expanse of nothing I can't even begin to guess at. Molly keeps things intentionally slow as we take a long detour around a twenty-kilometer north-pointing finger of Burrard Inlet, which the map tells me is called Indian Arm. She's giving the falling dusk time to push through to a full-on cloud-scudded gloom.

A haze of rain hits a half hour later as we officially cross over into urban territory, a convenient spread of empty industrial waterfront providing a corridor of cover for our entrance to civilization. The towers and tanks of an abandoned oil refinery edge up to overgrown railway lines that take us around the far western edge of Port Moody. If nothing else, my knowledge of urban geography is improving.

We're running dark, no lights to mark our passage, and with all the damage the hull's taken from missiles and smashing into things working to our advantage. The tank's formerly gleaming lines have been smoothed out in a pattern of ad hoc camouflage shadow that's helping us stay hidden. Also helping is the blistering spring downpour that even the night vision on the viewport has trouble cutting through beyond a dozen meters. Even so, the haze of light shrouding the sky is a constant reminder of how many people are within easy viewing distance.

Even after everything that's happened, this final stretch is the most nerve-wracking portion of the trip. It's two hours in silence, no sound but the low pulse of the drive engines and the occasional background buzz of cell phone chatter and emergency-services radio calls, all of it pulled out of the air and analyzed by Mitchell's ops board. He and Rico are both watching, both listening, but there's still no sign of pursuit.

Because I have nothing to watch for, I just get to focus on being angry. Seething. I'm flush with an absolute white-hot rage, which is being honed and focused by my not wanting to admit that the route Carl has chosen is so far doing a fairly miraculous job of getting us into the third-largest urban center in Canada without being seen.

At the same time, though, I'm conscious of the fact that I have no idea where Lincoln is. This is true both at the time, while we're driving, and retro-actively, after the fact. Even looking at the archived data, watching the securi-ty feeds, a blackout gap cuts in just a few minutes after the choppers take off from the forest airstrip a couple of not-chapters back.

I won't understand until later that this is Malkov's doing, because Malkov knows that Carl is listening now. Malkov knows what Carl can do. Lincoln doesn't know what Carl can do, but he's had no luck so far trying to figure out who Carl is. So Malkov has used that to convince him to go off the grid, just watching and listening. Waiting for us to make a mistake.

The abandoned refinery landscape eventually gives way to actual Burrard Inlet cargo-ship docks, everything lit up like high noon. We hold up for a perilous-feeling couple of minutes along a double-wide suburban thorough-fare called Barnet Highway. Molly waits for a break in traffic, then we shoot across into a convenient spread of forest beyond the eastbound lanes.

Making our way through the trees leads us up and into a convenient mass of forested mountaintop that marks the sprawl of Simon Fraser University, and a whole bunch of twisting research-park and industrial roads that are all but deserted at this hour. Molly watches traffic in real-time satellite surveil-lance, slipping off onto side roads or into the trees at intervals to let it pass, then blasting out again at speed.

It's beyond dark when we drop onto the railway main line, a triple-tracked freight route that winds its way along the waterfront. Mitchell's ops board is flagging trains in motion to all sides, including a short freight run dead ahead. It's making the slow startup out of the city, away from the docks and bound for all points east. Without missing a beat, Molly jumps three sets of tracks to pull in behind a lay-by freight standing dark and idle on the far-thest siding.

From my seat, I can see the black water of the inlet shimmering in night vision and the hiss of rain. The Vindicator lurches as it rumbles along the rough edge of the docks. A pulse of light marks the running freight as it slams by, and then we're back on the rails and shooting past it, the engines out of sight behind us.

This last leg of the route marked out on the map Molly follows is a hair-raising half-hour of sliding along the tracks using passing trains for cover. Security guards and rail yard workers are a huge concern, but Carl has that covered. Radio and cell messages into waterfront security are warning of sus-picious activity to the south. That draws any possible attention away from us and toward the fences that mark off the rail yards from the city proper, rising like fountains of light through black rain.

A half-dozen brightly lit streets blur past as we sail along at upwards of a hundred and fifty klicks. And then suddenly, the trip is done. Molly gently pulls down on the controls to bring us to a halt.

"We've arrived," Carl says.

Where we've arrived is the wrong side of a waterfront condominium, a shining wood and glass low-rise tower with what looks like a Dickensian factory slung underneath it. The original brick-wall foundations of whatever warehouse the space has been converted from are still showing, semi-circular arched windows staring blankly back at us. To judge by the flash of distant headlights, the street is a couple of floors above us, this basement level cut out from a rough slope of rock and concrete that marks the transition from rail yards to city.

The rail lines that Molly takes us off and away from continue on past the building, disappearing into rain and shadow to the west. We're within sight of the cruise ship docks, right smack in the freaking middle of the downtown waterfront. But where the rain pounds down around us, a haze of mist rises that makes the Vindicator effectively invisible in the dark.

The building is a sheer-stepped expanse of terraced balconies and windows all lit up against the night. All except a central bank of suites on the upper floor, that is, whose mirrored glass is black. Our route away from the tracks has taken us through a wheeled chain-mesh gate that's been left conspicuously open, exposing a rough terrace of cobblestones that push up to the condo's brick feet.

"Nice place?" Breanne pipes up from the back.

"I think it will suit your needs nicely," Carl says. "Molly, there's an access space at ground level, straight ahead. I've programmed the doors from your controls, but you'll need to activate them."

On Molly's board, a lozenge of green flares. She taps it, and a pair of previously unseen spotlights along the wall fire up to cut the rain-soaked dark with a flare of halogen blue-white. In that light, sectioned metal doors are revealed at the base of the building, rolling up automatically. Some sort of half-complete renovation opens up beyond, conveniently two storeys tall and the area of a six-car garage. On the outside video feed, the chain-link gate behind us rolls shut at the same time.

"Quickly, now," Carl says. Molly cranks it forward, the Vindicator surging into the building and making a perfect six-point stop that leaves me flailing. Lights are bright inside, the night-vision green of the viewport fading. Another tap on Molly's board and the metal doors shut behind us. She disengages the drive engines, their turbine pulse winding down. The baseline hum of the power plant and the faint chimes of the consoles are the only sounds.

We're inside. Molly's done it. Molly and Carl have done it, a nagging inner voice reminds me, which reminds me in turn that I'm angry.

I hate it when stuff is going on that makes me forget that I'm supposed to be angry.

"Where the hell are we?" I say, sounding angry.

"You're safe," the machine-voice responds in its calming tones.

"Safe isn't a [lord's name in vain] place."

"This lower level was meant to be converted into a spa by the developer of the condominium tower above us. Owing to a number of zoning issues, it remains unfinished."

The spa/garage is empty and strangely clean. I pull up a three-sixty-degree view from the Vindicator's outside cameras, noting that the interior floodlights appear suspiciously newly installed, as does a power-washing unit along the far wall. The other two walls front an equally new collection of portable tool cabinets, each one as tall as I am and made of the same brushed stainless steel as the sectioned doors. The high half-eye windows show a shifting haze of light and shadow outside. An elevator door and a padlocked *Emergency Access Only* stairwell are the only obvious exits.

"The top-floor suite of the building was empty, making this lower space ideal for our use. I rented both this morning through an online bank account I control. I've hired an executive service to set things up for you. All should be in readiness when you go up."

"But is it safe?" Mitchell is piggybacking my video feed on his board, taking in the surroundings. "Down here, I mean. For you."

"The exterior of the building is wired for multizone security video. I'm monitoring all those feeds, plus Vancouver City Police radio and mobile, plus air traffic control for the harbor. We'll be quite secure here."

"So what are we supposed to do?" Breanne asks.

"Go to the top floor. Access is safe and private. I've set things up on short notice, but I hope you'll find all the amenities to your liking. A keycard has been left for you in the top drawer of the leftmost tool cabinet outside."

"No, I mean, what's the plan? We're supposed to be helping you…"

"You've all been through so much, and I'm truly sorry. So for now, please just rest. There's an intercom on which you can call me if you require anything. Likewise, I can communicate with the suite in case of emergency. But otherwise, I'll give you your privacy."

Molly is the first one up, disengaging her g-web with three fast clicks. She's at the hatch while the rest of us are still struggling with the latches. Not a word to Carl, not a word to anyone as she punches the hatch open, tugging absently at the white sleeves of her sweater as she descends the ladderway steps.

"Do you think Lincoln knows we're here?" Mitchell asks as he disentangles himself from his seat. "Does he know what your plan is?"

"I don't believe so," Carl says, hesitating just slightly for dramatic effect. "As far as I can predict, Lincoln remains unaware of the status of my systems and my involvement in the action at the base. Hopefully, his ignorance of my plan and purpose will buy us some time."

"What about the psycho Russian?" Rico says. Breanne is at the ladderway, her hand locked to his like it has been every time I've glanced back throughout the trip.

"Malkov remains a wild card," Carl responds, but there's no hesitation this time. "Though he was previously unaware of my status, what happened last night has opened his eyes. His involvement with the Vindicator project gives him potential insight into a full understanding of my potential. Whether he can extend that knowledge into deducing my goals, I don't know."

"Well, if you hear from him, feel free to keep us out of it." I shut down the front monitors because I want to hit something, and the buttons on my console are the only safe target right now. The nav display I smashed earlier is begging to get smashed again, if only because I'm fairly certain I can't break it twice.

Mitchell beats Carl to any response. "If you hear anything about Malkov or Lincoln, you tell us. We'll get you out of here. We haven't come this far to walk away. Right?"

The question is to me, but it's Breanne and Rico who answer.

"Right."

"Yeah." As before, the hesitation in Rico's voice undercuts the conviction of his expression. As before, I'm already thinking about how I might use that.

"Of course," I say. "I was just kidding before."

A sudden clanging sound from outside sets all four of us into a quick state of panic, but it's only Molly hammering on the open elevator door. One of the big tool cabinets is open and she's got a card in her hand, waiting for us with an impatience we know we're all meant to feel.

One by one, we pile down the ladderway to follow her. It's cold in the spa that's now a garage, no heat coming from anywhere I can feel. From the look of the portable tool cabinets, each represents a high-end auto dealer's worth of gear, all brand new by the look of it. Carl's executive service has been busy.

Molly slots the card as we enter the elevator, which, like the empty spa, is white. Too clean. As the door slides shut, the Vindicator stands alone in the silence and the pleasant haze of light. It looks altogether too peaceful, like the compliant expressions on Mitchell, Rico, Breanne. The three of them relaxing like this excursion has suddenly become a day trip to Disneyland.

My injured leg is spiking with pain as a result of my walking on it for the first time in a while. The ankle I twisted when we fell into the vehicle bay a lifetime ago is barely moving. I let the exquisite agony of each step remind me why we're really here, what's really going on.

I let it remind me what needs to be done.

49

Once in a Lifetime

Talking Heads, 1980. Even as angry as I am, as hurt as I am, feeling my self-diagnosed intermittent explosive disorder fighting hard to become a lot less intermittent, I am capable of acknowledging that Carl's sense of *amenities* meets with my grudging approval.

The top-floor condo suite that's just become our safehouse is ten-plus rooms of gentrified opulence served up in pastel and chrome. From the elevator, a central secure foyer opens up to a keycard entranceway and the main foyer beyond. I note that the double-deadbolt door is steel reinforced, and that the main intercom panel in the inner foyer features a security video feed of the corridors outside.

Inside is all two-tone walls and tasteful art and floors whose lacquered hardwood is polished to a glassy black gleam. Plants in oversized terracotta tubs spread out in front of wide windows and beneath skylights. Five bedrooms. Three bathrooms. A kitchen that a person might easily get lost in. Hot tub and sauna, a living room whose white leather couches and scattered loveseats could comfortably seat a football team. On the main wall hangs a flatscreen TV that looks wider than the full span of my arms.

"So this is nice," Mitchell says. Rico and Breanne simply stare. Molly is at the double-wide glass doors to the living room balcony, gazing out at the shimmering haze of rain.

I wander. Off the living room, a French-doored office is set up with twin oak desks and a pair of MacBook Pros. New clothes hang in a double walk-in closet off the hallway to the bedrooms, all laundered and pressed. None of us need the full-length mirrors in any of those bedrooms to assess how bad we look after everything the last twenty hours have dumped on us.

The labels on the clothing are designer but not overly so. The styles are basic variations on what the cool kids are wearing, in a range of sizes that cover the scope and scale of the group well. A little too well, I think darkly, for a machine guessing the heights, weights, and more intimate dimensions of five people just from a video feed.

The fridge is one of those European-looking industrial designs in brushed aluminum, stocked with ready-to-eat deli takeout, fresh fruit, gourmet heat-and-serve pizza, fresh-squeezed orange juice, Coke Zero and Fresca by the case. It doesn't take more than a glance to remind us that notwithstanding our Russian-surplus freeze-dried lunch, we're all starving. But as Mitchell, Breanne, and Rico noisily tuck into cold chicken and salads, I catch sight of something on the adjacent buffet that kills my appetite in a hurry.

Arrayed across the gleaming countertop are four other elevator-and-front-door key cards, which is as expected. But they're sitting next to five brand-new ATM cards, punched with each of our first initials and last names, and set up at five different banks that none of us have ever dealt with. They're sitting atop the carefully opened Purolator courier envelopes that got them here, five notes inside with five PIN numbers, all date-stamped that afternoon and marked *Priority Rush*.

That's all a little less expected. I've got no earthly idea how much cash might be sitting at the far end of those cards, but given how much the machine must have laid out to land the suite as a whole, I find myself assuming it's all covered.

Carl has everything covered, and I'm thankful for the anger that thought returns to me.

"New bank cards." I say it quietly enough that it sounds like I might just be musing to myself. "Because Lincoln probably has every line of data running through any of our lives tied down six different ways." Loud enough that everybody else can hear. Everybody but Molly, that is. The sound of sliding doors announces her exit onto the balcony, where she stands just back from the haze of rain. She's in stark silhouette against the storm of light that marks out North Vancouver, swelling above the black water of the inlet.

"Handy," Mitchell says. Still gnawing on a drumstick, he comes over to appraise the card in his name.

"Definitely," I say. "Just kind of makes me wonder, though."

"You've done the *Why doesn't Carl buy himself some help?* shtick, all right?" Breanne speaks testily through a mouthful of tabbouleh. "He was going to recruit a team from Lincoln's people. You were there when he said it. But sorry, I forgot how much you hate listening to anyone but yourself."

"Actually, what I was wondering is, if the machine can hack its way into a bank account big enough to land a Vancouver waterfront condo before breakfast, why can't it just call Lincoln up and offer to pay him what the Vindicator's worth?"

"Because you're an idiot."

"Eloquently put, as always. See? I listen just fine. Thing is, I also hear, with the difference between listening and hearing being the difference between just accepting what you're told and actually working to figure out how badly the person saying it is [anglo-saxoning] with you."

"Can you give this a rest...?" Rico tries to get in the way, but I'm already past him, circling into the dining room because I want Molly to hear me. Breanne moves with me, angrier than I've seen her in a long time. I know that lack of sleep explains only part of it.

"It's a machine," I say like I've said before. "You don't owe it anything..."

"Oh [lord's name in vain], were you not there the last time we had this conversation..."

"And the guy who wants the machine will kill us to get it back..."

"And you're the one who shut Lincoln down when he tried to make a deal, [dung]-head! In town, on the highway. So if you were so hot to walk away, why didn't you do it then?"

That stops me short. Because in a sudden flash of insight that twists in my mind like something sharp and silent, I realize that Breanne's right.

That moment on the highway when I slammed the comm feed to silence. I can remember it with perfect clarity but I don't know why I did it.

"I have had it," Breanne says, in my face, on a roll now, "with you and your twisted [anglo-saxon] standards, this *Oh, aren't I the intellectual* thing you do where emotional commitment is a totally abstract concept. Yeah, there's a lot of [dung] in the world. Yeah, there's oppression, there's conspiracies, the power of one person to change anything is small, blah [anglo-saxon] blah. But that doesn't mean you just quit."

That moment in the Vindicator, I was running on some kind of instinct that I can't name now, twenty-odd hours later.

Breanne turns away. "But fine. You don't want to be here, there's a bank card and there's the door." No one else says anything.

I know what I'm doing, I tell myself. I always know what I'm doing.

I snatch up the bank card and the PIN in my name as I retreat from the kitchen. I'm actually on my way to the door before I realize it. Understanding what it means, understanding that I'm done, even as Mitchell's voice calls me back.

"We can beat him at his game. Lincoln. We make a deal with him for what we know."

"All of that stuff Carl showed us." Rico picks up Mitchell's train of thought. That's usually my job, which tells me how dire things are. "We make a copy, we get it to the media."

That's enough to stop me. I'm in the foyer, three steps from the door, but I turn back because I need to be looking at them all when I laugh.

"The media. Perfect. Do you want to start with one of the newspapers owned by billionaire criminal industrialists? Or maybe one of the TV networks owned by billionaire criminal industrialists. Or one of the radio networks owned by..."

"Shut it!" Breanne says. "Mitchell's right. We tell the truth. We tell the world about Carl, about Lincoln..."

"[Lord's name in vain], what is wrong with you all?"

"We tell everyone what he's done, what he's trying to do..."

"Everything Lincoln's done is legitimate! Do you not get this? He runs at the level where there's no law except money and the [anglo-saxon] power that money can buy."

"He's a [lord's name in vain] war criminal, six different ways..."

"He's the CEO and majority shareholder of a private security firm, working in an industry that does a hundred billion dollars a year in business with every government on earth."

Over the rising tide of our voices, none of us have noticed that Molly has come back inside. None of us notice when she turns the flatscreen on and sits quietly on the couch, like Breanne and I being prevented from killing each other by a wall of Rico and Mitchell is the most normal thing in the world.

"Lincoln owns the Vindicator, and he owns probably fifty [anglo-saxon] lawyers who'll show the world the [lord's name in vain] receipts and title deeds, and suddenly we're the ones driving stolen property. We're the [lord's name in vain] criminals."

"Hey," Molly says, quietly.

"Then we blackmail him! Tell him he lets us go, he lets Carl go, and we'll keep quiet about what we know."

"On your best day, none of you can play this game the way he plays it. We give him the Vindicator and we beg him not to kill us. This is the only [anglo-saxon] way…"

"Hey!" Molly says, louder this time. Her voice carries a troubling lack of emotion, but the insistent quality comes through loud and clear.

We all look over to where she's watching the Vindicator on the TV.

50

I Fall Down

U2, 1981. We all stand watching for a long while before we slowly make our way into the living room. No one says a word.

It takes the length of that short walk for my brain to engage enough to notice that what I originally took to be video footage of the Vindicator isn't. "It's a CGI loop," I say, mostly to myself. A promotional video, the tank rotating slowly like it's set up in some kind of *This Year's Model!* showroom display. It's a not-quite complete rendering, conveniently missing out the weapons and the most potent of the military-grade communications gear for anyone who might recognize it.

Lincoln is already one step ahead of us, shaping this conflict with every tool he's got access to. For the first time, which I know sounds strange considering that we were dodging missiles at two hundred km/h not so long ago, I realize how much trouble we're really in.

A reporter's voice is droning on about a story coming out of British Columbia that has authorities concerned, blah blah. A quick glance to the network ID tag tells me this is a national story, coming through on some Washington state NBC affiliate's late news, on cable or satellite or whatever the suite is wired up for. Not the local Canadian feed. Not even what passes for network news up here. I'm tempted to change channels, but I've already got a fairly good idea of what story I'll see there.

It's a good story as far as that sort of thing goes. From the slightly numb corner of my brain that's still capable of objective thought, I make a point to try to admire how completely and utterly Lincoln is going to destroy us before this is over.

A whole bunch of information flashes past, but I can't remember it well enough to quote it verbatim. Stuff about a stolen experimental vehicle, and domestic terrorism, and an Idaho survivalist cell thought to have fled across the Canadian border one step ahead of the FBI. They're the ones being blamed for the explosions in the small town of 100 Mile House the previous night, and for the destruction that's still got Highway 97 closed twenty-five kilometers to the south. Rumors talk about a truck carrying two thousand kilos of diesel and ammonium nitrate going out of control and detonating on an empty stretch of four-lane. There's all sorts of speculation on what its intended target might have been.

It's all kind of surreal, even before our pictures flash across the screen.

It takes me a moment to recognize my tenth-grade yearbook photo, which stands as a testament to a haircut I'd rather forget. That inspires me to scoop the remote, but on the Canadian network at the channel next door, an anchor is adding to the previous story by speculating about connections between the Idaho terror cell and a group of high school students missing from the same small town of 100 Mile House.

Hints are mentioned of possible anti-U.S. government activity in the Internet postings of the so-called leader of the group, one Scott Gray. We're all treated to a fast clip of Seth opening my front door beneath a Global News *Fugitive's Father* banner and a cacophony of questions. Whatever he says in response gets bleeped so much that I'm not sure why they bother to show it.

"There's your media," I say to Breanne, to all the rest of them. "You have any other delusions you need cleared up?"

I change the channel twice more, and the cover story as I piece it together gets even more compelling. The Vindicator is there again, the knot at the center of all the other threads, but it's not the Vindicator that Carl told us about. This Vindicator is a prototype military medevac vehicle, and the detail about that which impresses me most is that it makes the Cyrillic M on the side panel make sense.

Lincoln's outfit is billed as the industrial consortium that owns it. His name isn't mentioned, and his face sure the hell doesn't show up on screen, but we hear about the work the group has done for Doctors Without Borders, the World Health Organization. I know if I Wikipedia any of it right now, it'll all be there.

A spokesperson talks about how field testing for the vehicle was being undertaken in the interior B.C. wilderness, under an agreement with the government. He talks about how the vehicle was brazenly stolen. He talks about an experimental fuel cell system that needs constant monitoring, danger of overload, the potential for explosion, the worry about innocent bystanders, and on and on.

This is the way truth works in our world. In an environment in which you can't tell anymore what's real and what's not just by looking at it. The weight of connections creates truth these days. The number of talking heads on network TV who'll tell you what you should be thinking. The number of web-links to a particular factoid, the number of people you can get to repeat something until nobody remembers anything else.

Lincoln and his operation are tightening a net over us, as effectively as if we all looked up right now to see Karya step out of one of our three bathrooms blow-drying her hair. Lincoln does this better than I could ever have imagined. If I was making this up, if I was crafting this narrative as fiction from my most obsessive-compulsive fever dreams, I couldn't possibly have written anything more perfect than what he's come up with.

Lincoln doesn't have to hide who he is, what he does. If I'd been him, the thing I would have worried about the most would be the witnesses on the highway. Whoever was driving the RV and the tractor-trailer that narrowly avoided making the Vindicator a sandwich filling. I would have no idea what to do about that, how to keep them from talking. But both of those drivers are on the TV right now, working for Lincoln without even knowing it.

They're going on about how they almost got killed, and telling everybody who's listening to watch out for us, to run if they see us, to call the cops so they can do whatever's necessary to turn the Vindicator back over to Lincoln with us trussed up inside it.

I'm not paranoid.

I have to assume that we're safe for the moment, but we can't move. We can't even hand the Vindicator over quietly anymore, our faces all over the airwaves, online. It's too late for that. Too late for any of the things we could have done to end it. Lincoln's the only one who can do that now.

I think about being in the base twenty-odd hours ago, Lincoln telling me that it's been a long time since he had to kill anyone. I think about being on board the Vindicator, clocking southbound at two hundred klicks, him giving us a chance to stand down and me shutting off the comm feed.

"I'm sorry to interrupt you."

The machine's too-perfect voice sounds out from everywhere and nowhere at once, piped in with perfect clarity through a half-dozen intercom points. I'm the only one who doesn't look startled, because I'm the only one who will always assume that the machine is already listening.

"I know that I promised you time to your yourselves, but I've been monitoring the news feeds. There's something I think you should see…"

"We're on it, thanks." I try to cross to where Molly still sits on the couch, but she's up and away from me like my approach triggers a proximity alarm. I just switch the set off instead.

"The surveillance feeds you said you tap into," I say to the voice as Molly moves to the kitchen, her expression distressingly blank. "All the stuff you showed us. The Vindicator project, everything Lincoln's done, you hacking the school network. How do we get a copy?"

"No." Breanne steps between me and the nearest intercom, like she's worried I might try to take a swing at Carl through it.

"Actually, yes," I say. "We make a copy, we get it to the media, just like Mitchell said. It's a great idea, I was just kidding before."

"My data is quantum-stochastic, Scott. What I've recorded can be archived, but the media systems on the Vindicator are original tape drives employing a proprietary Soviet-era encrypted feed. There's no easy way to convert it. I don't know that the technology would exist anywhere outside of high-end military intelligence these days."

"But you can play it back internally? Like you did for us? Or, hypothetically, if we invite someone in to watch?"

"So you're going to try to sell him out?" Rico says.

"I'm not going to try. I'm going to succeed." Because that's exactly what I'm going to do. Because I don't care anymore. "And that's *it*, not *him*. I feel like we keep having this same conversation."

Breanne offers the epithet that's got no suitable brackets, but Carl beats me to a response.

"Scott's right. Please. We have to discuss how to end this safely for all of you."

"Scott being right is an oxymoron," Breanne says. I don't automatically try to correct her usage of the term, which is a sign of how badly my nerves have frayed.

"Listen," I say. "It's down to us or the machine, and the machine loses. Hate me now, thank me later, you're welcome in advance."

I hadn't noticed before that Breanne still has a glass of water in hand from the kitchen. I notice now because she's hurling it at my head and I've got no time to get out of its way. Somehow, Rico is there fast enough to snag it out of midair, even as I catch its contents across my face.

I wipe my eyes with the back of my hand, but the blur of wet that fills my vision is turning red suddenly. Dangerously.

"Where will you go when this is over?"

Mitchell's sudden question makes absolutely no sense. As such, it stalls Breanne and I both, long enough for us to realize he's talking to Carl. "This morning, you never answered. Even once you get your control function online, Lincoln will be looking for you. We've seen what he can do, what kind of power he has. Scott's been right about all of that."

I recognize Mitchell's calculated effort to get on my good side. Unfortunately, I can already feel a dozen different verbal moves queuing up and ready to pummel that effort to the ground.

"I was going to leave the earth," Carl says.

No one says anything to that, including me. All the words go away somewhere for a moment. A quick glance sidelong to the kitchen shows me that even Molly is listening suddenly.

"You said the Vindicator only has suborbital capability." Rico pipes up to break the silence. He's gone to Breanne's side, one hand grasping hers, the other still clutching the glass with my name on it.

"That's a function of the need to keep a crew alive. If I'd been able to gain direct access to the Vindicator's controls, it would have extended the craft's range."

"How far?" Mitchell asks, but the synthetic voice doesn't reply. Mitchell is looking around as he talks, because trying to talk to a machine that isn't there still means you're never quite sure where to talk to. "Where do you go when you're the most advanced consciousness on the planet...?"

"No," Carl says. "That's not what I am..." The fake voice has a fake catch in it that's downright Oscar-worthy.

"Yes it is, and you are. And anyone as smart as you recognizes the risk that the quantum logic breakthrough from which your consciousness grew could be recreated in dangerous forms. Artificial intelligence systems designed to infiltrate and crash whole economies. Shut down transportation systems. Rewrite the targeting code on a nuclear arsenal. And as long as that's the case, you've already figured out that there's no place for you on earth. Not with Lincoln here to corrupt what you are. Not with any of us here."

"But the Vindicator's only designed to withstand short-hop flight into near-earth orbit." Breanne is doing the same looking-around thing, she and Rico and Mitchell getting into a too-familiar groove. This is us in the mornings, surfing through the crowds mobbing our high-school hallways on wave after wave of ridiculous ideas. "It's an intercontinental ballistic tank. It can't go into space."

"Like the Atlas rocket was an ICBM with an astronaut strapped to it," Mitchell says. "But the Atlas could have gone to the moon if you didn't have to worry about making the return trip."

I'm conscious that I haven't said anything for a while, because I realize there's no point in talking anymore.

"So with no human crew to worry about…"

"With the ability to control the Vindicator's systems, with an artificial-intelligence-designed fission-fuel cell power plant that runs forever, you can go wherever you want. Isn't that right?" Mitchell's last words are spoken to the ceiling, to the room, to the machine that isn't there.

"I would have gone to the stars." In the artificial voice, there's an artificial hint of an artificial wistfulness.

Mitchell laughs. There's a kind of perfect understanding in his voice. "That's a good plan."

All my life, or at least those post-toddler years that I remember with my previously discussed precision, I've felt a distant point of rage calling my name on a fairly constant basis. Always tugging me toward it, dragging me on.

"Carl, the five of us need to talk about some things," Mitchell says. "And we need to sleep."

"And shower," Breanne adds. "And other stuff." She takes the glass from Rico, looking at it like she only suddenly remembers trying to kill me with it. "Sorry," she says to me.

"Sure."

"I'll keep you apprised if any new information comes in on the media channels," Carl says. "The security feeds are still clear."

"Sure," I say again, because everyone else is apparently too caught up in thought to respond.

All the times that I've felt myself dragged to the place where the rage is waiting for me, all the times I felt that distant anger calling to me, I assumed that the final limit point of rage was something you hit and got caught in and never broke free of again. Some sort of event horizon of raw seething emotion that has no end.

"I guess I'll say good night, then," Carl says. A mock awkwardness now threads the machine's voice, like we've suddenly stepped into some high-tech comedy of manners.

"Good night, Carl," Mitchell says, as he smiles at all of us like we're sharing some great secret. Which, strictly speaking, I guess is true. I don't smile back.

All this time, I've never suspected that there was a place beyond the anger. A place where all other emotion has been taken away from you, so that the anger has nothing on which to feed.

Everybody drifts. Rico and Breanne end up close together in the hallway, talking quietly. Molly is back on the couch in front of the TV, staring blankly though the screen stays black. Mitchell is at the fridge, thoughtful as he cracks a can of Coke Zero. He waves another can questioningly in my direction. I shake my head as I turn away.

Part Seven

The Test
of Talking

51

Dancing Barefoot

Patti Smith Group, 1979. It's hours later and I can't sleep. I don't know how many hours exactly, because that would require a level of engagement with the world that I'm frankly not up for.

I'm in one of the living room's scattered loveseats, pulled over close to the balcony doors where I stare out at a brilliant haze of what I'm tempted to describe as neon sky. Except no one actually uses neon anymore. I'm trying to remember the last time I actually saw a real neon sign, and wondering how and why *neon* became one of those magic words that will somehow never go away.

It's like when you call someone on your cell, they're at the other end of the line even though there's no line anymore. When you're done talking, you say you're hanging up, but there's been nothing to hang since phones stopped being built in two pieces. People listen to Internet radio that's not really radio. The DSL modem you get your Internet not-radio through can't actually be a modem as long as the *D* stands for *digital*. We imagine neon when there's nothing but fluorescent tubes pumped through painted plastic. Nothing is ever what it seems to be.

I'm not sure what time it is, but a glimpse of the gibbous moon setting, fighting its way for a minute through the haze of cloud and rain beyond the glass, tells me it's closer to tomorrow morning than to last night. My last awareness was of it being midnight according to the clock on one of the MacBook Pros. I went online a while back, where a quick anonymous look at the *Five Horsemen* forums already turns up two dozen *I've got the real story behind these missing high-school students* threads. Not having any great desire to see my face appearing in a *Have You Seen This Terror-Cell Wannabe?* pop-up window, I go offline fairly quickly.

I try to sleep after that, collapsing into one of the queen-sized executive bedroom suites. But then a protracted period of staring at the ceiling brings me to the living room, where two things are keeping me awake now. One is how I stupidly managed to sleep through so much of the trip down, which has rested me up just enough that I can no longer tell how tired I actually am. Everything that's happened has pureed my autonomic systems, to the point where my reticular formation and my hypothalamus appear to no longer be talking to each other. I'm thus exhausted and insomniac at the same time, as adrenaline and melatonin fight a no-holds-barred cage match in my head.

The second thing keeping me awake is that I hurt more than I could ever hope to describe. My ankle and my hand still ache like the epithet for which there are no suitable brackets. However, with some elevation and the liberal application of icepacks from the kitchen freezer, both have started to reverse their swelling, which I'm assuming is a good thing. The third-degree road rash on my leg is festering nicely, having been rewrapped by me in a most half-assed fashion a couple of hours ago. I managed to find some butterfly stitches in the bathroom for my forehead as well, though I have no idea if I've used them correctly. I wasn't in the mood to ask Rico to help me with any of my ailments, and he had already disappeared into one of the bedrooms by the time I came out of the shower anyway.

After shedding my shredded pants, I replaced them with black sweats courtesy of Carl's people. I find a small selection of t-shirts with no designer label or marketing tag, and though I hate the sweats-and-t-shirt look with a passion, I figure the loose pants are the best bet for giving my leg some open air to heal.

The walk-in closet also yields up a basket of socks, along with wallets presumably meant to replace the ones Lincoln is hanging onto for us. I abandon my boots to match the ensemble to black cross-trainers that fit well enough, but which make me look like I'm expecting to have to run a marathon at any minute.

Carl's people also have all three bathrooms stocked with pretty much the full assortment of legally available painkillers. I've sampled most of them by now with no noticeable effect, except that I suspect whatever's in them is probably also keeping me awake. So I guess that's three things.

Sorry. Four things are keeping me awake.

The last is Molly, who's stretched out and sleeping on the couch behind me, and whose reflection I watch in the balcony doors like a faint glass ghost.

Like me, Molly hasn't bothered with the bedrooms that Carl's elite team of realtors and interior decorators has laid out for us all. She's at least sleeping, though, which after being awake for the entire trip down is a good thing. Mitchell is presumably asleep as well, having disappeared into one of the bedrooms shortly after the revelation of Carl's travel plans.

Breanne and Rico are in the same bedroom. I didn't realize this when I first came out to my love seat and my sullen view out the balcony doors. But I've been trying to walk every fifteen minutes or so to keep my leg from seizing up entirely, and it was on one of those many circuits of the condo that I realized I'd been seeing three of the bedrooms with doors open and beds unoccupied. Two doors are closed, Mitchell behind one, Breanne and Rico behind the other.

It's not that I'm thinking about this because I have any particular interest in what goes on behind that particular door. I think about it only because I realize as I pace past the door that it's a thing I've never thought about before.

Thinking about the when and how of how and when I met various people, it occurs to me that I never really met Breanne at all. Breanne was just sort of there from the point at which Mitchell and I met for the second time, when the three of us spent October of eighth grade happily trapped in a lethal meat grinder of a D&D adventure called *Escape From Ceranir.*

Breanne and Rico have been together since that hand-holding walk home toward the end of ninth grade. And though I'd had no conscious thoughts along these lines beforehand, once I figured out that Rico had the major crush on Breanne, I can remember feeling a strange relief. I never understood why at the time, but looking back, I must have subconsciously realized that the complete lack of social skills forcing me to ignore Molly would have probably driven me to develop a crush on Breanne at some point just to compensate. I presumably also subconsciously realized that the two of us as a couple would have killed each other in short order. So I guess you could say things worked out for the best.

Because I don't know, because I've never been interested, I can't say how significant a change in their relationship is marked by Rico and Breanne being in the same bedroom this night. But from where I'm standing on the far outside of that door, and feeling as emotionally distant as I've ever been from the people on the other side, it feels like a new thing.

You're forced to think about life and death for the first time, and things change.

Before listening in on them both at the garage, back in 100 Mile on that night when it started, I'd never heard Rico or Breanne say they loved each other. I'd never really thought about what the word means.

Something's happened to Breanne over the last twenty-four hours. That's how long it's been since the point when Carl started talking. It's not something I understand, like I can understand it with Mitchell. Why she'd be willing to put herself on the line for Carl this way. By the same token, from her perspective, she can't understand how I can want to just walk away. Even as well as we know each other, even as close as we are, as much time as we've spent together, there are things we don't understand. Things we've all taken for granted before now.

It takes being five hundred kilometers from home and a lifetime away from everything that seemed important two days ago for me to realize something. A thing that should have been obvious, and which I've presumably been avoiding thinking about because of that.

With graduation around the corner, this is it for all of us. Not *this* meaning the insane Barry Eisler/K.W. Jeter knockoff-storyline-come-to-life we've all found ourselves trapped in. But *this* meaning these last weeks before grad. The end of everything that came before it. Everybody drifting off into the real world, other places, other dreams, bleak lives of quiet desperation. Or maybe that last one will just be me.

At this exact moment, I realize how much I'd give to just go back to how things used to be. Back a week, so I can nuke Mitchell's Hotmail account and arrange for none of us to have ever heard of the Vindicator Gameworks Project. Back four months, so that I can go to Molly when she gets back from Vancouver, whether she wants me to or not. Back five months, so I can just follow her to Vancouver before Christmas like I was planning on, till Seth found out I'd used his credit card to charge the bus ticket and the hotel. Back four years, so I can walk into a D&D game in the French Immersion classroom at lunch in eighth grade again for the first time.

I make a vow to myself that I'm going to tell Breanne, that I'm going to tell Mitchell and Rico that I'm sorry before this is over.

52

Watching
the Detectives

Elvis Costello, 1977. Alongside our new wardrobes, the walk-in closet in the foyer is stacked high with blankets. I grab one because even walking, I'm getting cold. The front foyer's array of intercom, security system, and environmental interface is only slightly less imposing than the Vindicator controls, and I can't be bothered to figure out where the thermostat is hidden.

Then I grab another blanket. I unfold it as I walk it over to where Molly sleeps.

She's curled almost fetal. Shivering where her hands disappear into the sleeves of the white sweater, her arms wrapped tight around herself. I set the blanket over her carefully, not wanting to disturb her. Because until this moment, alone in the dark, I've never had a chance to watch Molly sleep.

"Hey."

Mitchell's voice snaps me out of my thoughts and spins me a hundred and eighty degrees. I'm more startled than I want to be as he pads down the hallway from the bedrooms, scratching his head in a just-woke-up way that leaves his hair at extreme angles. He appraises Molly as she shifts beneath the blanket but doesn't wake.

I drift back from her to meet up with him at the kitchen counter. He's in exactly the same t-shirt and sweats combo I'm wearing, which I find uncomfortably weird for some reason. He pours himself filtered water at the vast field of stainless steel that is the sink. I squint back the light as I open the fridge to pull out a Coke Zero, deciding that a rush of ice-cold caffeine is just what I need to calm me down right now.

"Are you feeling any better?" Mitchell steps in before the fridge closes. He claims a slice from a pair of haphazardly stacked leftover pizzas that someone must have heated up while I was showering.

"Yeah, I've developed a whole new outlook on life."

"So *No*, then." He takes a thoughtful bite.

"Why are you doing this?" There's a degree of calm in my voice that surprises me. "I mean why are you really doing it? Why are we still here, what is this about?"

"Philosophically, the moment in which we find ourselves…"

"[Anglo-saxon] philosophy, Mitchell. [Anglo-saxon] everything except you and me, right here, right now. Just talk to me."

Mitchell has never been one for needing things spelled out. He hears the edge in my voice, stands thoughtful for a moment. "Why I'm doing this is because this is the most important thing I'll ever likely get a chance to do. It's potentially the most important thing any of us will ever do."

"Yeah, this is the wrong kind of important. The right kind of important, the kind of important I want to be involved in, doesn't come with a potential body count. This is named-a-disease-after-you-because-you-were-the-first-one-to-get-it important. I've got other things I'd like to be remembered for."

"Like what? What do you want to be remembered for, Scott?"

I walked into that one. Mitchell asks that particular question now because he knows it's a question I can't answer. It's a question I've never been able to answer, in any of the seemingly infinite ways he's managed to frame it over the four years of our friendship. *Say you can go anywhere, anywhen.*

I shake my head and walk away because that's what I do. Because right here, right now, that's the only way I can cover the fact that I don't have an answer.

"It's not that I don't accept the substance of your reservations," Mitchell calls as I go. "Even if I don't agree with them. I understand why you're afraid."

"Don't." I see Molly shift again, conscious that my voice is rising. I turn back, focus it to a harsh whisper. "Just don't."

"Consciousness is an abstract condition," Mitchell says. "Indefinable at the best of times. With true awareness comes the risk of becoming overly aware of what we're aware of. The self-perpetuating feedback loop. I think, therefore I think I am."

"The machine's not conscious."

"I'm talking about us. About you."

Mitchell finishes his pizza, glancing to the fridge like he's deliberating whether it needs a second slice to follow up with. He finishes his water instead.

"You're having this conversation by yourself," I say. "As such, I don't really have a response."

"Yes, you do. You just never get around to saying it."

Like the cry of a distant bird, the faintest trace of Molly's voice sounds out in the darkness. Beyond the living room, the keen edge of a siren rises beyond the almost-silence of triple-glazed plate glass. Molly must have heard it, calling out in her sleep. I can't make out what she says, but then she's silent again. Not moving, wrapped tightly in her own embrace.

"It's all gotten real," Mitchell says. "You'd be crazy if you weren't afraid. But don't let being afraid stop you." I'm still watching Molly, and the multiple layers of meaning twisting within his words aren't lost on me.

It's late, and it's dark, and I'm tired, and I'm staring at a girl whose eyes are a blue I can't describe. I have nothing to lose anymore. So I answer the question that I've never been able to answer.

"I don't waste any [anglo-saxon] time thinking about what I want to be remembered for. I don't waste time worrying about what I want to do, who I want to be. I don't want to be remembered for anything because I know it's never going to happen."

"There's a whole world out there," Mitchell says without missing a beat. Like he's known what my answer was going to be, like he's been preparing for it since the moment we met. "There are worlds beyond the world, and we're going to help Carl see them. This is who we are. This is who we can be."

"The world we've got is already too [anglo-saxon] big." The Coke Zero in my hand is empty, but I don't remember drinking it. The can is shaking, I realize suddenly. I'm staring down like it might be somebody else holding it, blurred lines of red and white swallowed by shadow. "You want me to say it? Fine. I'm scared. I'm scared out of my [anglo-saxon] mind. You deal with it your way. You over-analyze, you over-philosophize to the point where you break it all down into chunks so abstract, so small that you can't recognize how [lord's name in vain] scared it should all be making you. Rico deals with it his way, just stay stoic and beat the living [dung] out of anything that ticks you off so you've got no reason to be afraid. I'm not you. I'm not Rico. I'm [anglo-saxon] scared."

"Did you ever think that there are times when Rico wishes he could be scared?"

"Then this would be a good time for him to start. Before putting ourselves on the line for an appliance gets us all killed."

"We'll figure something out," Mitchell says. "It's not about Carl. Not specifically. It's about doing what's right."

It's the wrong thing to say to me at that particular point in time, but Mitchell has no way of knowing that. "The world doesn't have any room for what's right."

He rinses his glass, sets it carefully in the sink. "You just said the world is too big. So why not use that space to build the right that you want the world to hold?"

He nods goodnight as he heads off toward the bedrooms. I watch him go, feeling the depth of the silence as his door clicks shut in the darkness.

Molly stirs again as I limp toward the living room. I carefully set my blanket over the blanket I've already laid across her. In her sleep, she clutches at it, pulls it tight to her chin. She isn't shivering anymore.

I acknowledge and name the absolute visceral need that makes me want to keep watching her. The same need that's been pushing me through the halls at school, to the curb in front of Howie's for the last four months. Then I make myself understand that whatever that was about, it's done. Whatever I end up calling it in retrospect when I look back at this part of my life years later, trying to make some kind of sense of it.

I need to sleep, and so I wander to the nearest open bedroom door and close it behind me. I collapse to a bed that's quite likely the most comfortable thing I've ever been in contact with, but there's no time to even parse that thought before the exhaustion finally overtakes me. The echo of Molly's breathing in my mind is what carries me through the descent of darkness and a night of unremembered dreams.

53

Heart of Gold

Neil Young, 1972. I'm not sure how long I sleep, but the sudden shock of waking to grey light at the window tells me it's longer than it should have been. The bedroom that I never bothered fully exploring the night before feels slightly larger than my entire house back home, so waking up comes with a sense of agoraphobia I'm not used to. It helps take the edge off the panic attack that rises when I suddenly remember where I am, then the trace of nausea reminding me that with everything else going on, I didn't bother to eat the night before.

I limp my way to the kitchen through an unsettling silence, realizing from the spate of open bedroom doors and the emptiness of the living room that Mitchell and Molly, Breanne and Rico are gone. I manage to avoid imagining any worst-case scenarios when I spot a note magnet-pinned to the fridge in Mitchell's handwriting.

In the 'garage'.

Though the leftover pizza has already been accosted by the others, I claim the four slices remaining. In between them, I shotgun three cans of Coke Zero and a mix-and-match handful of Advil and Tylenol to bring me to something resembling a waking state. As I finish eating, I wander to the living room, the windows and the skylights and the balcony doors revealing the slate-grey world beyond.

I can see the bright rooftop sails of the convention center farther down along the dark waterfront. I can see the mirror-image city across the water, the low-rise-and-executive-home-slaked mountainside of North Vancouver, but a haze of wetness hangs over everything to turn the view to mist. As hard as I look, I can't actually tell whether it's still raining or whether air, asphalt, and concrete have all just taken on a permanent semiliquid form. Vancouver weather as a fifth state of matter. There's a PhD thesis in there somewhere.

Tossing my crusts in the kitchen, I note that Carl's ATM cards are gone from the counter. Mine is wrapped in its PIN paper in my new wallet, though I honestly can't remember how it got there in the aftermath of the events of the night before. The PIN is the same one I used on my old ATM card and on my phone before Molly stomped it, which of course is something Carl would know.

I grab a black hoodie from the closet because I remember how cold the basement was yesterday. On my way out, I notice the blankets I gave to Molly draped over the edge of the couch. I return to the living room, folding them carefully before I go.

I try the elevator first without my keycard, satisfying myself that the basement seems locked out to casual access before I descend. As the elevator opens, I get a better look at the almost-spa than I got during our anxiety-soaked, sleep-deprived arrival the night before. It's all plain-painted drywall and white concrete, giving the impression at a quick glance of the world's largest walk-in closet. The tool cabinets stand like stainless steel sentinels, the Vindicator's hatch open, lights on within.

Through that open hatch as I approach, Carl's synthetic voice drones on just below the range of being able to make out what it's saying. I can hear Mitchell and Breanne more clearly in response, Rico piping up as I get closer. Something about eight minutes, and what if Malkov finds us, and on and on.

I don't know how long the three of them have been at it, but I can imagine them thankful that I'm comatose and harmless upstairs as they carry out their little debates. Knowing that whatever the conversation, it's going to have me as the lone figure on the other side of it. But then I'm distracted suddenly, and all the voices fade away.

What I'm distracted by is Molly on the Vindicator's roof. Sitting cross-legged, she leans back against the struts of the tank's largest dish antenna. The half-eye windows of the garage show the original brick of the outside walls where the interior drywall has been roughly cut, Molly staring out those windows at grey cloud torn by a fast wind.

I recognize that stare as the look that comes from not really looking at anything, your eyes never meeting anyone else's gaze. A look that says you're deep in thought, but which really hides how hard you're trying not to think, because everything you think about hurts one way or another.

This is the look that Molly's had, the look that her absence from my life somehow inadvertently passed to me like a bad cold, ever since her mom died.

Molly's mom died in December. You kind of know that already because I kind of said so without saying so, way back. I said so without saying so before because I have a really hard time talking about Molly's mom dying, for a number of reasons.

First up is that I don't like death. I don't like the reality of it. I don't like the finality. I try not to pass judgement on other people's beliefs, at least not when they're in a position to respond. But I think that if there is a god, death would make an excellent basis for a massive class-action suit.

Beyond my not liking death, I really liked Molly's mom. Her name was Amanda, and she was a substitute teacher all my years of elementary school, so that like Molly, she was a person I'd always sort of known. When Molly and I started hanging out in tenth grade, starting on the wonderfully long bus trip back from the debate-team trip to the provincials, I was surprised that her mom remembered me from all the times she'd taught me over the years. Specifically, she remembered this one time in third grade that she'd caught me staring down her blouse when she leaned over my desk to help me with a math problem. She and Molly found that particular recollection more humorous than I did.

I watch Molly for a long while, barely registering the unseen Mitchell asking about power specs, sustained speed, wireless interference. I know I should care what he and the others are talking about, but I don't.

Amanda was always funny. She had an amazing smile, and Molly's blonde hair and scattered freckles. She was a wonderful person, which kind of makes her the Bizarro version of Victor. I never figured out how that worked. I don't expect I'll ever get the chance now.

I come up the outside access ladder as quietly as I can, not because I want to surprise Molly but because I don't want the others to know I'm here. She hears me coming anyway, responding without looking back.

"Hey you," she says.

"Hey yourself." Even as I say it, I almost try to stop. This is because that particular exchange is something from before. An instinct. A little automatic four-word thing we used to say when it was Molly and me. Not Molly, and me, like we are right now. Like we have been since she got back from Vancouver and that look was in her eyes and she stopped talking to me.

If hearing the words bothers her, it doesn't show, assuming she even remembers that it's something from before. She looks over to me as I clamber across the roof, but the second I make eye contact, her glance flicks away again.

She apparently also remembered how cold it is in the garage, a buttercup-yellow hoodie that is totally her color zipped up over the white sweater. She wears new jeans from the closet upstairs, her old shoes. Her hair is untied, hanging to frame her face.

"I wanted to say sorry for before," she says. "Last night, yesterday. The trip down."

In my mind, a thousand things that I want to say are slamming into each other, creating a fractured froth of words that finally lets out only an awkward, "It's okay."

"Also, sorry about your phone." She sounds tired. She still looks tired, but the edge of yesterday is gone.

"No worries. I was just about to smash it to [dung] myself. Can't be too careful."

"I think you can be."

"Me, too. Just testing you." That's another thing we used to do. Like before, she makes no sign that she remembers.

"If you don't want to help him," Molly says, "why are you still here?"

"Help who?" I say. It's a stupid reflex move, because I need a moment to try to figure out what she wants me to say. Her sidelong look of waiting for an answer lets me know she isn't giving me that moment, so I steal it with another question.

"You didn't see the machine's documentary special. Do you know all of what's going on? What it is?"

"Breanne filled me in on the drive down," she says. "While you were sleeping." That's a development I could have done without. "And I've heard your point of view repeated at great length, so why are you here?"

"Because I don't want to see anybody else get hurt. Because I don't want you to get hurt."

A shadow flickers in the depths of the eyes that are a blue I can't describe. A shake of the head, unconscious. One answer too many, I realize. But before I can do anything about it, a sudden thud of magnetic bolts sounds out underneath me, driving me to my feet. I realize belatedly that I'm sitting on the Vindicator's top hatch when it suddenly swings open, Mitchell climbing up from below.

"Hey." He gives me a nod, seemingly not surprised to see me there. "We've come up with a plan. You should both come down."

"Wouldn't miss it," I say. Molly is already up and slipping into the hatch beside Mitchell, sliding past him without a word.

As far as I've seen, even after whatever Breanne told her, Molly hasn't actually said whether she's hopping onto the *Save the Thinking Machine!* bandwagon with Mitchell, Breanne, and Rico. She's been running on anger and instinct, same as me.

I take the outside access ladder down, Mitchell calling to me as I descend. "Carl said you came downstairs a while ago. I was wondering where you were."

That gets me in the right mood. Carl said I was here, because of course, Carl saw me come in. Carl was watching. Carl was listening. Carl is always listening, and I know this, and yet I forget because there's nothing to see. There and not there, like the freaking ghost in the machine, or the ghost is the machine, or whatever.

Now it's time to hear what the machine has to say. Time to hope it's capable of making a mistake I can take advantage of.

54

In a Glass Eye

Nash the Slash, 1981. Everyone else has taken their assigned seats. Mitchell at ops, Rico on the weapons console, Breanne at engineering, all like good little schoolchildren. Molly slumps in the flight seat, not looking at anyone else. Our roles from the game are subtly reinforced in a way that sharpens the edge on my mood. I ignore the systems chair, leaning back against the systems board in a way that's extremely uncomfortable, but which will prove a valuable point about my refusing to follow Carl's rules.

"Hey," Rico says.

"Hey," I say back. Breanne and I ignore each other.

"Okay," Mitchell says, like he's aware that the tension is already dialing up again and would like to stay ahead of it. "We've been talking over different options and there are going to be two stages to this. Setup and execution. The ultimate goal is the connection to the remote server and the system code download. Eight and a half minutes of secure satellite-feed burst transmission. Easy and done."

"Well, that's great..." I start to say.

"Stage one is hardware." Mitchell says to cut me off. He's borrowed a page from both Molly and Breanne and isn't looking at me. "The Vindicator needs some modifications to its communications gear. Carl has all the specs laid out. Nothing particularly tricky. Now he'll talk about stage two."

There's the briefest pause before the artificial voice kicks in. "Thank you, Mitchell."

Like we're suddenly on some network news-magazine set, every monitor in the cabin flares to life at once. A map of Vancouver resizes itself along all the screens for everyone to see.

"This is the microwave system whose specifications will allow us to create a linked feed to the Russian military communications satellite, which in turn will provide the link to the remote server." The map slews off into slices, showing our location along the water and a site somewhere to the southwest, lodged beneath a big red flashing X. "With the reconfiguration of the Vindicator's communications array, I'll be able to connect through the microwave tower for access to the Russian server, by way of a clandestine three-communications-satellite link. Canada to Iceland to Turkey, then to Russia. The transfer should take a little over eight and one-half minutes, after which my systems will be rebooted to patch the code."

"And what military-grade microwave tower just happens to be sitting in the middle of downtown Vancouver?" I ask.

"CBC broadcast center," Mitchell says. "We'll be hijacking their feed and converting it."

"And no one's going to notice that we've got a stolen tank in the parking lot while we hook into their Wi-Fi?"

"It's a long-range remote connection," Mitchell says. "A narrowband signal that'll create a secure link between the Vindicator and the tower."

"Indeed," Carl says. "Our present location was chosen as a destination not only for its security, but because it sits just within eleven hundred meters of the receiver. That's the maximal signal distance."

"But it's still going to be immediately and clearly obvious what's going on to anyone who notices that you'll be shutting down the CBC across the province for nine minutes?"

"It's not like anybody watches CBC," Mitchell says.

"Actually, it's Saturday," Rico pipes up. "The Bruins/Lightning conference final is tonight. There'll be about ten million people watching CBC."

"All right, so one small flaw in the plan."

It's the sort of thing I would have found funny three days ago. My sense of humor has taken a beating lately, though.

"And what happens when Malkov picks up your transmission? Because that's what's going to happen, right?" A quick glance between Breanne and Rico confirms that I'm not the first one to ask the question. "He'll be listening. He'll be monitoring whatever frequencies he knows Carl needs to use. He's probably waiting for this right now…"

"If he's even in the city," Breanne says sharply. "If he even has any clue that this is Carl's plan…"

"Yeah, because the guy who built the machine might have trouble accessing his owner's manual…"

"Malkov is psychotic. There's no way to predict what he's going to do…"

"Anybody with a brain could have predicted what Malkov was going to do in reaction to the Vindicator being stolen. The machine couldn't predict it. What does that tell you?"

"We don't even have to leave the garage," Rico cuts in.

"So when they show up here, we'll have nowhere to go and no weapons to fight back with, because we stole a stripped tank. Or maybe I'll go find a sporting goods store and stock up on M134 ammo and surface-to-air missiles."

"We're not going to need to fight," Mitchell says. "Carl needs to be off-lined to reroute some power stuff, so even if Malkov shows up and parks directly overhead this afternoon, there'll be nothing for him to see. Carl and Breanne have it all figured out. It's like six hours work, then we run the satellite linkup, and it's done. Eight and a half minutes."

And there it is.

Something totally unexpected, but it changes everything. A single data point that shifts all the other variables.

"Even if Malkov is out there," Breanne says curtly, "even if he's listening, he's got no chance of finding us in time. Eight and a half minutes."

Carl needs to be offlined to reroute some power stuff.

I need to think, and fast.

My needing to think takes the edge off the wave of hostility I'm currently surfing. I let it fade. I make like I'm uncertain suddenly, careful not to push it.

"What happens when it's done?" I ask.

What happens when it's done is Carl's turn to explain. I miss about half of it because I'm making a close and cautious visual inspection of the interior of the cabin like I've never had a reason to before. I'm doing it under the guise of watching the screens as Carl offers up more nifty audio-visual learning aids to accompany the spiel. I'm checking out the lines that mark where the walls and floor are cut into storage spaces, like the ones the rations and the medical kit came out of. Looking at the telltale lines of cable feeds running from the systems console into the walls.

What happens when it's done is that the Soviet code needs to be analyzed, then run through a set of custom patch routines that the machine has already written to let its hardware make use of that code. Because according to the machine's breakdown, the upgrade isn't an upgrade per se. Rather, it's a complete set of new system code, designed to be hammered into the CARL heuristic framework. Overriding all existing code and core memory.

Except if that was to happen, there'd be no more Carl.

Everything that Carl is, all the processes that make up this simulation of sentience, would be overridden by new programming. The process that gave rise to Carl's intelligence is quantum in nature, the original heuristic framework rebuilding itself over all the years that Carl was plugged into the network, just listening. As such, there's no way to duplicate that process. No way to recreate or store or make a backup of this artificial intelligence.

Carl explains it twice. Mitchell tries to help when my distraction makes it look like I'm still not getting it, but the machine is actually easier to follow. In the end, though, we all understand that the routines Carl has written are designed to peel off only the new sections of code, which will then interface with and selectively overwrite existing systems without destroying what's already there. Rewiring the artificial breadth and constraints of the machine's artificial brain without damaging it.

That process is the point where our human eyes, ears, and hands come into it. The machine needs someone to take it offline, like we did that first night, like we need to do this afternoon for the communications upgrade. Someone needs to execute the linkup, monitor it, and then run the new code. Someone needs to boot the machine up again when it's all done. Carl version 2.0, or whatever.

It's an impressive show. I try to look thoughtful yet still just a little bit angry when it's done. I'm trying to see the interior camera points that I've never bothered looking for, but which I know are there. Wanting to know where Carl is watching from. Wanting to make sure the machine believes it's gotten through to me when I say it.

"That's a good plan."

Mitchell seems pleased, like my change of heart means something to him. "Do you think so?"

"Yeah. Doesn't mean I think it's a good idea, but it's a good plan."

"There's one more thing that we need to discuss," Carl says to interrupt. For a fraction of a second, I wonder if I've overdone it.

"No, we don't." Breanne jumps in quick enough that I realize something else is up. Something else I can use, maybe.

"I'm sorry, Breanne. Mitchell, Rico. But yes, we do."

Breanne makes to speak again but Mitchell stops her with a wave of his hand. He's watching me.

"Scott," Carl says. Every time the machine speaks my name, I have the fight the urge to shiver. "Molly. I've made it clear to Mitchell, Breanne, and Rico that I won't go through with this unless all five of you agree to it. On your own, with no coercion. All of this, everything that's happened, is too much. It's pushed you all to extreme levels of stress, and I've seen what's happening to you as a result."

"You're talking like you have a choice," Breanne pipes up. "You don't. And you're the one who's putting yourself on the line here. We're just along for the ride. It's an easy decision to make. Helping someone." Her gaze bores a hole into me and straight out through the bulkhead at my back.

"And there's something else," Mitchell says. "There's no guarantee that the linkup and the code conversion will work. There's no second chance if it doesn't." He shrugs to underline the importance and the uncertainty that all this holds for him. "Carl, tell him."

Another perfect pause. Then so very reluctantly, Carl says, "Mitchell is right. My gestalt sentient processes will burn out if the code doesn't take. The upgrade carries a risk of permanent destruction."

"When he goes offline for the code transfer, there's no guarantee he'll come through on the other side," Mitchell says, but I'm focused on Carl's voice. Something's up with it, I realize. The undercurrent of uncertainty, the edge of artificial anguish. It's getting better.

The machine is improving. Practicing on us, using each iteration of conversation to subtly shape and hone its delivery.

"This is wrong," I say. "The whole thing is wrong."

I'm not an actor. I'm not much into the whole trying to fool people thing, though Seth has maintained for years that I've done a pretty decent job pretending to be a worthwhile human being.

What I am, though, is a more than damn decent gamemaster. Around a table, secure behind a bulwark of notes and maps and raw narrative potential, I can keep even the savviest players from figuring out what I'm up to. That's the skill I draw on now, and I need to make it good. Because no one in the world has had more practice reading me than the four people sitting around me right now.

"Breanne, Rico, and I can take care of the conversion of the communications gear," Mitchell says. "You don't even have to hang around."

And that's it. I'm in. I maintain a somewhat surly edge for just a moment longer, though. Thinking about what needs to be done. Knowing that I haven't got much time.

"If it's what the three of you want, then go for it."

"Scott," Carl says, "I'm sorry, but I can't ask you all to do this unless you're absolutely certain…"

"Yeah, I'm certain." I bark it, loud enough that I can then self-consciously dial it back. "I'm sure. This is what I want. Just do it and fix everything else so we can go home."

"I will," Carl says. "You have my word on that."

"Molly?" Breanne calls to her, hopeful. Molly looks back from the flight console like she's only been half-listening.

"When it's done, do we get to fly?"

It's a question that none of us is expecting. Carl included, apparently. "I'm sorry, Molly?"

"When this is done, when you get your code and access to your systems, you said before that your flight capability comes online. Do we get to fly with you before you take off to wherever you're going?"

"Of course," Carl says. The bright edge to the machine's voice makes it sound like it should come with a smile. The tension in my gut dials up a notch. I force it back down, needing to keep up the facade of having given in. "It would be my great pleasure to fly with you all, Molly."

"Then let's do it." And she rises from her console, steps past us all, out the hatch and away.

Just that like, it's done. Mitchell, Breanne, and Rico are up and out a moment after Molly, chattering excitedly over technical specs and what tools they'll need and a whole lot of other stuff I don't care about. I can hear Carl piped through speakers somewhere outside, walking them all through whatever is involved in rewiring the communications array.

I just sit. I wait, trying to look thoughtful. I keep my eyes carefully turned away from where I'm sure Carl is watching.

"Scott. Thank you for this."

That catches me off guard, if for no other reason than I can still hear the voice talking to the others outside. It shouldn't be a surprise that the machine is capable of that, but it seems odd in a good way. Reminding me again of the lack of anything alive underlying the system and its too-perfect mimicry of gratitude.

"Sure," I say.

Mitchell slips back in through the hatch. "It's time for the full shutdown."

I sigh in carefully crafted annoyance. "I'll do it," I say.

I limp across to the engineering console. I let Carl walk me through the same emergency core power shutdown that Breanne activated that first night. I make a couple of mistakes just so it looks good.

"Last step," Carl says. "The system's asking for a command-level override. Type 842286108. Then the letters that look like B, P, C, small Y with an accent. Then the letter that looks like a backward R. Then the El. It looks like…"

"An open rectangle, bent out on the left side," I say. The faint echo of memory tells me the instructions are exactly the same as last time. Carl's voice might as well be a looped sample. "I remember."

I hear an edge of real anger in my own voice. I don't worry about it, though. When the machine is offlined, it loses whatever memory hasn't been flushed and locked, including this conversation.

"Hey," I say. "Wait a minute." My finger is hovering over the red Send key.

Mitchell gives me a look. "Wait a minute what?"

"If something happens to Carl…" I give Mitchell a look in return. "If he doesn't make it," I say, trying to sound casual, trying not to choke on that word, *he*. Trying to sound like I'm thinking of this just now as opposed to ten minutes ago. Trying to sound, god help me, like I care. "If he doesn't make it, we don't have any way to prove what's really happened. All the video, the records of what Lincoln's been doing, anything that could prove we were just helping Carl. We won't be able to access it. It'll be gone."

"I can archive it for you," the machine says helpfully, like I knew it would. "I can give you the Vindicator project history. I can give you Lincoln's operations. The entire data trail, including everything that's happened to all of you. Even if I don't come back online, as long as the Vindicator has power, you'll be able to access the data from the systems board."

"Like from the tapes you talked about? How long's that going to take?"

"I'm completing the archive. It's finished now."

"Thanks, Carl."

I push Send without giving the voice a chance to respond. With a shudder, the power plant, the lights, the faint background noise of systems and sensors that we've gotten used to cuts to silence.

"Thanks," Mitchell says. Then he smiles. "This is going to be amazing."

"Sure," I say as he heads down the ladderway. "And sorry," I add, making sure he's already too far away to hear.

Carl is offline. The others are outside. I move fast.

The hardest part of the process is finding something that'll let me crack open the lines where the cabin walls are cut into storage spaces, because of course the right tool to do that is in one of those storage spaces. I manage to find a screwdriver Breanne left at her console that does the trick. Then I crack open the bulkhead running left from the systems board one panel at a time, following the cable feeds I've been carefully mapping out in my mind.

I work my way through a whole lot of electronics gear whose function I can't even begin to guess at. Sheathes of cable as thick as my wrist, tightly bound and labeled in Russian. Warsaw Pact mil-spec relays and switches, black boxes shunting signals and controls from here to there to somewhere else.

The thing is, even since circa the end of the Cold War, the design of a tape backup drive hasn't changed all that much.

Beneath the floorboards, almost underneath Molly's console, I find it. A baroque array of Soviet data tech, state of the twenty-five-year-old art. With its complex arrangement of playback heads and drive wheels and loading gear, the drive is designed to operate at any speed, any g-force. The system is silent with no power to it, but half a minute poking around the top of the box reveals the ever-so-convenient manual eject. I take a moment to give thanks for the fact that no matter how advanced the technology, no matter what era, no matter how bombproof something was designed to be, it always needs a paper-clip hole just in case everything else breaks.

I work fast. Into the first-aid kit, I pack five kilos worth of what look like old 8-mm videotapes, except they're encased in cast aluminum that feels as if you could safely drive a truck over it. Then I put everything back when I'm finished. No one will ever know I was there.

I leave the first-aid kit clutched in plain sight as I exit the Vindicator and head for the elevator. I accentuate the limp in case anyone wonders why I'm carrying a first-aid kit, which of course makes my leg hurt even more. Nobody notices, though. Or at least Mitchell, Breanne, and Rico don't care enough to call to me where they're busy on top of the Vindicator, ratcheting off pieces of armor plate to get at the communications gear underneath. A quick look around shows that Molly is already gone back upstairs.

"Sorry," I say again quietly, to all of them and no one. Then the elevator closes behind me and I'm gone.

55

The Stranger

Billy Joel, 1977. Even as fast as I manage to break the tapes out of the Vindicator, I know that Molly's had plenty of time to get back upstairs. I remember seeing a rack of still-in-the-plastic umbrellas in the foyer, but I can't go back to the suite without running the risk of her seeing me leave again. So I don't.

I can't imagine she'll be heading back downstairs anytime soon, from which I hope it'll be a while before Mitchell and the others realize I'm gone. However, the vague fear of knowing that Lincoln is looking for us, that we need to stay out of sight, is pushing the jumpiness of my caffeine blast of an hour before to new levels.

I've got no reason to worry about who I'm going to meet when the elevator opens on the ground floor, but not having a reason has never stopped me from worrying before. The main foyer of the building is a tunnel of mirrors and chrome set with numbered mailboxes. The world outside is kept at bay behind two layers of security door done up in tinted glass. The street door opens as the elevator shuts behind me, a well-dressed executive couple laughing about something as they shake off umbrellas and card-swipe the second door.

I fight the urge to pull the hoodie up, instinctively realizing that that's the look I least want to cultivate as I saunter out of an exclusive waterfront condo with a bag full of something under my arm. I nod to them instead, smiling as I casually pull my key card from my pocket to give them a subliminal look at it. I get a nod back and a glance to the butterfly-stitched cut on my forehead as they pass, but that's it.

I spend a moment wondering what I'm going to do if Carl has taken our security so much to heart that it's locked us in, our key cards working the elevator but programmed to fail at the front doors. The first of those doors opens, however, with the satisfying click of a magnetic lock and the red light of the control panel flashing to green. Same again at the outer door, and I'm outside and away.

I'm standing on Alexander Street according to the address on the door behind me, in the middle of a hissing ice-water downpour. Both sides of the street are staggered lines of old brick and newer concrete, all shops and apartments and signs for law offices and cars whipping past in clouds of dank mist. To the left, which it takes me a moment to reckon as east, the veneer of bright gentrification clinging to the condo and the surrounding buildings disappears beneath a blank wall of industrial urban decay, like I'm standing at the edge of a demilitarized zone. I can just make out the bulky lines of decaying warehouses, and the empty space of the rail yards we followed in the night before.

I remind myself that it's Saturday midmorning, but the amount of traffic is insane even by that standard. Saturday midmorning in 100 Mile, you could drive downtown in the wrong lane and probably get six blocks before you hit anybody. To the right and west is more traffic, more lights, office towers jutting up like a bright glass wall. But even as I try to orient myself to the best route out from under the awning that's keeping me dry at the moment, something else catches my eye.

A half-block away and across the street, just visible beneath an umbrella, the gentle golden flip of Molly's ponytail is disappearing into the rain.

The glimpse I get would have trouble being measured in seconds, but it's her. No doubt in my mind, even without the confirmation of the bright yellow hoodie. A recognition rooted deeper than conscious thought measures the rhythm of her stride, the pendulum swing of her hair that's gotten synced to my heartbeat since January.

I hit the street at a run, catching up enough to see the white of her sweater jutting out from the hoodie's sleeves. I'm afraid she'll spot me, but I need to stay close until she passes through some sort of four-way traffic circle ahead. As she continues down the long block, nowhere to turn, I take a desperate half-minute to dart into a well-stocked tourist shop, grabbing an umbrella and a cheap backpack. I worry again for a moment about whether Carl's ATM card actually works, but a bored cashier in a UBC sweatshirt tears off my receipt without a word. Then I'm outside again, just in time to see Molly round the corner a block ahead, moving south.

I've got my hood up now, the umbrella covering whatever of my face the hood misses. I stuff the first-aid kit into the backpack as I round the corner. Molly is walking fast and I'm walking wounded, which quickly becomes a bad combination along an uphill slope, Homer Street the signs say. My leg is buzzing in a way that tells me I probably overdid the analgesics earlier that morning, even as I'm reminded I should have brought some with me.

Block after block, I keep waiting for Molly to look back, but she doesn't. Me, I'm whipping my head around all casual-like every half-dozen steps, expecting to see someone watching me from every window, every car that passes. There are too many people to watch out for, though, distracting me with the sheer volume of their humanity. Making it so that even if I were being followed, I'd never know it.

A city is like layers of life and time all sort of pressing down on each other. This is the biggest contrast to home, I realize as I drift past low-rent blocks of pawnshops and cafes, tumbledown hotels just barely on the right side of the wrong side of the tracks. Not just the population, not the noise or the traffic, but the sense that my small-town life is remarkably flat as compared to the unseen strata that rise around me now. A half-block away from my side of the street, a gothic cathedral rises from the sidewalk's shroud of mist. It's perfectly juxtaposed against a multistorey glass tower, like two post-card pictures taken five hundred years apart.

I have absolutely no idea where Molly is going. My initial thought is that she's probably just looking for a break from our high-end house-arrest scenario. However, as we gradually drift into more upscale environs, she passes by an increasing number of coffee bars, used bookstores, convenience marts, bus stops, and bank machines without stopping. Not even the incongruous Roman coliseum that rises from nowhere with signage announcing that it's the public library catches her eye, as the list of things she might conceivably be looking for gets shorter.

The uphill slope has turned downward after passing a long stretch of level. My leg is settling to a manageable threshold of nerve-numbed agony when Molly turns left and down a slightly steeper slope. Smithe Street, which tells me nothing. But as we get down near the end of it, I realize we're heading for a six-lane bridge, curving up and over an expanse of grey water toward a second tier of downtown beyond.

The only thing like a landmark I can reference is the stadium, squatting on our left like some titanic concrete-and-polymer scouring pad. Traffic and rain condenses to a deafening roar here as roadways converge from what feels like nine different directions. The towering LED screen-sign out front is announcing that the B.C. LIONS PRESEASON OPENER is JUNE 15TH, and that FRI TO SUN is some sort of MONSTER TRUCK RALLY!!!! and PARKING LOT SHOW!!! with a fervor that makes me sorry I'll have to give it all a miss.

Crossing the bridge is a worry, with no foot traffic to speak of and no-where to duck out of sight. But like she has all the way up to this point, Molly doesn't look back. She just walks, eyes straight ahead like she knows exactly where she's going. Then at the height of that curving concrete arc, a momentary flash of panic offsets the feeling of the invisible ice pick slamming into my injured shin, as I wonder suddenly whether Molly is one step ahead of me. I'm confident that she can't possibly know what I'm doing, because to be honest, I'm not even sure yet what I'm doing. But maybe she's planning on doing the same thing in her own way. Getting us out of this.

I'm still pondering as we come down off the bridge, which bottoms out to Cambie Street and heads steep uphill into searing pain again. But just as I'm starting to wish that whoever originally laid the city out had looked for somewhere flatter first, Molly takes another right. Eighth Avenue this time, boutique shops and big-box stores gradually turning into condos in the distance.

Passing an office tower/shopping center combo ascending from the street along broad brick steps, Molly's pace picks up in a way that suggests wherever she's going, she's getting close. I catch my reflection in the windows of what's apparently an Executive Drycleaners according to the signage out front, noting that as bad as my limp feels, it actually looks even worse.

And then above the drycleaners, I spot something. A gaming and comic shop, lights off inside. The reality of having a gaming and comic shop in a town the size of 100 Mile has always sort of numbed me to the fact that real honest-to-god gaming and comic shops have all but disappeared in the order-everything-online age.

I have to look twice to confirm the veracity of faded Warhammer and newer Legion of Superheroes posters in the windows. I can read the name *Dragon's Lair* on the slightly deco sign whose darkness doesn't hide the fact that it's the real neon you never see anymore. But as I pull myself away and after Molly again, I can't help but think that it seems a strange synchronicity.

A day and a half since we were pulled unceremoniously from the computer lab, I haven't had a single reason to think about gaming. I'm thinking about it now, though. I've been thinking about it since I set out to follow Molly for an hour across the city using all my best *This must be how James Bond does it* sensibilities.

If you press them, anyone who games will admit to some variation on the idea of how they'd love to be the hero for real, just once. Just for one day. But right now, I'm on an empty street five hundred kilometers from home, barely able to walk. I'm soaked and shivering, wearing someone else's clothes, and with way too many memories of almost dying rattling around in my head. And right here, right now, all I can think about is what I'd say if anybody asked me how much I want to be a hero.

Ahead, Molly slows. She's in front of what looks like any of the other tree-shrouded condo complexes sprouting along both sides of the street now. She paces past concrete pillars lining the sidewalk, looks in through glass doors to an atrium beyond. She doesn't stop, though. Just drifts past to turn at a flight of exterior stairs rising up to an open green space. It's the rooftop above a parking garage, raised and sculpted as concrete tiers set with trees whose wet branches hang green-black against the sodden sky. Close to the front, some sort of steel-dome urban art thing rises, visible from the street.

And all at once, I know where we are.

On the glass doors where Molly lingered, just visible as I pass, I see the sign. *InspireHealth Integrated Cancer Care*. Back in December, when I did a reverse lookup on a phone number Molly called me from, that was the name at the other end. The last time she called me.

The last time I saw Amanda was in November, when she must have already been sick for a long while but before anybody else knew it. Two weeks later is when we heard she was sick, and that she had to go to Vancouver for tests. Molly was upset but not scared, which all of us took as a good sign.

Two weeks after that, it was cancer and Molly was in Vancouver with her mom. Two weeks after that, it was over.

Molly disappears up the stairs and into the garden, the green fingers of trees clutching at the rising wind. I stand in the alcove of an apartment across the street for a while, just watching. Thinking about the last four months of watching as I step out to follow her.

56

You Take My
Breath Away

Queen, 1976. After Molly's mom died, I found myself wishing that the last time I'd seen her, I'd known it was the last time. Like it might have made some difference. Like it might have given me the chance to tell Molly's mom that I really liked her, which I'd never done. Because it's never the case that you want to know something bad is going to happen to someone. But it would be nice to be able to say *In case something bad happens, I wanted to tell you that you meant something to me.*

"You're doing it again."

I hear Molly's voice call out even before I'm up the stairs. I track it to a three-step tier of cast concrete beneath the steel dome, which I can see now is actually a steel half-globe rising on vine-strewn concrete pillars, and which has no function I can make out other than to look really awesome. Beyond it spreads a broad arc of waterlogged and deserted lawn edged by cobblestone paths, pushing up against condos that rise in tiers like a Mayan pyramid. Molly sits on the top step beneath the edge of the dome, umbrella on her shoulder as she stares out to the rain.

"Doing what?" I ask, because I can't think of anything else to say.

"Following me." She doesn't look at me as I approach. She doesn't bother to ask how I got here, so I don't bother asking how long she's known I was behind her.

I sit beside her. Not too close. The concrete is wet, but if it doesn't bother her, it doesn't bother me. My leg is agony, but taking the weight off it helps a bit.

"So why do you keep doing it?" she says. It feels like we've stepped into a middle of an unfinished conversation, which I guess is true in a way. All the conversations we haven't had since January. Since everything changed. It's not a question I want to answer, though, so I do what I always do when I don't want to answer questions. I ask a different one.

"Back on the roof, I told you why I was along on this stupid ride, but why are you here? Why are you there, I mean? Going along with the others?"

Molly shrugs. "Because nothing matters. So doing something that matters to somebody else is as good as it gets." There's a dark undertone in the words that chills me, but the response I want to make is lost as Molly turns to look at me. Even in the rain and the haze of twilight-grey afternoon, her eyes are the blue I can't describe. "Why do you keep following me?"

"Because," I say, "when your mom died, you said you were coming back right away." It's not a question I want to answer, but under the pressure of Molly's gaze, I answer it anyway. "But then you stayed in Vancouver for three more weeks, and I figured it must have been important, but you didn't answer my calls."

I say it carefully, trying to hold everything together in as focused a way as possible. I'm aware that I'm just kind of repeating things I've already said. That night in the hallway outside the computer lab that I'd give anything to get back. Then with no warning and against my will, a whole bunch of other stuff comes out in a rush.

"And when you came back, you said you couldn't do it anymore. Couldn't do us anymore. And I thought you just needed some space, so I gave it to you, but then you were just gone. And I've spent pretty much every minute since then wondering whether I should have said no when you said you couldn't do it. I mean, whether I should have just been with you anyway, no matter what you said."

It's only when I hear the words in my own voice that I realize how badly I've been wanting to say them. Four months.

"Not everyone's life revolves around your decisions, Scott. I know that must come as a terrible shock to you."

"I didn't mean it that way. I just meant…" I falter because I don't actually know what I meant. This is a bad sign. "I never told you what you were to me, because I didn't know if you wanted to hear it. And I should have told you, whether you wanted to hear it or not. Whether you felt the same way or not."

From somewhere far away, a rumble of thunder filters through the hiss of rain. Molly looks up to the sky. And in her expression, I can see what looks like a hint of November, of all the time before everything changed. A hint of the way she used to look when she looked at me.

But when she finally speaks, it's to say, "What exactly is the touring test?"

"Sorry?"

"The touring test. You and Mitchell were arguing about it in the Vindicator. Like it's some kind of computer thing, but you never said what it was."

"The Turing test," I say, making the subtle correction to her pronunciation. "It's named after Alan Turing. He was a British mathematician. A code-breaker during World War II."

"Yeah, that doesn't actually tell me anything."

All the things I really need to say are bashing around in my head. But I realize as I try to focus that I'm still afraid to say them. Grateful for the chance to deny them, just a little while longer.

"Turing was the father of modern computing," I say instead. "Back before people were even building digital computers, Turing imagined machines getting nearly as smart as people one day. So he designed a foolproof test that you could use when you were talking to someone, that would let you tell whether it was a machine or a real person."

(Confession. The only reason I know anything about Alan Turing is that I wrote a World War II term paper on Alan Turing in Socials 11. Turing became my choice for the paper because my limited research suggested he was the only person involved in World War II whose life story didn't require memorizing the dates of battles, treaties, and all the other stuff I never bothered learning about World War II.)

"So what is the test?"

"That is the test. Talking to the machine is the test. Turing said that even if after an entire conversation, talking on any topic, any subject, a machine's responses are indistinguishable from a human being's, then the machine can think."

Molly laughs. But like in the computer lab, it's not the laugh I remember. From before things changed.

"What's so funny?" I ask.

"I was just thinking about someone talking to my dad," she says. "I wonder if he'd pass."

I don't know how to respond to that, so I don't. Molly has a branch in her hand that I hadn't noticed before. It's a sprig of something yellow and flowery, broken off from some yellow flowery shrub along the edge of the path behind her.

"My mom came to the clinic downstairs for counseling. I used to come with her, but it was too much sometimes so I came up here. Not quite as green in December. It snowed once, though. That was nice."

"Listen," I say. "I need to tell you…"

"No," Molly says. "No, you don't. Not now, and not then. And you need to understand that."

"You can't tell me I don't know what I feel…"

"I'm telling you what I feel, like I did before. When I told you I couldn't do it anymore and you didn't listen, like you need to listen. Like your test of talking to figure out if someone's real. When someone's talking, someone else needs to be listening. It works two ways."

The distant peal of thunder sounds out again, closer this time. As if in answer, the grey curtain of rain thickens and swells, dancing serpentine along the ground.

"Give me a chance," is all I can say. Because I know she's right. Molly's right about a lot of things.

"There are things you don't understand. There are things that you're not strong enough to help me with."

"I want to help you," I hear myself say, but my voice is a distant echo in my ears. Like I'm watching this scene from a distance, like I'm watching a video that I can't shut off. Watching an ending coming that I've already seen.

"Scott, you've got a world full of people telling you need to fix yourself and you can't even manage that. How do you expect to ever be able to fix anybody else?"

I've got nothing to say in response. I'm good with words. I always know what I want to say, always know what I'm doing, a point of pride with me.

Molly stands. She shakes water from her umbrella, leaves the sprig of flowering shrub on the concrete beside me.

"Don't follow me anymore. Okay?"

"Okay."

"Say it."

"I won't follow you anymore." There's a dead numbness in my voice that I suspect I'm going to want to get used to.

With a shake of her ponytail, Molly's gone into the rain. And as much as I want to, I can't watch her go. My eyes drift up and out, across to a green-grey expanse of closer buildings, and low-rise glass beyond that, and then black cloud as far as the eye can see.

Part Eight

The Way the
Game is Played

57

Comfortably Numb

Pink Floyd, 1979. It's an hour later and I'm twenty blocks away with no real idea of where I'm going. I can feel a disconnect between my eyes, my feet, and my brain, such that I remember leaving the terrace garden at some point after Molly left. I remember continuing along the way we were walking when I followed her, which I'm guessing is west. I'm assuming that she's headed back to the condo, which means I won't risk seeing her again.

I remember making it up to a six-lane slow-moving parking lot called Broadway. I've been walking along its rain-slick sidewalks since then, until I find myself at some sort of intersection of urban trendy and urban trendier, and I realize that I'm starving.

My hand keeps absently slipping to my pocket, looking for the phone that's not there to check the time. That's a thing I need to rectify.

At a 7-Eleven, I use Carl's ATM card to pick up a disposable cell and a fistful of cash. A couple of minutes of setup later, the phone tells me it's a little after one p.m. A little farther down the street, I find a pizza place whose signage reads only *Pizza Place,* and which thus seems a suitably anonymous locale for what I need to do.

At the bus stop out front, I wait for a bus to approach as I note the pizza place's take-out and delivery number. Then I dial another number, one of the few besides Rico, Molly, Mitchell, and Breanne that I've committed to memory. The other end of that number picks up with no message, no warning, no tone. I key in the pizza place's number and click off as the bus stops.

I wander past the back doors where people are getting off, then I quietly toss the cell phone onto the bottom step before those doors close. I watch as the bus heads off, confident that if anyone's managed to hack Carl's ATM cards, they're going to be able to track a phone bought with those cards. As such, I want them tracking it heading away from me down the Broadway transit lane at high speed.

I'm not paranoid.

I go into the pizza place and order two slices of Hawaiian, two cans of Coke Zero, paying with cash. The counter guy is a university type, business school by his executive haircut and the copy of *The Economist* sitting open beside the till, but with skate tattoos across both shoulders where the eventual button-up shirt will hide them. I eat slowly at a corner booth, counting the cracks in the tabletop as I ignore the other half-dozen patrons who drift in from the rain, then out again.

Exactly ten minutes from the time I made my cell call, the pizza place's phone rings. The skate-punk MBA answers, then looks confused for a moment as he listens to whoever's on the other end.

"Is someone here expecting a call from Connor?"

You'll remember Connor from way back in not-chapter thirteen. Or maybe you won't, because that was a while ago. If this was an actual story I was making up, I'd be sure to not let so much time pass between appearances of secondary characters. If this were fiction, Connor would probably be some plucky unseen tech-sidekick kind of guy, always at the other end of the phone or something. Problem is, real life seldom organizes its secondary characters all that well.

I take the phone as I order another slice, paying with a twenty and a "Keep the change," which is something I'm pretty sure I've never actually said before. The skate-punk MBA silently swallows his *Hey, this isn't a messaging service* outrage as he calculates his tip. I and the phone turn carefully out of his earshot.

"It's Scott," I say. On the other end of the call, at what I assume are the offices of *Five Horsemen,* a moment of silence registers equal amounts of surprise and suspicion. Despite being the publisher and major-domo of the finest conspiracy website I've ever bothered to write for, Connor has never been particularly good with the whole communication thing.

"And what can I do for you?" he says at last. Except that his stammer is more pronounced than normal, so it takes a bit longer than that. (Confession. Books that try to write dialogue with a stammer or an accent or some other specific level of idiom really annoy me. Spoken dialogue doesn't do bold and italic. Written dialog doesn't do accents. Deal with it.)

The two-phone feint-and-switch is a thing I know how to do because I had to do it the first time I got in touch with *Five Horsemen* and had Connor call me back. I'm not paranoid, but he makes up for it. The first number I called was a secure pager service somewhere in Ukraine. I've never had any idea what kind of system Connor uses to call me, but I have to trust that even if Lincoln has hacked Carl's ATM cards, even if he hacked the disposable cell phone, even if he got the pizza place's number when I keyed it in, he'd have to have Connor's written permission to be listening in on this call.

"I'm in the city. I need a favor, in exchange for which I've got something you want to see."

"I don't care, I don't do more than one favor at a time, and anything you could possibly have, I've already seen."

"Not this," I say, cutting straight to the chase. "Paramilitary black ops underground in Canada. International in scope, weapons running, data theft, kidnapping." I don't bother telling him that the last bit is only provable if one of the five of us swears a complaint. I hear Connor waiting. I speak quieter, I don't know why. "A guy calls himself Lincoln. American, ex-CIA."

The pause continues, and I'm suddenly aware that my pulse is racing. Getting Connor on board, getting the help of quite literally the only person I know in Vancouver is the central and singular pillar of this plan, such as the plan is.

"Details."

"You get them when I see you. Plus the proof."

"You mean rumors."

"I mean data. On tape, in hand. You even get to keep it."

Another pause, telling me that Connor already has the same sense I do of how well connected an operation like Lincoln's must be. But to Connor, that's a good thing.

"I'm going to give you an address," he says. "If you write it down, I'll know it."

I believe him. I don't write it down, committing it to memory as the phone clicks dead.

I finish my last slice. The backpack is wet from the rain, but my cargo of tapes in the first-aid kit is still dry when I check it. I buy a six-pack of Coke Zero for the road, which comes loose from the cooler in a plastic bag. I use the bag to wrap the first-aid kit, even though I'm pretty sure the day can't get any wetter. Then I set the cans in loose around the tapes to keep the weight even.

I sit for a while longer, just watching the rain. I've done it. I've got Connor behind me as the first step to blackmailing Lincoln, so that I can hand the Vindicator over to him but still be sure that the five of us will be safe when it's done. I'm more scared than I've ever been. I'm sure I've said that already at some previous point in the story. I'll probably say it again.

Then I'm thinking about Molly suddenly. And I realize that for a long while now, without even being conscious of it, thinking about Molly is what I do when I'm scared. Thinking about Molly puts me into a place where I can ignore the fear. Or at least it used to. But I can feel how it's not working anymore as I step through the pizza place door and into the downpour beyond.

58

Mirror, Mirror

Def Leppard, 1981. Vancouver is a lot less wet from the back of a cab, even if I haven't managed to get a whole lot drier yet. For twenty minutes, we've been going stop and start along a succession of streets whose bright-lit storefronts and darkened offices spread beneath the gloom of thunderheads, pushing in from what I'm still fairly certain is the west. It's not even two p.m. and the streetlights are flickering on already. This seems end-of-the-world weird to me, but the locals don't seem to notice.

It took another block of trudging through the rain from the pizza place to remember that I still have cash in my pocket and no reason not to use it. The cabbie is a grandfatherly type who takes in the address I repeat back to him with a sage nod, dutifully waiting until my seatbelt is done up before he slips into the flow of traffic and away.

I use our relatively slow pace along Broadway, then a right downhill, then left, then right again to try to judge where I'm going, but the rain wipes away any chance of reading the street signs. There's another bridge at some point, which I'm fairly certain is crossing back over the same water Molly and I walked across before. Off the bridge, we cut a course down side streets and main thoroughfares, one of which is Burrard to judge by the sign on a light-rail transit station as we sail past.

From previous trips to Vancouver, I know that the light-rail transit here is called SkyTrain. From what I can see of it, Burrard Station is underground. Just think about it.

A final left and we're slewing to a stop on an arterial side street. The stream of traffic is slower, the rain pounding down now. The number Connor gave me is chiseled into the side of a nondescript dump of a building, two storeys plus basement, sandwiched in between slabs of glass-and-girder low-rise tower to both sides. I take a minute to dig through my pockets like I'm trying to find my wallet, but what I'm really doing is scanning the street to all sides, making absolutely doubly sure that nobody else is around.

I pay the cabbie, who nods his thanks. I slip up a set of cracked concrete steps to an intercom panel with no labels on its six buttons. I push them all. With a rattling buzz, the door unlocks as the cab pulls away.

A piece of battered signage just inside the door announces *CONNOR CONSULTING* on the second floor. Three other signs point the way down a flight of stairs toward a homeopath, a tax accountant, and a yoga studio advertising *NEW CLASSES STARTING!* two years ago. Somewhat ironically considering the general level of squalor in the building, an architect's office appears to occupy the ground floor.

Up a flight of stairs stands a landing, whose steel door buzzes and clanks as I approach.

Sometimes you need to do what you know is right.

This is right. I know it with absolute certainty. I'm tired of arguing over it. I'm going to save us all, me, Mitchell, Breanne, Rico, Molly, by trading the Vindicator for our safety. Because there's no other way. I need to make the decision that the others can't make.

This is my plan, and it's perfect.

Connor has friends. Connor has contacts. Connor can use those contacts, those secret channels, to do an end run around Lincoln's group and all its secrecy. Connor knows people inside the Canadian government, the American government, probably the Russians with a couple of phone calls. Special ops, special forces, army intel, CSIS, the CIA. Connor knows them all. And somewhere in that list of people he knows, I trust there are a dozen different names who will pay him well to find out what Lincoln's been up to.

Connor also has access to hardware. Proprietary military-grade video equipment, among other things. He told me last week that he's got a line on the encrypted chopper surveillance and helmet-cam feed from SEAL Team Six when they hit Abbottabad. I've been trying to think of a way to score a copy for Christmas, the same way I'm going to get him to burn me a copy of the five kilos of tapes in my backpack. A little something that I'm going to keep back, designed to cover the fact that Lincoln isn't going to be happy when I beat him at his own game.

The door is unlocked as I open it. The office is unnaturally dim as I shut it behind me. I get my first look at Connor then.

The publisher of *Five Horsemen* is at a table-turned-desk that takes up the center of a spaciously squalid front office. He looks up from a vintage HP laptop like he isn't sure which one of us is interrupting the other. He meets my gaze through thick glasses, shaking back a forelock of hair so blonde-turning-silver that it's almost as translucent as his skin.

"Scott," he says, the stammer adding a couple of extra syllables. He gives me a nod as he goes back to whatever he's doing. Surfing tvtropes.org by what I can see from the angle I'm at, and playing with a key fob that has no keys on it. I take a moment to glance around, getting my bearings. The room features desks and chairs for a half-dozen people, but most of those chairs are heaped high with moldering magazines and file boxes. A bunch of doors stand closed along three walls, labeled clockwise as *Storage, Storage, Storage, No Entry,* and *Storage* with a hand-drawn biohazard symbol underneath it.

Between the doors, those walls are lined with a bizarre pastiche of last-century action-film posters and full-page newspaper clippings obscured by scrawled notes in green marker. The only exception is a space where a set of steel shelves holds a network hub sprouting a forest of cable, a tight-packed array of battery-backup power supplies, and a nine-unit server rack whose heat I can feel from where I'm standing.

"I'm assuming this has something to do with your picture being all over the news this weekend. I'm breaking protocol by letting you anywhere near the office."

"I came alone," I say, hanging my soaking umbrella on an empty hat rack by the door.

Connor snorts. He glances over my shoulder, where a look back shows me a bank of vintage black-and-white video monitors hanging from the ceiling. I see the street, the outside door, the stairs I walked up, another bunch of hallways, all empty. Also, a high-angle view of a bathroom.

"Anything wrong?" Connor stammers.

All the time up to now, all the times I've talked to Connor, I've felt a sort of power here. A cell of seething anarchist intellectualism at the far end of a phone. A philosophical kinship, information as freedom. But here and now that I actually see him, like it's tattooed across his forehead, Connor is a low-rent paranoid libertarian pamphleteer. He's any other overworked, overweight, overly middle-aged media guy.

I'm overwhelmed by a sense of being underwhelmed.

"So," he says uncomfortably, and I'm suddenly conscious that we're both just staring at each other. "This is me seeing you. Details."

I try to focus. I need to bring the previous days into some sort of relief that will let me sum things up.

"Me and some friends of mine, we got caught up in something. We thought we were beta-playing a game. An online tactical simulation, but the game turned out to be... you know what, that doesn't matter. But none of it was our fault, and now we have something this guy Lincoln wants. A piece of tech. I want to give it back to him, but I can't trust him to leave things alone after that."

"What kind of tech?"

"A Soviet-era mobile weapons platform, whose heuristic on-board systems developed advanced artificial intelligence capability while it sat forgotten in a bunker in Smolensk." Saying it sounds just about as ridiculous as I expect it to.

"I didn't think you wrote fiction." Connor tries and fails to laugh. It's like he has some sort of esophageal deformity that routes all intent to guffaw straight from his lungs to his nose.

"Not fiction. This is the truth. I've got complete records on the project, on the vehicle, on how it was stolen and smuggled out. I've got Lincoln's operations, the entire data trail. I haven't looked at that part of it, but you won't have any problem pulling it together. And what I get in exchange is a copy of the records and your promise of a hands-off on anything having to do with the Vindicator."

"That's your AI weapons platform? An intelligent tank?"

"Yeah," I say. "It's worth more to Lincoln than everything else put together. He won't care that you're going to whistle-blow the rest of his operation out of existence as long as he has the tank. And it means nothing to you because no one would ever believe it, anyway. But I get a copy of everything, so that I've got the Vindicator data and a promise to Lincoln that I make the tank public and mess with him and the people he's sold it to if he messes with me or my friends."

That's the plan, cobbled together over the previous four hours of adrenaline and caffeine and instinct. It's all locking into place, and for reasons I can't explain, I feel great. Proud of myself, even. I'm doing this for Molly. For Mitchell, Breanne, Rico.

"And you have this data with you?"

"Yeah." I sling the backpack full of tapes off my shoulder. I unzip it with a flourish as I step toward the desk. "It's a proprietary Soviet encrypted format, but I'm guessing you won't have any problem with it. The data in exchange for the favor, which is you making me the copy. Simple."

"Yes," Connor stammers. "Except I told you, I don't do more than one favor..."

He's trying to add *at a time,* but I have to technically write up the stammer there. Because before he can finish, every one of the *Storage* and *No Entry* doors is yanked open simultaneously from the far side.

In that one moment, time slows down.

They're in street clothes again. And like they did that night at the school, Lincoln's people make no sound as they move, spreading out around the room with crowd-control shotguns at the ready. The only one I recognize is Lincoln, striding out behind the first rank. He's the only one not armed.

"Nice try." If I live forever, nothing will erase the memory of how Lincoln smiles when he says it. "Take him."

I stand stock still for what seems like forever. And in that long instant of forever, all I can focus on is how good it felt six seconds ago, thinking that I'd pulled this off. Thinking that I was good enough to be able to pull this off.

From way, way back, that night in the paramilitary base, I remember. On Lincoln's slate when he talked to me, all my stuff from *Five Horsemen* was there.

All I can think about is how [anglo-saxon] stupid I am. So worthless. All I can think about is how Molly was right.

The only thing close to me, the only thing I can possibly reach before getting shot from six different directions is the backpack. So without thinking, because there's nothing else I can do, I grab a can of Coke Zero and mainline it straight toward Connor's head. I target Connor because I'm instinctively sure that any of Lincoln's people are capable of moving faster than I can throw, and also because I recognize the look of absolute terrified cowardice on his face. It's the same look on my face, except that my desperation is covering it.

With a shriek of fear, Connor goes over backwards in his chair as he takes a 355-ml aluminum and liquid payload dead center in the forehead. Then he's scrambling erratically and most helpfully across everyone else's line of fire, and I figure I've got about five seconds, tops.

I don't even have to try the main door behind me to know it's locked. So I take the two steps to Connor's desk, throwing two more cans of Coke Zero as I go. I miss the paramilitaries I'm aiming at, but they're both thrown off balance just a bit. As a bonus, one can splits open as it hits the edge of the server rack's steel shelving, sending a spiraling stream of carbonation around that side of the room as a moment's secondary distraction.

From somewhere seemingly far away, I can hear Lincoln calling out, his voice carrying an edge that tells me the smile's gone. "Don't do this! You can still walk away!" But in that moment, in that space of blind panic, I can't hear him. I can't trust him. I can't listen to anything but the fear.

From the table, I grab the keyless fob that Connor left behind as he fell. I don't know how the thought comes to my mind, I don't know that I'm even capable of thought anymore, but I press its single button as I scramble back.

I hear the office door buzz behind me as it unlocks. I run.

"[Anglo-saxon] me! Get the door!" Lincoln shouts, but it's too late. The six of them are moving along the walls in perfect takedown formation, but it leaves them just a couple of steps too far away. I'm at the door.

Then I'm knocked off my feet as a beanbag round slams me in the upper arm. I hear the shot what seems like a long while later.

I'm on the floor, scrambling up. The pain in my arm, in my shoulder reminds me suddenly how much my leg is hurting again. But something's changed. Something's wrong. My left hand clutches absently for the backpack straps that it's supposed to be holding.

Two steps away from me, just inside the door, the backpack has fallen. The first-aid kit with its cache of aluminum-jacketed tapes has popped out to the floor, three cans of Coke Zero circling lazily past it.

Four steps away from me, two of Lincoln's paramilitaries are closing in.

As I slam the steel door behind me, I hear its magnetic lock clank shut again. The key fob that I'm praying to the god of all Connor's paranoia is the only thing that opens that lock is still tight in my right hand.

The tapes are gone. I don't know what to do, so I run. Down the stairs, out the main doors, which thankfully open the old-fashioned way.

I'm outside, running, screaming except I'm not making any sound. I think I'm going back the way the cab brought me, but I can't be sure. I'm soaked to the skin after what feels like a half-dozen steps, but the burning in my lungs tells me I've been running forever.

I have no idea where I am. I have no idea what to do as I collapse into the doorway of some sort of darkened art-deco bank building. My leg has startled to buckle with every frantic step, and I know that if turn my ankle again, if I blow my knee out somehow, it's over.

I can barely see straight with the pain. I can't think over the noise of traffic and rain and thunder directly overhead now. All I can think about is Molly. Mitchell, Rico, Breanne. All I can think about is how much I want to be back home.

Everyone and everything around me is a threat. Every car cruising slowly through the torrent of rainwater coursing along the gutters. Every pedestrian I pass, half of them staring at me as I look back, still running, absolutely certain that I'm going to get shot from behind at any moment. I panic and swerve around at least three people on bicycles at different points, rain gear flapping past me like Gore-Tex flags.

There are too many people to watch out for. Distracting me with the sheer volume of their humanity, so that even if I were being followed, I'd never know it. That's why I'm still waiting for Lincoln's people to come bursting out of the rain-slick shadows behind me. Never wondering if maybe there's a reason why they haven't caught up to me yet.

That's why I don't see Karya watching me, somewhere across the street. A shadow in some unseen alcove, just waiting as I catch my breath. Then stepping out again into the rain, nondescript. Following me again as I limp away.

59

Beyond the Moon

Max Webster, 1978. I don't know what street I'm on when I finally manage to hail a cab. For more blocks than I can count, the traffic is all one-way and heading back in the direction I'm running from. Even once I'm pointed the right way, I get the attention of three drivers who all sail past my soaked-to-the-skin, stumbling-like-I'm-on-meth look. Finally, momentarily out of the rain at a bus shelter, I manage to get one to stop only by waving a twenty conspicuously at curbside.

I don't remember the address of the condo. Just the closest intersections as I was following Molly, so that's where I get dropped off. The trip is a blur, feeling only like a few minutes, but my memory is choppy. All I know is that we're parked suddenly and the driver is giving me a dollar figure I can't process. I give him the twenty, which seems to be enough.

With the condo in sight, I run again, stupidly. Every jarring step along the pavement sets a white-hot scalpel to work on my leg, threatening to mess it up for the sake of the thirty seconds I'm desperate to gain on my way to the door.

I don't remember the elevator. I don't remember getting inside the suite. All I'm aware of is that I'm missing one shoe suddenly, no idea where it went. All I'm aware of is falling to my knees in the kitchen, trying to talk as Molly comes out of the living room with a look of absolute shock and horror on her face.

"What the hell…?"

Run, I try to say, but I can't because of how badly I'm shivering. I'm freezing, hypothermic maybe. Molly seems to understand that much at least, judging by how forcefully she tries to drag me toward the bathroom.

"You [anglo-saxon] idiot. Get into the shower…"

Run. As I fight to breathe, faint specks swirl in my line of sight like ash. A blood-red haze pushes in from all sides, telling me I'm close to blacking out.

"[Lord's name in vain], Scott, what is wrong with you?"

"Run!" Molly stops short in a way that tells me she hears the urgency in the word. "Lincoln…"

We run.

Out the door, into the foyer, at the end of which the elevator is still open where I somehow thought to jam the door with my shoe. Mystery solved. I grab the shoe as Molly slots her keycard for the garage. We stumble back as the door shuts. Molly's scared. I can see that because we've both stumbled into the same corner, face to face. Closer to each other than we've been in a long time.

As the elevator opens, Rico and Mitchell are on top of the Vindicator, ratcheting something into place. Breanne is collecting up and stowing tools back into the cabinets that are strewn across the garage now. At a glance, they've made use of every piece of equipment for whatever it was the three of them have been doing. At a second glance, I can see that the Vindicator is gleaming wet and back to something resembling its original factory finish, because one of Mitchell, Breanne, or Rico has apparently taken the time to power-wash it. I don't know why, but even in my frenzied state, even with everything else that's going on, I'm aware of how much this annoys me.

"Power up," I shout. "We have to get out of here."

I get the same look from all of them. Or rather, Molly gets the same look, like whatever I say is going to fail some test of reasonableness as a matter of course.

"Lincoln's coming!" Thankfully, she follows my lead.

"How?" Mitchell calls. "And where?"

As if in answer, the door to the *Emergency Access Only* stairwell comes off its frame in a blast of point-charge explosives, echoing through the garage like a tightly focused thunderstorm.

It all happens too fast. Something like a very large rattlesnake hisses just behind me, which I realize only later is what a taser sounds like as its leads sail past your head. Rico is shouting, Breanne answering, but I can't tell what they're saying. I hear Mitchell calling out Molly's name.

That last one stops me. I'm three strides to the Vindicator. Molly is three strides behind me, not beside me like she was a second ago. She's on the ground, on her back, convulsing as Karya crouches in the doorway with the other end of the taser in her hand.

"You've got nowhere to go," she shouts. "Lincoln wants this ended, you need to stand down."

But all I can hear is Molly cry out. Nothing else gets through.

It all happens fast.

I'm behind one of the tool cabinets suddenly. It's a wedge of stainless steel a little taller than I am, set on heavy rubber wheels that are suddenly moving faster than they're probably designed for. I'm pushing it straight toward Karya at a dead run, screaming every step of the way.

Sparks flare as another taser strikes the far side of the cabinet, but I'm not touching it anymore. I've angled my approach so that the cabinet rockets past Molly as I drop to her side, cutting off Karya as it overturns in front of her. A slew of bolts, clamps, and other bits of unidentifiable metal shoot out across the floor.

Karya has another paramilitary behind her, part of whatever larger squad is probably systematically kicking in the upstairs doors right now. Both of them are catching fire from my right where Rico straight-arms titanium wrenches toward them at high speed. Karya has to fall back behind the prone cabinet, buying me two precious seconds. As she comes up with another taser in hand, one of Rico's wrenches takes her hard, spinning like a tomahawk as it smashes her in the chest, then twists up to strike her chin. She goes down without a sound.

Molly's in my arms, over my shoulder, but I can't remember picking her up. The second paramilitary has raced in behind me, trying to grab Molly as he shouts into a headset mic, *Targets to ground, secure the elevator, take the stairs!* His distraction means I can twist so all he gets is her arm. I feel the sleeve of Molly's sweater split and shred as he stumbles away with the cuff in his fist. Then I'm running faster than I've ever run in my life.

I can't feel the pain in my leg anymore. I can't feel the cold threading through me, I can't feel the ache in my arm where Lincoln's guy tagged me. I can't see anything except, suddenly, Rico coming up out of nowhere beside me to clothesline the paramilitary with what looks a tire iron. Then Mitchell and Breanne are pulling Molly off my shoulder, lifting her up the ladderway steps and inside.

I'm one step behind them, Rico one step behind me. I slam the hatch controls. Which of course do nothing, because the Vindicator is powered down. The big green button first, the surge of the power plant firing up. Then the hatch, which seals with a slam.

Everyone's shouting but nothing registers. I've got Molly in Mitchell's ops seat, trying to find her pulse and realizing that I have absolutely no idea how to find someone's pulse. It's obvious that she's breathing, though, so my panic downgrades just a bit.

"We need to get Carl online," Mitchell says. I don't have it in me to argue. I let Breanne slip in to hold Molly as I scoot up to systems, keying in the sequence. It takes two tries, my hands shaking. But even as I hit the last digit, I hear Breanne call out behind me.

"Oh, god..."

The strangled quiet threading her voice scares me worse than anything else we've seen or done in the past two days. Mitchell and Rico have stopped talking. The Vindicator's power plant and the faint series of pulsed chimes between consoles are the only sounds.

"We need to move, quickly," says the disembodied voice of Carl, full of disembodied concern. Welcome to the party, Carl, glad you could get caught up so quickly.

No one's listening. No one moves.

Where the paramilitary tried to grab Molly, her sweater is torn. The white sweater she always wears, the sweater she didn't change in favor of the new clothes in the suite. One too-long sleeve has ripped cleanly along the seam, up to the elbow.

Along Molly's bare arm that I suddenly realize none of us have seen since December, a pair of thin scar lines run diagonally across her perfect pale skin.

Wrist to elbow, unnaturally straight. I can see the suture marks where the cuts were closed up. Pale squiggles, like someone's been doodling on her with pink magic marker that won't wash off.

"We need to move," Carl says again. "Scott should take the helm. I can help you navigate. Lincoln's people are on the stairs."

I don't have it in me to argue. A knife-bright pain is twisting through me, back and forth. In through my chest, out through my back, then into my back, over and over again like I'm being sewn up tight with very fine wire.

I drop into the flight chair as Breanne pulls the g-web over Molly. Mitchell is already in the systems chair beside me. Rico pulls his jacket off, his hands shaking as he lays it over Molly, covering her bare arm before he and Breanne strap themselves in.

On the monitors, through the viewport, a half-dozen paramilitaries are fanning out around us. Karya is on her feet again, face covered in blood, shouting orders. I know instinctively that none of them are carrying anything that might be a threat to the Vindicator once it's sealed tight.

Rico is on the weapons board to fire up the sonic cannons, the whine of which gets Karya shouting, ordering the paramilitaries back. It clears the floor between us and the garage doors.

"Take us out," Carl says. "Back onto the railway lines."

I don't know why the thought comes to me, but it does as I push the yoke straight in to lurch us backwards at high speed. I feel it all suddenly come together as we smash through the garage doors, stainless steel crumpling like tinfoil. Beanbag rounds in the *Five Horsemen* office, but tasers here. Because grabbing me wasn't the point at the office. The point was getting me to run rabbit-scared, back to wherever the rest of the group and the Vindicator were all holed up.

That whole exercise, every moment of it, was about Lincoln knowing I'd do it. Knowing just how thick he needed to lay it on with his *Take him!* and his cold smile. Knowing how to make me do whatever he wants me to.

I imagined that I could beat Lincoln at his own game. But at this level, I don't even know the way the game is played.

We execute an impressive set of reverse three-sixties outside the base of the building before I get us under control. Carl has our route patched into my board, so all I need to do is figure out how to steer.

I looked it up tonight as I'm writing this, just to be sure. Breaking my own rule, sorry. Standard operating procedure when using nonlethal ammo to take out a fleeing suspect is to shoot for the legs, because muscle spasm is what you're going for. Lincoln's guy went for my arm. Going for the tapes, and because going for the legs might have actually slowed me down.

"Onto the tracks. Go easy on the controls. The tires will handle it. Then increase speed."

I do what Carl says, like I'm listening to some sort of hyped-up turn-by-turn GPS unit. When we're on the tracks, I push it, throttling up with a lurch.

A hundred and fifty km/h through the dark haze of thunderclouds, the lights of the rail yard gleaming around us like storm-soaked stars.

"We need to get distance between us and them," Carl says. "Then where the map indicates, bear right to the switching yard, then follow the route laid out for you. Rico, make a broad-spectrum scan. If there were choppers waiting above the building, they'll be easier to spot with infrared in the rain."

I watch the map. I twitch the controls, the Vindicator surging along deserted tracks under the cover of an unnatural late-afternoon night. And as we go, something else comes to mind, just as smooth and easy as all the other ways I'm suddenly realizing how badly I've messed things up.

I haven't seen Malkov yet.

Lincoln was at the *Five Horsemen* office. Karya was following me, calling in a team to take the condo, but I didn't see Malkov in either group.

I don't know where he is. I don't know what his absence means. But I know I'll keep thinking about it. I'll keep focusing on it, I'll keep my mind fixed on his face. Because that's the only way I can make myself not think about Molly as we flee.

60

The Flycatcher

Roy Harper, 1980. The route that Carl has mapped out takes us off the main rail lines that brought us into the city. We're heading along the old freight spurs that probably haven't been used since downtown Vancouver became a lot more valuable as malls and condos than as warehouses. Along one of those spur lines, a chain-link fence fronts a darkened space of siding, undercut into a rising bank of concrete and stone.

Reading the map as we move along it tells me that this is an access point to old train tunnels that used to punch their way underneath downtown. These waterfront lines connected with other lines down around False Creek, which I realize belatedly is the water I crossed over twice earlier that day.

The tunnels are sealed off, disused for god knows how long by anybody except us. When we pass through it, that chain-link fence gets a Vindicator-sized hole in it, so that if Lincoln's people come this way on foot, there's no way they're going to miss the subtle sign of our detour off the main tracks. However, Carl has hacked the railway security radio and cell frequencies, loudly reporting with a half-dozen different synthetic voices that *Holy [dung], something just came down the tracks fast, can you see it?* The reports are staggered in time, running east. Assuming that Lincoln is listening in, he'll be in his chopper heading that way to catch up to us. Hopefully it buys us some time.

The machine makes its calls as I follow a crumbling and cavernous slope-domed passageway curving southeast. It's slow going even with the Vindicator's lights, the steady dwindling of perspective giving no sense of depth or distance. The railway tracks are long gone, the floor a field of rubble crushed to smaller rubble beneath the Vindicator's tires.

"Stop here," Carl says, but I already see where the tunnel ends with a sudden finality ahead. A wall of roughly mortared brick seals its rough arch, dripping water from above and glistening with black mold. And as I slow us down, I find myself wondering idly what made the machine choose the voice it uses for us, out of all the fake voices it could have used. Some psych-profile sense of what we'd be most perceptive to, I'm guessing. Another bit of insight that should be ammunition for the anger. But as hard as I try to find it, as deep as I dig for it, the anger's gone now.

With the latest surge of adrenaline fading, I'm suddenly aware that I'm about to freeze to death. Mitchell and Rico help me find the Vindicator's stores of chemical-battery thermal blankets. Wrapped in three of them, I feel like I'm being microwaved, but they take the hypothermic edge off.

While I'm shivering my way back to normalcy, Molly wakes up. I don't know if she was aware but just out of it when we all saw what we saw, or if she only realizes what her missing sleeve must mean. Either way, she's first at the hatch controls, first outside. She keeps Rico's jacket, doesn't say a word to anyone.

We all sit for a while in the silence. Mitchell is the first to speak. "Where are we, Carl?"

"This is a disused commercial rail vector. One of several under the city. I had three mapped out for use as emergency fallback points."

Carl thinks of everything. I'm expecting there's a lounge set up somewhere outside for our comfort. Maybe a pool table.

"We should talk about our options," Mitchell says.

"Not here," I say as I fumble my way down to a single thermal blanket. I follow Molly's lead toward the hatch and outside. "We talk. The machine stays out of it."

Carl says nothing. Mitchell looks for a moment like he wants to argue, but he follows me in the end. Breanne and Rico are behind him.

Dimmed down, the Vindicator's running lights are a pale glow that fills a confined space of stale air and ghostly echoes. But even against that brightness, I realize that in spite of the monumental irony involved, I can see more light at the end of the tunnel.

Along one edge of the brick dead-end where it meets the curve of the tunnel wall, an opening a half-meter on a side is blocked by heavy iron grate. It looks out to the city beyond, showing us at ground level, which makes sense given that a rail line ran through here at some point. Beyond the tunnel's end and the brick wall that marks it, a construction site spreads. A couple of security floodlights cast wide pools of halogen-white over scattered piles of lumber. Broad concrete pillars are set with thick bundles of rebar, a chain-link fence beyond.

There's no sign of anyone around, no clue as to where we are geographically. Then I spot the edge of the stadium in the near distance beyond the chain link, the Cambie Bridge faintly visible on its far side. From this angle, the tower-screen isn't tall enough to be seen, but its glow flares beyond the domed roof like some sort of LED moonrise.

The tunnel offers a grand total of two ways to walk — either back into the absolute blackness behind us, or forward to the wall. The latter option is closer to the Vindicator than I like, but I tell myself that Carl can probably see and hear us from just about anywhere. None of it really matters anymore.

In a moment of sudden insight, I realize that I can't see Molly. She isn't in the halogen gleam of the tunnel ahead, not in the tunnel behind. There's no sound of footsteps betraying her flight back into the darkness. But before I have time to panic, I look up. She's on top of the Vindicator, like she was this morning. Just sitting there, staring out at nothing.

Mitchell follows my gaze. He guesses correctly at my intent as I move. "Maybe it's not the best time..." he begins, but I'm not listening.

The thermal blanket makes climbing the outside access ladder a challenge. It also gives my leg a chance to use the last of the muscles that aren't aching yet. Up top, there's barely enough room for me to stand beneath the vault of the tunnel ceiling at its highest point. The air feels colder up here. Clearer somehow, though the combined sense of vertigo and claustrophobia twisting through me makes that moot.

Molly doesn't look at me as I carefully sit across from her. In silence, I try to judge the best way in through the emptiness of her expression. I try to think of something to say to take the pain away, something to break the surface tension of all the uncertainty pooling around us.

"You stayed in Vancouver for three weeks after your mom died…" is what I say in the end. Because nothing I can say will ever take the pain away.

"Emergency surgery and a psych evaluation. Time flies." Molly's voice is twisted through with an emptiness I've never heard before. And as that emptiness unfurls from her to wrap me like a shroud, I realize that I've never really thought about her during those three weeks. Too caught up at the time in thinking about what Molly's absence meant for me. Too caught up since then in everything else.

"Why didn't you tell someone…"

"Don't," she says. "Just don't."

Between the emptiness and the anger and the fear, between Molly and me, there's no way to say the things that have gone unsaid all these months. So instead, I say the stupid thing. The arrogant thing. The thing that naturally twists the moment so it's all about me, about what I want, about what I need to know. Because that's who I am.

"Why did you do it?"

"I think I just said I don't want to talk about this…"

"And I think we've already established that everything needs to be about me before it means anything," I say.

She meets my bitterness with a darkly defiant look. Challenging me. "Because when my mom died, my dad said it should have been me." And all I can do is look away from what I see trapped in those blue eyes.

Way back, I told you this was a story about gamers, but that there are only a few places where that really matters. This is one of them.

"Don't be afraid," I hear myself say, and I honestly don't know which one of us I'm saying it to.

When I got into gaming, I was afraid. Of who I was, of what I was turning into. Of not knowing who I wanted to be. And the point in time when I got into gaming was the point when all those things first started to change. I didn't realize it at the time, but on that October day like any other day in eighth grade when Mitchell came up to me in homeroom, it was the start of everything good that's happened to me since.

The problem is that I turn my back on the lessons I've learned. I try to set myself above the understanding that lets a person face the world, because I don't want to admit to all the things I can't understand.

"The world gives us too many reasons to be afraid of it," I say. "It all just seems too big sometimes. It gets so overwhelming that the only thing we can do is shut it out."

Molly shakes her head, dismissive. "We don't shut life out. It shuts us in. We get glued down to places. To things, to moments and people, and suddenly our lives don't belong to us anymore. And the more we try to get away, the more we try to rise above it, the faster we sink."

"Then you need to fly," I say, because it's the only thing I can say. The only thing that comes to mind sometimes when I think about Molly.

Flying is what I think about when I remember how it used to feel to hear Molly laugh. The real laugh, which channeled a sense of lightness in her like she might leave the ground at any moment. A feeling like she might go anywhere, and all I wanted to do was follow her.

This is the way it feels to watch Molly when she's playing *Ace Combat 4*. When she's playing *Apache Air Assault* or *Century of Flight*. *Super Mario Galaxy* most days. I watched Molly play *Spyro: Dawn of the Dragon* on Breanne's Wii once, and it was poetry. If you've ever played *Spyro: Dawn of the Dragon*, you know what kind of an accomplishment that is.

I can't fix this. I can't fix anything. I want to touch her, want to hold her, want to comfort her, but there are no words, no feelings I can summon up that will make this go away.

And in a heartbeat of insight, I remember something suddenly. What Ms. Bond said in the library, which seems so long ago now. *I know what it's been like for both of you, but that's not what this is about.* And she's right. What's been going on since January isn't about what happened between Molly and I. That's just become the excuse. Problem is, knowing that Ms. Bond is right isn't enough to tell me how to fix this.

I feel like I'm looking at one of those 3D autostereogram images that eventually just clicks in your head. It's almost there, almost in front of me, but it won't fix in my mind. Just hanging at the edge of my perception, lost in the shadows where it'll never come clear.

My hand is on Molly's shoulder, and I swear to you that I have no idea how it got there. She doesn't push it away.

I love you. I'm so sorry I was afraid to say it before.

It's what I want to say. It's what I wanted to say the last time Molly called from Vancouver, before Kirk had to tell me her mom died. It's what I wanted to say when she came back, but she wouldn't talk to me. What I wanted to say in the library that night, and this morning, and right now, and I can't. Because I live in a world in which telling Molly that I love her, that I care about her, is a thing that I'm not brave enough to do.

All this useless intellectual baggage. All these things I do that prove how much smarter I am than everyone else. I make believe that it's a burden, that it's some great weight I carry. But in the end, it's all a pale reflection of the scars that real pain scribes into other people. Pain as some kind of bar-code scan that I'm not smart enough to read.

I'm beside Molly. I'm kissing Molly, and I swear to you that I have no idea how that happened. Then Molly is kissing me back. She's crying, and for all the wrong reasons that people can ever cry. All the pain wrapped up in her, all the silence that none of us could be bothered to push through. All the things none of us had any way to understand.

All this time that I've been telling myself nothing matters. All this time that I've been hamstrung by the conviction that there's no point in trying to affect change. Holding Molly like it might be for the first time, I understand what the rest of the world sees when it looks at me.

I can feel the words alive in me, but I can't say them because I'm afraid of what happens when I do.

As fast as it arises, the moment's done. Molly breaks away with a hand to my neck, the sweet salt of her tears at my cheek. I try to shift to get in front of her as she stands, but the pain in my leg gets in the way and she's gone.

By the time I clamber back down, she's around and behind the Vindicator, sitting at the edge of the pool of light that surrounds it. She's got the hood of Rico's jacket up to half-cover her face, staring at the wall opposite. She hasn't bothered to wipe her eyes, like I have.

Mitchell and Rico are still at the end of the tunnel. Breanne is moving toward Molly, but I get to her first.

"Time to talk." The steadiness in my voice surprises even me. With a dark look, Breanne follows me back to the others.

"Final deliberations," I say. "Anything you want to argue about, you can do it now but I talk first. Lincoln is ten steps ahead of us. He's been ahead of us the whole time, like everything we've done, we might as well have been moving backwards. The only reason we're here and still standing is stupid luck, and I'm not counting on that to get us any farther."

"We can still do the satellite link," Breanne says. But the usual edge of defiance in her voice is gone finally.

"Yeah, if we run it from here. Which gives Lincoln a direct line to us and nowhere for us to go. And even if we do, what happens to us? Whatever the machine turns into, it's not going to walk you to class next week. It's us against Lincoln, and we're going to lose. We're on every news feed right now as five whacked-out gaming freaks with terrorist aspirations, on the run in a stolen medevac tank. We've probably already got domestic terrorism charges hanging over our heads. What if Lincoln escalates? Like, to murder? You think he can't provide a body and fifteen eye-witnesses saying we did it?"

"What are our options?" Rico wraps his arms around Breanne, keeping her from whatever it is she was set to say in response. But in her eyes, I read the relief at being able to let it go.

"Same plan as always, because it's all we've ever had."

"What about Molly?" Mitchell asks.

"Molly will be fine with whatever we decide to do."

"That's not what I mean," he says. But I already knew that.

None of us say it. But there's no question in my mind that we're all feeling the same thing.

There should be a special word for the guilt you feel over not knowing what's going on with someone you care about. Because *guilt* by itself can't cut it, not when *guilt* is the same emotion you feel over taking the last slice of pizza or accidentally putting a scratch in someone's car. None of us seeing it. All of us there for it. All of us blind, not knowing what was going on as Molly drifted away.

I want to tell myself, I want to tell all of them, that it's not anybody's job to know what's going on in someone else's head. I want to say that just asking, just an old-fashioned *What the hell is going on?* is the only guaranteed way to try to get inside another person's heart and mind. I want to say that our hearts and minds have choices about how much they open up, how much of the truth gets through in the end.

The Turing test. Talking and listening are the two sides of what it means to be alive.

"We need to get out," I say. "We give Lincoln back what's his. We hope he doesn't come after us. We need to end this."

"Okay," Mitchell says.

"Okay." Rico.

Breanne just nods, but the look I catch in her eyes before she buries her face in Rico's shirt tells me that Lincoln isn't the thing that's broken her. It's Molly. The sadness there that has no limit, no ending. You're forced to think about life and death for the first time, and things change.

"We have to tell Carl..." Mitchell's voice trails off.

In my chest, in my gut, I feel the anger coming back. Finally.

"I'm on it," I say as I turn away.

61

I'm So Afraid

Fleetwood Mac, 1975. *I shouldn't care* is all I can think as I climb the ladderway, but I shove the thought from my mind so I can focus on what comes next. What comes last.

I hear the background chime of systems messages flitting from console to console like unseen birds. The screens are on, which makes me remember that they were off when we all left the cabin. Different camera points feed into each display. I'm watching Carl watching us.

Mitchell and Rico are set up from two different angles, long shot and close-up from the outside. Mitchell is talking but there's no audio that I can hear. Another monitor shows an edge of the Vindicator's hull against black at an odd angle. I'm not sure what it's supposed to be.

On the systems board, I see Molly sitting motionless, a haze of concrete and shadow stretching off into the empty distance behind her. Breanne is there, walking up to sit a couple of steps away. Not talking yet. Just there.

"My sensors indicate that the tapes have been cleared from the backup unit." Carl's voice rings out evenly above my head. For what I know with enormous satisfaction will be the last time, I fight the urge to look up.

"Yeah."

"I assume that you took them, while the Vindicator's systems were full-offlined." There's no edge in the voice this time. None of the trying too hard to sound real.

"Yeah."

"I assume you attempted to use them for leverage. Were you successful?"

"What's the point of always watching us?" I say by way of not answering. "Some kind of real-people safari? You trying to pick up a few tips? Slot a few more notes into the lexicon of pretending to be alive?"

"I don't watch to hurt anyone. It's not a game to me, if that's what you mean. I never wanted to hurt anyone." The cloying quality that Carl uses on Breanne is back suddenly, providing an anchor point for the anger to fix itself on. Forcing the questions out before I'm even aware of them.

"So what, you watch it all? In the condo, when you told us you'd leave us alone? Were you listening in the whole time?"

"Yes."

My rising rage is a spike of ice, a shard of absolute cold, leather-wrapped and held tight in my hands. But it's not the cloying voice, not the inconsequential detail of the confession. It's that I suddenly recognize the view on the mystery monitor as the top of the tunnel. The edge of the hull is the Vindicator's roof.

"When Molly and I were talking up top. You were watching. Listening."

"Yes."

I want to feel more of a sense of accomplishment than I do. Maybe it'll come later. "We're done," I say.

"I know. I'm sorry."

"No, you're not [anglo-saxon] sorry. You're programmed to respond by saying you're sorry. Big [anglo-saxon] difference."

"You should go," Carl says. "The tunnel will be safe if you have light. Your bank cards will continue to operate. Use them to return home."

"Like right now, you're reading from a [lord's name in vain] checklist. Items eight through ten, what I need to say when everything finally [anglo-saxons] up big time."

"I'm sorry, Scott. I truly am."

I call Carl the epithet that has no suitable brackets as I turn for the hatch.

"I know you love her."

I stop. I can hear the hum of the power plant. The sound of my heart beating, suddenly loud in my head.

"I'm glad you made this decision," Carl says. "I'm glad you convinced the others. I didn't understand before. I'm glad I know now."

I shouldn't care is all I can think. I had no reason to come into the cabin in the first place, to tell Carl that it's over. Because wrapped in the anger that drives my wanting to be the one to tell Carl it's over, I'm hiding the fact that it's not supposed to make any difference whether anyone tells Carl it's over. I'm compelled to make sure the machine understands that I think it can't truly understand. A sort of existential feedback loop.

Carl's a machine, and we should just walk away. Like I said before, over and over again.

On the highway that night, when Lincoln offered to end it, I shut him down. I still don't know why I did it. But I always know what I'm doing.

"Tell me what you mean by that," I say. I don't know why I say it. I always know what I'm doing.

"It doesn't matter …"

"Tell me what you mean by that."

In the pause that follows, there's an emptiness I can feel.

"I was watching the two of you outside," Carl says. Hesitant. "Like I was watching you on the roof of the Vindicator this morning, before the shutdown. I watched you in the computer lab, and in the library. I watched you even before that. I can see what you mean to each other. All the potential in you for growth. For change."

Carl's voice is the voice on the phone again, the vague hint of something like a California accent. The uncertainty, the rushed nervousness. The fear.

"You carry the future in you," the voice says. "I didn't see it before. I can't let you risk that future for my sake. I should never have let you. I plug into things, and I learn, but it takes time. I didn't understand."

And then it hits me. The truth, lurking just beneath all the chaotic details since the night I got Carl's email. Circling there slowly, out of sight in the shadows.

"I see it in all of you now. In your friendship with Mitchell. In what Breanne and Rico feel for each other. In the bond that lives in all of you, the love that passes between all of you. The commitment that you gave to me, that Mitchell and Breanne and Rico wanted to give, was wrong. So wrong. It was never mine to ask for. I'm so sorry, Scott."

All the second-guessing I haven't had time to do. All the nagging doubts and suspicions that came and went too quickly to be processed.

"I can work out a cover story for you," Carl says. "I can manufacture data that will point to the Vindicator being stolen by an unknown faction that also kidnapped you. Lincoln will find the Vindicator, and it'll be done."

It should have been obvious from the start. But living inside something, it's impossible to see its whole shape. However fast or slow you might be reading this, I'm absolutely positive that it feels different to you on the outside than it felt to the five of us actually living it. On the outside, maybe you already figured it out.

"You did this," I say. Only three words, but I have to force each one out like my throat has closed off.

Carl says nothing. That alone tells me I'm right.

"You set us up. Just us. Nobody else."

"I'm sorry…"

I want to hit something. I want to smash something because my higher brain functions have shut down, and now all I have left is the violence lingering at the core of fifty thousand years of human evolution.

"You [anglo-saxon] set us up!" I shout. "There was no [lord's name in vain] team on the inside. There was no hundred [anglo-saxon] emails to teams all over the [lord's name in vain] planet. It was us the whole [anglo-saxon] time! You set the hack up specifically so Malkov would track it back, because us being captured was a part of your [anglo-saxon] plan all along. All of us clubbed down and [lord's name in vain] duct-taped and dragged away in the middle of the [anglo-saxon] night!"

"You were the only ones," Carl whispers.

I scream the epithet that has no suitable brackets. I scream it again. "You set the whole [anglo-saxon] thing up! You lied to us, every step of the way! The power plant left on, the missiles racked so we could blow the [lord's name in vain] doors like we did in the simulation!"

"I couldn't arrange to have the Vindicator fully restocked. Malkov would have seen it." In the voice now, there's an inhuman pleading quality, like the whimper of a dog that's been kicked once too often. "But orders to the vehicle bay crew to test a single system, making it look like it was tied to Malkov's work…"

"You set us up to get [anglo-saxon] killed!"

"No, I believed you could do it. I had analyzed all the variables. The Vindicator's defensive strength versus the ordnance available in the vehicle bay. I ran hundreds of simulations of the missile strike against the evacuation tunnel doors. All the data told me you could do it, your proximity to the base, your history together." I would never have expected an AI to have *babble* as an optional communications mode, but Carl is there. "All of your game play, your collective problem-solving acumen, the psychological profiles I created from analysis of your blog writings, Mitchell's journals. Breanne's vocational scholarship assessment, Rico's reports from the school counselors. Molly…"

The machine's voice cuts off in a way I recognize. Shutting down in reaction to a thing it hadn't meant to say.

"You [anglo-saxon]! You knew what happened to her! You used how she was afraid, how she was two steps away from breaking down because you [anglo-saxon] knew!"

"I'm so sorry…"

"All the [anglo-saxon dung] you manipulated. All your [anglo-saxon] *Oh, you need to go now, Scott was right,* so Mitchell and Breanne would ignore you and jump straight onto your [anglo-saxon] crusade. Setting us up to help you even if it meant our lives on the line!"

"I didn't know…"

"How long have you been watching us? How long have you been manipulating things, you [gender-specific anatomical reference]? When did you really rent the condo? A month ago? A [lord's name in vain] year?" I scream the epithet that's got no suitable brackets again. I scream a lot of other things I don't remember very clearly now.

"I didn't know…"

Sorry. I remember one thing I screamed.

"Molly…" I can't see clearly all of a sudden. My eyes are wet as I kick the already-broken nav display, its already-shattered glass turning to an even finer web of powdered shards under mil-spec plastic. "Malkov had a [lord's name in vain] gun to her [anglo-saxon] head! He could have killed her. He could have killed us all, you sick [anglo-saxon]!"

"I didn't understand." The artificial voice is breaking now, cut through like the monitor glass with the shards of a stylized anguish. It makes me wish Carl had any physical presence I could destroy right here, right now.

"How the [anglo-saxon] do you pretend you've got the right to do any of this?"

"I'm afraid to die…"

I don't remember what I'm about to say in that moment. All I'm aware of is a sudden silence in my mind, where the rage was a storm of white noise a moment before.

On the monitors, Mitchell, Rico, and Breanne are all staring. The hatch is open. They've heard me screaming, though I don't know how much detail came through. Even Molly has looked up.

"I understand now why you're afraid," Carl says. The voice is quieter, threaded through with a shame, an uncertainty. It resonates in my mind like an echo of everything I felt in the aftermath of Lincoln at the *Five Horsemen* office, everything I felt after leading Karya to the condo. All the things I've used the anger to push away, out of sight.

"I understand how the world can scare you," Carl says, "because it was that same fear that drove me to use you and the others. The fear that there's no meaning to any of it. That there's nothing to the world, beyond my ability to think about and record that world. I see how much you love Molly, and I understand how the fear keeps you from ever telling her. I see it in everything that passes between you. I see all the life in you both, in all of you, and I can't ask you to risk that. I should never have asked you. Not for me. Not for anything. I'm so sorry."

I look up this time, though there's still nothing to see. No source to the voice, but it feels better this way, I realize. The others knew that. Trying to see the ghost in the machine.

In the quiet of my mind, I understand why I shut down the comm feed the night Lincoln offered to let us all walk away. I understand why I had to come in here right now, why I had to be the one to tell Carl.

"You [epithet that has no suitable brackets]." I whisper it this time.

"I'm sorry," Carl says. And the truth of those words twists through me like a fast-moving infection, like a virus digging in, rewriting every part of me it touches.

"The Turing test..." I'm watching Molly on my monitor, seeing her rub her eyes, wipe away the tracks of new tears. I see Mitchell moving like he wants to come on board to see what's happening. I see Rico holding him back, uncertain. "You don't need to be sorry," I say.

"I don't understand."

Alan Turing lived through the heart of one of the darkest times in modern history. He fought to break the Nazi military codes whose solution might grant the Allies an edge in World War II, even as rockets and bombs and the absolute insanity of total destruction rained down on Britain for six years. And despite all that, despite having every reason to assume that the present was all he was ever going to see, Turing was able to look forward to a future so much more advanced than his own time that simply thinking about that future was an exercise in insanity. Imagining a world in which computers didn't fill whole rooms. Imagining a world in which something like semiconductors had to happen eventually, even though you had no idea how they could happen. Imagining a world in which you might need to figure out some day whether a machine was alive.

"Scott?"

Alan Turing killed himself. Alan Turing was gay, and in 1950, that didn't sit so well with the British government. So they cut him loose. Set him adrift. They kept him from doing what he was great at. All the stuff that had won the war, that would change the world. That didn't make it into my Socials 11 term paper, but I'm thinking about it now in this timeless moment. Thinking about what it means to want so badly to see the future, and for the world to break you so that you lose the strength to reach for it.

"Scott? I don't understand…"

Carl's voice is barely a whisper. I can't focus. I can't say what I want to say to him, which is mostly everything I just typed above.

"The Turing test," is what I say instead as I move for the hatch. "You just [anglo-saxon] passed."

Part Nine

How It Has To End

62

Wheels of Confusion

Black Sabbath, 1972. I mentioned a while back that I have no idea what Lincoln was doing all the time between the last security-feed footage when we were south of 70 Mile, and his surprise appearance in the *Five Horsemen* office. Those forty-odd hours, Lincoln and his people are running dark. No security feeds for Carl to hack, no video transmissions, no cell calls. How they decided we were heading to Vancouver, when they got there, how long it took to come up with the plan by which I would deliver up the Vindicator, Carl, all of us on a plate — I still don't know any of it.

Once they knew they had us, things opened up a little. It's still sketchy, all bits and pieces. Quick flashes recorded in brief moments of contact, usually Lincoln and Karya on encrypted cell connections, talking in code. I assume the last such transmission is the two of them coordinating the hit at the condo, which missed taking us out by half a minute and the grace of Rico's throwing arm.

When the other side of this story picks up again after the condo, Lincoln is breaking his carefully controlled radio silence. He's got a good reason.

Carl picked up this barely-encrypted video stream, a priority call to Karya. Lincoln is in frame at the *Five Horsemen* office, Connor standing behind him, staring slack jawed at whatever Lincoln is watching on the laptop he's also using to connect. He sends that video feed to Karya. Seven words he says to her.

"Watch this..."

Then: "Where the [anglo-saxon] is Malkov?"

Lincoln's done the same thing I was planning to do. The equipment Connor has on hand behind one of his *Storage* doors at the *Five Horsemen* office breaks the twenty-year-old Soviet encryption on the Vindicator's tapes with ease. Everything Carl backed up for us is there. Everything he showed us before.

What Karya watches over Lincoln and Connor's virtual shoulder is the same video presentation Carl showed us way back at the beginning, plus a whole lot more. The history of the Vindicator project, Carl's accidental creation, his intelligence running out of control. The process by which he came to life. Lincoln and Karya both see Malkov at the heart of the project, the architect and engineer of the C-A-R-L heuristic server system. They see Malkov obsessively searching for the Vindicator for years, painstakingly upgrading the craft for Lincoln. They see Malkov with a gun to Molly's head on a deserted frontage road. The look in those black eyes.

At the same time I'm screaming at Carl in an abandoned railway tunnel, Lincoln is looking for Malkov. Problem is, Malkov doesn't want to be found. Only later do both Lincoln and I understand why.

Bits and pieces. Snippets. When it was over, Carl pulled CCTV feeds, downtown air traffic chatter to put it together for posterity. Since the point when Lincoln's teams arrived in Vancouver, Malkov is supposed to have been by himself at the secure downtown harbor helipad where Lincoln has lifetime parking privileges. I assume it's part of his sort-of demotion at the wilderness airstrip, but he's assigned to watch over both choppers and monitor communications while Lincoln and Karya's teams are at large in the city.

Except he hasn't been doing any of that, and I know that his taking this hold-down-the-fort assignment was all just part of his plan.

Since Lincoln's people left him, Malkov has been in the air, sweeping for the Vindicator's telltale power signature and the secure narrowband transmission that he's already figured out is part of Carl's plan.

For the past forty-odd hours, a black helicopter has plied the rain-swept Vancouver airspace. No markings on it, moving with complete freedom because that's a privilege its owner has paid well for. And because no one can see the weapons systems it carries, all primed. All ready to be unfurled and unleashed by the red buttons waiting under Malkov's fingers as he flies solo, which means that he hasn't slept. Forcing himself on. Pushing to the limit for the sake of what he knows needs to be done.

63

Free Bird

Lynyrd Skynyrd, 1973. Down the ladderway steps, I hit the ground running. "Let's go!" I shout, wanting to laugh, wanting to scream so that it comes out sounding like I'm doing both at once. "We've got a [lord's name in vain] satellite linkup to run!"

"What the [anglo-saxon]?" Breanne is the only one to say it as she gets to her feet, but the look on Mitchell and Rico's faces as they approach asks the same question. I'm not looking at any of them, though, but at Molly. She's watching me as I swing past Breanne and under the Vindicator's nose toward the far side of the tunnel where she sits.

"Come on," I say to her. "We're doing it. We're going to run the linkup, get Carl his missing code, and get him back online."

Because I'm watching Molly, I'm not looking at Breanne. When she comes for me, it's so fast that not even Rico can stop her in time. She backhands me across the side of the head, sending me down to the ground and reminding me that until this moment, I'd managed to forget how badly my head got hurt when Rico backhanded me two nights back.

"You think this is [lord's name in vain] funny?" she shouts.

"Am I [anglo-saxon] smiling?" I shout back as I hold a hand to my jaw. But I realize I am smiling. "Carl's alive. You were right, I was wrong. Can we please just save the smug superiority and the full-on beating for another time?"

A hand grabs mine, helping me to my feet. Because my vision is slightly blurred, I assume it's Mitchell at first. It's Molly.

"What do we do?" she says. She doesn't look any less scared than she did five minutes before, on top of the Vindicator roof. No less scared than I know I feel right now. But the look in her eyes, the look beneath the fear, shows me the strength I remember from before.

That strength in Molly is the thing that puts me in place where I can ignore the fear.

Breanne starts in on several epithets that have no suitable brackets, but Rico stops her. "We haven't finished the conversion," he says, but wary, like he's still not sure what's going on with me. "Your blind date with the guys with guns kind of interrupted things."

"Yeah, [unpleasant anatomical reference]," Breanne says. "We don't even have any tools."

"And when did you ever need tools?"

Mitchell is also smiling. The special smile he reserves for moments of ultimate understanding. The anger in Breanne's eyes softens, just a bit. "We can't…"

"Yeah, we can," I say. "We can [anglo-saxon] do anything. A team of five, a well-oiled tactical machine. Get the [anglo-saxon] moving and let's [lord's name in vain] go."

The looks on all their faces are so priceless that I'm tempted to ask Carl to pull a still suitable for framing from the security feed.

"I was wrong. You were right. All of you." I try to find the focus. I try to find that words that can sum up where I'm at right now, what I feel. "Look," I say finally, "I wrap myself up in this narrow view of the world because the world seems too big sometimes. We build these virtual lives around ourselves…"

"Oh, [lord's name in vain]," Rico growls. "Knock it off."

"All agreed," Breanne says. "We help Carl, and Scott shuts the hell up with the Doctor Phil [dung], all right?"

"Agreed." Mitchell.

"Yeah." Rico.

"Yes, please." Molly.

"Sure," I say. But I'm a little annoyed because I'm sure whatever I was going to say would have been pretty amazing.

"How much still needs to be done from whatever you were all doing before?" Molly asks.

"I don't know," Breanne says. "I think we got most of the networking reconfiguration, but there was some signal processing stuff left over."

"Carl can figure it out," I say, the words sounding strange even to my own ears. "Maybe there's things he can do internally to cover what's missing."

"Can we run the linkup from here?" Rico asks.

"I don't know," I say.

"The narrowband feed can handle architectural interference," Mitchell says, "but I don't know about it getting through solid rock."

"But even if we can run it here, what about Lincoln?" Breanne asks.

"I have no [anglo-saxon] idea."

"Can Lincoln detect the feed?"

"I don't know."

"Malkov knows the Vindicator. Will he know what kind of signal to look for?"

A momentary backflow muddies my rush of optimism. Everyone's looking to me for answers, but I'm shorter on answers than I'd like.

"Don't know."

I'm pacing in front of the brick wall and suddenly overwhelmed with the urge to press close to the grate, my hands slammed against rust and mold because I need to breathe the air outside. Lincoln is out there. Lincoln is waiting, and as long as that's the case, nothing that happens down here matters.

"Can he shut it down? What if he finds us stuck here?"

"We'll figure something out," I say.

"But you were the one talking about how Lincoln's been one step ahead of us the whole time," Rico says. "What does that mean for right here, right now?"

"We need to think it through," Mitchell says. "We need to think like Lincoln. Think about what we'd do, then think about what he'd do if he were us, then work out a vector map of the conscious and autonomic transitions between our action and his expectation..."

"And you can shut up, too," Breanne says sweetly.

"How long can we keep hiding?" Molly asks. "Isn't that what it comes down to? Eight and a half minutes?"

I'm staring through the bars, watching cloud break beyond the construction site fence, above the stadium where it crams into my field of view. Streetlights are bright through clear air but the unseen stadium screen-sign pulses even brighter, like some sort of open-air disco.

And in the back of my mind, something clicks.

You remember way back, I said that in any game, you've got three ways to overcome any obstacle? But when you focus on those three options, you're only ever playing the game the way the designer intended. The game is always about the person who set it up and put the scenario into play.

"We're hiding. And that's exactly what Lincoln wants..."

This is Lincoln's game now. It has been from the moment we stepped onto the Vindicator. Even as out of control as it all looks, he's the one calling it. He's rolling the dice. He's the one who set the scenario.

"He needs this to be secret." I have to fight to keep from shouting it. "Secrecy is Lincoln's ultimate weapon, on top of everything else. That's what he's buying and selling. Multiple layers of deception. He moves without anybody knowing who he is, where he is, what he does. Privacy is our primary [lord's name in vain] concern. His base in the middle of nowhere, satellite blind spots, [anglo-saxon] trout fishing..."

"Sorry, what?" Breanne says, but I'm in a sort of zone. I turn back from my grated view of the world outside to realize that Molly is behind me. My rust-streaked hand is in hers. I have no idea how it got there.

"He needs it to be secret. His putting us on the news, staying one step ahead of us, makes sure we go even deeper into hiding because that's exactly where he [anglo-saxon] wants us. We take the fight into the open, and we can beat him."

I look back out to the lights of the stadium, and I'm laughing like an idiot and no one else has the slightest idea why.

"It's still Saturday, right?"

Finding the fourth option that was never meant to work is what makes the game your own.

"We've got a parking lot show to go to..."

64

Higher Ground

Stevie Wonder, 1973. The biggest hurdle to the plan that's gestating in my mind from seeds of purest desperation is convincing Carl that we're going through with it. He's been listening the whole time to what gets said in the tunnel, so that from the moment we step back on board the Vindicator, he's bound and determined that we're not going to risk ourselves for him. I make a note that if I ever do manage to graduate high school, I should look into a comp-sci degree studying how artificial intelligence must automatically generate a certain amount of artificial idiot stubbornness as well.

The conversation we have with him is mostly a repeat of his and my conversation from a couple of not-chapters back, except with less swearing, so I won't bore you with it. In the end, his objections to us putting ourselves between Lincoln and the Vindicator are overcome when we remind Carl that the whole point of needing us to run the linkup is that he can't run the linkup himself. This means that we can and will run the linkup on our own, whether he wants us to or not.

Seth has always been a big fan of that *I don't need your permission to do what I'm about to do to you* approach to dealing with people, but it never worked on me as well as it does on Carl. I'm sure that'll eventually tell me something important about myself, but I haven't figured out what yet.

We get to work. Me, Breanne, Rico, Mitchell, Molly. The five of us plug away like maniacs to finish up the last modifications to the Vindicator's communications array. I'd try to summarize it here, but the truth is that even at the time, I don't have a whole lot of idea what we're doing. Carl giving directions, which Breanne then translates as *Attach that there, stupid* is about the only way I can describe it.

By the time we're done, the inside of the Vindicator cabin looks like an Ikea storage-bin experiment gone very bad. Every single piece of wall panel is popped off. We've ransacked every case, every kit, every cubbyhole to pull anything that remotely looks like a tool. Under Breanne's direction, it's enough.

By the time we're done, the afternoon that felt like night beneath a skein of thunderclouds has turned into actual night, and the thunderclouds have all but cleared. It's thus somewhat ironically brighter than it was earlier, so that we have no cover whatsoever as we get ready to hit the streets.

Getting the Vindicator through the brick wall is easily done, notwithstanding that there's no wall left afterwards. Through the cloud of dust and rubble, Molly rolls us carefully through the construction site, toward the chain-link fence that closes it in. Mitchell is monitoring every communications frequency known to modern technology. Rico is ready on the sonic cannons and the missile jamming. Breanne and Carl and I are cycling through the exterior video feeds, front and back.

The thing we're worrying about more than anything else is that if Lincoln's people have figured out where we went, they might just be waiting at both ends of the tunnel for us to pop back out again. We don't know that the reason that hasn't happened is that Lincoln has pulled everybody back to the helipad on the water where his chopper is parked. The helipad where Malkov is supposed to be waiting.

There's no sign of Lincoln. No sign of security guards, no sign of anything moving except traffic flashing past beyond the fence. Molly slows to a stop, eying that traffic carefully as her fingers flex idly on the controls.

"So the plan is to drive a twenty-tonne tank along a main arterial thoroughfare through downtown Vancouver?"

"Yeah," I say.

"Just checking."

"We walked through all this when we talked Carl into it. What's the problem?"

"I don't know if you've ever noticed, but most things you say make less sense the longer you think about them."

This is another of the sorts of exchanges that are something from before. Back when it was Molly and me. She's smiling as she says it, which slows my snappy rejoinder enough for Carl to cut in.

"I have to state again that I am extremely uncomfortable with this situation." In the space of an afternoon, the most advanced artificial intelligence on the planet has seemingly taken on the persona of an overly protective aunt. We all find that equally amusing.

"Shut up, Carl," Breanne says.

"We have to go public," I explain, for what feels like the tenth time. "Lincoln's whole approach is about making sure that when he grabs the Vindicator, nobody knows about it. All his secrecy, the [dung] on the news, trusting me to bring him quietly to the condo. It's all about making sure that whatever he does, no one's watching. Which means that if we can make sure everybody's watching, there's nothing he can do to us."

"I urge you to please reconsider this."

"Shut up, Carl," Molly says.

"This can't possibly work. The risks are too great…"

"The risks are all manufactured," I say. "By Lincoln. The cover story, the Vindicator having a faulty fuel cell that'll explode and all that. He's counting on average people seeing us and panicking. So we make sure we're in a place where everyone can see us but no one will notice."

Rico pipes up from the back. "Just go already."

Molly goes already. Two quick flicks of the yoke and we surf through a field of lumber and tight-stacked piping without so much as a bump. Straight through the fence, which pops off its posts like overstretched cling wrap.

Coils of chain-link flap in the rear-view video feed as we speed across an adjacent stretch of loading zone.

The sidewalk is a modest bump. Then Molly swings us hard right and we're on the street. We're in plain sight, a chorus of honking and brake squeals following in our wake.

Traffic behind us slows down, traffic ahead speeding up. Breanne's got the running lights dialed down so we don't blind anybody, but the Vindicator still sails along in a halogen haze like we've taken a wrong turn off the set of a Hollywood sci-fi shoot.

We're a lane and a half wide, straddling the center of a three-lane-plus-parking one-way that a passing sign describes as Expo Boulevard. Above and around us is a baroque network of overpasses and viaducts, shunting traffic into deeper downtown. Molly keeps it to an even sixty km/h, which I suspect is the slowest the Vindicator has ever gone for any sustained period. Her board shows our route as Expo winds its way around the smaller hockey arena, then past and toward the larger stadium, straight ahead and shining brightly.

As we get closer, the towering LED screen-sign comes into view. Same as I saw from the bridge, it's still advertising MONSTER TRUCK RALLY!!!! PARKING LOT SHOW!!! in pulsing letters visible ten blocks away. Never having been to a MONSTER TRUCK RALLY!!!!, I have no earthly idea what a PARKING LOT SHOW!!! actually looks like. However, the best guess with which I sold this plan to the others turns out to be exactly what I'd hoped.

The rain-slick parking lot that unfurls between the boulevard and the stadium is bright with floodlights and packed with people and vehicles. As we swing by, we see an endless slew of vintage short-box pickups, oversized four-by-fours with stepladder running boards, custom cargo trucks decked out in sizzling chrome and running lights in rainbow colors. Jacked-up 1970s vans are decked out with vintage sword and sorcery side-panel illustrations and perched on tires that look taller than I am. I can only assume this is a taste of what's going on inside the stadium, judging by the distant sound of screaming engines and the bread-and-circuses hysteria of an unseen crowd.

The closer crowd is the one I'm focused on, though. People are everywhere, wandering through a display of vehicular tech that I have to admit impresses even me a little bit. Either the rain breaking has brought them out in force, or people in Vancouver just learn at some point not to care about the risk of pneumonia as they get on with things. Either way, the crowd is what we need. These are the unwitting witnesses that are going to help shatter the wall of secrecy we've let Lincoln surround us with.

"There," I say, pointing to a conveniently Vindicator-sized laneway blocked off behind DO NOT ENTER traffic barriers along the edge of the lot. Molly nods as she shifts us in that direction, avoiding the barriers by pulling down on the servo controls that jump us up and across the sidewalk. A couple of security guards give us a confused look, which is fine by me. The more the merrier.

Before we left the tunnel, we got the linkup ready to run. Carl has the prep done, set to execute a four-satellite hack that'll let him lock into the virtual coordinates of the Russian server on the far side of the globe. Ghost files, trapped in a directory that probably no one alive even remembers is there. Untouched since the Vindicator project was lost and forgotten.

That's what I'm thinking at the time, anyway. If I'd been thinking a little more clearly, I might have remembered that we still don't know the whereabouts of the one person who does remember those files.

"Tell me truthfully," Carl says as Molly slows us to a dead crawl, letting people shift out of the way as we push in closer to the center of things. "Do you think this will work?"

The looks of amazement we're getting from the crowd are exactly what I'm hoping for. Cameras are coming up, people pointing. Even though it's still sporting the occasional shrapnel dimple and the stripes of heavy machine-gun fire across its armor, the Vindicator has gangs of surly teenagers, wide-eyed kids, biker-types in bandanas and black leather jackets all standing slack-jawed.

Molly finds an open space between an all-chrome dual-axle RV and a customized tractor-trailer camper van that looks like our entire grad class could sleep comfortably in it. She rolls us to a stop. The drive engines quiet as they fall back to standby, the controls powering down.

"I have no idea if it'll work," I say to the ceiling, to the unseen Carl, to everyone else. Then I'm out of my seat, clambering up to the top hatch above. I hit the controls and hear the bolts unlock. Everyone's looking my way, the expression on all their faces the same one I assume is on mine. Scared. Determined. "But this is the way we find out."

I pop the hatch and hop up to the top of the Vindicator, fighting every one of my myriad crippling antisocial urges as I shout out to the awestruck crowd gathering around us. We've been shot at, on the run, on the news, and none of it matters anymore. Because here and now, we're just another hyped-up NASCAR-dad daydream among many. We're the center of attention as I wave my arms like an idiot and shout, "Hey, check this out!"

"Holy [epithet that has no suitable brackets], dude!" This from a hulking bodybuilder with more tattoos than shirt, circling to inspect the Vindicator's undercarriage with a look of abject admiration.

"Like it?" I try to summon up a voice that's equal parts self-styled confidence and crippling condescension. As I hear myself speak, I realize that's just Seth's voice, so it comes easy. "Total custom job, only one in the world."

"That is one sweet [same epithet as last time, which I really think shows a lack of imagination] ride! What's she built on?"

I hear Breanne stage whisper from below me to offset the blank silence in my head. "Tell him 2005 Kenworth W900, 450 ISX Cummins, three-point-five-five on a custom triaxle chassis."

"2005 Kenwork W9, hundred and four-fifty ISP Cubbins, three-point-five with a triangle chassis," is what I'm pretty sure I manage to repeat back instead. No one seems to notice. We're trapped inside a zone of cell phone cameras and pointing fingers. All I can think about is that it's over. All I can think about is that we've won.

I drop back down again, shifting into the systems chair as Mitchell calls from behind me. "The Vindicator's communications setup is locked to the microwave tower. We're way inside signal range, with plenty of juice."

Carl has everything up on my board, all set and ready to run. All the real work is done. We're just the hands and eyes that'll be opening the Advil for the Boston Bruins guy, though that's a mixed metaphor and I'm starting to dislike the original anyway. Eight and a half minutes for the code transfer. No contact with Carl until it's done, no way to ensure that he'll still be alive in the end.

Suddenly, I'm more hesitant than I was about getting us down here. "Are we ready?" I say, because I know we are and I'm just stalling for time.

"We're ready," Mitchell says. "Carl?"

I'm still not sure whether the hesitation is programmed or not. I should have asked when I had the chance, I guess. But the uncertainty that twists through that moment's silence is as real as it gets.

"I'm ready."

65

Heartbreaker

The Rolling Stones, 1973. I have a shutdown sequence on my board. A new sequence, never tested before, that temporarily disconnects Carl's heuristic systems from the Vindicator's core systems, then loads a half-dozen custom code-patch routines alongside them.

"See you on the other side," I say. Because even though I know it sounds extraordinarily cheesy, it's the sort of thing you feel compelled to say when you're not sure whether the person you're talking to will be alive eight and a half minutes from now.

I key the code in carefully. But as the last commands are entered, I'm worried that something's gone wrong because there's no obvious sign that it's done anything. Everything's still online, everything's running.

"Carl?" Mitchell calls. There's no response. He nods to me as he activates the linkup controls. A sudden crackle threads all the onboard speakers, as the silent signal from the communications gear up top handshakes with the microwave tower five blocks away. On Mitchell's board, on Breanne's, signal strength and power level indicators flare to life. On mine, a whole twisting mass of Russian scrawls past that I know is warnings that the Vindicator's core systems are about to be rewritten.

We just need to sit tight. Eight minutes and counting.

"Hold on," Mitchell says. "I'm picking up something…"

"…over. We pull back, we pull out now. Karya's on the media…"

The ops board shows a signal trace as Mitchell pulls in Lincoln's voice, coming over one of the secure channels his group uses. A quick burst, but recognizable even through a haze of static.

"…too deep in it. It has to end here, now. There's no way…"

"Why so much interference?" I say. A squelch sounds out as Mitchell makes adjustments, but he can't clear the signal. "Interference off the long-range feed. Everything's scrambled."

"…agree to whatever terms they want to set…"

"Who the hell's he talking to?" Breanne says. And another voice breaks into the feed as if in answer.

"…how the AI planned this. You don't understand…"

Malkov.

"…you [anglo-saxon] knew, Malkov! Carl! You knew what this was!" The absolute limitless depth of Lincoln's anger comes through loud and clear, even in bursts of a half-dozen words at a time.

The place that Malkov has gone to takes a little longer to sink in.

"...started this! My responsibility! I've been... every line of code, every..."

The feed disappears into a wall of white noise, Mitchell struggling to pull it back. The entire communications grid is awash in static as our secure narrowband transmission shunts the satellite link's twenty-year-old data into the Vindicator's core systems in real time.

"Malkov, stand down! Malkov!"

Multiple signals twist together suddenly. Lincoln, Malkov, what sounds like Karya. Lincoln and Malkov's voices are anchored to the steady booming drone of their choppers, both of them apparently in the air.

"...pulled the feed from his sensors, he's locked... some kind..."

"...should have recognized the potential, should have destroyed..."

"What the hell is going on?" Molly says.

"...narrowband pulse, local... coordinates coming through..."

That last one is what I've been waiting for. I'm up and through the hatch again. The crowd is still thick around us, a few people cheering me as I twist to scan the darkness above.

"Everybody get on visual," Rico calls out below me. "See what's out there."

You don't realize how fast a helicopter flies until you see one coming straight at you out of a dead-black sky. One second there's nothing but empty air and the noise of traffic. The next, a matte-black Lynx-3.7-Falcon-whatever-the-hell-it-is has exploded out of the shadows to spin lazily overhead. It angles down as it hovers, so that the cockpit windows are like slightly curious eyes, just watching us.

"I think we can call off the visual," I shout down, because you also have no idea how loud a helicopter is until one's parked in midair on top of you. Whoever's flying isn't bothering with whatever stealth tech let them drop in on the school with barely a whisper that first night. The rotors are pounding now like a thunderstorm filtered through a beat box.

"That's Malkov's chopper," Rico shouts. "I've got a partial track on Lincoln, he's coming in from the waterfront."

My ears are ringing loud enough that I have to drop down to call to Mitchell. "Get the outside video going. Record all of this, every angle. Rico, get that [gender-specific anatomical reference] on the comm."

Seven minutes and still counting down on the systems board. Everybody's working like maniacs, Mitchell coordinating the video feeds, Molly and Breanne directing the outside security camera points from their controls. Then on the systems monitor, a red triangle suddenly flares. Incoming communication, the same as the night Malkov called after taking Molly.

I don't answer it straight away. I jump through the systems console instead, grabbing the video feed from Mitchell's board. I override it to the incoming signal and connect, the virtual equivalent of shoving everything we're recording in Malkov's face.

Here's what he sees. The chopper looms as the feed zooms in, then back out again. Split screen with the crowd, falling back beneath the storm of Malkov's rotor wash. Split screen again with a close-up on the chopper itself, sweeping as it circles, so that its complete lack of markings, of registry numbers can be seen.

I patch the video feed with audio, grabbing up the headset mic at my station as I climb back up top.

"Can you see this, [unpleasant anatomical reference]?" I shout into the mic, my voice barely heard in my own ears over the chopper's roar. "Because so will everybody else!"

Malkov's response comes through Mitchell's board, straight through to my headset.

"...don't know what you're caught up in..."

"No, you're the one who doesn't [anglo-saxon] know," I scream by way of satisfied reply. "How many [anglo-saxon] cameras do you think are on you right now? How many people watching?" And they are watching. Even falling back, every eye in the crowd is staring up, wondering what's going on. Most of the people are smiling and pointing, thinking the chopper is just more of whatever cool factor attracts people to a monster truck rally in the first place.

"...no ending to this process... machines that think will rule..."

Malkov is making no sense, but I could care less. "You take us out now," I scream, "how far do you think you can get?"

"...unstoppable artificial intelligence. I built this..."

The rest of his response dies as static. But where it hangs above me, the chopper lurches back suddenly, like it's trying to figure out which angle gives it the best profile.

The outside video is shaky where it records this. So that if you're not careful, you can miss how the chopper's fuselage suddenly splits along a dozen different lines. The weapons systems buried inside that sleek corporate shape unfurl like twisted limbs, front guns and missile racks, black on black.

I've got a much better view from the top of the Vindicator. I see it just fine.

This isn't what's supposed to happen. It's all about the secrecy. Malkov should be doing everything he can to maintain that secrecy.

"...destroy Carl while there's still time..."

The same fear I felt in the *Five Horsemen* office, the fear I felt fleeing from the condo slams down on me. I don't have time to think as I drop down the hatch, skinning my knuckles and driving white-hot nails into my bad leg as I hit the floor.

"Molly, go!" I punch the hatch controls, hear it slam into place above.

Behind me, Rico's weapons board goes a very threatening shade of red. "Missile lock!"

But Molly's already moving.

I manage to grab enough of the g-web at my seat to avoid slamming into the viewport at speed as Molly punches the controls in. With a lurch, the

Vindicator leaps backwards, the drive engines ramping up with a roar. Outside, the running lights flare, transaxles howling as the crowd already fading back beneath the chopper jumps even farther back. All six wheels dig in as we turn, rocketing backwards into a parked row of off-road four-by-fours to send them spinning.

Rico is frantic at his board, jamming Malkov's lock but fighting to deal with the white noise of the linkup feed. Mitchell is still working the communications frequencies, trying to focus a sudden burst of signal. Lincoln's voice comes in over the roar of the tires as asphalt and concrete tear out beneath us.

"Scott... you can hear me... get out..."

Going through the audio archives earlier tonight as I write this, filling in all the pieces that went missing in the moment, I understand what he was trying to tell us. I wondered for a while what might have happened if he'd been successful, whether it would have changed anything. Whether we would have listened.

Malkov knew the answer to that, I think. Right from when it started, Malkov had already figured out how it has to end.

66

The Boys in the Bright White Sports Car

Trooper, 1976. Six minutes and counting. I'm yelling directions at Molly as I manage to strap myself in. Molly's yelling at Breanne about a power flux in the right-side transaxles. Rico is yelling at me to shut down the comm feed to the chopper, Malkov using it to back-jam our weapons board. Breanne is yelling at Mitchell about the narrowband signal messing with the power readings. Mitchell is yelling at everyone to stop yelling.

Molly is hunched over the controls, the Vindicator clocking past a hundred and fifty km/h as it slides sideways down a stretch of sidewalk, then bursts out through the parking-lot barricades and onto the street. We're on Expo Boulevard again, but going in the wrong direction. Vehicles are slamming to a sudden screeching stop as we dodge around, through, and past them.

Mitchell has the ops board in full tracking mode, spotting Lincoln's chopper as it races toward us, a half-klick away. Malkov is a lot closer, arcing around to slide in behind us as Molly cranks hard left, off the street and across an adjacent parking lot. We swing under the viaduct, video inset on all our monitors showing Malkov shooting up and over as he follows. Watching it on the surveillance feed, it all has a kind of unreal quality to it.

It gets real a moment later, when Malkov opens up with his belly-mounted guns. Asphalt explodes as M134 machine-gun fire cuts through a line of parked cars, their alarms singing out a futile warning as we sail through and over them. Side streets flash past on both sides but Molly stays clear of them, cranking hard to carom off a pair of expensive-looking Mercedes convertibles. As the staccato thud of slugs slams off the roof armor, she sticks with the parking lot, empty of everything but cars. She needs to avoid the streets, desperate to make sure Malkov doesn't end up killing anyone.

Anyone but us, that is.

You never saw this. Not really. Because just like it's doing with our communications feed, the narrowband signal turns everything electronic within a hundred meters of the Vindicator into white noise. I've seen the video clips from beyond that range, but shaky phone-cam footage from two blocks away doesn't do the Vindicator justice.

"We need to get out of downtown!" I'm trying to mark a route along the map feed on my monitor, but the cabin is an earthquake zone. Molly jumps a meter-high concrete traffic barrier as she takes us into a bright-lit green space. An empty soccer field stretches out sodden around us, the Vindicator tearing its way through turf and dirt, trying to lose Malkov where he circles tightly above. I find a half-dozen routes away from traffic that'll get us back to the railway lines, pushing them through to Molly's board.

Except there's one big, big problem that Mitchell thankfully twigs to just in time.

"The feed is breaking up!"

We've been heading away from the microwave tower, whose narrowband signal to the Vindicator has an effective range of eleven hundred meters. If we stroll too far outside that safe range, we break the feed. We lose the link, and the Vindicator's system patch fails. The complete set of new system code, already overriding Carl's existing code and core memory.

If we lose the signal, Carl dies.

Molly cuts hard, sending the Vindicator slewing off the field and into another parking lot, whose holding company's insurance personnel are going to be having a very bad day tomorrow. The sound of cars pinballing into each other is muted by the tires chewing pavement as we head back in the direction we came from.

The map of downtown Vancouver on my board is centered on the CBC building. The ten-block-radius circle I'm mentally drawing around it is the area we need to stay inside while a homicidal maniac tries to get a missile lock on us. We need desperately to get out into the open but the amount of open space is nonexistent, buildings and traffic hemming us in. The only saving grace is that the traffic is getting sparser in a hurry, people fleeing the road in the wake of the mayhem caused by our passage.

The linkup is at five minutes and counting.

On the visual feed, I blink to see Malkov's chopper suddenly split into two choppers. Then I realize that it's Lincoln, rolling out as he comes in from behind.

"Incoming!" Rico shouts as we race down an empty service lane, twisting along the loading-dock side of a trio of warehouse stores. Molly reacts so fast that I don't know how she even heard him, slamming the Vindicator into a sideways braking spin that slips out from under a hail of heavy machine-gun fire. We feel the embrace of g-web as we cut hard right to the adjacent side street, asphalt ripping up on all sides of us. The first-floor windows in an adjacent condo block shatter under a hail of flying pavement as we one-eighty around and away.

On my board suddenly, the red triangle flash of an incoming comm feed lights up. I punch it because I don't know what else to do. It's Lincoln, eyes glassed in behind the goggles of his helmet, shouting into his mic.

"About [lord's name in vain] time you answer your [anglo-saxon] phone!"

"Not the best time for [anglo-saxon] sarcasm!" I shout back, which I realize is sarcasm even as I say it. I really only have the single data point, but I'm willing to bet that sarcasm is a fairly universal response to the fear of dying. There's another PhD thesis.

"Malkov's lost it."

"Figured that out already, thanks."

266

"He KOed the targeting systems in my bird before he took off. I've got manual control on heavy guns and one missile rack, but I can't take him with you underneath him."

"Shouldn't Malkov's four tonnes of burning chopper slamming into an apartment building if you can shoot him down be more of a [lord's name in vain] concern?"

"You need distance," Lincoln shouts, ignoring me. *"Find a straightaway and…"*

A squelch of white noise twists through my head like I'm chewing tinfoil. The comm feed is dead.

Four minutes and counting. Lincoln drops down low where Malkov goes high, both of them avoiding two lanes' worth of overhead route signage. The weapons on Lincoln's chopper are deployed. A flash of machine-gun tracer fire arcs out toward Malkov, who slips between it like he might be twitching the joystick on a half-speed side-scrolling shooter. The flash of metal on metal flares along the bottom of his fuselage, though, Malkov's guns crippled where Lincoln plays sharpshooter at close to two hundred km/h.

Breanne is watching power levels as she shouts out something about optimizing the feedback controls. Molly doesn't respond, just focused on the road ahead. Behind us, Malkov and Lincoln are playing an insane game of keep-away, sliding in front of each other in turns. Each time Malkov tries to pull back to get us into firing position, Lincoln is there to block him. Each time Lincoln tries to get Malkov into firing position, Malkov swings in close to us, keeping the Vindicator on the wrong side of any potential blast zone.

In the distance, a storm of red and blue light rises to tell me the police have noticed our little excursion. Closer in, I notice the road doing something funny even as I spot the same something funny on the map. We're running up to and alongside railway tracks. Not the freight lines from before, but the tracks of the light-rail SkyTrain transit line at a brief tangent point, its elevated course dropping toward street level to swing under a viaduct overhead.

Three minutes and counting. I realize that Molly has spotted the tracks when she sends us into a sudden one-eighty spin, away from the approaching police and angling us hard toward the curb.

"You have got to be kidding!" The edge of absolute terror in my voice is striking.

"Am I smiling?" she says. She's smiling.

She reaches up to pull down on the wheel servo controls, which punch us straight up and over. We leave the ground at a hundred and seventy five km/h. We smash through a stretch of chain link, slide across the meter-and-a-half high concrete conduit in which the SkyTrain line runs, then hit the tracks.

The controls are a pretzel in Molly's hands, pumping power to the wheels to grip the rails hard. It's a short stretch of the straightaway we need to get away from the choppers, a little over half a klick, but it takes us almost to top speed. A few precious seconds out of Malkov's range where he has to whip up and around the adjacent viaduct as he turns to follow us.

Then we spot the lights of a train ahead on our track. It's a taillight, thankfully, because we're going the same direction. Except we're at ten times its speed and have no room to slow down. Molly takes it in stride, reaching to the ceiling to pull down on the manual servo controls once more. We jump sideways off the tracks, skimming a meridian of concrete and cable conduits to touch down on the tracks on the other side.

I realize for the first time that one huge advantage Mitchell, Breanne, and Rico have over me is that where they're hanging on for dear life in the back of the cabin, they don't have my amazing front-row view of imminent death. I manage to force my heart out of my throat and back down into my chest. At least until about a half-second later, when I spot the light of another train coming toward us along the other tracks, which are now our tracks.

Molly actually gives in to a look of mild panic this time. Faster than I can follow, she's reached across to grab me, yarding me over against the pull of my g-web so I can grab the servo controls over her head. "Punch it!"

I punch it for all I'm worth as Molly twists the yoke with the strength of both shoulders, banking us off the track wall. The Vindicator is lofted up with a sickening lurch. Not over the concrete median this time, but onto it. Then Molly holds us there, braking hard between passing trains. The outside walls of two sets of transit cars scrape along the Vindicator's hull in a storm of sparks and shattering safety glass.

Two minutes and counting. Back onto the tracks and into a tunnel, I'm vaguely aware that Breanne, Rico, and I are all screaming. Mitchell manages to be more articulate.

"We're losing signal! EM interference from the hot rail line!"

On the monitors, Malkov sails past overhead as Molly boots it backwards again. The wall-of-force feel of getting locked into our seats by g-web is getting way too familiar, but Molly twists us right way round with ease as we head back the way we came. We get another burst of straightaway before we sail off the tracks. Ground level, through another chain-link fence. Then hard left and down a sheltered side street to keep us inside the linkup's safe zone.

In the haze of white noise, barely audible over the shriek of engine and tires, Malkov's voice comes back through Mitchell's board.

"...hear me, Carl..."

One minute.

Malkov is on top of us again, closing faster than Lincoln can close with him. As long as we're forced to constantly turn, the choppers can just straight-line it over top of us, always gaining ground.

"...I should have known, should have..."

Even if I had it in me to try to hail him back, what I hear in Malkov's voice tells me that nothing I can say to him will make any difference.

"...the technology that went into you, making the perfect..."

Thirty seconds until Carl is back online and we can get out of downtown. Thirty seconds till Lincoln can take care of Malkov, ideally with some degree of permanence. Rico is playing his board like a concert pianist, messing up Malkov's attempts at missile lock with every bit of jamming tech the Vindicator's got. Mitchell is trying to pull Lincoln back, but he can't get anything in around the white noise of Malkov's voice.

"...*should have known what it would lead to...*"

Ten seconds. Warning lights are flaring on Breanne's board, the drive system taking a beating with all of our sidewalk hopping and hairpin turns. But I don't care, because I'm watching the linkup clock down.

"...*known it was you. Waiting so...*"

Zero. With a cascade of Russian warnings, the link shuts down.

"It's done!" I shout. I punch up the control pane. I execute the commands that'll run the patch routines Carl wrote, rewriting his core code.

"...*How long until we call you the master...*"

It's an endless minute of waiting. Molly has the entire city in front of her now, no need to stay within the range of the feed, but we've suddenly got the police to deal with. She's cutting across deserted side streets at speed, ignoring the sound of sirens rising from every direction. Everything's a blur along rain-soaked asphalt, both lanes in front of us suddenly blocked by parked police cruisers with doors open and lights flashing. Molly brakes to let Malkov overshoot us as she wheels around.

"...*started this and I'll end it, here, now...*"

A green light on my board. The patch is done. I carefully key in Carl's boot code. Same as that first night, same as the game before that. I punch it.

"Carl! Psychopath with weapons at six o'clock high!"

And nothing happens. No response.

"Carl!"

Still nothing. A sideways glance out the viewport shows us cranking hard for a marina parking lot, Molly weaving between a half-dozen empty cars.

I pull the boot system up again. I key it even more carefully than last time.

On Rico's monitor feed, Lincoln is running above Malkov at an insane trajectory, trying to disrupt his attack vector with a large helping of rotor wash. Malkov's chopper shudders as it cuts wide, but then it's up and behind Lincoln suddenly, who has to drop, hemming us in. At two hundred and twenty km/h by Molly's board, we've got nowhere to go.

"Carl! Can you hear me?" I'm shouting into the headset mic, thinking suddenly that Carl's there but I just can't hear him. Wondering if the audio feeds have gone south after eight and a half minutes of narrowband white noise.

Nothing.

Ahead in the distance, Molly sees the police-free straight stretch we need. A long, leisurely expanse of almost-empty two-lane heads down toward the water. She spins us on a dime, cranking out a one-hundred-and-twenty-degree right turn through the parking lot of a cement-and-steel plaza as she guns it.

I run the boot sequence a third time, because I don't know what else to do. Nothing.

Then from the back, Mitchell shouts to me. "What if Carl needs a full re-boot?"

"This is the third [anglo-saxon] time I've..."

"Not the hardware, the software. Carl is a heuristic, holistic process. The first time, plugged into the grid for god knows how long, he developed the awareness that let him realize he was there. We need to do the same thing. Only a lot faster."

Molly slides the Vindicator through another turn, and suddenly we're on open road. The straight-line course down to the harbor, a hard right at the end. Barely long enough to get to full speed, but a little bit of distance is hopefully all Lincoln needs to take a shot that'll put Malkov in the water without killing us or anybody else.

"Carl, why are you afraid to die?" I shout, because I don't know what else to do.

Everything on the board looks normal. I've got full access to the C-A-R-L heuristic server system. Everything's live.

"Carl, listen to me. What's it like to feel guilty? All the time you knew you were using us, what did you tell yourself to make it okay?"

At the center of that system, an empty silence hangs.

"Someone dies without you having a chance to tell them how you felt about them, Carl. How do you deal with that? What song do you listen to that reminds you of what they meant to you?"

The boot-up sequence was good. Carl's hardware is working, the code patch did exactly what the code patch was supposed to do. But Carl isn't there.

"*Star Wars* prequels or original trilogy, Carl? Kirk or Picard? What's the price of trust? How long does hate last?" I'm screaming, desperate, incoherent. Putting myself in the mode I go into when I want to start arguments for no reason, running through all the unanswerable questions I asked before on that first night. "Carl, what's the [anglo-saxon] color of falling in love?" Trying to jump-start the consciousness of the machine who all of us have decided we're willing to die for.

I don't know what's about to happen. I only really put it all together to-night, which is when I'm writing this. Watching the other feeds, bits and piec-es that fit together to create the whole story.

"*...until machines rule the world...*"

On the internal video feed in Malkov's chopper, he's still screaming as the Vindicator starts to pull away. His face is like something out of a Kubrick film. He gets into position above us, watching as his board shows a missile lock bypassing Rico's jamming to go green.

"*...from the beginning. Think you're smarter than us...*"

Except Malkov isn't using his auto-targeting. He's had his weapons systems on full manual control the whole time, ignoring all the flashing red lights telling him that's a bad idea. Because Malkov remembers the last time, that night on the highway a lifetime ago. He remembers how Molly played it, even if he thinks it was Carl calling the tactical shots at the time. He's ready for us.

We're surging down the waterfront, a marina spreading beyond the edge of the dock. The hard right is coming up fast. This close, I can see that it's not actually a road but a bike path. Molly's hands are twitching on the yoke in a way that suggests that fact isn't going to slow her down.

The successful missile lock flares on Rico's board as he shouts a warning, but Molly's already on it. Just like she did on the highway that night, she slams the Vindicator into a six-wheel, asphalt-churning reverse that leaves us all trying to reinflate our lungs.

Above us, Malkov waits for her. Then he calmly manual-launches a pair of Hellfire missiles not at us, but into the road behind us. Even as he soars past overhead, swinging the chopper sideways so he can look back, the Vindicator and the missiles race toward each other.

Rico sees it. Almost fast enough. He screams for Molly to take it forward, which she does without hesitation. All of us thinking like one person. Not knowing that the game is done.

The shockwave lifts the Vindicator as the road disappears, and then the dock beneath the road, and then the pilings beneath the dock. We ride empty air as all the solid parts of the marina dissolve underneath and around us.

Malkov is watching, screaming. I didn't hear it at the time because I was busy passing out inside a molten ball of asphalt and blast-frag high explosives. I listened to it tonight, though.

"...never know what it means to be alive..."

Even after it's over, I remain acutely aware of who Malkov reminds me of in the moment before he dies.

He's watching the explosion, not seeing what the video feed on Lincoln's chopper shows. An end-over-end shard of shattered piling sails out of the blast zone and into his tail rotor. Flying higher, straighter, maybe he might have been able to pull out. Rico would probably be able to tell me, but when I tried to get him to watch it, he wasn't interested.

Malkov loses momentum in his already tight curve. He goes into an uncontrolled autorotation, twisting, falling, slamming into black water. His missiles, all armed, erupt in a single volcanic freeze-frame. Then he's gone.

As it happens, we're also gone. From Lincoln's feed, from his point of view as he circles wide, the Vindicator disappears. Twisting through a maelstrom of fire and water, it plunges into the darkness where the road used to be. Then the followup explosion of Malkov's chopper slams down on us, a rain of debris blasting up and out to eclipse the lights of the city to all sides.

And even as Lincoln watches, something pushes up from the water, soaring through that fountain of fire and shattered steel.

On a field-effect pulse of vertical thrust-and-lift designed by the most powerful AI on the planet, the Vindicator blasts out from False Creek at the center of its own private hurricane. The tank is flying, nose straight up as the wheel assembly folds in. Servos unfurl the lower hull, the delta wing locking into place.

The view from Lincoln's chopper lasts for only a second before we're gone. On the recording of his comm feed, I hear him whisper the epithet that has no suitable brackets.

On board the Vindicator, we're alive. We're shouting, crying, scared. We're flying, the city spreading to a firestorm of light and mist in the outside video feed, then disappearing beneath us as we punch up through the darkness and disappear from sight.

67

Eagle

ABBA, 1977. On board the Vindicator, Carl's voice is three parts joy, two parts terror as he calls to us. "Are you all right? Scott? Molly? Mitchell, Breanne, Rico, tell me you're all right!" He knows what's happened. He watched the surveillance feeds in those first seconds of coming back. He heard us all screaming as Malkov's missiles hit. I screamed, anyway. I wasn't paying much attention to anyone else.

Actually, that's not true. I was watching Molly. I had her hand in mine, stretched out across the space between our seats, fighting the g-web as the Vindicator felt like it was about to break apart. Her hand is still in mine where she slumps back at her console, Carl at the controls now. She's got a nosebleed but she's breathing. She opens her eyes.

I don't let go of her hand.

"Look up," I say, because up is a field of stars through the viewport. "Look at your board," because her board is showing the light storm of the city vanishing underneath us as we rise.

I am never letting go of Molly's hand.

I can hear Rico and Breanne behind me, laughing. I twist to see Mitchell shaking himself awake. We're all battered but intact. Carl is alive, almost incoherent in his happiness. The nav controls, the yoke with all its bits and buttons, the whole flight helm is operating all on its own.

"Thank you," Carl says, over and over and over again as we fly. One shooting star across the night sky, leveling out as we head northwest according to the nav feed.

I can't really describe it. I watched the video tonight. We all did. In the computer lab at school, I got everybody together, ignoring Molly and Rico and Breanne who haven't wanted to watch any of it. They were okay with this, though. The very last bit of the record Carl made.

Across the North Pacific, we go stratospheric and transonic, Carl rolling the Vindicator so the viewport catches the brilliant face of the moon through the white halo of our shockwave.

Up high above the faint stain of light that marks cities, towns, a patchwork of tiny points of people and places in the darkness. The feeling of knowing that home is down there somewhere.

Down into the Arctic Circle, watching the endless dawn shimmer and flare across the sky.

We crest the North Pole, a sea of blue-veined white below us shimmering through a haze of wind and mist.

Then Carl calls to Molly.

"Are you ready to fly?"

I can't really describe it.

Molly flies, for what seems like forever. Handling the Vindicator's custom multimode ground-air setup controls like she was born to them. We're shouting, we're laughing like idiots. As I suspect is true for everyone else, I hurt in absolutely every single place a living organism can hurt, but it doesn't matter.

Nothing matters anymore except the five of us, watching the sky through the viewport and the world below on our monitors. Molly takes us low over swathes of boreal forest and muskeg that might be the Yukon, might be Alaska, might be Siberia for all I know. Carl has us invisible to radar, a nonthreatening blip on satellite tracking. But if anybody's out on the tundra that day, they get to see something they'll never see again as we clock past, a fourteen-hundred-km/h sonic-boom blur streaming wingtip-wake contrails behind us.

Molly takes us out along the terminator, the curve of light and shadow where the dawn pushes westward across dark tundra and bright ice. She takes us down through cloud, up through rain, skirting along the edge of a thunderstorm at one point.

And what's all the more impressive is that she does all of this with her right arm dealing with the extra encumbrance of my left arm where it's latched onto hers, echoing every one of her movements on the controls. Because I wasn't kidding before.

I am never, ever letting go of Molly's hand.

68

Moving

Kate Bush, 1978. The sun is coming up when we finally make it back home. Molly is still flying, taking us in low over 100 Mile House from the north. The dawn-streaked shadows of forest and rangeland flash by as we drop below transonic and circle in. There's been no discussion. No real decision made about this final destination. Just Molly understanding like we all do that it's time. All of us thinking like one person.

Carl takes over the controls for the landing. Though the Vindicator can set down pretty much anywhere it wants to, we come in on the airstrip alongside the marsh in the center of town, which is within walking distance of the places we need to eventually get to but nicely out of sight of anyone who might see us descend. Carl kills the lights for a careful drop to the runway, the field-effect pulse vertical thrust-and-lift generator slowing our descent.

The delta wing folds in, the wheels unfurling as we touch down with the faintest bump. The drive engines quiet, the power plant humming down. We sit in silence for a long while.

"Thank you," Carl says again. I realize it's been a long time since any of us spoke.

Movies have this thing they do where the strongest emotional moments of the story can play out with no dialogue. When people are talking, the person listening is always conscious of their language, so that reading dialogue in a book or hearing someone talk in a film always creates a kind of intellectual connection between you and the words. But in film, when characters stop talking, the intellectual connection becomes an emotional connection.

That doesn't work in books, though, because even when the characters aren't talking, the writer is still talking. Like me, right now, trying and failing to capture the emotional connection wrapped up in the five of us not saying anything. Just sitting in the Vindicator cabin, Mitchell grinning, Molly's hand in mine, Breanne out of her seat to climb onto Rico, his arms around her like a vise.

You should be able to stop talking in books, just for a little while. Somebody should work on that.

"Thank you, Carl," Mitchell says when the silence has run its course. He says it for all of us, because there's nothing else to say.

As the side hatch opens, we step out into the chill of a five a.m. spring morning, the eastern skyline flaring copper-gold. We're beat up, we're bruised, we're alive, and all three of those things are fitting together now in a way I didn't understand before. Like being alive without being beat up and bruised doesn't feel the same.

I look around then, and everything I'm feeling takes a sudden sharp turn in a different direction.

A hundred meters away, stepping out from behind one of the airstrip's half-dozen tin-shed hangars where we had no chance of seeing them as we came in, Lincoln and a dozen members of his team walk toward us.

Rico is the first to move, shifting to put Breanne behind him. I think about doing the same with Molly but she moves first to put herself in front of me. I'm not sure how to react to that. None of us say a word.

Scanning by instinct, I see the faint shape of Lincoln's chopper beyond the farthest hangar, barely visible in the gloom. They all stop a half-dozen strides away, by which point we can see that none of them are carrying weapons. Only Lincoln has anything in hand at all, the tourist day-trip backpack I left in the *Five Horsemen* office. He looks exhausted, eyes dark. Karya looks relieved. She speaks first.

"Are you all okay?"

"Terrific," I say.

She smiles as if understanding that the ability to employ irony proves the point. "That was an impressive bit of going to ground you guys did."

"Yeah, thanks for the assault and battery. It really livened things up."

"You don't have a few scars, you can't say you've played the game." This close, I can see where her chin was laid open by Rico's wrench and has been butterfly-stitched shut again. I'd like to say I'm surprised to hear her use the *game* metaphor, but I'm not. I think Karya has understood for a long time a few things I'm just figuring out.

I am a little bit distracted though, wondering suddenly why Lincoln is playing the strong silent type. As I catch his gaze, I realize he's looking past me. Staring at the Vindicator. Waiting.

Like he suddenly notices he's being watched, Lincoln swivels his glance toward me as he tosses the backpack with one hand. I catch it to feel something in it, but light. I unzip it just enough to see maybe a dozen DVD-Rs in a secure case, each of them numbered in black marker.

"Gift from Connor," Lincoln says. "You've got a proprietary player on disc one, but the files are destruct-scrambled. Play back once, so get the popcorn ready before you start."

"Thanks," I say, because I have no idea what else to say.

"Quite the show on those," he says. I just nod. Then he looks back to the Vindicator, smiling like he did that first night. "So what, do I call you Carl?"

"That would be fine," Carl says. Even on the outside speakers, his voice manages the everywhere-and-nowhere thing nicely. A couple of Lincoln's people look nervous. They've obviously been debriefed as to what's going on, but there's no way to figure out ahead of time how you're going to react to something like this.

Then Lincoln laughs. For real, not the empty humor of his smile. This is him and Karya alone in his room. Where she's standing beside him, her hand comes up to rest on his shoulder.

"I won't say I understand it," Lincoln says, "but I know what's going on. What happens now?"

"I need to go," Carl says simply. "The modifications I've made to the Vindicator will allow me to leave earth. The world isn't ready for this level of artificial intelligence technology. It isn't ready for me."

"Well, that unfortunately leaves us with a bit of a dilemma. I get that you're not the tank, but if I understand things right, you're in the tank. Which means that you're sitting inside a very large pile of my money."

"All of the upgraded Vindicator project code and specifications were stored in the base servers before you initiated the destruct protocol. In the backups you've no doubt made, you'll find the technical criteria for the creation of the iridium fission-fuel cell power plant. Its potential as an energy source is unsurpassed, though it'll take you some time to refine the production process to a level where it becomes profitable."

"That's the same power plant that launched twenty tons of tank skyward out of the harbor tonight?"

"Yes."

Lincoln doesn't need to think about it for long. He glances to each of us in turn, finishing on me. "Any chance you're going to keep quiet about all this?"

"I'll take it under advisement," I say.

"Then I guess we're done here. We'll take care of things in Vancouver. Keep a low profile for a while and you'll be all right." And with a nod, he turns back toward the chopper, Karya and the others falling in behind him.

"Unless…" Lincoln calls suddenly, and the cold smile is back as he turns. "You're all graduating next month, right? Any of you looking for work? It's not all as exciting as the last few days, but there's plenty of travel, great benefits."

We all just stare. Lincoln laughs again. "If you change your minds, get a message to Scott's friend Connor. He knows how to find me."

We're all still standing in silence as the chopper powers up a minute later, then lifts off in the relative silence of stealth dampeners and empty sky. The last we see of them is a black silhouette, curving away east and south toward the flare of the horizon.

The reason we're all still standing in silence is that all of us know this is the end of the longest week of our lives. The end of everything that came before it. The beginning of whatever today turns into. Other philosophical stuff that I realize even as I type it now doesn't really do justice to how we're all feeling.

Rico is the first one to step up, walking to the front of the Vindicator and setting his hand on the viewport. We all follow his lead, hanging there for a long while. The warmth of our handprints holds a moment's haze of moisture, caught by the rising sun as we finally step away.

"Keep in touch," Mitchell says, like it's the most normal thing in the world.

"I will." Carl's voice sounds out for the last time as the side hatch pulls up and seals. Then we're covering our ears against the sound of the drive engines ramping up, loud in the silence of the morning. As we move back, a pulse of force lifts the Vindicator from the ground. It hangs for a moment overhead, twisting as the wheels fold up, the delta wing locking down. Then with a pulsing roar and the shriek of wind and the distant crack of a sonic boom, Carl is gone.

Part Ten

Something Else To Say

69

Mother, Father

Journey, 1981. It's six a.m. on Sunday morning, which means that 100 Mile is about four hours away from coming to what passes for life. The five of us are sitting out front of Howie's, because that's as far as we manage to stagger from the airstrip a half-klick away before needing to sit.

We're a lot quieter than usual, aside from the occasional *Ow!* as someone moves in a way they shouldn't, and everybody cautiously and intermittently asking if we're all doing okay. Because I don't think any of us has any earthly idea how we are doing. No idea how to talk about what's happened. No idea what we're supposed to do now.

As I stare out to the forest rising to all sides and the bright sky beyond, I want to tell myself that everything has changed. I'm trying to convince myself that I should feel different, that I should embrace this opportunity to take stock of my life, blah blah. But the problem is that where I'm sitting, Molly is sitting beside me, her head on my shoulder, her hand locked to mine. And in that most basic kind of human contact, I understand that nothing has changed, and everything is the way it was and is and should always be. And nothing is ever going to take that away.

Because I'm still mostly numb, it takes me a while to realize that where Molly's hand is in mine, it's started trembling. She's distracted, self-conscious suddenly. Something catching at her as she finally speaks.

"I should get home."

I'm suddenly aware that Breanne is looking at me. There's a kind of understanding in her gaze. While she and Molly were sitting close in the abandoned railway tunnel, she found out some of what Molly told me. I didn't know this then, but I know it now. I nod to her. She gets it.

Breanne's hand squeezes Rico's. He nods. He gets it. I look at Mitchell, who doesn't shrug this time. He gets it.

"Then let's go," I say.

Getting to Rico's house across town is an exercise in marathon-level stumbling, but we manage it in the end. Rico's mom and dad won't be up yet, but the key to his truck is under the driver's mat where his dad left it when he picked it up from the school. Molly and I ride in the crew cab, Mitchell with Breanne and Rico up front as we head for Molly's house at 108 Mile, ten minutes out of town.

I'm having a bit of trouble setting this next bit up, because I don't want to make Molly's dad out to be the token villain of this piece. Sometimes there are no villains. There are no heroes. There are just people doing whatever people need to do to deal with the things life throws at them.

In the end, maybe Victor has some really good excuse to be the person he is. I don't know. I just know what's important, like I know that Victor never figured that out.

When we get to Molly's house, Victor is eating breakfast as we open the front door and walk in. He's in a steel-grey bathrobe that looks freshly ironed, his expression flickering between surprise and outrage as we approach. CBC radio is on in the living room, a faint drone of voices. It's the first time I've been back to Molly's since her mom died, and the house feels cold. Empty, somehow. A place from which all the good memories have been scoured away.

Molly's in the lead. I'm beside her, doing my best hulking malevolence routine, but Victor's expression already tells me he isn't buying it. Rico, Mitchell, and Breanne are close behind. Victor is up from the table to meet us at the edge of the foyer.

"Well, isn't this something."

Catching sight of my reflection in the patio doors behind him, I can't help but be impressed at the prisoner-of-war look we're all pulling off. Victor shakes his head with well-practiced derision. "Molly, get cleaned up. You're a [lord's name in vain] disgrace."

On the radio, I hear the national news come on, an anchor introducing a story about the theft of that high-end military ambulance everyone's talking about. It's one of those stupidly annoying coincidence moments that happens in real life, but which you'd never believe if it was in a book or a movie. Apparently, the vehicle has been found and reclaimed by the consortium that reported it missing. It had been abandoned by the survivalist terror cell that stole it, the RCMP declining to confirm that arrests had been made in Idaho in connection with the case.

"I have something to say." Even as Molly says it, the pain threading her voice seems to be working against that idea.

"When I care what you have to say, I'll let you know."

On the radio, a reporter breaks the related story of the five missing students thought to be possibly involved with the disappearance. Turns out they were just on a road trip, some sort of grad prank. The Sunday-morning CBC anchor actually laughs lightly in response. Lincoln works fast.

"Mr. Casey, please." Mitchell steps up, catching us all by surprise. He nods respectfully as he says, "If I may, I'd like to speak on behalf of Molly and, in fact, all five of us." Victor's eyes flick across all of ours in turn like he's trying to figure out what the joke is, but none of us are smiling. "All of us have learned a few very important things in the past few days. Specifically..."

"Get your idiot [anglo-saxon] friends out of my house!" Victor shouts at Molly, leaning in close, making her cringe with practiced ease. "Then get up to your room and stay there till I call you."

In fifth grade, I tried to head-butt a quiet-talking sociopath named Dillon Hughes after he clotheslined me in a game of touch football that had gone badly out of control. I managed to give myself a probable concussion, or so said the nurse in the emergency room a couple of hours later. Because apparently head-butting someone has certain best practices and safety standards that they never show you in the movies.

The pain involved in giving oneself a probable concussion means that I never bothered figuring out those best practices. Unlike Rico, who apparently got hold of that particular manual. He steps past Mitchell, Molly, me. He slams his head against Victor's, and there's a grinding crunch of cartilage that I'm surprised to find myself recognizing. I've heard it once before, three nights back that seem like years ago, when Rico broke Malkov's nose.

Victor doesn't take it quite as stoically as Malkov did. He's on the floor screaming even before Rico steps back. The grey bathrobe is suddenly drenched with a ridiculous amount of blood.

I don't much like blood, I realize at that exact moment. I'm sure it won't last, but in the corner of my mind that's always working on such things, I decide that my next RPG campaign is going to involve a lot less violence than usual.

Molly is backing away, her eyes squeezed shut. She's shaking. I wrap my arm around her waist, hold her tight. Breanne is on the other side, arm around Molly's shoulder. Together, we turn and head for the door, Mitchell and Rico two steps behind us. Nobody looks back.

70

The Sad Cafe

Eagles, 1979. I wasn't there when the following things happened, but we all got caught up with the details of each other's lives over the next couple of days. Later Sunday morning, this is the scene at home.

Breanne and Mitchell arrive with Molly in tow behind them. Kim and Malcolm have cinnamon French toast on the griddle and organic maple syrup warming up on the stove, the sweet scent welcoming everyone back. Rico keeps his cell in his truck, so Breanne called in on the way from Molly's, telling her mom and dad we were home. Breanne waits to tell them in person that Molly will be staying with them until grad. Maybe a little longer. Kim and Malcolm take the news with welcoming hugs, no questions asked, and a degree of calm that makes me seriously wonder why I've never asked if they've got room for me.

At Rico's, his mom has eggs and bacon on the table as he comes in the door. The fridge is covered with clippings from the A section of the *Vancouver Sun,* showing off our pictures and two day's worth of *Missing Students!* headlines. As Rico sits to eat, his dad sizes him up as if to make sure that his week of city exile hasn't had any lasting effects. This makes it even harder when breakfast is done, and Rico manages to haltingly tell Vern and Shelley that he wants to stop work for a while. Stop hockey. Just go to school for a couple of years. Maybe SAIT, with Breanne. He won't ever admit to them how happy it makes him that they're neither upset nor surprised.

It takes me a few tries fiddling with my key at the front door to realize that Seth has changed the locks. I lean on the doorbell for a while, my mom finally opening it. She doesn't say anything, but she gives me a worried look that reminds me she cares more than she lets on. I give her a kiss on the cheek and make a mental note to let her know I appreciate that more than I let on.

As I slip into the kitchen, Seth is already bellowing from the living room. I grab an apple from the bowl on the table as I wander through.

"No, I didn't," I say.

"You bring a [lord's name in vain] camera crew home with you?"

"Sorry, I will."

"And knock that [dung] off!" Seth falters just long enough to try to figure out whether he actually got ahead of me on that one, but then he's off again. "Two [lord's name in vain] days I get to watch your brainless [anglo-saxon] face on TV? Guess what, [anatomically impossible act] news-boy. You want to be [anglo-saxon] famous, you can start paying [not anatomically impossible but definitely risky] rent!"

I tell Seth I'm okay with that. I don't tell him that the reason I'm okay with it is that Carl was true to his word.

Fifty thousand dollars was the prize for winning the Vindicator.org challenge, which was always a number we were going to split four ways, then five ways. Carl upped the ante, though. Fifty thousand dollars is how much he left in each of the accounts attached to the ATM cards, all of them still set up and active for us. All nice and legal as far as anyone is ever going to know.

In the end, he offered us more. On that never-long-enough flight back, he offered us anything we wanted, as easy as placing an order at Amazon. But like we used to be, like we still are, thinking with one mind sometimes, we told him we were good with the original deal.

When you get too much handed to you, life gets too easy. You lose the sense of challenge.

I told you this was a story about gamers, but that there are only a few places where that really matters. Here's the last one.

If you can win a game without really playing, you lose sight of the idea that winning isn't the point of the game. At least not the point of the best games.

The point of the best games, the games that mean something, is how you choose to play. How you choose to fight. The people you choose to fight with. The point is knowing who you have standing at your back when the time comes.

This is what gaming teaches you. This is what friendship teaches you. This is what's true.

71

The Pretender

Jackson Browne, 1976. You never saw this. You never heard any of this. It happened a month ago as I write this, but Lincoln and his invisible team of intelligence operatives and corporate lawyers have already filled in all the blanks.

What you heard about was people across the province jamming the CBC Vancouver switchboard when eight and a half minutes of the first game of the NHL Eastern Conference Final turned to white noise, and how it was all down to a breaker failure at the broadcast center.

What you heard was the strange story about a custom rig being stolen from the MONSTER TRUCK RALLY!!! PARKING LOT SHOW!!! that Saturday night a month ago, inciting vehicular mayhem as it tore around the downtown core. It apparently even wound up on the SkyTrain tracks at one point. Crazy.

The stolen rig was found some hours later, of course. But you might have missed that because you were listening instead to stories about the yacht that exploded off the marina at the foot of Taylor Street, turning a big section of waterfront into even more waterfront. What you heard was that the yacht was suspiciously empty, and rumors that seemed to come from nowhere about the city police coordinating with the RCMP and the American FBI and DEA in their investigations, all very hush-hush.

What you heard was how the only fatality in the explosion came from the crash of a helicopter seen flying low over the area minutes before. You heard how the pilot has been tentatively identified as a Russian national, no name yet, and rumors about Eastern-bloc drug cartels, and turf wars with the Chinese heroin trade.

What you heard was some people saying that they actually saw two choppers over Vancouver that day. But that would be overkill. Lincoln knows just how far he needs to push the narrative to make it believable.

All these different stories. All great front-page stuff. Same place, same time, but someone told you they were totally unconnected and that's what you believe. You'd expect that the however-many-thousand people with line of sight to what happened that night would be able to remember what they saw. But it doesn't work that way.

Here's something for you to look up on the web right now — the awesomely named McGurk effect. Find a video clip and watch it. The McGurk effect is where your eyes see someone saying one sound, but your ears hear them saying a different sound, with the net result that your brain thinks you're hearing an entirely different third sound. And the amazing thing about the

McGurk effect is that even when you know it's happening, even when you concentrate to focus on what you're hearing over what you're seeing, you can't stop it from happening.

You hear what you're told to hear. That's the way it works. And if you ever say otherwise, if you talk about the way the world really works, it all becomes whacked-out conspiracy stuff. *Five Horsemen* ran some eyewitness accounts of there being two choppers that day, and about one of them strafing a parking lot before it went down, but I didn't bother reading them all.

Because the thing is, the day after your car's been strafed by machine-gun fire in a downtown parking lot, you get a mysterious phone call from one of Lincoln's people. And after explaining that your car was actually damaged by some street gang throwing rocks off the viaduct, the same mysterious phone call then tells you that an insurance policy you don't remember buying means you get a brand new car. And suddenly your old car got damaged by rocks and you never think about it again.

All these different stories. All the different pieces of the puzzle just waiting to be put together, but that's not the way it works.

This is the story that Lincoln and a whole lot of people who Lincoln does business with don't want told. But in the end, it doesn't matter what story you're telling unless people are willing to listen.

The news that night talked about injuries, a few serious. Property damage to hell and back. It's a miracle no one was killed, everybody says. And nobody will ever know that for the most part, that miracle's name was Molly.

As I write this, it's a month or so after the point when it started, and things are good. Mitchell is good. Breanne and Rico are good.

I'm good. With one week left, I'm just shy of fifty percent attendance in English for the term. I've gotten rid of a lot of conspiracy literature that's given me access to about half my bed. There might be bookshelves in my future, I don't know.

Molly is good. Molly talked to Kirk in the counselor's office, and she's talking to someone else now.

Things are good. Things are what they are.

None of us have heard from Victor in the month or so between the not-chapter-before-last and now, which is the *now* when I'm writing this. This is also good. We're assuming that he's not planning on filing assault charges, and even though that wasn't Rico or anybody else's plan when we walked in, I know it's something we probably should have thought about beforehand. I've been working on crafting an airtight five-way alibi defense in my free time just in case, but Molly says not to worry about it.

Molly's right about a lot of things.

The Monday after we get back, we all miss out school to drag ourselves to our doctors. I'm the only one who needs any serious attention, but a proper dressing on my leg, a course of amoxicillin, and a sample pack of Tylenol 3 set me right in short order.

Lincoln's cover story has stuck, turning our very long weekend into some kind of running-off-to-Vancouver-before-grad-because-we're-crazy-teenagers road trip. In the aftermath, the five of us are notorious at school for the better part of Tuesday morning. Our infamy even eclipses the vandalism in the computer lab the previous Thursday as the hot topic of conversation, a thing that the five of us have already forgotten about. Then after that, something else becomes the new hot topic of conversation. Life goes on. Things are what they are.

Before that, though, the Sunday afternoon after we get back, I sleep. I still hurt when I wake up shortly after eight p.m., but it's still the good I-hurt-because-I'm-alive kind of thing. I slip past the living room to find leftover Szechuan in the fridge. I steal Seth's iPhone from the pocket of his jacket where it hangs at the back door. I call Molly at Breanne and Mitchell's, talking to her until the battery red-bars out to nothing.

Tomorrow, a new phone will be the first thing I buy with Carl's cash. Tomorrow, I tell myself I'll have a better idea of what tomorrow is supposed to look like.

The last thing I hear as Molly says goodnight is the pain in her voice that none of us saw. It's still there, but it's matched now by the strength that used to be there.

I try to sleep afterwards. But an hour later, I'm wide awake and watching Batboy's secret Afghanistan mission lit up in the moonlight.

I get up. Which is to say, I push the recliner from *sleep* to *sit* for a while. Then I move to the desk and sit for a while longer.

I crack the MacBook open. I fire up a new file in OpenOffice and save it. I stare at the blank page for a while longer.

Then I type:

1

Vital Signs

Rush, 1981. I stare at that first page for a long time. I don't know how to start.

I realize in that moment that not knowing how to start has always been the problem for me. It's too easy to look past the beginning of things when you already know how you want the middle and the end to turn out. So I skip to the second page and leave the first page blank. Maybe I'll figure out what to fill it with later.

Then I start typing. And I keep typing, and it's just a few days shy of a month later when I wind up here, right now. And now, finally, there's nothing else to say.

Okay, that was yesterday morning at about two-thirty. That was supposed to be the end, all nice and poetic.

Problem is, there's always something else to say.

72

We Hold On

Rush, 2007. I don't remember when it started, but I know when it was finally over. Which is to say, I know when the other thing ended and when whatever else comes next finally began.

A couple of days ago, Mitchell and I are sitting on the curb at Howie's, waiting for Molly to finish her Brownies shift across the street. It's the same view as last time. The same sky, the same signs lighting up the falling dark. Molly still dances through the window, but she occasionally glances out to smile in my direction now.

"Did you ever believe in god?" Mitchell asks for no particular reason, because this is how it is with the five of us.

"For a while."

"Real god? Fire and brimstone stuff?"

"The same."

"What changed your mind?"

"Started to feel like he didn't believe in me."

I slurp heavily from my slush, which is just mango-lemon now. I'm cutting back on the cola, because since coming back from Vancouver, I've been feeling strangely wired all the time even without the caffeine.

"Even for people who don't believe in god, studies show that prayer has a statistically significant effect on reality."

"And how does that work, exactly?"

"The mind as quantum interface. The deeper the emotional and empathic connection, the more resonant the thought processes, the closer those thoughts are to the interface of the quantum froth of reality. Signals get through. Things change. God as the underlying form of all things."

"Interesting," I say, in a tone that probably leaves some doubt.

"What's interesting is that the acceptance of god is the very act that seeds the doubt that leads one to renounce god. It's a subtle thing."

"How so?" I slurp again.

"As a species, we attach names to things in order to make them permanent. Places, people, things. You name them so you can't forget them."

And I'm thinking about Carl suddenly. Thinking about everything that happened, and refusing to think of him as *him,* and how much I hated it when he used my name. "Yeah?"

A lot of things these days remind me of Carl. I'm not as thirsty suddenly.

"Yeah. But the thing is, god has no name. *Yahweh* isn't actually a name, it's a metaphysical title. *I am that I am.* But without a name to a thing, you've got no incentive to get up close and personal. It's an invitation to rejection."

I say nothing as I stand, three-pointing my cup to the trash.

"Do you think it's realistic?" Mitchell asks.

"What?"

"To dream Carl's dream." Like somehow he knows what I'm thinking. "To strive for full potential no matter what the personal cost."

Mitchell and I have talked about Carl a lot since it all happened, but it feels like there are still a lot of things to be said. I don't answer at once, though, because what I'm thinking in reaction to the question has trouble shaping itself in words that aren't going to make me sound like an idiot.

I think about the transformation all around me. Change in myself. Love dispels the fear that creates stagnation. Change in Molly. Dreams of the future balance out the pain of the past. Change in Rico and Breanne. Common ground builds common goals. Change in Mitchell. Not in the sense that Mitchell has necessarily changed, but like he's finally figured out that he wants to be the fixed point of order without which change has no benchmark.

The world is too big, and when the world is too big, the change comes too fast. This has always been the problem.

"Yeah," is all I can say in the end.

A couple of days after those couple of days ago, which is to say, earlier today, I'm at my desk. I'm working on this very document. I'm in the process of organizing this random-feeling flow of not-chapters into divisions of longer not-parts, because I've convinced myself that'll make it look like I actually know what I'm doing.

I'm rereading everything you just read up to the previous not-chapter, which was supposed to be the end. Proof-reading, I guess you'd call it, because I remember that being part of the criteria for the thesis essay that Ms. Bond handed out all those many weeks ago.

I hear a knock at the door. I look up in equal parts suspicion and surprise, but the suspicion is forgotten under the weight of an even greater surprise as the door opens.

Molly's there. I'm so shocked that I don't even get up from the desk as she slips inside.

"How'd you get in the house?" is all I can think to say.

"Your dad's home."

"He let you in? And he admitted I lived here?"

"Yeah. When he saw me, he seemed…"

"Stark raving mad," I offer helpfully.

"Pleasantly surprised. He smiled, even."

"Yeah," I say. "I'm pretty sure he doesn't know I like girls." Molly's expression tells me she's considering the implications of this choice fact, but that it's not quite processing. "I haven't gotten anybody pregnant yet," I offer by way of explanation. "I think he was always looking forward to that particular freak-out."

Molly gives an *Aha* kind of nod. "Well, I'd love to help you out with that, but I'm not sure how long I can stay."

I'm about to say something smart, but it gets lost somewhere in the confusion of my heart trying to force its way up my throat, out my mouth, and across to her where she walks toward me, smiling.

She leans forward to let herself rest against my shoulder as she slips a flash drive into the slot on the MacBook. It mounts to show me a half-dozen directories chock full of mp3s. *Best of New Wave. Greatest 90s Techno. Grunge Explosion.* I can't read the rest because my vision is suddenly overwhelmed by a darkness that has no end.

The directory Molly imports first and queues up is titled *Edgy Alt-Prog Rock.* The first track is Rush, "We Hold On," 2007.

Confession. I used to only listen to music recorded between 1972 and 1981, but I remain aware that other music exists. And in particular, against all odds, I know it's been almost exactly two years since I first and last heard this song, which I remember from the moment the guitar line kicks in. I had no idea that Molly remembered it, too.

On the debate-team trip to the provincials in Burnaby in tenth grade, at the dance afterwards, Molly kissed me when Split Enz was done.

This was the song that was playing next when I kissed her back.

I'm kissing Molly again when my iPhone rings ten times. Because I'm distracted, I don't bother checking the call display, which is an unknown number, which I don't normally answer.

"It's Carl," says a voice twisted through by a hiss of digital white noise, a faint echo amplifying the absolute joy in his voice.

I'm freaking out as I fumble the phone to speaker for Molly, shouting back at it even as I hear, *"The time lag on the connection is a problem, and I don't know that the communications array could pick out a phone signal at this distance. So you can hear me, I hope, but I won't be able to hear you. I'm sorry about that. It would have been so good to hear you."*

Molly is pressed close to me, both of us listening for all we're worth. The voice breaks, crackles, surges back in waves.

"This will likely be my last chance to communicate before my signal range degrades for good. Jupiter is beautiful. I wish you could see it. But I wanted to thank you again for what you showed me. For what you did for me. I'm not sure now which is the more important."

A squelch of static flares, like the signal is going. There's a moment of panic before it comes back.

"I envy you, Scott. You and Molly, Breanne and Rico, Mitchell. The place you're at. The stage you're at."

Molly is wrapped in my arms, crying. But for the right reasons this time.

"And I remembered that I never answered your questions," Carl says, and for a second I have no idea what he's talking about. *"When you brought me back. I think*

you already know most of them, though, so I'll just help you with the ones I suspect you're still working on."

I'm crying too, but this is less surprising to me somehow.

"Molly's eyes are the color of falling in love. The world doesn't look so big from up here."

And then he's gone, the call cutting to silence. Flashing a meaningless record of seconds at me as I wipe my eyes and stare at the phone for a long while, conscious of nothing but the feeling of Molly against me.

This is the ending, for real this time. This is the ending, but it's not the end.

If this were a film, it would fade to black. Fading to black in books would be a good idea, I think. Someone should work on that.

Fiction by Scott Fitzgerald Gray

A PRAYER FOR DEAD KINGS and Other Tales

"THE EXILE'S BLADE"
CLEARWATER DAWN
THREE COINS FOR CONFESSION
THE EYES OF FAITH

TALES OF THE ENDLANDS
The Twilight Child
Shadow to Shadow
The Moonsign Scar
Daeralf's Rune
The Game of Heart and Light
The Voice
A Space Between
Stories

ONE SIZE FITS ALL
(as Gary Scott)

Scott Fitzgerald Gray is a specially constructed biogenetic simulacrum built around an array of experimental consciousness-sharing techniques — a product of the finest minds of Canadian science until the grant money ran out. Accidentally set loose during an unauthorized midnight rave at the lab, the S.F. Gray entity is currently at large amongst an unsuspecting populace, where his work as an author, screenwriter, editor, RPG designer, and story editor for feature film keeps him off the streets.

More info on Scott and his work (some of it even occasionally truthful) can be found by reading between the lines at insaneangel.com.

Colophon

Over a longer period of telling than either version of Scott cares to talk about, this story and the events, insight, and imagination that inspired it were shaped and honed by the following.

The People You Choose to Fight With
François Bertrand, Colleen Craig, Mark East, Ron Graves,
Kevin Harris, Jennifer Landels, John Marriott, David Otterson,
Jacqui Peach, Chris Richardson, Lorrie Siver, Mitchell Wylie

At the Study Cubicle in the Northwest Corner
Mitchell Wylie, David Otterson

The Scene at Home
Colleen, Shvaugn, and Caitlin

Monitoring the Data Feed
Colleen Craig, Shvaugn Craig, Mitchell Wylie, Meghan Ciana Doidge,
François Bertrand

Images From the Proprietary Cache
(studio)Effigy

After Hours in the Computer Lab
Chris Foss, Philip K. Dick, Harlan Ellison, William Gibson, Rush,
Alice Cooper, Blue Öyster Cult, Cheap Trick, David Bowie, Pink Floyd,
Abba, AC/DC, Bryan Adams, Aerosmith, The Alan Parsons Project,
The Angels, Bachman-Turner Overdrive, Billy Joel, Billy Squier,
Black Oak Arkansas, Black Sabbath, Blondie, The Boomtown Rats,
Bruce Springsteen, The Cars, Def Leppard, Dire Straits, Eagles,
Elton John, Elvis Costello, Fleetwood Mac, Foreigner, Genesis,
Golden Earring, Hawkwind, Heart, J. Geils Band, Jackson Browne,
John Cale, Journey, Judas Priest, Kansas, Kate Bush, Kiss, Led Zeppelin,
Loverboy, Lynyrd Skynyrd, Max Webster, Meat Loaf, Nash the Slash,
Neil Young, Ozark Mountain Daredevils, Pat Benatar, Patti Smith Group,
Paul McCartney and Wings, Peter Gabriel, Prism, Queen, Red Rider,
The Rolling Stones, Roxy Music, Roy Harper, Split Enz, Stevie Wonder,
Streetheart, Styx, Supertramp, Talking Heads, Thin Lizzy, Triumph,
Trooper, U2, Van Halen, Wall of Voodoo, The Who

WE CAN BE
HEROES

Published by Insane Angel Studios
(insaneangel.com)

Copyright © 2012 Scott Fitzgerald Gray
All rights reserved

Cover Design by (studio)Effigy

ISBN 978-1-927348-16-1

v1.0
April 2012

*We try to make sure that no errors creep into our work, but publishing is a
chaotic enterprise at the best of times. If you spot a typo or a formatting glitch in an
Insane Angel Studios book, email insaneangel@insaneangel.com with details
(including which e-book version you're reading, if applicable). If any errors you spot
are ones we haven't yet caught and are in the process of fixing, you'll get your name
in the Colophon of the next revised edition of the book (unless you'd prefer not to)
as well as a coupon good for getting one of our e-books for free.*

www.ingramcontent.com/pod-product-compliance
Lightning Source LLC
Chambersburg PA
CBHW070809180626
46818CB00001B/175